"I meant it when I said that I've got you."

With his free hand, Sean tucked a strand of hair behind Sierra's ear, tracing his thumb over her cheekbone. His eyes drifted down to her lips, and he couldn't fight it anymore. Clearly he was hell-bent on destruction tonight, because for the first time in his ten years as a bodyguard, he was going to kiss a client.

Cupping her cheek with his uninjured hand, he slowly dipped his head and gently, tenderly closed his mouth over hers. She responded immediately, returning the kiss with a soft sigh.

Finally he was touching her and tasting her just the way he'd wanted since the day they met. Finally, and it was a thousand times better than he ever could've imagined. And he'd spent a lot of time imagining it.

It was the best wrong thing he'd ever done.

NECESSARY RISK

Tara Wyatt

FOREVER

NEW YORK BOSTON

Copyright © 2016 by Tara Wyatt
Excerpt from *Primal Instinct* © 2016 by Tara Wyatt
Cover design by Christine Foltzer
Cover art by Tony Mauro
Cover copyright © 2016 by Hachette Book Group, Inc.

Forever
Hachette Book Group
1290 Avenue of the Americas
New York, NY 10104
forever-romance.com
twitter.com/foreverromance

First Edition: February 2016

Forever is an imprint of Grand Central Publishing.
The Forever name and logo are trademarks of Hachette Book Group, Inc.

The publisher is not responsible for websites (or their content) that are not owned by the publisher.

The Hachette Speakers Bureau provides a wide range of authors for speaking events. To find out more, go to www.hachettespeakersbureau.com or call (866) 376-6591.

ISBN 978-1-4555-9027-8 (mass market); 978-1-4555-9026-1 (ebook)

Printed in the United States of America
OPM
10 9 8 7 6 5 4 3 2 1

For my husband Graham, who makes all my heroes look like chumps. I love you. Go Team Falcon!

ACKNOWLEDGMENTS

This book was a long time in the making, and it wouldn't have happened without the love, support, and encouragement of so many people.

First and foremost I would like to thank my family for supporting my dream of being a published author. Thank you to my husband, Graham, my parents, Cathy and Gerry, my brother, Wes, and my extended family, as well as my in-laws, for your love, support, and continued enthusiasm. A huge thank-you to my sister-in-law Samantha Wyatt for being one of the first people to read the book and to cheer me on, and to Joan Wyatt, who was one of my earliest fans, and who is missed every single day. A special shout-out to my dog Schroeder, who endured many walk-less days and was by my side almost constantly while I wrote.

I'd also like to thank my best friends, the Thursday Girls—Amanda, Robin, and Sarah—for putting up with months of neglect, whining, and me going on and on about made-up people. You guys are awesome, and I'm lucky to have such amazing girlfriends.

A special thanks to my fantastic critique partners, Erin Moore and Harper St. George, without whom this book would've been impossible to finish. I'm so incredibly lucky to work with you talented, smart, amazingly supportive ladies.

Thank you to my agent, Jessica Watterson, for believing in me and my writing, and for helping to make my dreams come true. Thanks to my editors, Lauren Plude and Alex Logan, for all your hard work. The book wouldn't be what it is without you. And thank you to my Hamilton Public Library coworkers, who have cheered me on tirelessly from day one.

I have made so many amazing friends while writing this book, and I feel so incredibly fortunate to have people like Jenn Burke, Kelly Jensen, Kelly Siskind, Brenna Mills, Amanda Heger, and many others in my corner. Twitter friends *are* real friends! I would especially like to thank Shannon Richard—you are a new friend, an awesome friend, and a keeper. I'm so glad to know you.

Finally a huge, enormous, elephant-size thank-you to the Toronto Romance Writers, especially the wonderful, lovely, and talented Juliana Stone. I would not be where I am today without your kindness and support. You are amazing, and I'm lucky to know you. I would also like to thank Morgan Rhodes, Eve Silver, Molly O'Keefe, Maureen McGowan, and Nicki Pau Preto (who gets me like WHOA—I love you, bae).

Oh, and wine. Can't ever forget the wine.

CHAPTER 1

Sierra Blake glanced up at the bank of lights, and tiny dots danced in front of her eyes. People didn't often realize just how hot stage lights could be. The expression "basking in the spotlight"? That stray *s* had to be a typo, because it was more like "baking in the spotlight."

"Sierra, what do you think separates you from other child stars?" The 90's Con panel moderator directed the question at her, smoothing a hand down his tie as he glanced at the index cards clutched in one hand. She took a breath, the prickling threat of sweat teasing along her hairline. God, was she relieved she didn't have to do this daily anymore. She smoothed her hair over her shoulder and ran her hands over the skirt of her cream-colored silk dress. Hundreds of eyes locked onto her, and a zing of adrenaline shot down to her toes.

She bit her lip and fingered the shooting star pendant at the base of her throat. "You mean, how did I avoid living 'la vida Lohan'?"

Laughter bubbled up from the audience, and she relaxed

a little. Although it was par for the course at events like this, she'd always hated that question and the quagmire of emotions it dredged up.

She took a deep breath and dove in. "Quite frankly, being a child star is pretty messed up. You're working with adults, keeping adult hours, making adult money, and trying to live up to the expectations of everyone around you. Any kid would find that kind of pressure confining. And that's where the rebellion comes in. Drinking and drugs and sex. And all of this is happening when you're trying to figure out who you actually are. How are you supposed to do that in that environment?" She paused, contemplating how much to share.

"But you didn't go down that road," prompted the moderator.

"I didn't. I think part of the reason is that *Family Tree* was an ensemble show." She looked across the stage at her former costars, smiling warmly. "There wasn't one star carrying everyone else. We were a group, and the older actors looked out for the younger ones. I think the shock of suddenly being in the spotlight was easier to absorb when it was shared between all of us."

"That's definitely true," interjected Rory Evans, one of the other stars of the show. "We all bonded in that environment, and we became a pretty tight-knit group. We were a support system for each other without really even realizing that's what we were doing."

"Totally." Steven Simmons nodded. "We were a crew. No one had pressure on his or her shoulders to make the show a success. I think part of the reason it was a success was that the bond Rory mentioned shone through on the screen. We were all friends."

"We're all *still* friends," said Rory, taking a sip of his water. And it was true. Rory was a good friend, who'd seen her through the loss of a parent, through a change in career, from her teens to her thirtieth birthday just a few months ago.

"For sure," said Sierra, grateful that she hadn't had to shoulder the question on her own. "I can't speak for everyone else, but I think if I'd started in movies instead of on a TV show with the cast we had…" She shrugged. "Well, I don't know. I might've given Lindsay a run for her money."

"We all might've. In fact, some of us tried," said Steven, looking around innocently and drawing laughter from the audience. Although he had it together now, the antics of his early twenties were well documented.

"We did," said Sierra, her fingers once again straying to her star pendant. Rory reached over and squeezed her knee, giving her an encouraging nod. "You know the drinking, and the drugs, and the sex that I just referenced? All of that was true, at least for me. There was a period, between when *Family Tree* ended and when I started working on *Sunset Cove*, that I…" She trailed off, her fingers knotted together. "I lost control. I was seventeen, and my dad was dying of cancer. I was trying to figure out…well, everything, I guess. I was lost. Scared. So I drank, and I partied, and I hooked up with boys, trying to find a way to quell the fear that my world was about to end. Keep in mind that I also lived in a world that completely facilitated this behavior. It didn't matter that I wasn't legal, I had no issues getting into bars, finding someone to sell me pot, or getting boys' attention. That whole Hollywood world was so toxic. I didn't realize it at the time, but it was. Especially for a scared, lost kid. Everything came crashing down when my dad died, and then I had a pregnancy scare."

She forced herself to take a breath, and Rory gave her knee another squeeze. "I'm telling you all of this to partly explain that in some ways, I'm not so different from other child stars. I was messed up. And that toxic environment is why I'm not really in that world anymore.

"When I thought I was pregnant, I went to Choices. For anyone who doesn't know, Choices is a nonprofit organization that provides confidential reproductive, maternal, and child health services at low or no cost, and has centers across the country. I didn't know where else to go. I didn't want to tell my mom. I didn't even know if I was pregnant, and I was too chicken to go buy a pregnancy test. What if someone recognized me?

"I was able to take a test there, and it turned out that I wasn't pregnant, which was a relief because clearly I would've been ill equipped to deal with an unplanned pregnancy at seventeen. I didn't have my own life together. How could I even think about a baby's life? The support I received at Choices played a huge role in turning my life around. They offered me counseling, birth control, and support at a time when I felt alone and scared. So after I finished working on *Sunset Cove*, I went to college, and now I work for Choices. I'm proud to be their spokesperson, because I know firsthand what a difference they can make in someone's life. Frankly, I—"

"Shut your fucking mouth, whore!" A male voice erupted from the crowd, and stunned silence fell over the audience. Sierra froze, her mouth still open. A chill ran up her spine as a feeling of naked vulnerability engulfed her, pinning her in place. Rory's hand tightened on her knee and she scanned the crowd, but with the bright stage lights, she could see only the first few rows of people. Everyone else was hidden, shrouded in the shadows and beyond the reach of the lights. She glanced at Rory and the panel moderator, unsure what to do next. She'd spoken about Choices in public dozens of times, and no one had ever hurled obscenities like that at her.

And that's when something heavy, soggy, and cold slammed into her chest. It was as though someone had hit the slow-motion button on her life, and she felt as though she were suddenly underwater, dizzy and unable to get enough oxygen. Slowly she looked down, and all she could see was red, blooming in large patches on her dress, soaking it through. She ran her trembling hands down her torso, trying to figure out where all the blood had come from. But there was no pain, and the blood was cold.

Not her blood.

Shaking, she stood, and that's when she saw it, crumpled at her feet. A diaper with an exploded red dye pack. It was supposed to look like a bloody diaper. And someone had thrown it at her. A boiling anger ate at her chest, and her cheeks burned with humiliation. She clenched her jaw against the hot, stinging tears prickling her eyes.

"Oh my God, are you OK?" Rory's hands were on her shoulders, and the slow motion of the moment morphed into fast-forward. She shook again, a shiver racking her as a wave of dizziness washed over her, making the room tilt nauseatingly for a second. She nodded, her chest tingling hotly as her mind scrambled to make sense of what had just happened. The overwhelming urge to get the hell out of there took over, and she spun, almost tripping over the chair she'd just been sitting in. Shoving it aside, she ran offstage, needing to get away from the lights, away from the exposure.

Just away.

* * *

Sean Owens pulled his sunglasses from his face, squinting against the bright Los Angeles sunshine as he strode toward the back entrance of the convention center, slipping them into the pocket of his suit jacket. He scanned the small aboveground employee parking lot, on the alert for any unusual activity, but nothing stood out. The standard perimeter check complete, he reached into another pocket for his phone, ready to check in with De Luca, the new guy on his team, before heading back to the office.

Before he could send the text message, the nondescript door at the back of the convention center flew open, slamming against the brick wall with a sharp bang, and he tensed, his hand edging toward the Glock 19 in the shoulder holster under his suit jacket. A woman came rushing out, one hand clutched to her chest, her face pale.

She was covered in blood.

Ten years of training and carefully honed instinct kicked into high gear, and he rushed toward her, his legs kicking into motion before he even had time to think about it. He raked his eyes over her tiny body, trying to figure out where all the blood was coming from, and if it was hers. She wasn't moving as though she was injured. She almost collided with him, but he anticipated her and braced his hands in front of him, his fingers curling lightly around her upper arms to steady her. She gasped and looked up, and a pair of bright-green, terrified eyes met his. Immediately he looked behind her, trying to determine if someone was pursuing her.

"Are you hurt? Is this your blood?" he asked, keeping his voice calm as he held her steady, his eyes still scanning the area for potential threats.

She shook her head, the ends of her golden-brown hair brushing against his fingers.

"No," she said, her voice strained. "It's dye."

He frowned and once again scanned the area behind her as he swapped places with her, putting himself between her and the door.

"Are you all right? You're not hurt?"

She laughed, the sound shaky and hollow. "Am I all right? Not really. But I'm not injured."

Sean's heart eased out of his throat from where it had leaped at the sight of a woman covered in blood running out of the convention center. But only slightly.

She pulled away, moving back a little. "I need to go."

He nodded, wanting more than anything to help her. "Where? I can drive you."

She took another step away from him, one eyebrow arched, a frown on her face. "Yeah, I don't get into cars with strange men, but thanks for the offer." A bit of color returned to her cheeks, making her green eyes look even brighter.

"Understandable. My name's Sean, and I'm a security expert." She eyed him warily, and he continued. "A bodyguard. I'm here at the convention to check on a new member of my team, see how he's doing with a client." He slipped his hand into his pocket and fished out a business card, handing it to her, wanting to earn her trust. Even though she was uninjured, his instincts told him that she needed him. She studied the card with narrowed eyes for a second before crossing her arms over her chest.

"This doesn't prove anything. You could've had these made."

He bit his lip, trying to suppress the smile he knew wouldn't get him anywhere. But he couldn't help it. Not only was she cute, she was smart.

"I just…" She toyed with his card, running it back and forth over her knuckles. "I just need a minute."

"Why don't you sit down?" He gestured to a bench several feet away. She glanced from him to the bench before finally nodding. Still keeping himself between her and the door, he let her lead the way. She sat down heavily, her

elbows on her thighs, her face in her hands. He eased down
beside her, sitting so as to block her from view of the
convention center's back door. He watched as she took several deep breaths, and his chest tightened slightly. She was
scared, and upset. Even if she didn't trust him, he could protect her from whatever had her so upset, and no way in hell
was he going to leave her on her own. He couldn't. Not
only was it his training, but there was something about this
woman. He couldn't put his finger on it, but he felt drawn to
her. Wanted to protect her and look after her.

The parking lot was quiet except for the distant rush of
traffic from the front of the convention center, the rustling
of the leaves of the trees lining the parking lot, and a bird
chirping softly somewhere above them. Her slender shoulders rose and fell as she took several deep breaths, and he
said nothing, giving her space. After a few moments, she
straightened and leaned back against the bench, smoothing
her hands over her stained dress that had once been white or
yellow. It was so ruined, he couldn't tell for sure. Her eyes
raked over him, and he let her look, hoping to put her at ease.
Finally her eyes met his.

"What happened?" he asked, needing to know so he
could keep her safe.

She sighed heavily, and her shoulders relaxed, easing
down from around her ears. "I was speaking at the convention," she said, gesturing to the building behind them, "and
someone threw a diaper full of dye at me."

"Someone attacked you with a diaper?"

She nodded, her bottom lip caught between her teeth. She
looked up, her eyes once again meeting his, and there was
that tug in his chest again. That pull.

"Why would someone do that?" he asked, propping one
ankle on his knee and threading his fingers together, forcing

his body into a relaxed posture to hide the tension radiating through him.

"I guess because I have some unpopular opinions."

"About?"

"Equal access to birth control and family planning. I'm a spokesperson for Choices, the women's health nonprofit." She looked down at her splotchy dress and sighed again, rubbing a hand over her face.

"Ah. Explains the diaper." The knot between his shoulders loosened just slightly. Chances were this was nothing more than idiot protesters, looking to make a point by embarrassing her. He looked back at the door again, but there was no sign of anyone following her.

Her lips moved, a tiny ghost of a smile. "I'm sorry I kind of accused you of…lying, or whatever. I didn't mean to be rude. I'm just…"

He held up a hand. "No apology needed."

She glanced down at his card, still clutched in one hand, now slightly crumpled. "I've heard of Virtus," she said, referring to the security company he ran with his father. The blue-and-gray logo was emblazoned across the top of the card he'd given her. She extended her hand across to him. "I'm Sierra, by the way."

He nodded. In the back of his brain, he'd recognized her almost immediately, but his concern for her had taken precedence over everything else. "I know. I'm Sean." He enveloped her small, delicate hand in his, and a warm, electrical tingle worked its way up his arm. Slowly she pulled her hand back, and damn, the friction of her skin against his felt good.

"I know." She held up the card.

He rubbed a hand over his cheek, his closely cropped beard bristling against his fingers. "Right. So, any idea who might've attacked you?" He scanned the quiet parking lot again. No way in hell was anyone getting close to her right now.

She blew out a slow breath and shook her head. "Not a clue." Some of the color dropped out of her face again, and he knew he needed to keep her talking. The urge to comfort her was nearly overwhelming. He couldn't change what had happened to her, but he could try to make the present suck a little less. He wanted to ask her about her own security, if she had anyone working for her, but thought that might come off like too much of a sales pitch, and that wasn't what she needed right now. So he headed in another direction.

"Were you on a panel?" he asked, tipping his head toward the convention center.

She nodded. "Yeah. *Family Tree* reunion. We do it every year for 90's Con."

"I remember that show. You were cute."

She smiled, fully and genuinely this time, and that smile aimed in his direction felt just as good as the slide of her hand against his. "Thanks. It was a long time ago. I'm surprised people are still interested in it twenty years after the fact, to be honest. Surprised, but glad."

He tilted his head, considering. "People grew up watching that show. I know I did."

Her eyebrows rose, and she leaned toward him slightly. "You did?"

"Sure."

"I guess I thought...I don't know. That it was mostly dweebs who watched it. It was kind of a goody-goody show." She shrugged, wrinkling her nose. Fuck, she was cute. His chest tightened again, but this time there was something else there along with the protectiveness.

He arched an eyebrow. "Who's to say I wasn't a dweeb?"

She laughed. "I seriously doubt that." Her eyes skimmed down over his body again, this time leaving a trail of heat in their wake.

"And why's that?" His eyes met hers, and a flush crawled up her neck and to her cheeks. Her eyes dropped to his mouth, just for a second, and something hot and thick pulsed in the air between them. She tucked a strand of hair behind her ear, and his fingers itched to repeat the motion.

Damn. She wasn't just cute. She was gorgeous.

"You don't look like a dweeb," she said softly.

Several feet away the door swung open again, and Sean leaped to his feet, putting himself between whoever had emerged and Sierra. She stepped out from around him and into the arms of Rory Evans, her former costar and...what, exactly?

"I've been looking for you. Are you OK?" he asked as he held her.

She nodded, and Sean was surprised at the jealousy swirling through him at the sight of this woman—who was pretty much a stranger—in someone else's arms.

"I'm OK. I just needed some air."

Rory smoothed a hand over her hair, completely ignoring Sean. "The police are here, and they want to get a statement from you about what happened."

She nodded again, and started to walk back toward the convention center. Turning suddenly, she laid a hand on Sean's arm, giving it a squeeze. She smiled up at him and it was as if someone were squeezing his heart with a fist.

"Thank you, Sean." Her hand lingered on his arm for a second, the air between them once again thickening.

How good would it feel to pull her into his arms the way Rory had just done? At least there she'd be safe. "You're welcome. Listen, if you ever...need anything, give me a call." He pointed at the card still in her hand, reluctant to let her go, but knowing he needed to get back to the office. Trying to reassure himself she'd be all right, with her *friend*, or whatever the hell Rory was to her, and the police. "You sure you're OK?" he asked, wishing he could go back inside with her to keep an eye on her. Not wanting to let her go. It felt…wrong.

Another fierce tug yanked at his chest.

"Yeah. I am." Her eyes held his for a second, and then she turned, slipping her arm into Rory's.

Sean pushed a hand through his hair as he watched Sierra walk away, his heart punching against his ribs as she glanced back over her shoulder at him one last time before disappearing back into the convention center. He took a deep breath, and then another, and then he walked back to his SUV. He looked back over his shoulder, contemplating going inside, just for a few minutes, just to make sure everything was under control…yeah. It couldn't hurt. He'd taken a few steps back toward the convention center when his phone rang, vibrating in his pocket.

"Owens."

"Who are you sending on the Robinson job?" his father asked, no greeting, just a barking question. Typical.

"Davis and Anderson. Why?" Sean's jaw tightened, tension seeping down his neck.

"You don't think it needs a third?"

Sean shook his head, irritated but not surprised that as usual, his dad was questioning his judgment. "It's a pretty standard job, so no. I think Davis and Anderson can handle it just fine, and keeping it to two keeps it within Robinson's budget."

"Uh-huh," said his father, sounding unconvinced. "This goes wrong, it's on you."

"It'll be fine. They've got it, and I'll check in with them regularly," said Sean, yanking open the door to his SUV and dropping into the driver's seat. He rubbed a hand over his mouth, used to his dad's blaming him for everything that went wrong. But just because he was used to it didn't mean it went down any easier.

Especially the blame he deserved. After all, it was his fucking fault his mother wasn't around anymore.

Phone jammed between his ear and his shoulder, he pressed the ignition button and tugged his seat belt on.

"You check on De Luca?"

Sean grimaced. "Didn't get the chance. Something else came up, but I'll check in with him by phone. I'm sure he would've made contact if there were any issues. I'm on my way back to the office now. Did you get the proposal I sent about the revised marketing plan?"

His dad sighed heavily. "It's a waste of fucking time. Not to mention money."

Sean leaned his head back against the seat, his jaw clenched tight. Nothing was ever good enough. "Let's talk about it back at the office."

"Fine. But it'll take a lot to convince me you can pull it off."

Sean almost snorted. Story of his fucking life, right there.

CHAPTER 2

Sierra walked up the short path from her driveway to her front door, keys jingling in her hand, watching as the sleek black sedan from the car service backed out of the driveway. She shivered as an early-summer breeze ruffled the leaves of the massive sycamore tree in her front yard. It was early June, and the temperature had dipped into the sixties as soon as the sun had set. The soft, sepia-toned glow of dusk enveloped the house, painting the white exterior a muted pink. The house was small compared to most of the others on her street, but it was hers, and it had been home since she'd bought it five years ago. Cozy and warm, it was her sanctuary. Especially on days like today. All she wanted was a bath, a glass of wine, and to snuggle up in bed with a movie. She'd managed to get most of the dye off her skin with a makeup-removal wipe, but her dress was ruined.

She dumped her purse onto the table in the entryway, flipping on the light switch beside the door. Her purse, too heavy as always, tipped sideways, spewing its contents across the small table, her phone clattering noisily against the wood as a tube of lipstick made a break for it down the hall. Grumbling, she bent to collect the spilled items, pausing at the slightly crumpled business card.

Sean Owens.

Professional Bodyguard and Security Expert.

Blood rushed to her cheeks, even though she was alone, and she tapped the card against her lips, replaying the all-too-short interaction with Sean, who had to be one of the most gorgeous men she'd ever seen. The thick dark-brown hair, short on the sides and a bit longer on top. The short, neatly trimmed beard that covered his jaw and framed his full lips. The coffee-colored eyes, warm and rich, with little lines crinkling around the corners. The hint of a scar curving across his left cheekbone and toward his ear, intensifying his rugged appeal. He'd been wearing a navy blue suit, and her stomach did a slow turn as she remembered the way it had clung to his broad frame, emphasizing his wide shoulders. He was tall—very tall, well over six feet—and built, and she'd be willing to bet he had something *very* good going on underneath that suit.

And then there were his hands. Holy hell, those hands. Large and strong, all wide palms and long, thick fingers. Goose bumps danced up her arms as she remembered the heat that had radiated outward over her skin at his touch. Oh, God, and that smile. Crooked and confident, with straight white teeth.

She could sum up the entire package in one word: *yummy*.

The truth was, she hadn't stopped thinking about him since she'd walked back into the convention center. While talking to the police about the attack, she'd been thinking about Sean. While assuring Rory and Steven she was OK, she'd been thinking about Sean. While on her way home, speaking with her director at Choices on the phone and reassuring her she was fine, she'd been thinking about Sean. His name buzzed through her brain, over and over again.

She couldn't explain it, and the fact that she couldn't unnerved her a little. There'd been something so easy, so simple about sitting with him. He was a total stranger, yet she'd felt completely comfortable with him, and sure, it had something to do with the fact that he was drop-dead gorgeous, but there was more to it than that. He'd had a quiet confidence that was immensely appealing, and he'd projected—without even trying, it seemed—the ability to take on the world one-handed and win.

He'd earned her trust in under five minutes, which wouldn't be weird, except for the fact that her trust wasn't something she gave out freely. And certainly not so quickly.

Something about him had grabbed her and wasn't letting go.

She stood, and the hairs on the back of her neck prickled, an eerie tingle running down her spine. She frowned, her eyebrows drawing together as she tried to place what was triggering the feeling that something was amiss.

Oh, shit.

Her alarm hadn't chirped when she came in the door, reminding her to disarm it. She checked the display panel and pressed her fingertips against her mouth, heat prickling across her scalp. It had been disarmed over an hour ago. She distinctly remembered setting it before leaving.

And she lived alone.

Her pulse sped up and her lungs constricted, refusing to pull in enough oxygen. All the anxiety, all the fear, all the awful helplessness of that afternoon came roaring back, and any sense of calm she'd managed to restore vanished. With a trembling hand, she grabbed her phone from the table and cautiously made her way deeper into the house, dialing 9-1-1 and leaving her thumb poised over the call button. She took quiet, cautious steps, listening for anything out of the ordinary. Every single hair on her body stood at attention.

With each step, the muscles of her legs felt less like muscles and more like Jell-O, and her stomach churned uncomfortably. A creeping, prickling sensation teased along the base of her neck as she reached the semi-dark kitchen. Her phone clutched in one hand, she grabbed a kitchen knife from the block on the island with the other, her eyes darting into every corner. A car alarm went off outside and she shrieked, nearly jumping out of her skin and dropping the knife, sending it skittering across the tiled kitchen floor. Quickly she bent and scooped it up, her heart racing as she stepped into the dining room off the kitchen.

She froze at the sight of the message left for her, scrawled across the far wall of the dining room in bright-red paint.

BABY KILLER

Unable to contain the terror making it impossible to move, to breathe, to think, she screamed.

* * *

"Drink?" True to her rock-star reputation, Taylor Ross always had plenty of alcohol on hand, and tonight Sierra was beyond grateful for it.

Taylor didn't wait for Sierra to answer but headed right for the fridge in her large open-concept kitchen. Overnight bag over her shoulder, Sierra followed her, watching Taylor's slender six-foot frame as she opened the fridge, her long blond hair falling in messy golden waves down her back.

"God, yes." Sierra tossed her bag onto the floor and swung herself onto one of the chrome-and-leather stools lined up in front of the stainless steel island in the kitchen. "Please."

While Taylor opened a bottle of wine and retrieved glasses, Sierra dropped her head into her hands, bone-deep exhaustion weighing on her like lead. Her head throbbed, a hangover from the overdose of adrenaline she'd experienced. And yet she still had the energy to feel angry and violated.

Because feeling angry and violated was better, easier to handle, than feeling helpless and violated. Anger she could do something with. She could harvest strength from anger. But that sickening, crumbling feeling of powerlessness? There was nothing she could do with that except fall apart. And falling apart wasn't an option.

Taylor folded herself onto the stool beside her and pushed a full glass of wine toward her. She looped an arm around Sierra's shoulders and pulled her close, pressing a kiss to her temple.

"I'm sorry, babe. This sucks."

The simple tenderness in Taylor's words unknotted something deep in Sierra's chest, and her throat thickened, her eyes stinging with unshed tears. Unable to help it, she started to shake, and with a single blink broke the dam. Setting her own wine aside, Taylor wrapped her arms around Sierra, and for several long moments, she did nothing but hold her, rubbing a soothing hand up and down her back as she sobbed.

"Yes. This does suck," Sierra managed to rasp out between shuddering gasps, her face buried against Taylor's shoulder. She allowed herself the luxury of a few more shaking sobs and then forced herself to take a deep breath, the air bursting into her aching lungs. Pulling back from Taylor, she wiped at her cheeks with the backs of her hands, the peace of catharsis settling over her.

"Thank you," she said, and then took a healthy gulp of her wine.

Taylor rubbed her arm. "I don't even know how many times you've been there for me, Si. You're my girl, and anything I can do to help, you just let me know." She gave her arm a squeeze and Sierra shot her a weak smile, beyond grateful for Taylor's friendship. For nearly ten years they'd been best friends, almost like sisters, and given everything that had happened, Sierra couldn't think of anywhere she'd rather be. "So what did the cops say?" asked Taylor. "Beyond the fact that you shouldn't stay in your house tonight?"

Sierra took another sip of her wine, and then blew out a long, slow breath. "Like I'd want to stay there after what happened." She shook her head, anger tightening its grip once more. "They said that it looked like someone had tampered with the alarm, and they were still dusting for fingerprints when I left. But the cop said he wasn't optimistic. Chances are if someone's smart enough to disable an alarm, they're smart enough to wear gloves."

"Do they have any idea who might've done this?"

Sierra nodded, picking idly at a thumbnail. "They think it might be this wacked out pro-life activist group called Sacrosanct. In other cities they've attacked people associated with Choices, but it's never happened here in LA. The police are looking into if Sacrosanct has set up some kind of satellite branch here."

"Fuckers." Taylor shook her head, her lip curled in disgust.

"They also asked if I could think of anyone who has a grudge against me."

Taylor tipped her head and held her hands out in front of her, palms up. "You told them about Jack, right?"

Sierra fought the urge to roll her eyes. "Just because we had a bad breakup doesn't mean he's out to get me."

Taylor arched an eyebrow, her long slender fingers drumming against the stainless steel island. "He was pretty pissed when you dumped him, Si. And he never supported your work with Choices."

"I know. That's part of the reason I dumped him."

"The rest of the reason being that he's a manipulative, controlling asshole who never deserved you and treated you like a decoration?"

Sierra felt herself smile, just a little. "Pretty much, yeah. But still. Breaking into my house and writing 'baby killer' on my wall? Throwing a diaper at me in public? That's not really his style. I know you were never his biggest fan, but you've got to admit that this doesn't seem like something he'd do." Sierra's relationship with Jack had been one of those relationships that start out great, but then turn into a game of Jenga. Slowly and surely he'd pulled out brick after brick, each one a bit trickier than the last, and she'd let him, leaving the foundation shaky while shit piled on top. Eventually he'd pulled the wrong brick, and the whole thing had come crashing down. She'd left him, even though he was good-looking, charming, smart, and successful.

As Sierra had found out over time, he was also a bag of dicks.

Taylor pursed her lips, and after a second she half nodded, giving in. "I guess not. It all seems a bit beneath a state senator, doesn't it?"

Sierra nodded. "And I haven't even talked to Jack in

months. The cops said this all fits with Sacrosanct's activities in other cities. Jack might be a jerk, but he was never violent or threatening."

"He may not have been violent—and seriously, that's like, the only nice thing I can say about him—but he is a jerk. Who told you you'd regret breaking up with him." Taylor leaned closer and pointed at her own chest. "In my book, that's a threat."

"So he'd publicly attack me? Several months after I broke up with him? That doesn't make any sense. Trust me, defending Jack is the last thing I want to do, but I'm pretty sure we can rule Senator Shithead out."

Sierra's phone rang, buzzing softly against the island's surface. When she checked the call display, she shot Taylor an apologetic smile. "It's Mom. I have to take this."

Taylor waved her away, topping up their glasses as Sierra padded through the living room, the overhead light winking against the row of gold records hanging on the wall. She swiped her finger across the screen to answer the call as she stepped out onto the terrace.

"Hi, Mom."

"Oh, honey. I got your messages. Are you OK?"

Sierra swallowed around the lump that formed in her throat at the sound of her mom's voice, which was tight with worry. "Yeah, Mom. I'm OK. Just a little shaken up. I'm staying at Taylor's tonight." As she rehashed the day's events with her mom—the attack, the break-in, what the police had said—she paced slowly around the terrace, her eyes roaming over Taylor's backyard and the view of the Hollywood Hills and Los Angeles sprawling at her feet. The famous white Hollywood sign glowed in the distance. Standing outside in the cool night air, the city pulsing with life around her, cars crawling by in the distance, she suddenly felt small and alone.

Untethered and insignificant. She slipped her free hand into the back pocket of her jeans, and her fingers bumped against the stiff paper there. Pulling it free, she studied the card, the blue-and-gray Virtus Security logo visible even in the terrace's dim light.

"So, anyway, the cops are looking into Sacrosanct," she finished, chewing on the inside of her lip as she stared at Sean's card.

Her mother let out a long sigh, and Sierra rubbed at her chest, feeling guilty that her mother was worried about her. "Honey, are you sure you want to keep going? You could just quit working with Choices and then everything would be OK."

Sierra bit her lip and tipped her head back, squinting to make out the few stars visible against the light pollution seeping up into the night sky. Maybe her mom was right. Maybe she should just walk away from Choices for her own safety. In one day she'd been attacked and had her home violated and vandalized. Clearly someone was targeting her because of her work with the organization. And now she was scared, angry, and likely giving her poor mother an ulcer.

But deep in her heart, she knew that walking away wasn't the right thing to do. Not for her, because she didn't want to give in to the harassment and let whoever was doing this to her win, and not for Choices. Keeping her chin up, refusing to be bullied, and sticking with Choices was the right thing to do, hard as it might be. She looked down at Sean's card again, her mind made up.

"I'm sure, Mom. This is important to me, and if I let them scare me away, what does that prove? That doesn't help anyone."

"It helps me sleep at night, for starters."

Sierra closed her eyes, wincing at the guilt slicing through her. "I'll be fine, Mom, I promise. I'm hiring security."

"I think that's a good idea. At least until this all blows over."

"Yeah. Me too."

"I love you, honey. Give Taylor a hug for me, and promise me you'll be safe."

"I promise, Mom. I love you too." She disconnected the call and stepped back into the house, the night air following her in.

"How's Renee?" asked Taylor, plopping down on the leather sofa in her living room and extending a wineglass toward Sierra. She took it, sitting down beside Taylor and tucking her feet under her.

"Worried. She wants me to quit working for Choices."

"I can understand why. What are you going to do?" Taylor sipped her wine as she crossed her long legs.

"I feel bad that she's worried, but I can't just leave Choices. Not only is that unfair to them, but then I've let myself be bullied and the assholes win. So I'm going to keep working with them, and hire security." She handed Sean's card to Taylor, who glanced at it quickly.

"I think I've heard of Virtus…yeah. I think I've seen one of their billboards or something. This logo looks familiar. You know this guy?"

"I just met him today, at the convention center."

Taylor shot her a teasing smile. "Big *Family Tree* fan?"

Sierra laughed, relaxing into the couch. "Actually…" She trailed off, dropping into the memory of meeting Sean again. How hot and protective and in control he'd been. Her stomach swirled as she conjured up the way his hands had felt on her skin, the delicious way his eyes had crinkled when he smiled, the way she'd felt instantly safe and comfortable with him…

"Uh, hello? Earth to Sierra. Where did you go?" Before she could answer, Taylor plowed ahead, her eyes wide. "Is he hot?" She picked up Sean's card from where it lay between them on the couch and pointed it at Sierra. "He *is* hot, isn't he?"

Sierra's cheeks heated and she snatched the card back. "Yes, he's hot, but that's not why I want to hire him." He'd made her feel so safe. Protected. While sitting with him, she'd known that he wasn't going to let anything happen to her.

"Oh my God! Look at you!" Taylor slapped her leg playfully, a wide smile on her face.

"What?"

"You're all swoony."

Giving up any pretense, Sierra let her head tip back against the sofa and rolled her neck to look at Taylor.

"Tay, you should see this guy. *Hot* doesn't even scratch the surface."

Taylor took a sip of her wine. "Start from the beginning, and tell me everything."

CHAPTER 3

Sean took a deep breath, inhaling the scents of fresh-cut grass, old leather, and cooling evening air. Metal baseball bats clanged softly together in his gear bag as he walked across the diamond to his team's bench, puffs of dust swirling up around his feet with each step. Dozens of spectators dotted the bleachers of Pote Field, chatting among themselves and watching the players set up. Dropping his gear by the bench, Sean bent over to unzip the bag.

"Hey, man. Glad to see you didn't get stuck at work. For once." Antonio Rodriguez, one of Sean's oldest friends, clapped him hard on the back, a bat tipped casually over his shoulder.

"What do you mean, for once? I've only missed a couple of games." Sean straightened, shoving a pair of black-and-white batting gloves into his back pocket, mentally tallying how many games he'd missed since the start of the season two months ago.

"Actually you've missed six." Antonio leaned against the

chain link fence separating the bench from the diamond, studying Sean.

"Shit. Really?" Sean shook his head. "I'm sorry, man. Work's been crazy lately. I didn't mean to—"

"Hey, look! It's the ghost! How you been?"

After exchanging greetings with a few of the other teammates, Sean pulled his cleats out of his bag, dropping down onto the bench to lace them. "So how's it going? You good?" he asked, glancing up at Antonio.

"Yeah, I'm good. Caught a few big cases at work."

"Oh yeah? Anything interesting?"

"Dude, it's Major Crimes at the LAPD. It's *all* interesting."

Sean stood, brushing his hands over the pants of his uniform. "Lap?"

Antonio nodded. "Yeah. You should probably warm up nice and slow. Get all that rust off you."

Guilt gnawed at Sean, and he shoved a hand through his hair before tugging his cap down over his eyes. "I know. Some stuff's come up at work, and—"

Antonio blew out a breath, his lips flapping together. "Man, you work too much."

Sean didn't say anything. What the hell was he supposed to say? Antonio was right. He probably did work too much. He prided himself on his work, and if a client needed him, he did his best to be there. Over the past several years, he'd taken on more and more responsibility at Virtus, and now that meant not only working with his own clients, but supervising a team of four other bodyguards, and making decisions about staffing, company expenditures, and training. His dad expected a lot of him, and Sean expected a lot of himself, so it worked—from a professional standpoint, at least.

From a personal standpoint, things were a big fucking mess, and there was really no way to fix it. Unless someone had a time machine, Sean and his father were both stuck, living with what had happened over ten years ago now.

It was the only time Sean had failed to protect someone. And he lived with the guilt every day, regret and remorse eating at him like a cancer. So yes, he worked a lot, and yes, he took his job damn seriously. Never again would he fail someone like that. No matter the cost.

Jogging side by side, they traced the perimeter of the field. The diamond was nestled into the southeast corner of Griffith Park, and to the east, the Hollywood sign glowed faintly pink in the fading daylight. Sean barely registered the famous landmark as he jogged, having seen it thousands of times. He'd grown up in Los Angeles, and he was numb to the exotic allure it held for tourists. A large hill separated the baseball diamond from the golf course on the other side, dotted with trees and shrubs. The sun dipped behind the horizon, painting everything a hazy pinkish-yellow hue. As they passed the stands, Sean could feel Antonio's eyes on him.

"Hey, is Jana coming?" Antonio asked, slightly out of breath. He was having a hard time keeping up with Sean's long, easy strides.

"Oh. Uh, no."

"She busy?"

Sean glanced sideways at Antonio. "We're not seeing each other anymore."

"What happened?" They each grabbed a glove, and Sean picked up a ball and tossed it to Antonio, who backed away several feet before throwing it back. Other members of the team hung around, stretching and talking, a few others also tossing a ball back and forth.

"Nothing. She just…I had to cancel a few times for work. She couldn't deal with my schedule."

"Can't say I blame her," said Antonio, his voice flat as he shot Sean a pointed look. "That's too bad, man. I liked her."

"Yeah, me too." Sean adjusted his cap, tugging it lower over his eyes. He and Jana had only dated casually for a few months, and he couldn't honestly say he'd been surprised when she'd pulled the plug. It wasn't the first time his schedule had made trying to date pretty damn difficult.

"Don't take this the wrong way, bro, but you need to loosen up a little. I get that your job's important to you. Trust me, I do. But you gotta live your life too, man, otherwise what's the fucking point? I'm not saying take it less seriously, but you need to check your priorities. Work-life balance, man. Google that shit."

Sean just laughed, knowing Antonio was right, but also knowing he probably wasn't going to be changing his schedule. Protecting people, helping them through difficult, sometimes dangerous, situations, gave him a sense of purpose. Each person he helped earned him the tiniest measure of redemption. And making sure Virtus remained one of the best private security companies in California eased some of his guilt. Sometimes. So he worked his ass off because he didn't know what else to do with himself.

By the time the game ended, the sun had set completely and the floodlights had switched on, illuminating the field in a harsh white flare of artificial light. Sean peeled off his batting gloves and dropped them into his bag.

"Victory beers at Frank's Bar. You in?" Antonio's car keys jingled in his hand.

Sean nodded, a grin spreading across his face. "Yeah, sure. And beers are on me, since I've been MIA lately."

Antonio clapped him on the shoulder. "Hey, you wanna buy us all beer, you can disappear as often as you like."

Frank's Bar and Grill was a tradition for the team. After every game they gathered to either celebrate or commiserate over burgers and beer. Frank reserved a section at the back for them every Wednesday, knowing they'd be in.

Red vinyl booths lined the walls, with thickly shellacked wooden tables and chairs filling the floor space. A long, wide bar dominated the left side of the room, with a row of wooden stools standing at attention in front of it. Frank waved from behind the bar as the team filtered in, and he turned up the volume on the classic rock pumping from the speakers, already compensating for the cacophony of over a dozen men celebrating and blowing off steam.

Sliding onto the chair next to Sean, Antonio elbowed him. "You got any new celebrity stories?" A few other heads swiveled in his direction at Antonio's question, and Sean smiled, shaking his head slightly. They were all under the impression that being a bodyguard was something glamorous and exciting, and asked him often about the celebrities he met. He shared stories when he could, but only within the bounds of confidentiality. There was something hilarious about a bunch of guys who lived within spitting distance of Hollywood asking him for celebrity gossip, thinking he was connected, and he was having too much fun to disabuse them of the notion. He actually didn't deal with celebrities that often. While Virtus had several actors and musicians as clients, the majority of its business came from politicians, business executives, and athletes, and from acting as a security consultant for various events.

"Actually, yeah, I did meet someone today." And damn if something tiny and light didn't flutter in his chest at the thought of Sierra, weighted down only by the accompanying brick in his stomach as he remembered how scared she'd looked at first.

Antonio rolled his eyes and set his beer bottle down. "Are you gonna make us guess?"

Sean sat back in his seat, his fingers wrapping around the neck of his beer bottle. "It's no fun if you don't." He smiled and brought the bottle to his lips.

"Man or woman?" asked one of his teammates.

"Woman. I met her at 90's Con."

They all threw out incorrect guesses, Sean shaking his head at each name. "I'll give you a hint," he said, taking another sip of his beer, and he didn't realize just how tense his shoulders had been until they started to relax. "I bet at least one of you had that famous poster of her wearing a red bikini."

"Sierra Blake!" Antonio shouted out her name, and the entire team agreed with his guess. The red bikini hint had given it away. Any straight male between the ages of twenty-five and forty knew that poster. It featured an eighteen-year-old Sierra, tanned and smiling, wearing a tiny red bikini and washing a car. It had been a promotional tool for a cheesy prime-time soap, *Sunset Cove*.

"So are you working for her?" a teammate prompted. Sean picked at the label of his beer bottle, the tension returning to his shoulders. No, he wasn't working for her.

And everything about that felt wrong. Helping her, looking after her today, had felt good. Right. She'd seemed OK when she'd gone back into the convention center, and he really hoped she was. And even more than that, he wished he had a way of finding out whether she was, in fact, OK. She was clearly strong and intelligent—not to mention beautiful—and it wasn't that he didn't think she could look after herself.

He just wanted to do it for her.

The same tug in his chest he'd felt that afternoon pulled the air out of his lungs, and Sean finally recognized it for what it was.

Need. The need to protect her and keep her safe. The need to comfort her. The need to be near her again, and to touch her again. These urges swirling through him, they weren't wishes, or wants, or ideas. They were needs, the way food, water, and air are needs.

Quickly Sean recounted a watered-down version of the story of how he'd met Sierra, simply indicating that she'd had a run-in with some protesters, and was upset. She'd been embarrassed enough; he didn't want to get into the gritty details of the attack.

He was protecting her, even when she wasn't around. Even when he'd probably never see her again.

The tug was almost painful.

"What was she like?"

"She was great. Upset about the protesters, but also really nice." Sean paused, searching for the right word, but there wasn't one. He wanted to find a word that summed her up, that wrapped her neatly into a little package, but he couldn't. She'd seemed a lot of things to him. Smart. Warm. Funny. Sexy. Vulnerable. Strong. Fucking adorable.

Beautiful.

"Is she still hot? I can't remember the last thing I saw her act in."

Sean rubbed a hand over his mouth, smiling. "Yeah. She's still hot." A round of approving noises rose up from his teammates.

"I heard about her getting hit with that diaper at the convention. Poor girl." Mike, the oldest member of the team, shook his head sadly.

"She handled it really well," said Sean, a wave of pride washing over him at how strong and together she'd been despite what had happened.

"She single? Married? What's her deal?" Antonio asked, nudging Sean.

"No idea." He picked at the label on his beer bottle again as his jaw tightened, the image of Sierra walking back into the convention center with Rory searing through his brain.

"Isn't she dating that state senator? The one who was on the cover of *Men's Health*?" asked another teammate.

"Jack Nikolaidis?" Sean sat up a bit straighter, and a drop of condensation from the beer bottle rolled down over his fingers, mirroring the cold trickle working its way down his spine. Through work, Sean had heard whispers that Nikolaidis wasn't quite what he seemed. Some of the other politicians he worked with had mentioned rumors about corruption, and bribery, and maybe even criminal ties. But they were just rumors, and a lot of people loved Jack. He was attractive, wealthy, well-educated, and charming. Some even thought he might be the next governor of California, if he played his cards right.

"Not anymore. They broke up a few months ago now. The rumor's that he wanted to settle down, have a family, and she wasn't interested, so when he got too serious, she dumped him," said Mike, leaning forward conspiratorially on his elbows. "Didn't exactly paint her in the best light, but given that he's a politician, and he's the one who got dumped by a beautiful woman, I'm sure his people are spinning it." He was met with several puzzled, surprised looks. "What? My wife has a subscription to *People*."

Shortly after, the guys began to clear out, and Sean pulled out his wallet and threw down enough to cover the team's tab. Antonio waited for him, and they walked out to the parking lot.

"Seriously, man. I'm really glad you came out tonight. It was good seeing you."

"Yeah, I'm glad I came out too. It's been too long."

Antonio shot him a pointed look but didn't say anything, letting his raised eyebrows do all the talking for him.

"Listen, can I ask you a favor?" asked Sean as they slowed, nearing their cars.

"You did just buy me a beer, so shoot." Antonio leaned against the bumper of his sedan.

"That story I told you about Sierra Blake and the protesters…" He trailed off and shook his head, trying to organize his thoughts. Trying to differentiate the intense need to protect Sierra from the instincts he'd spent the past decade honing. Trying to figure out if thinking about the attack left him unsettled because there was more to it, or because it had involved Sierra.

"Yeah? What about it?"

"I don't know. But there's something about it that isn't sitting right with me. Something's off." He rubbed a hand over his mouth, thinking, trying to pin down the feeling. But like most gut feelings, it was slippery, and wouldn't hold still long enough for him to get a good, hard look at it.

Antonio tilted his head, squinting against the parking lot's lights. "What? You don't think it was protesters?"

"No, I do. I just…my gut's telling me that something's up. Can you poke around a little? See if anything shakes out?"

Antonio pushed off the bumper of his car. "Sure. No problem. She file a police report about the attack?"

"I would assume so. She talked to them after."

"I'll pull it. See if I can get you a copy."

"Appreciate that, man."

"Don't mention it. I'll let you know when I've got

something for you." He studied Sean for a few seconds with a long, appraising look, one eyebrow raised, his lips pressed into a thin line. He opened his mouth, but then quickly closed it again.

But it didn't matter. Sean knew exactly what he'd been about to say.

And even if Antonio was right, he didn't want to hear it.

CHAPTER 4

Sierra stepped off the elevators and onto the tenth floor of the office tower at Sunset and Vine. A pair of sleek glass doors stood in front of her, the large *V* from the Virtus logo frosted onto the glass, winging up on either side over the polished metal door handles. She'd thought about calling and making an appointment, but the truth was, she wanted to see Sean again, and she figured this was her best course of action.

Assuming he was even here. If he wasn't, then she'd call the number on his card. She stepped into the brightly lit office space, morning sunshine streaming in through the floor-to-ceiling windows lining the far wall, and a single, disconcerting thought ran through her mind.

I might not be able to afford him.

A circular stainless steel reception desk sat just to the left, two women behind it wearing Bluetooth earpieces and typing rapidly as they listened and spoke. Behind them an open-concept area was a hub of activity, people talking, pointing at monitors, drinking coffee, answering ringing phones. The activity was centered around a cluster of glass-and-chrome desks laden with computer equipment, including huge monitors. A little farther back, blue-and-gray couches sat grouped around low-lying black tables. To her right and across from the reception desk there was a small waiting area, furnished with simple gray leather chairs and glass-topped coffee tables stacked neatly with magazines. A huge flat-screen TV was mounted to the far wall, currently tuned to CNN. Behind the reception desk and to the left of the open-concept area sat a bank of offices, enclosed in walls of glass. The walls were each emblazoned with the Virtus Security logo about halfway up, the blue and gray crisp against the spotless glass. The entire space was bright, modern, professional, and sleek.

She'd been about to step up to the reception desk when one of the glass doors toward the back of the bank of offices swung open and Sean strode out, deep in discussion with another, younger man. Sean held a tablet in front of him, pointing at it and clearly explaining something to the employee, who watched Sean with rapt attention, nodding rapidly at everything he was saying. She could see the employee's lips move, forming the words "Awesome, thank you," before he took the tablet back and headed for another glassed-in space across the room. The glass of these walls was frosted for privacy, the door marked with "Conference Room" in simple, modern lettering.

She watched as Sean slipped his hands into his pockets and started back to his office, only to be waylaid by another employee who waved him over and pointed at his computer screen. Sean leaned down, one hand braced on the desk, the other pushing through his hair and messing it up a little. In a simple light-gray suit, white shirt, and sage-green tie, he looked incredible. Blood warmed her cheeks as she studied him, watching the easy way he interacted with the other employees, the way the fabric of his suit jacket stretched across the wide expanse of his back. She liked watching him move, talk, work. His confidence and competence were both palpable; it was the way he carried himself, the way everyone around him seemed to defer to him, the way he had solutions to everyone's problems.

He stood, his hands on his hips, holding his open suit jacket back to reveal a flat stomach, trim waist, and narrow hips. An employee said something that elicited a laugh from Sean, and the sound that reached her was warm and rich. She wanted to wrap herself in that sound, it was so appealing. He turned again to go back to his office, the wool of his suit hugging his ass and showing off rounded muscle.

Holy gorgeous, Batman.

She took another step forward, now at the reception desk, when he stopped and slowly turned, as though he could feel her gaze on him. From across the space, his eyes met hers, and her stomach exploded into butterflies, while at the same time relief flooded her. The knot she'd been carrying between her shoulders since the attack yesterday afternoon loosened, just from being in the same room with him.

She didn't care what it cost. Even if she had to take out a second mortgage on her house, she'd do it to hire this man to protect her.

His face creased into a smile, and he closed the distance between them in several long, quick strides. The smile faded as he approached, his eyes roaming over her.

"Sierra. Is everything OK?" he asked, his brow furrowed.

She couldn't suppress her shaky laugh, and she pressed her fingers to her lips. "Not really, no. Can we talk?"

"Absolutely. Let's go to my office." He gestured for her to go ahead of him, and with a hand on the small of her back, he led her through the bustling space and to the office she'd seen him emerge from a few minutes ago. The lettering on his door spelled out his name, as well as "Director of Operations and Strategic Planning." The other offices belonged to the directors of finance and accounting, information technology, and human resources and training. The last office, the biggest, was empty, but she noticed that it belonged to Patrick Owens, whose title was simply "President."

She pointed at the next office as she followed Sean in, the buzz of the rest of the office dropping away as the glass door fell silently closed behind them. "Are you related? I noticed the same last name."

He nodded as he sat down on the gray sofa against the far wall, gesturing for her to sit down beside him. "Yeah. Patrick's my father."

She lowered herself down onto the sofa, and then reached into her purse for the folder she'd brought with her.

Sean leaned forward, once again frowning in concern. "Did something else happen?" His eyes skated up and down her body, and she swallowed, her mouth suddenly dry. She took a breath, forcing herself to focus.

"Last night I came home to discover that someone had broken into my house. The police think it was probably the same protest group who attacked me at the convention yesterday."

Sean's mouth pressed into a firm line, his eyes darkening slightly. But he said nothing, waiting for her to continue. She passed him the folder, and he flipped it open instantly, his eyes scanning rapidly over the copy of the police report she'd brought with her.

"Someone wrote 'baby killer' in huge red letters across my dining room wall." He nodded, indicating that he was listening even as he read. He rubbed a hand over his mouth, and the butterflies she'd been trying so valiantly to rein in escaped, fluttering helplessly through her stomach and chest. Swallowing, she continued. "I set the alarm when I left, and it was disarmed an hour before I got home. The front door was still locked. I don't know what the hell's going on, and it's freaking me out."

He looked up from the police report, anger hardening his features. "They're messing with you. Trying to scare you."

She took a breath, and her words tumbled out in a rush. "I'd like to hire you, if you—"

He cut her off by gently laying a hand on her knee. Warmth radiated outward from where he touched her. "Yes. Absolutely, yes."

It must've been only a few seconds at most, but the seconds stretched out, warm and slow, as his brown eyes held hers. The weight that had been pressing down on her since the attack yesterday afternoon lifted, and she suddenly felt as though she could breathe again. She swallowed and Sean took his hand back.

"Thank you. I'm not sure what you charge, but…"

He cut her off again, this time with a wave of his hand. "We'll figure something out." He smiled, a slow quirk of the corner of his mouth, and heat spiraled through Sierra's body. "I'm glad you're here, and that you're OK."

"I've been a bit of a target ever since I started working for Choices a few years ago, but nothing I couldn't handle. Nasty e-mails, comments online, that sort of thing. I knew I was opening myself up to that kind of stuff when I agreed to work with them. Some people see it as a controversial topic, so I expected the hate mail and the online stuff. But

I've never had anything like this happen before. I've never felt genuinely afraid before." She ducked her head, inhaling a few quick breaths to try to dispel the sting of tears pressing at her eyes.

"Hey." Sean's deep voice was gentle. With a featherlight touch, he tipped her chin up. The sensation of his skin on hers sent sparks shooting up her spine, and she bit her lip. Sean tracked the movement with his eyes before flicking them back up to hers. He shifted almost imperceptibly closer. "I'm not going to let anything happen to you. I promise. From here on out, I've got you." Her breath caught in her chest and she nodded, the movement brushing the tips of his wide fingers against her chin. "For the record, I think what you're doing is brave. It takes guts to stand up for what you believe in. It takes strength."

His words washed over her, replenishing her resolve to keep working for Choices. "Thank you," she said, her voice a little hoarse. She cleared her throat. "That means a lot to me. I was starting to question if I was doing the right thing." She wanted to close her eyes and press her face into his palm, but he dropped his hand, once again quickly taking it back.

"That's only natural, given everything you've been through in the past twenty-four hours."

She nodded, twisting her fingers together. "So...what happens now?" she asked, glancing out at the office space.

"We work in teams. I'll be lead on this, meaning I'll be with you 24/7, and another guard will rotate on and off."

"24/7?" she asked, licking her lips as more of her tension melted away. How was it possible that she barely knew him, and yet he made her feel so safe?

"I'd feel better being on-site at all times, yes. There will always be someone in the house with you, either me or someone from my team. We don't know who we're dealing with, and until we do, I'm not going to risk leaving you alone."

Her stomach did a slow turn at the protectiveness in his voice. "I have a small guesthouse you can set up in, if you want."

"It's close to the house?" he asked, eyebrows raised.

"My property actually isn't that big. The previous owners converted the pool house into a little guesthouse. Unless you'd rather be in the house."

"As long as it's close enough to the main house, the guesthouse should be fine for when I'm not on shift. Hang on a sec." With a reassuring smile, he pushed off the sofa and strode over to his glass-and-chrome desk. He picked up the phone and hit a button. "Morning, Cassie. Can you round up Alpha Team and send them into my office? Thanks." He hung up and sat down in the leather desk chair, the chair squeaking in soft protest against his weight. He was so...*big*. Tall, and broad, with a wide back and masculine hands.

Her stomach swirled as something hot and sweet flamed over her skin, and she recognized it instantly as lust. She let herself luxuriate in it for a few seconds, wondering what he'd look like with his shirt off, if his hair would feel as thick and soft between her fingers as it looked. If he was...proportional.

Oh, sweet Jesus.

Sierra watched as a few of the guys broke away from the grouping of computers in the center of the office space and headed for Sean's door, not waiting for an invitation to come in.

"Sierra, this is my team. Carter Davis, Ian MacAllister, Zack De Luca, and Jamie Anderson." He turned to the men, who stood in a cluster of suited muscle by the door. "Sierra's a spokesperson for Choices, and she's now been the target of two attacks, both in public and at home. She filed police reports for both incidents, but she's understandably concerned for her safety until whoever's harassing her is neutralized."

Sierra studied the group of bodyguards as Sean brought them up to speed on her case. Carter was huge, about as big as Sean, with medium-brown skin and short black hair. He shot Sierra a smile as Sean introduced him. Ian, on the other hand, didn't smile, only gave her a curt nod. His reddish-blond hair curled around his ears, his blue-gray eyes piercing. She got the distinct sense he was someone you didn't mess with.

The other two guards, Zack and Jamie, seemed much less intimidating than Carter and Ian. Zack was tall and lean, with an almost cocky confidence in the way he carried himself, despite the fact that he appeared to be the youngest of the group. With thick dark-brown hair, light-brown eyes, and a killer smile, he was almost as hot as Sean.

Almost.

"Hey. Sorry this is happening to you," said Jamie, the last guard. With his blond buzz cut and kind blue eyes, he looked like the hottie next door.

They made an impressive team, fit and confident. And in Ian's case, a little scary.

Sean glanced down at the folder in his hands before speaking. "I'll go over to Sierra's place with her to check it out and get set up. I'll take a look at your schedules and other client bookings to work up a schedule of shifts and text you with your assignments. I'd also like to take a look at your alarm system," he said, turning to her. "I want to know how exactly it was tampered with. You ready to go? Did you drive here?"

She shook her head. "No, I took a car service."

"I'll drive you home."

As the team filed out, she bent to retrieve her purse from its spot on the floor by the couch. She spun and almost slammed into Sean, who was just coming around from behind his desk. His fingers curled around her shoulders, and he held her steady, pulling her against him to prevent her from stumbling.

The air between them changed, becoming thick and heavy as his gaze dipped from her eyes to her mouth and back again. His grip tightened slightly on her shoulders, a sharp contrast to the way he'd pulled his hands back before.

"You OK?" he asked, his thumbs tracing little circles on her shoulders.

I will be if you kiss me.

Sierra couldn't remember the last time she'd been this drawn to someone, this trusting, and so quickly. It was both thrilling and unnerving.

"Sean," she said, her voice barely above a whisper. His eyes darkened, and she knew he felt it too, the heat swirling in the air around them, drawing them together. His chest rose and fell slowly as he took a breath, and then he released her, stepping back behind his desk.

Or maybe he wasn't feeling it too, and she was projecting her loneliness-driven lust onto him. Before she had time to analyze his quick retreat, the door to his office swung open again, and Sierra knew immediately that the man in the doorway had to be Sean's father, Patrick. He had a head of short, thick salt-and-pepper hair and had the same large build and brown eyes as Sean. There was a definite resemblance, and Sierra had to admit that Patrick was quite attractive for a man who was probably in his mid-sixties.

Sean and his father locked eyes, and the air in Sean's office once again shifted, the pressure dropping as though a storm were about to hit.

"Sierra, this is my father and the founder of Virtus, Patrick Owens," said Sean, gesturing toward his father. She shook Patrick's hand, and he gave her a polite smile. "This is Sierra Blake. She's our newest client."

Patrick's face remained neutral. "Would you excuse us for a moment, please, Ms. Blake?"

She looked at Sean, who gave her a reassuring nod. "Uh, sure. Sean, I'll meet you in the waiting area?"

"Sounds good. This will just be a minute. Help yourself to water, coffee, anything you need."

As she made her way to the waiting area, she glanced back over her shoulder, and although she couldn't hear anything, she could tell Sean and his father were arguing. Sean's posture was tense, his jaw clenched as he braced his hands on his desk, leaning forward toward his father, who was talking and gesturing emphatically. Sean kept shaking his head, disagreeing with whatever Patrick was saying. Patrick pointed in her general direction and she felt suddenly guilty, although she was pretty sure she had nothing to feel guilty about. She scurried back to the waiting area, feeling like both a spy and a delinquent.

"Don't worry about that," said Jamie, falling into step beside her as she headed for the coffee machine in the far corner of the waiting area. "It's just what they do. Even though Patrick officially retired two years ago, he's having a hard time letting go. I don't think he got the memo that being retired means you *stop* coming to work."

Sierra took a mug from the basket beside the machine and slipped it under the dispenser. She selected a pod and pressed the button on the machine, feeling relieved that she hadn't gotten Sean in trouble. Relieved that he'd said yes to the job. Relieved that he'd be with her, looking out for her until the harassment was over. And she barely knew him.

Barely knew him, but knew that she trusted him.

And wanted him.

Oh, God help her. She was in some serious trouble.

CHAPTER 5

Sean rolled his SUV to a stop in Sierra's driveway, taking in the small but pretty white house that sat on a quiet street in the Hollywood Hills. A large sycamore tree cast shade over the front lawn, the leafy shadows almost reaching the street. From the front everything looked secure, but he'd need to do a thorough walk-through in order to assess the security she had in place. He glanced over at her as she unbuckled her seat belt and hopped out of the SUV. But instead of making her way toward the front door, she paused, her bottom lip caught between her teeth. He followed her out of the SUV and locked it behind him, coming around to her side of the vehicle.

"I haven't been back inside since the break-in," she said, tipping her head toward the house. She wrapped her slender arms around herself, her green eyes bright.

For about the hundredth time that morning, Sean sank into the feeling of relief he'd been carrying around ever since he'd set eyes on Sierra standing by the reception desk. The relief—that she was safe, that she'd come to him for help—had been almost overwhelming in its intensity. And now that he had eyes on her and knew she was OK, he *would* protect her. He trusted his team, but he wasn't willing to take the risk of leaving her in someone else's hands. He couldn't.

The instinctive protectiveness he felt toward her ran deep, and he hadn't realized just how deep until he saw her again this morning. He was determined to keep her safe, and if he ever got his hands on whoever was doing this, he'd beat the shit out of them. But now that she was officially a client, it also meant that she was off-limits. Not only was it incredibly unprofessional to get involved with a client, it was distracting. And distraction would be dangerous, for both of them.

He knew it wasn't going to be easy to ignore the chemistry sparking between them—hell, he'd wanted to kiss her in his office—but he didn't have a choice. The fact that she was now a client was a big-ass "Do Not Pass Go" sign.

He gave her a reassuring smile. "It'll be OK. And it'll be good for me to see the damage." She nodded and led the way up the path to her front door. As they walked, Sean's eyes roved over the property, looking for potential vulnerabilities.

"Do you have motion-detecting lights?"

She shook her head. "No. The outdoor lights are on a timer, though."

He nodded, listening, as he slipped his phone out of his pocket to take pictures and make notes. "We'll get you some motion detectors, and the indoor ones should be on timers too, for when you're not home. And we should upgrade these to floodlights." He frowned, looking into each corner of the porch, and then stepped back to study the exterior of the house again. "You don't have any security cameras, do you?"

"No, just the alarm. It's just me, and it honestly never occurred to me to get security cameras."

"You live alone?" he asked, even though he'd already picked that up from the police report. He just wanted it confirmed.

She nodded. "Yeah. I've lived here for five years now."

"I'll add security cameras to the list. I've got some gear in my trunk. Once we've finished our walk-through, I'll set them up for you."

They reached the porch, and his eyes immediately went to a plastic rock sitting by the welcome mat. He stooped down and picked it up, flipping it over and extracting the hidden key. He held it up between his thumb and forefinger, one eyebrow raised, and Sierra cringed.

"I don't think I need to tell you that having this here is a terrible idea, right?"

She blushed slightly, looking sheepish. "I actually kinda forgot that was there."

He handed her the key and the plastic rock with an impatient grunt. "Ditch the hide-a-key."

He turned his attention to her front door, studying the handle and hinges. "We can upgrade this too. I've got some reinforcements I can install that will make it more resistant to being kicked in. New hinges and screws, a thicker dead bolt."

Her eyes widened, and she clutched the plastic rock to her chest. "You think someone would try to kick in my door?"

"It's not likely, but to keep you safe, I need to be prepared for anything this protest group might throw at you."

Her brow furrowed, tension written across her pretty face. Shit. He hadn't meant to scare her. Before he could stop himself, he tucked a strand of hair behind her ear, his fingers lingering on the delicate skin there. "Chances are, no one's going to try to kick down your door. And if they do, that's what I'm here for. I'm not going to let anything happen to you. I get that you're scared, but I promise, I've got you."

She closed her eyes for a second and pressed her cheek into his palm. She was so small, so sweet, so undeserving of any of this shit that his heart ached a little for her while the rest of his body roared to life, heat pulsing low in his gut and tightening the muscles there.

Fucking hell. One touch, and he was ready to pin her up against the wall.

"I'm really glad you're here," she said, sighing heavily. Reluctantly he pulled his hand away, struggling to maintain any semblance of professionalism.

"Let's go inside. I want to take a look at that alarm system."

She unlocked the front door and he followed her in, turning his attention to the small panel on the wall beside the door.

"I assume this came with the house, considering it looks like it's about twenty-five years old," he said, once again tamping down the tiny surge of anger pushing up through his chest. Her security was mediocre at best.

"Yeah. It's active, though."

"Right, but these are easy to tamper with. All you have to do is take the battery out to bypass having to put the code in." He pushed a hand through his hair. "Who knows both your code and that you had a key hidden on your front porch?"

She crossed her arms. "No one who'd write 'baby killer' on my wall, I can promise you that."

"This all needs to be upgraded. I have a system we can install for you. It connects with the security cameras, locks on every window and door, and the motion-detecting lights I'm going to install for you. I'll show you how to use it once it's set up. And don't give your code to anyone."

"Right, but I—"

He didn't give her the chance to finish. "Sierra. Do not give out your code. Ever."

She studied him, her lips slightly parted. After a second she nodded.

"Show me where the vandalism happened."

She tipped her head and led him through a sunken living room, the height of the ceiling accented with dark criss-crossed wooden beams. Two worn, comfortable-looking chocolate-brown leather couches sat at right angles to each other, orange and tan throw pillows scattered over them. Dark wooden wainscoting, matching the ceiling beams, came halfway up the wall before meeting wallpaper that looked like thick linen. It was warm, and welcoming. Nicely furnished without being pretentious. Comfortable and lived in—it was neat enough without looking like a showroom. The art on the walls and the books lining the shelves in the living room confirmed that she was smart and had good taste.

They crossed the living room and went into the kitchen, which was a large, open space with gray granite countertops, stainless steel appliances, and white cabinets. A massive island dominated the middle of the room. As they walked, Sean made a mental note to make sure the windows in the living room and kitchen all had functioning locks and to discuss the possibility of upgrading all the windows on the main level to laminated glass, which was much more diffi-cult to smash.

He followed her into the dining room and sucked in a sharp breath. Even though he'd known it would be there, seeing the words *BABY KILLER* scrawled across the wall in red paint, the color eerily bloody, had him grinding his teeth. His heart punched at his ribs, anger once again taking over.

As he looked at the damage, anger didn't seem to be a big enough word to encompass everything he was feeling. He could barely breathe around it, it was so suffocating. He paced, shoving a hand through his hair, trying to stay calm, rational.

Easier said than done, because it pissed him the fuck off that someone had done this to her. When he got his hands on these assholes, there'd be hell to pay. In the meantime Sierra was his to protect, and he'd make damn sure she stayed safe.

* * *

Sierra's shoulders slumped as she surveyed the damage to the dining room a second time. She didn't even care about the vandalism. She could repaint. But repainting wouldn't erase the sickening sensation that her home had been violated. Her sense of sanctuary had been shattered, and the comfort she'd once associated with her home was gone. She wasn't sure if that feeling could ever be restored.

She knew that she wouldn't have been able to come back here so soon if it hadn't been for Sean. She'd been too chicken to come back by herself, and now she was grateful she didn't have to face the damage alone. A muscle ticced in his jaw as he looked around the room, his hands on his hips. He turned to look at her, and something in his expression softened, just slightly.

He reached out, as though maybe he was going to lay his hands on her shoulders, but then shoved his hands into his pockets instead. "We don't need to stay in here. Let's go back to the kitchen and talk."

She poured them each a glass of iced tea and they settled on opposite sides of the island. His phone buzzed and he shot her an apologetic smile as he reached to check it, scrolling quickly through an e-mail or a text. She watched his hands as he worked, riveted. She was quickly becoming obsessed with his hands. How they looked. How they felt. She wanted to learn a lot more about his hands, but he kept taking them away. She didn't know how to read him. She knew there were sparks between them, and was positive he'd felt that almost magnetic pull too. And yet she could tell he was holding himself back.

Still reading, he absently rubbed a hand over his mouth, and her stomach clenched and swirled. It was almost unfair how gorgeous he was. She'd never experienced such raw lust for someone before. But she knew that it already went deeper than lust, because his appeal was more than skin-deep.

He looked up and their eyes locked. Oh, God, this man was doing stupid things to her insides, turning her inside out and tying her into knots while her stomach dipped and swirled as though she were on a roller coaster.

Needing something to do, she reached for her glass, but instead of closing her fingers around it, she managed to knock it over. She braced, waiting for it to smash onto the tile floor, but the crash never came. Lightning-fast, Sean shot out a hand and rescued it without even spilling a drop. With that lopsided smile, he set it down on the island.

Those goddamn *hands*. So much strength and power, and so much control. A hot thrill worked its way down her spine as she imagined them on her, touching her, taking off her—

"Someone from our tech team is going to come by shortly to help me get your security cameras and alarms set up. And as soon as Zack gets here, I'll go grab my stuff from my place, and then I'll install your new lighting."

She took a sip from her rescued glass, listening, unable to take her eyes off him.

"I'll be staying in your guesthouse, and as I said, there will always be someone in the house with you. If you need to go somewhere, I'll go with you, and we may take another member of the team as well, depending on what's going on. Even for mundane stuff like groceries or running errands, we need to have a security plan. I know it sounds excessive, but until the cops are able to arrest whoever's doing this, I'm not taking any risks with your safety."

"I don't think it sounds excessive at all," she said, shaking her head. "Given what's happened, it makes me feel better." She felt safe with him around, with his obvious security expertise. She knew, without a doubt, that he could protect her from Sacrosanct.

"Good. If you have any questions, or need anything, just let me know."

She had questions and unfulfilled needs that she'd be willing to bet good money he could help her with, but she had the feeling her rapidly growing crush on him wasn't what he was talking about.

"I'm going to read over both police reports from yesterday, see if anything jumps out at me," he said, setting his phone back down on the island and taking a sip of his iced tea.

"I can get you a copy of the first one."

"I've got a connection at the LAPD. He already pulled it and e-mailed it to me. I've also got him doing some digging on Sacrosanct to see what we can find out."

"The cops seem fairly certain that's who's behind this." She traced the tip of her finger through the ring of condensation from her glass.

He nodded slowly. "Can you think of anyone else who'd target you like this?"

"No. I think the cops are probably right about this being

Sacrosanct, and if not them, then some kind of copycat protest group."

"If you think of anyone else we can look into, let me know. We've got a private investigator on contract who can dig into places the cops sometimes can't."

"I will. Thanks." They sipped their iced teas in silence for a moment, but there was an easy comfort to it, which was crazy, given that she'd known him for less than twenty-four hours. At this time yesterday, she hadn't even known he existed. Today she couldn't imagine not having him around.

He pointed to a framed photograph on the shelf that held her stained and dog-eared cookbooks. "Is that you?" he asked, pushing away from the island to examine the picture up close. She leaned an elbow on the island, appreciating the chance to watch him unnoticed.

"Yeah, me and my dad. I was fifteen in that picture." In the photo, she and her dad wore matching aprons, flour streaked across her cheek and his forehead. He had an arm around her, and she was laughing. "It was Christmas Eve. We were making gingerbread cookies."

He picked it up and studied it, that lopsided smile making another appearance. "It's a great picture. You look really happy."

"I was. That was a few months before he got sick." She moved around the island, coming up beside him. She glanced at the picture she'd looked at thousands of times, trying to see it through fresh eyes.

The smile dropped away, and he set the picture back down. "Sick?"

A heaviness she'd long grown used to settled over her like dense fog. "Yeah. Pancreatic cancer. He died when I was seventeen."

His eyebrows drew together and he looked at the picture again. "I'm sorry." He paused for a second before continuing, tension pulling at his features. "I know how hard that is. I lost my mom about ten years ago."

She reached out and laid a hand on his arm, loving the feel of the hard muscle there, taking a small measure of comfort in the solid strength beneath her fingers. "I'm sorry. Was she sick?"

The corners of his mouth pulled down. "No. It was a car accident."

She gave his arm a squeeze. "I'm sorry."

He laid a hand over hers, his thumb tracing lightly over her knuckles, sparks arcing out over her skin at his touch. "Thanks."

"You know, people say that time heals, but I'm not so sure, because I'm always finding new ways to miss him." She swallowed, the small black knot right in the center of her chest squeezing tight. "And then it hurts all over again."

"I don't think it ever gets easier." He glanced away, his eyes soft and sad. "It's something you carry with you everywhere. Always."

She could almost feel the pain shimmering off him and she squeezed his arm again, knowing how much it helped to have an anchor against the grief that still rose up occasionally and caught her completely off guard. She raised her hand and laid it flat against his chest, the steady rhythm of his heart beating against her palm. The light in his eyes shifted from sadness to something dark and hot, and he dipped his head slightly, moving the tiniest bit closer. With him so close, every one of her nerve endings uncurled and stretched toward him. He was so tall, so *big*, that she wanted to lose herself in the shelter of his gorgeous body, to wrap herself around every part of him.

The doorbell rang, the chimes echoing through her silent house, and Sean pulled away.

"That's probably Zack," he said over his shoulder as he moved away and through the house.

Sierra spun and braced herself against the counter, trying to catch her breath. Trying to quell the fear that while this man could be very good for her, he could also be very, very bad. She'd spent months rebuilding the walls around her heart that Jack had managed to tear down, and now in less than a day, Sean had already started chipping away at them.

CHAPTER 6

Soft golden candlelight threw flickering shadows against the walls of Sierra's bedroom, deepening the peaks and valleys created by her rumpled sheets. Sean smiled down at her, propped up on one elbow, the sheet falling over his hip. The candlelight did his broad, muscled chest all kinds of favors, and she ran the tips of her fingers up his arm, enjoying the play of warm skin and hard muscle beneath her fingertips. Beneath the sheets, he slid a hand slowly up the outside of her thigh.

A fly buzzed somewhere, the sound stopping almost as soon as it had started.

Sean's hand continued its slow path up her thigh, and her legs fell open. She wanted everything he had to give. She was selfish and needy, and she'd take it all, over and over again. His fingers teased the seam where her hip joined her thigh, inching lower.

The fly buzzed again, louder this time. The edges of the room faded, and she dug her fingers into the sheets.

With a knowing smile, Sean dipped his head, his lips almost brushing hers as his fingers caressed her inner thigh, so close to where she wanted them.

Touch me. Kiss me. Take me.

Sierra's eyes popped open as her phone vibrated on the bedside table. With a soft groan, she pushed herself up to a sitting position and reached for her ringing phone, wishing she could simply sink back into the dream, where it had been just she and Sean.

Oh, God, those hands. She sighed out another little moan and checked the call display, grimacing slightly when she saw her agent's name on the screen. She hadn't spoken to her in months, and she knew Linda had been annoyed with her when she'd turned down the last audition Linda had booked for her. She wasn't acting much these days, and as far as Sierra was concerned, that was just fine. She made a very comfortable living off the residuals from both *Family Tree* and *Sunset Cove*, which allowed her to devote her time to Choices. Rubbing a hand over her face, she swiped her finger across the screen to answer the call.

"Good morning, Linda."

"Oh, you *are* alive. I was starting to think you'd kicked the bucket, since you haven't returned any of my calls."

Sierra grimaced. "I've been busy. What's up?" She swung her legs over the side of the bed, kicking her feet and trying to ignore the weight low in her stomach. Linda never called without an explicit purpose. Her time was far too valuable.

"Are you free for lunch today? I'd like to meet with you. I've been making some calls, and I have a potential audition I want to talk to you about."

"Oh, uh, today? I'll have to check with my security people." Her mind flashed back to her dream and her stomach clenched.

"Since when do you have security people?"

"Since I was attacked in public and my house was vandalized."

"Is this related to all that Choices stuff?"

"Yeah, it is."

"Well, that doesn't surprise me. I don't know why you waste your time with that when you could be acting."

Sierra pressed her mouth into a thin line, not wanting to get drawn into a fruitless argument with Linda, who continued without waiting for a response from Sierra.

"Just meet me for lunch today. I promise this is something you'll be interested in. It's more Gloria Steinem, less rom-com."

Her curiosity won out over her reluctance, and she found herself nodding. "Yeah, OK. I'll see what I can do. I'll call you if I can't make it." Sierra slid her feet into a pair of slippers and made her way out of her bedroom, slowly descending the stairs into the living room with the phone still pressed to her ear.

"Perfect. Meet me at Kismet at one o'clock. Ta."

Wondering if she'd made a mistake by agreeing to meet with Linda, she shuffled into the kitchen and started the coffee maker. While she waited for her mug to fill, she checked her e-mail on her phone, sorting the messages into work and personal folders. Once her coffee was ready, she wrapped her hands around the mug, inhaling the warm aroma.

Weak sunshine filtered through the kitchen windows that looked out onto her backyard. When she'd first walked through the house five years ago, she'd loved it and had been pretty sure she wanted to call it home. The backyard had sealed the deal. A long rectangular pool sparkled in the middle of the yard, surrounded by terra-cotta patio stones that branched off to form a path toward the small guesthouse in the far right corner. Rosebushes and various potted shrubs lined the pathway and patio, and a row of low, chubby palms stood along the edge of the property. Beyond the pool the Hollywood Hills rose up, smeared with greenery, mansions, and hazy sky.

About to take that first fortifying sip of her coffee, she froze, the mug halfway to her lips.

A pair of large hands appeared on the edge of the pool, followed by a pair of strong, cut arms, and finally one of the most chiseled bodies she'd ever seen in her life.

Sean hauled himself out of the pool, water dripping off him and onto the patio stones. His black swim trunks clung to his narrow hips, revealing ripped thighs and a muscular ass. He walked over to the patio table, checked his phone, and then dove gracefully back in.

The sexiest man she'd ever seen was swimming laps in her pool. She took a sip of her coffee and continued to watch him, letting her mind slip back to that dream. Her imagination hadn't done him justice. She'd known he was fit and strong given the way his suit fit him, but knowing and seeing were two completely different things. His body was incredible. He just looked so...*strong*. And big. And gorgeous.

After several minutes of hard swimming, he hauled himself out again, muscles straining as he pulled his large frame onto the patio stones. He shook his head, flinging out water droplets that sparkled in the sunlight. The moment could've been more perfect only if it had been happening in slow motion with "Whatta Man" playing in the background.

If it hadn't been clear enough given that dream, it was now undeniable. She'd never been more attracted to a man in her life. And sure, the unbelievable body and gorgeous face were a big part of that, but there was more to it than simple lust. Because while she'd never been so attracted to a man in her life, she'd also never been so instantly trusting of one, and the knowledge that she trusted him completely despite having known him for less than forty-eight hours was unsettling. Trust had never come easily for her, and here she was, giving it freely and unquestioningly.

Maybe it had something to do with how safe she felt around him. How protected and secure he made her feel just with his presence. After the attack and the vandalism, she'd been sure that she'd never feel at ease in her home again, but last night she'd slept like a baby—albeit a horny one—knowing that he was less than a hundred feet away in the guesthouse, and that a member of his team was spending the night on guard. The attack and the break-in had left her feeling vulnerable and powerless, and now she felt sheltered and safe. He'd spent the rest of the afternoon yesterday in jeans and a T-shirt, installing security cameras and motion-detecting floodlights and working with some guys from his company to get the new alarm system set up and linked with everything. Her garage now looked like the inside of some top-secret command center. She liked seeing these different sides of him: the professional in a suit, the handyman in jeans, the athlete in swim trunks. She was collecting all these different pieces, holding on to them, wanting to know what she'd see when she had them all.

He was just doing his job, and maybe everything he'd done for her wasn't a big deal to him, but it was a big deal to her. Almost effortlessly, he'd restored something taken from her.

She could feel herself sinking, getting pulled into something she wasn't sure she could handle. Maybe she was confusing lust for something more. Maybe she was making the mistake of letting her attraction to him and her recent loneliness cloud her judgment, and seeing things that weren't there.

Maybe it would be safer if she kept a little friendly distance between them until she got a grip on how she felt about him and how he made her feel.

And yet…it was only being friendly if she took him a cup of coffee, right?

She grabbed a pod and brewed a second cup.

Sean picked up a towel from one of the patio chairs and began drying himself off, his muscles flexing beneath tanned skin as he moved the towel from his hair down his torso and over his legs.

Oh, God. She'd never wanted to be a towel so badly in all her life.

Watching him, she felt a warm tightening between her thighs, accompanied by a tingling pulse low in her belly. Sean was still toweling off when she stepped out onto the patio stones, the freshly brewed cup of coffee clutched in her hands.

"Morning," she said, trying not to stare. "I thought you might like some coffee."

He smiled at her and took the offered mug. "Thanks. You sleep OK last night?" A droplet of water fell from his hair and onto his shoulder, sliding down over one of his gorgeously defined pecs and into the dusting of dark hair that arrowed a path down his abs and into his swim trunks.

She had the sudden urge to trace the trail left by the drop of water with her tongue.

"Sierra? You OK?"

Her cheeks hot, her eyes flew up to meet his. An amused smile tugged at the corners of his lips as he waited for her answer.

"Oh yeah. I'm good," she stammered, tucking her hair behind her ears. "Did you, um…did you sleep OK?"

"Just fine." He took a sip of his coffee, still studying her. The strap of her tank top slipped off her shoulder, and his eyes tracked the movement, lingering on her bare skin. An electric current ran up her spine, and her lips parted slightly, the air suddenly too thick to carry enough oxygen.

He reached out and gently slipped the errant strap back into place, the pads of his fingers grazing her neck and collarbone. She wanted to arch into that touch, needed more of it, but he pulled his hand back and took another sip of his coffee.

"My agent wants to have lunch with me today. Can we do that?" she asked in a rush, her skin still tingling from the contact.

He tipped his head and then nodded. "Shouldn't be a problem. Anything else you need to do today? Appointments or anything?" he asked.

"Not an appointment, but it's my friend Chloe's birthday tonight. I'm supposed to meet up with her and a couple others for drinks at the Chateau Marmont."

Sean frowned, his lips pressed together tightly. He took a sip of his coffee and grimaced slightly as he shook his head. "No. It's not a good idea."

She felt her shoulders drop slightly. "But you'll be with me. It'll be fine."

"It's a public place at night, and I wouldn't even know who or what to be on the lookout for. For your own safety, it's best if you stay home, where I can control the situation. There are too many moving pieces, too many unknowns for me to think it's safe for you to go to a bar right now, regardless of whether or not I'm with you."

"Oh." Disappointment pulled at her, and she sighed heavily, but then frowned as she looked up at him. "So what makes this different from the lunch meeting with my agent?"

"The time of day, the location, the activity. There's a difference between a business meeting in the middle of the day between two people, and drinking in a crowded bar at night with a group."

"The attack at the convention center happened in the middle of the day."

He tipped his head, agreeing. "True, but the point of the attack wasn't to hurt you. It was to humiliate you in a public place. We don't know what they have planned next, or who they even are. Better to play it safe and minimize the risks. Invite your friends here. Then we're both happy." Another drop of water fell from his hair and onto his chest, landing with a tiny splash beside his right nipple. Her blood hummed in her veins in response.

She sighed again. "I'll see if I can convince them to change their plans for me, I guess. I feel bad asking them to, though." A surge of anger pushed up through her chest, not because of Sean and his security protocols, but because of the situation that necessitated them. Not only was Sacrosanct trying to intimidate and humiliate her into shutting up, but it was negatively affecting her day-to-day life. All because she felt that women should be allowed to decide what happened to their bodies.

Assholes.

* * *

He watched as Jonathan Fairfax circled him, stalking closer like a wolf hunting its prey.

"What do you mean, you don't have the money?" Fairfax batted at the overhead light, sending it swinging back and forth in an arc of light and shadow, adding to his dizziness. He shifted in his chair, the wood hard and unforgiving underneath him. It creaked slightly, and he cleared his throat.

"I don't have it right now. But I'll get it."

"You have no fucking clue who you're messing with, do you?" Fairfax's voice was quiet and menacing, the words spoken with deadly precision.

A chill ran across his skin, the hairs on the back of his neck standing at attention, because he knew exactly who he was messing with. A bead of sweat rolled down his back, and he clenched his jaw, trying to suppress the tremor threatening to shake his skin free of his bones. "I'll get you the money. I swear."

Fairfax frowned, looking both unconvinced and unimpressed. "Let me ask you a question. Do you think it's fair that we held up our end of the deal and got you exactly what you wanted, and now you can't pay us for services rendered?" He nodded at someone behind the chair, and suddenly a plastic bag came down over his head, clamped in place with strong, immovable hands. He struggled for air, kicking out his feet as his lungs burned, his vision blurring around the edges. After a moment the bag lifted, and he sucked in a lungful of air, sputtering and gasping as his pulse thundered in his ears.

"Answer me. Do you think that's fair?"

He shook his head rapidly, spots dancing across his field of vision. "No."

Fairfax smiled, all tanned skin and white teeth. "I'm so glad we agree." The smile still in place, he leaned down, his hands braced on the arms of the chair, his face inches away. "You will pay me every cent you owe me with interest, you fucking worm, or I will end you, slowly and painfully. The next time I set eyes on you, you better have my money. Don't make me break your fingers. I hate resorting to clichés."

He nodded. "I'll have it. I promise."

And he knew exactly where he was going to get it.

CHAPTER 7

Sierra stepped into the restaurant with Sean and Jamie at her back, a sea of customers enjoying their lunches before her. She glanced over her shoulder at Sean, who sent her a reassuring smile. Not only was she not looking forward to the meeting with her agent, but she suddenly felt open and exposed. Her eyes darted around the restaurant, looking for…something. Anything out of place. Her shoulders stiffened as she realized how right Sean had been about the potential danger in public spaces right now. She didn't even know who or what to look for, or what they'd do next. Fear mingled with anger, and she gripped her purse a little tighter.

"Relax. You're fine. Jamie and I have got you." Sean's deep voice was quiet, and it washed over her, unknotting the tense muscles in her back and shoulders. He laid a hand on her lower back and guided her farther into the restaurant. "I'll be at a table nearby, and Jamie will be watching the doors. If it wasn't safe, I wouldn't have let you come." She glanced back at him again, and his hand pressed a bit more firmly into her back, warmth radiating out from his touch and relaxing her even further. She nodded, gratitude that he was here and trust in his ability to keep her safe extinguishing the anxiety eating at her chest.

She caught Linda's eye and waved, weaving her way through the maze of square tables, each topped with a pristine white tablecloth. The sun streaming in the front windows reflected off the wine bar on the opposite wall, illuminating the elegant space done in shades of cream and tan. Nearly every table was full, mostly with industry types conducting business over twenty-five-dollar salads that wouldn't have satisfied a rabbit. As she approached the table, a waiter appeared and pulled her chair out for her. She smiled politely and took a seat, watching as Sean settled himself a couple of tables away. Close enough to protect her, but far enough away to give her some privacy. The low buzz of conversation, clinking glasses, and scraping chairs hummed through the restaurant, shrouding them in a hush of sound.

Linda tucked a smooth strand of ice-blond hair behind one ear before taking a tiny sip of her water. "Sierra, sweetheart, how *are* you?" Her well-preserved face barely moved as she spoke. Her head swiveled around, taking in Sean a few tables behind her. One slender eyebrow arched inquisitively. "You weren't kidding about the security."

"I'm fine, Linda. And no. I wasn't kidding. After what happened the other day, I'd be stupid not to have security."

Linda flipped open her menu, her thin lips pursed. "Hmm. Well. You could just, you know. Quit. Then you'd be out of danger, right?"

Sierra bit back the scoff rising up in her throat. "If I quit, they win. And Choices loses. I refuse to let some whack-jobs have that kind of power."

"I just don't understand why you'd put yourself at risk for them."

"Because I understand the importance of what they do, Linda. And I'm not going to let these bullies scare me."

"But you already are scared, darling. I can see it. You're pale. You look tired. You keep looking at your bodyguard as if you're terrified he's going to leave."

As Linda spoke, Sierra realized that her eyes had, in fact, drifted back to Sean. Almost guiltily she pulled them away, not sure what to do with the realization that she needed Sean around to feel OK. That she'd attached herself to the safe harbor he provided like a barnacle to a ship. Eventually, mercifully, this would be behind her, and then he'd move on to another job.

Oh. The thought hurt like pressing on a bruise, tender and sore, purple and black around the edges.

Oh.

Pushing the thought away, she flipped open her menu, which was divided not by type of cuisine but by type of diet. Raw, vegan, gluten-free. Only in LA was this completely normal.

"I can get you work. Real work," continued Linda as she pulled a script out of the briefcase tucked against her chair.

"My work at Choices *is* real work."

"It puts you in danger, and makes you almost no money."

"I'm not hurting for money, Linda. You see my residuals. I'm doing just fine." She certainly wasn't rich—especially by Hollywood standards—but the residual payments from both *Family Tree* and *Sunset Cove* brought in a few hundred thousand dollars a year, which was plenty. In fact, those residuals were pretty much the only reason she even still had an agent. She'd bought her house outright, and didn't have any extravagant expenses.

Well, aside from what was likely to be a whopper of a bill from Virtus. She'd done a little Googling, and figured her weekly tab would be somewhere around ten thousand dollars.

So far it had been worth every penny.

"Why do fine when you can do great? Take a look at this," Linda said, sliding the script across the table to Sierra. "This is right up your alley."

Before she could reach for the stack of pages, the waiter approached to take their orders. Linda ordered the "farm lettuce special," which was basically a head of lettuce with salad dressing. Salad dressing on the side, of course.

"And for you?" The waiter turned to Sierra, pen poised over his notepad.

"I will have the portobello mushroom chicken, and a glass of sparkling water. Thanks." She snapped her menu shut and eyed the script in front of her warily.

"It's not going to bite you. Just look at it."

She hesitated, running her thumb over the chunky edge of the script, flipping the corners up with a soft burr of sound. "Linda, I appreciate this, but I'm not really acting much right now."

Linda sighed heavily and reached across the table, opening the script and tapping a manicured finger over a name on the front page. Elle Breccan. Sierra frowned slightly. That name was familiar. Why? She racked her brain, trying to pull the information free.

"The film's called *Bodies*," said Linda, continuing to leaf through the pages like a saleswoman presenting a brochure. "It's based on a true story. Remember that human trafficking ring that was discovered in Atlanta a couple of years ago? The film focuses on Elle Breccan, the lawyer responsible for both discovering it and saving all those girls." Linda looked up, sending Sierra a meaningful look. "Even though she got shot and almost died in the process."

"Wait, you think I could play Elle Breccan?" She remembered the story now. Breccan had discovered an underground ring of over two hundred massage parlors that served as a front for sex trafficking. Girls as young as eleven—many of them immigrants, both documented and undocumented—had been abducted from their families and forced into the trade, often being sold to the highest bidder. Breccan, the assistant US attorney for the area, had done everything in her power to stop it.

"Absolutely. You're in your thirties now, so you could play someone up to forty."

Sierra rolled her eyes, knowing there was little she could do about the pervasive ageist sexism in Hollywood. She pulled the script toward her and began flipping through the pages, a tiny spark of excitement flaring up inside her as she read.

"Are you interested?" asked Linda after a few minutes. The waiter returned with their food, and Sierra moved the script to the side. She cut a piece of her chicken and chewed thoughtfully.

"Intrigued," she answered finally, flipping through a few more pages. It had been years since she'd acted, but this story…it was incredible. Not only was Elle Breccan a compelling character, but the story was one that needed to be told. At first glance the script looked solid. Well written and dramatic without being preachy.

"Just promise me you'll think about it. I can get you on the list to audition, but I need to know soon."

Sierra felt herself giving in, her interest in the project winning out. "I promise I'll consider it." Linda's face lit up in triumph, and Sierra felt compelled to add, "I'm not saying yes or no, just that I'll think about it."

Linda speared a chunk of lettuce and pointed her fork at

Sierra, smiling confidently and looking completely pleased with herself. "I told you it wasn't a rom-com."

* * *

Sean's gaze roamed over the restaurant, returning every thirty seconds or so to Sierra, who was deep in conversation with her agent, a script open on the table between them, their plates now empty. He made eye contact with Jamie, who was stationed at another table by the door, and he nodded. The restaurant was busy, but there were no threats. Maybe he'd overreacted, telling her she couldn't go to the Chateau Marmont with her friends. She'd been so disappointed. He glanced at her table again, and her eyes met his for a second before she returned her attention to the script. Something hot and possessive seared through him, and he knew he'd made the right call.

Keeping her safe was *everything*. It was the *only* thing.

His phone buzzed from inside his suit jacket pocket, and he pulled it out, his eyes still scanning the restaurant as he answered.

"How're things going with the Blake job? I noticed you pulled a lot of resources in for this," said Patrick by way of greeting. The man was physically incapable of saying hello.

"Everything's fine so far. Equipment's all installed, and we've got the rotation going, so between the guards and the surveillance, I feel we've got a good handle on the situation."

"No further signs of the bastards, huh?"

"Not so far. I talked to Antonio, and they're still investigating. The cops have been looking into Sacrosanct for a while, but they don't have enough evidence to move on them."

"Are we sure it's Sacrosanct? Could it be anyone else? She got other enemies?"

"Sacrosanct makes the most sense, but it's possible the harassment could be coming from somewhere else. Antonio's looking into it, and I've also got Clay checking on a few people."

"People like state senators?" Patrick's voice was crisp and sharp.

Sean grimaced. "Just covering all the bases."

"If Jack Nikolaidis finds out you're having him investigated, shit's gonna hit the fan and splatter all over you."

"Clay's good, Dad. Discreet and smart. Nikolaidis will never know."

"But you think he's involved?"

Sean rubbed a hand over his mouth, the back of his neck prickling. "I don't know. He and Sierra dated, and it ended badly."

There was a moment of silence before Patrick spoke again. "Yeah, OK. That's worth looking into. You just pray he doesn't find out."

"He won't. I trust Clay."

Patrick grunted before changing the topic. "Priestley was in this morning, looking for you."

Sean glanced at the ceiling and shoved a hand through his hair. "Why?"

"Probably because he wants his job back."

Sean laughed, one short, bitter burst. "He burned that bridge. Hell, he didn't just burn it, he blew it the fuck up. No way is he coming back."

"We should give him another chance. With his military experience, he was a damn good bodyguard. Smart. Brave. Tough."

The ease with which his father complimented someone

else ate at Sean, but he shoved it down, ignoring the acidic churning in his stomach. "He was also reckless, with a temper. I almost lost an eye because of him."

"But you didn't."

"*But I didn't*? That's your defense? Jesus." Sean forced himself to take a breath, not wanting to get drawn into the usual argument right here and now. "The answer's no. Colt Priestley is never coming back to Virtus. He's too much of a liability."

"Fine. But I like him."

Of course he did. A muscle in Sean's jaw ticced. "Great. Go have a beer with him then, but he can't have his job back."

"Keep me updated on the Blake job." And with that his father hung up. Apparently he was just as allergic to *goodbye* as he was to *hello*. Not to mention the myriad other things he never said.

Sierra caught his eye and tipped her head toward the door, indicating she was ready to leave. After dropping a five on the table to cover his coffee, he slipped his phone back into his pocket and met her at her table. Her agent had already left, and with a script tucked under her arm, Sierra headed for the door, an unreadable expression on her pretty face. The tug in his chest was back as he watched her walk toward the SUV. There was something in the closed-off expression of her face, the tight line of her shoulders, that made him want to reach for her.

Goddammit. His need to protect her was tangling up with his attraction to her into a knotted snarl he didn't know how to unravel.

He held the rear passenger door of his SUV open for her, and she slipped in without a word. He paused as Jamie dropped into the front passenger seat, pulling the door closed behind him.

"You OK?" Sean asked, bracing his hands on the open doorframe, not for balance but so he wouldn't reach out and touch her. He couldn't seem to help himself anytime he was close to her.

She chewed her lip and ran a finger over the script in her lap. "I might have an audition."

His eyebrows rose. "And that's not a good thing?"

"No, it is…I just…" She shrugged. "I don't act much anymore, and this is potentially a really good opportunity for me. Especially given how everything's going with Choices right now." She frowned, twisting her fingers together.

"You're having doubts."

She looked up and met his eyes. "Maybe. Everything's upside down right now. I walked away from acting years ago, and now I've got this audition. Working for Choices means a lot to me, but maybe I'm crazy for putting myself at risk for them. My mom wants me to quit. Linda wants me to quit. Maybe they're right." She bent forward, dropping her head into her hands. "God, I feel horrible for even saying that out loud."

"Hey." Almost of its own volition, one of his hands slipped free from its grip on the vehicle and he slipped it under her chin, tilting her face up. "Do you want to quit?"

Determination shone in her eyes, and she didn't hesitate. "No."

"For what it's worth, I think what you're doing is brave. Not everyone would stand by a cause they believe in after what you've been through. The fact that you are…" He took his hand back and slipped it into his pocket. "It says a lot about the kind of woman you are."

"What kind of woman is that?" she asked softly, her eyes skimming down over his body before returning to his face.

"A smart and strong one, who refuses to be bullied.

Someone who stands up for others, and who does the right thing, even when the right thing is hard. Someone who has strong values and ideals, and who sticks to them, even when things get tough." At some point during his little speech, his hand had come out of his pocket, because it now rested on her knee, his thumb tracing small circles on her soft skin just below the hem of her skirt. "I think you're incredible."

She laid her hand over his and squeezed, warmth flooding through him at the contact.

"Thank you," she said, her eyes bright, her words quiet. She squeezed again.

Holy hell, did he want to kiss her. Kiss her until she wasn't scared anymore, until neither of them could breathe, until he heard his name dropping from her swollen lips.

But that simply couldn't happen. So with a small smile, he pulled his hand away and dropped into the driver's seat of the SUV, hoping his heart would eventually slow the hell down and some of his blood would start flowing back toward his brain and away from his swollen cock.

Jesus. He'd be lucky if he didn't have permanent zipper-teeth marks indented into his dick. And all she'd done was touch his hand.

Somehow he managed to wrench his attention away from the situation in his pants and the woman who'd inspired it and eased the SUV into traffic without killing them.

CHAPTER 8

Thanks for changing your plans, Chloe. I really appreciate it," said Sierra as she pulled her friend in for a hug. After her lunch meeting with Linda, she'd called Chloe and explained the situation, asking her if she wouldn't mind celebrating her birthday at Sierra's instead of the Chateau Marmont. Chloe, sympathetic and sweet as always, had agreed instantly. Sierra had spent the afternoon arranging to have cupcakes and other treats delivered, even sending Jamie on a decoration run because Sean wanted her safe and sound at home as much as possible.

The sound of raucous laughter erupted from the living room, and Chloe smiled.

"I see Taylor's already here," she said dryly.

"You're actually the last one to arrive for your own party." Sierra took the bottle of wine Chloe held in her hands and led her into the living room. "You know, you didn't have to bring wine, seeing as I'm the one who insisted you come over."

Chloe shrugged and tucked a strand of her gorgeous

cinnamon-colored hair behind her ear. "With everything going on, I figured you could use it. You're OK?" she asked, concern filling her wide hazel eyes.

Sierra nodded and patted her arm reassuringly. "I've got top-notch security, and the cops are looking into the attacks. I'm OK." She glanced around, taking in the newly installed security cameras, the slightest twinge of claustrophobia stealing her breath for a second. Zack approached with a rueful smile.

"He's got to check you and your purse. I'm really sorry," said Sierra, heat prickling her neck.

"No problem." Chloe gamely held her purse out to Zack. Once he was finished, she stepped into the living room with Sierra, Zack's gaze following her. With her golden-brown skin dotted with freckles and her startling hazel eyes, she was stunning, but didn't seem to realize the effect she had on men. She and Sierra had been friends for over twenty years, having grown up together. Chloe's father, Julius Carmichael, had been one of the executive producers on *Family Tree*, and while Chloe didn't act, she'd been around the set quite a bit. She was only a year younger than Sierra, and they'd both been grateful for another kid to play with during the downtime on set. They'd bonded over Barbies, Polly Pockets, Disney movies, and trying to play jokes on the older kids. Even as Sierra had drifted away from Hollywood, going to college instead of pursing an adult acting career, she and Chloe had remained close. Chloe's father was still one of the most powerful television producers in Hollywood, and she was following in his footsteps, writing scripts and working with him on different projects.

Chloe was greeted with a rousing chorus of her name, and she moved deeper into the living room to accept hugs and birthday wishes from Taylor, Rory, and Alexa Fairfax.

Sierra ducked into the kitchen to pop Chloe's bottle of pinot grigio into the fridge, needing a second to catch her breath. The anxiety she'd been fighting back all day had resurfaced, making her stomach churn and her chest tighten. She felt trapped in her own home, hiding and forcing her friends to accommodate her. She wrenched open the fridge and shoved the bottle of wine inside, slamming it shut with satisfying force.

"Whoa. Should I start hiding the steak knives?" Sean's voice came from behind her, and she spun to see him leaning against the island. Something funny tightened in her stomach when she laid eyes on him, a sensation in direct opposition to the anxiety she'd felt a moment ago. He wore a black T-shirt that hugged all those muscles in all the right places and a pair of worn jeans, and despite her frustration, she felt herself smiling. Curiosity and humor danced across his face, his eyes crinkling slightly as he watched her.

"No, I'm good. Just feeling a little…" She gestured around her. "Cooped up, I guess." She grabbed a cupcake from a nearby tray and peeled the wrapper off, taking a healthy bite. The cream cheese frosting was slightly tart and perfectly sweet, melting on her tongue with the red velvet cake.

Sugar always made everything better. Temporarily at least.

"But you get that this is what we need to do right now, right? It's for your own protection."

"Of course." Her eyes met his. "I trust your judgment, Sean."

"Good."

"Doesn't mean I like any of this, though."

"Maybe you should take the wine *out* of the fridge, then. If the door still works," he said, his tone light. She tried to stifle it, but she laughed, a brightness filtering over her at his gentle teasing.

Sean's phone buzzed, and he yanked it out of his back pocket. As he studied the screen, he ran a hand through his hair. In the bright lights of the kitchen, she noticed a few sparse strands of gray threading through at his temples. Her fingertips tingled with the urge to touch his hair, to sink her fingers into it.

"Sorry," he said, looking up from his phone and shooting her that lopsided smile that sent heat flushing through her.

She waved away his apology. "So I thought you would've retreated to the guesthouse." Zack was on duty tonight, and just as he'd done with Chloe, he'd briefly checked each guest as they'd come in, which had been beyond embarrassing, but each of her friends had tolerated it with good humor. Except Taylor, who'd immediately turned it flirty and dirty, inviting Zack to frisk her, among other things. By far the cockiest of Sean's team, he'd flirted right back.

God, she loved her friends. Not everyone was lucky enough to have such a supportive, fun, tight-knit group. She was beyond grateful to have them in her life. A little bit more of her anxiety slipped loose, and her shoulders felt lighter.

Sean shrugged, the black cotton of his T-shirt pulling tight across his strong, wide shoulders. "I thought I'd stick around, keep an eye on things for a bit."

She tipped her head to the fridge, which was well stocked with appetizers, a fruit tray, drinks, and various other goodies. "Help yourself to anything you want."

He smiled. "Thanks. But I just had dinner, so I'm good."

"Not even a cupcake?" She picked one up from the tray on the counter and walked over to him, holding it out. It was as though her skin were sensitized to him, and the closer she got, the more her nerve endings came to life, stoking the heat curling slowly through her. She couldn't remember the last time she'd wanted a man the way she wanted Sean. He was gorgeous, and kind, and strong, and her body craved him with an intensity that was both thrilling and a little frightening. Just looking at him sent her heart racing and her stomach swirling with want, not to mention the warm throbbing that settled right between her legs whenever she was near him. Or thinking about him. Or dreaming about him.

Maybe her body was trying to tell her something her stubborn brain—or was it her heart?—was refusing to accept: that she could be vulnerable with him, and it wouldn't blow up in her face and leave her collecting the scattered shards of her heart. He'd already seen her at her most vulnerable, at the mercy of whoever was trying to scare her, and he'd taken her vulnerability and cradled it in those big strong hands, protecting her and making her feel safe and secure.

Maybe it was time to explore another kind of vulnerability.

I think you're incredible. His words from earlier echoed through her, strengthening the shimmering strands of trust arcing delicately between them.

"I don't really eat sugar," he said, setting his phone down on the island and leaning back on his palms. His shirt clung to his muscled frame, and she believed him. You didn't get the body of a Greek god with cupcakes.

"Never?" she asked, and began peeling the wrapper from the cupcake, the accordion folds popping out rhythmically.

"Not usually." He licked his lips, his eyes darkening slightly. "Maybe you should take one to Rory." He tipped his head in the direction of the living room.

"Rory can get his own cupcake."

Sean arched one eyebrow. "So you guys aren't…" He

trailed off, but he didn't need to finish the question. Sean cared if she was single or not. And he seemed a little jealous that she might not be. She squared her shoulders, feeling suddenly both light and bold.

"Rory's just a friend. I'm single." She swiped her finger through the icing on top and sucked her finger into her mouth. His lips parted slightly as his grip tightened on the island, his knuckles almost white. "It's very good," she said sweetly, once again holding the cupcake out to him.

"I don't doubt it." His voice was low, a little rough, and he cleared his throat. She stepped closer to him and set the cupcake on the island. As she reached past him, her breasts brushed his chest, and she didn't step back. Instead she laid her hands on the island on either side of him, close but not touching. She looked up at him, trying in vain to read the expression on his face.

"But you don't want the cupcake?"

He took a breath, and her breasts pressed into his chest again. And then his hands were on her, circling her waist and pulling her against him. Big and strong and warm, they felt so good on her, as though she could melt into a puddle of bliss under his touch. There wasn't a part of her that wasn't alive and fully awake. He smelled so good, a lingering hint of aftershave clinging to his skin, blending with the clean-laundry smell of his T-shirt. She wanted to bury her face in his chest and breathe him in, but couldn't seem to tear her eyes away from his face. When he spoke his voice was still low, and a little strained. Heat flashed in his eyes.

"It's not that I don't want it. It's that I shouldn't have it. Trust me, there's a difference."

"You can't always deny yourself what you want."

"No, but in this case, I have to. Cupcakes are…off-limits.

No matter how much I want one." His grip tightened, and he pulled her more firmly against him.

Oh, sweet Jesus. He was hard, thick and big, his cock straining against his jeans and pressing firmly against her hip, and try as she might, she couldn't suppress the tremble coursing through her. He *was* just as affected as she was. So why was he holding back, telling her no?

The tips of his fingers grazed the top of her ass, and even through her jeans, she could feel that touch searing through her, tying up her insides into ridiculous knots of lust and need. Like a sunflower stretching toward the sun, she arched up onto her toes, her eyes glued to his mouth. Just one kiss. One little taste of that gorgeous mouth. His breath was warm against her face, his eyes hooded.

Cold air swirled around her as he set her away from him and stepped away, pushing a hand through his hair. A pained look flashed across his face, his brow and jaw tight. "No, Sierra."

She stood glued to the spot, trying to understand. "Why?" Realization flashed through her. "Oh, God. *You're* not single, are you?" Her voice was barely a whisper. Sean didn't wear a wedding ring, but that didn't mean he wasn't in a serious relationship. She'd just assumed, with the chemistry between them, the flirting…shit.

He sighed heavily and shook his head. "No, I'm single." He shook his head again and planted his hands on his hips. "You're a client, and I can't cross that line."

She pressed her hands to her cheeks, suddenly mortified at the way she'd just come on to him. "Oh. I'm—I'm sorry. I shouldn't have…I just thought…," she stammered, her face on fire. Her skin hurt, shame and regret crackling over her. She felt like a creep who'd sexually harassed her bodyguard.

He stepped back toward her and eased her hands away

from her face. She trembled slightly, ready to come out of her skin with how much she wanted him, with how much every single touch nearly undid her. "Don't be." He held her eyes with his. "You didn't misread anything, I promise you. But you're a client. As much as I might want…" He trailed off and his jaw tightened again, the cords of his neck straining visibly as he fought for control. "*Everything*, it can't happen." His voice was low, almost a whisper, and fierce, matching the hot intensity shining in his eyes.

She nodded, trying not to sink into the disappointment threatening to suck her under like quicksand. "I understand." She couldn't ask him to compromise his professionalism just to satisfy the lust swirling between them.

He cradled her face, his thumbs tracing lightly over her cheekbones. "I'm sorry."

She nodded, loving the friction of his hands against her cheeks. "I understand," she repeated, disappointment and the tiniest sting of rejection eating up all the oxygen in her lungs. She felt a tiny part of herself curl away.

He studied her for a second longer with those deep-brown eyes before releasing her. "Go. Enjoy your friends."

She backed away, nodding weakly, before making a beeline for the powder room. Safely shut away from everyone, she forced herself to suck down several deep breaths and then splashed cold water on her face.

A jumble of emotions swirled through her, all blending into each other until she didn't know how to feel. Disappointed. Rejected. Embarrassed. And yet she knew, somehow, that his working for her wasn't the only reason he was holding back. He'd wanted her. She'd felt how turned on he was. But she'd also seen something in his eyes. Given the number of walls she put up around herself, she was pretty good at recognizing them in others.

After patting her face dry, she emerged from the bathroom, feeling slightly more together despite the wet heat still pulsing between her legs. She sank down onto the couch beside Alexa, snagging a handful of pretzels.

"Hey, you OK?" asked Alexa, rubbing a hand over Sierra's arm. Sierra just nodded and chewed, managing a half smile around her mouthful of pretzels. She'd known Alexa almost as long as she'd known Chloe. The youngest member of their little group, Alexa had played Sierra's younger sister on *Sunset Cove*, and unlike Sierra, she was still acting. The Fairfaxes were one of the most famous Hollywood families, on par with the Barrymores, the Hustons, and the Fondas. Alexa's father, Jonathan, had won his second Oscar last year.

"OK, now that everyone's here, I'd like to propose a toast." Rory stood with his tumbler of scotch clutched in one hand. "To our lovely birthday girl. May the next year bring you happiness, health, and success."

"And a hot, well-hung boyfriend." Taylor winked as she raised her beer bottle.

"We love you, Chloe. Happy birthday," said Sierra, and they all clinked their glasses against Chloe's, who stood and hugged each of them tightly.

"I'm so glad you were able to make it, Rory." Chloe gave Rory's shoulder a squeeze. "I thought you were supposed to be in New York."

"I'm headed back tomorrow. Filming got pushed back a couple of days, which worked out great for me. You know I hate to miss a girls' night."

"You do make a pretty great girl," said Taylor.

"He's an honorary girl!" Alexa scrunched up her nose, clinking her glass with Rory's.

Rory batted his eyes and settled back on the couch. "Why,

thank you. This doesn't mean I have to start shaving my legs, does it?"

They all laughed, and once again Sierra felt grateful to have each of them in her life.

"How's your album coming, Taylor?" Sierra asked.

Taylor took a long pull on her beer before answering. "Don't ask. Everything I write comes out wrong, and that's when I can write anything at all. I sometimes think winning that damn Grammy was the worst thing that could've happened. Now I'm too up in my own head about everything, and I know I'm putting way too much fucking pressure on myself. But I don't know how to unwind, get out of my own way…"

Taylor trailed off as Zack walked quickly through the room on his way to the kitchen, probably to check in with Sean. Sierra didn't miss the way Taylor's eyes tracked him, traveling up and down his body as he walked.

"No," said Sierra, pointing at her. "Behave."

Taylor held up her hands in defense. "I'm behaving. For now." She glanced toward the kitchen before leaning forward, her forearms braced on her slender thighs, a mischievous smile tipping her mouth up. "He's pretty hot, though. I make no promises of behaving in the future."

Sierra just shook her head and smiled. Taylor was going to do what she wanted anyway, and they were all adults here. Mature adults, fully able to control themselves.

She'd just keep telling herself that until it felt true.

* * *

Sean stood in the kitchen, hard as concrete and trying to get his heart to ease out of his throat. Fuck, that had been close. He'd been about half a breath away from kissing her senseless. He'd never kissed a client before, and he sure as hell wasn't going to start now. He was thirty-five years old, dammit, not a horny teenager, and he needed to get a handle on himself. As tempting as she was, he couldn't let himself get distracted. And yet he knew there was more to his hesitation than distraction.

He couldn't fully explain it, but there was something about Sierra that appealed to him on pretty much every level. Yeah, she was sexy, but it was more than that. She was smart, and unwilling to back down in the face of harassment, and she took her work seriously. She was funny, and cute, and he felt so fucking good around her. Something about her just made sense to him. He felt completely torn, struggling to reconcile his need to protect her with his need for *her*.

It wouldn't be so difficult if the attraction were only physical. But it wasn't. He could fall for her. And that was something he wasn't looking for. A complication he didn't need in his life.

He paced to the edge of the kitchen, his gaze darting repeatedly to the tray of cupcakes still sitting on the counter. He turned away from them.

"Ugh, I saw Jack's stupid interview on TV the other day. I don't understand how someone can be so charming and so repulsive at the same time," said Taylor, and Sean paused, feeling only slightly guilty for eavesdropping.

Sierra laughed. "Ha! It's called politics."

"You did the right thing," said Alexa. "He never supported you or your work. I don't care how hot he is, he wasn't good enough for you."

"Thanks. I'm inclined to agree," said Sierra. "We started off so great. I thought maybe…we had a future. That I'd found something worth hanging on to. And then he turned out to be such a colossal asshole. I still feel so stupid for falling for his whole act."

Rory chimed in. "You're being way too hard on yourself. He didn't treat you right. I'm glad you broke up with him."

"Me too. God, he was pissed. I think he was surprised that I actually left him."

"He's spoiled and rich, and used to getting what he wants," said Chloe. "It doesn't matter how pissed off he was. Dumping him was the right thing to do."

"I still think you should tell the cops about him," said Taylor, and Sean stood up a little straighter, a chill creeping down his spine. "He told you you'd regret breaking up with him. And now this creepy shit is going on, directly related to your work at Choices, which he always hated."

Sean slipped farther back into the kitchen, his mind buzzing. He drummed his fingers on the island, feeling restless. He picked up his phone and checked his e-mail, then dialed Antonio's number, pacing slowly through the kitchen as he listened to it ring.

"Detective Rodriguez," Antonio answered, his voice brisk.

"Hey, man, it's Sean. You have a second?"

"Sure. What's up?"

"Just wanted to know if you'd made any progress or found anything interesting with the Blake investigation."

"We're still looking into Sacrosanct. They've been active in San Francisco, and we have confirmation that they've set up a branch here in LA. Can't link them to anything yet, even though my gut tells me that they're behind this."

"You remember the other night, we talked about how Sierra dated Jack Nikolaidis?"

"Sure."

"Apparently he was directly opposed to her work with Choices, and when they broke up, he threatened to make her regret it."

"Oh, really? Huh. Well, isn't *that* interesting," said Antonio, and Sean could almost hear the wheels turning from his end of the phone. "Thanks for letting me know."

"I've got one of my guys doing a little discreet digging too. Thought it would be worth mentioning. I know he's popular, but I've heard rumors that he isn't quite what he seems. Bribery. Corruption. Maybe worse."

"Nikolaidis might be the media's golden boy, but everybody shits somewhere. I'll keep you posted. Thanks for the heads-up."

"No problem. Thanks for looking into him. The sooner we get this wrapped up the better. I want these assholes caught." No one messed with his girl and got away with it.

Fuck. He was thinking of her as his girl, and damn if that didn't feel good.

He ended the call and, with a quiet growl, snagged a cupcake off the tray and headed for the guesthouse.

CHAPTER 9

Sean popped the last bite of cupcake into his mouth as he closed the door to the guesthouse behind him, sucking a bit of icing off his thumb. He locked the door behind him and tossed his keys onto the kitchen counter. They landed with a loud, echoing skitter, the sound jarring in the dark silence. Pushing a hand through his hair, he flicked on the lights, illuminating the small space. The guesthouse was laid out like a bachelor apartment, albeit a really nice one, with large windows, hardwood floors, granite countertops, and a walk-in shower worthy of a five-star hotel. A walk-in shower that was calling his name, and he yanked his shirt over his head as he walked toward the bathroom at the back of the space.

He tossed his shirt on the queen-size bed nestled into the far right corner, hidden from the living room with sliding glass panels. He was already missing his California king. His feet hung off the end in a queen, and he'd woken up this morning sprawled across the mattress diagonally on his stomach, the sheets twisted around him, the muscles in his back and shoulders complaining loudly.

He shucked his jeans, socks, and boxers, tossed them on the bed, and padded naked into the bathroom.

As the jets of hot water cascaded over his tense shoulders, he tried to relax, knowing Zack was on duty in the house tonight, doing regular sweeps of the property and monitoring the security cameras. Trying to convince himself that concern for Sierra's security was the main reason for the tension radiating through him.

Fucking hell, but he'd wanted to kiss her. That he'd been able to pull away had been nothing short of miraculous.

Tilting his face up to the spray, he closed his eyes and let the water wash over him. He adjusted the knobs, making the water as hot as he could stand it. Even though he'd done the right thing, he'd seen the pained look in her eyes as he'd moved away from her.

But he couldn't get involved with a client. It was unprofessional, and he needed to focus on protecting her. He couldn't do that if he was letting his dick do the thinking.

And yet…he couldn't stop thinking about the look on her face as she'd stared up at him, her green eyes dark, her lips parted, her cheeks flushed. Mentally he rewound the situation, allowing himself the luxury of imaging the outcome if he'd let things play out differently.

He'd have kissed her, gently at first, almost teasing, before slipping his tongue into her sweet little mouth and kissing her hard and deep. He'd have slipped his hands under her ass and lifted her, her legs sliding around his hips, his throbbing cock cradled against her. He'd have laid her down on that island and stripped her shirt over her head. He'd have buried his face in her delicate neck, tasting the skin there before traveling lower, palming her small, perfect breasts as he traced the outline of her nipples through her bra with his mouth. She'd arch up into his mouth, and he'd suck her deeper until she writhed beneath him, her legs still hooked around his hips.

He looked down at the bar of soap in his hand and shook his head. And then he slicked it over his palms.

He braced his forearm against the wall of the shower while his opposite hand slid down between his legs to grip his hard cock. As the spray from the shower pounded his shoulders and back, he stroked himself, one long, slow, teasing pull. His balls were heavy and ached for release, despite the fact that he'd already satisfied himself that morning before his swim. He'd woken from a dream about Sierra, almost painfully hard.

In the dream she'd slipped into the guesthouse in the middle of the night, completely naked, and had begged him to fuck her. Begged him, pleaded with him, told him she needed his cock inside her *now*. He'd bent her over the edge of the bed, hands spanning her small hips, and had lined himself up with her hot, slick entrance, ready to thrust into her, when he'd woken up.

He pumped his fist up and down, his eyes closed while thoughts of Sierra filled his head. Her mouth around his cock. Taking her from behind, her pert ass bouncing against his hips as he slammed into her. Pushing her legs apart and tasting her, discovering what sounds she made when she came for him. What she would look like riding him, small breasts bouncing as he watched his cock disappear into her body. What it would feel like to hear her call out his name, shaking and sweating and completely satisfied. His breath came faster, and he swelled, his lust for her so raw and sharp it hurt. With a rough grip, he pushed himself to the edge, stroking faster. Pressure coiled at the base of his cock, and with the fantasy of climbing on top of Sierra and sinking into her tight, wet depths as she cried out for him, he grunted and came, his cock pulsing in his fist.

His chest heaving, he leaned his forehead against the slick tiles of the shower. His head didn't feel any clearer. Not at all. But at least the ache and the tension had dissipated. For now.

After toweling off and pulling on sweatpants and a tank top, he grabbed a beer from the fridge. Settling himself on the couch, he flipped through the channels until he found ESPN and the tail end of the Dodgers game. He took a long pull on his beer, wishing he could have more than one. But even though he was off duty, he couldn't allow himself to indulge.

Seemed to be the theme of the night.

Never in his ten years as a bodyguard had he struggled so much to maintain a professional relationship with a client. And it wasn't for lack of opportunity. Over the years, he'd had his share of clients come on to him, and he'd never been even remotely tempted to give in.

With Sierra, everything was different. From the moment he'd laid eyes on her, there'd been something about her that had drawn him to her. Something almost intangible yet magnetic. An instant connection of some kind that he'd never experienced with anyone before, and especially not a client.

If anything happened to Sierra because he let himself get distracted, he wasn't sure he could survive it. He'd failed to protect his mother years ago, and he was barely living with the pain and the guilt of how he'd failed her. He saw it in his father's eyes, that undercurrent of disappointment that was always there. He saw it in himself, in the way he held himself back when it came to relationships. And there wasn't a damn thing he could do about it because he couldn't change the past.

He took another pull on his beer, absently rubbing a hand over the center of his chest, trying to soothe the soft, dull burn that seemed to be permanently lodged under his sternum. The game went to commercial, and he flipped a few more channels until he landed on a syndicated repeat of *Family Tree*, which had aired for almost ten years in the nineties. The scene featured Steve Simmons and the actress who'd played Sierra's older sister, as well as a five- or six-year-old Sierra, who'd just caught her siblings breaking something and trying to cover it up. Mouth wide, she planted her little hands on her hips and said, "You're gonna be in soooooo much trouble!" The last word came out like "twuhble," upping the cuteness by another factor.

Tiny Sierra was freaking adorable, with her pigtails and big green eyes, and freckles dusting the bridge of her nose. Even though the show was dated and corny, he found himself smiling as he watched. It was hard not to when she was on-screen. She was sweet and cute with a little bit of attitude. She laughed at something, and he noticed that her nose scrunched in the exact same way it still did. Maybe someday, when Sierra had kids, *this* was what her daughter would look like.

For some reason that thought made his chest hurt even more.

* * *

Sierra sang along to the Jackson 5's "I Want You Back" as it played from the small wireless speaker on her kitchen counter, basking in the morning sunshine streaming in through her kitchen windows. Spending time with her friends last night had been exactly what she'd needed to lift her out of the funk she'd been slinking around in for the past couple of days, and she felt recharged.

She poured pancake batter onto the hot griddle and

checked the frying pan next to it, inhaling deeply as the scents of frying bacon and freshly brewed coffee mingled together, and she thought of her dad. When she was a kid, he'd made a huge breakfast every Saturday morning, usually bacon, eggs, hash browns, and pancakes. Coffee for him and her mom, hot chocolate for her and her sister. After breakfast she'd curl up on her dad's lap, her older sister beside them on the couch, as they watched Pee-wee Herman or cartoons, laughing themselves silly. Her dad had done a mean Pee-wee impression, and it had never failed to send her into a fit of teary-eyed giggles.

She missed him every single day, and she found herself missing him even more in light of recent events. She missed the calm, warm stability he'd provided. She missed his voice, his laugh, the security of his arms around her. He'd died over ten years ago now, and it still hurt. Losing him was the hardest thing she'd ever gone through, and she hadn't handled it well. No one told you that grief wasn't an emotion but an entire state of being, forced on you by the loss of a loved one. It wasn't something you felt, but something you lived through and with, day after day, month after month, year after year. She'd made mistakes, a string of bad teenage decisions, but in the end she'd come out on the other side of her grief ready to take her life in another direction.

Her dad had missed out on so much, and she hoped he'd have been proud of the decisions she'd made once she'd made it through the fog of grief. He'd always supported her acting, but she had a feeling he'd have been even prouder that she'd gone to college. That she had a career that gave her life real purpose and meaning.

That she was happy, most of the time.

She stretched her arms above her head, spatula still in hand. As the song launched into the chorus, she brought the spatula back down and held it in front of her, using it as a microphone, singing at the top of her lungs and dancing along. She executed a fast spin, almost losing her balance as her socked feet slid against the tiled floor. She froze, dropping the spatula with a small squeak, as she registered Sean standing in the doorway, watching her and looking achingly sexy in a simple black suit and white shirt undone at the collar, a light-blue tie clutched in one hand.

He stared at her, and she felt suddenly self-conscious in her messy bun, oversize T-shirt, panties, socks, and nothing else. His eyes slid down her body, lingering on her legs before migrating back up to her face, his gaze leaving heat tingling across her skin. For a second, maybe longer, they locked eyes. Sierra could feel the electricity arcing in the air between them, and the hair on her forearms stood on end.

Sean cleared his throat and shoved his hands into his pockets as he stepped into the kitchen. "Sorry. Didn't mean to startle you."

She bent to pick up the spatula, and when she stood up again, she found his eyes once again on her. Heat pulsed between her legs as she imagined how good they'd feel wrapped around him.

She reminded herself of the way he'd rejected her yesterday as she reached for the mugs. "Would you like some coffee?" she asked over her shoulder.

"Please. Man, that smells good."

"Are you hungry?"

Before he could answer, his stomach growled loudly, and they both laughed, some of the tension ebbing. She shot him a smile, hiding everything beneath the surface: how badly she wanted him, the tiny twinges of fear that she was already in over her head with him, trusting and wanting too easily when she was still smarting from the rejection yesterday.

She clung to that rejection, unsure if she was pissed or relieved that it gave her the chance to strengthen her defenses. He'd started to tear down those carefully constructed walls so easily that a little distance was probably a good thing.

"I'll grab you a plate."

As she brewed him a cup of coffee, Sean sat down on one of the stools lined up in front of the island. She got three plates down, for her, Sean, and Zack. He deserved a nice hot breakfast too, after spending all night on duty and putting up with Taylor's flirting. Although he hadn't seemed put out by the flirting. No, he'd been flirting right back, and pretty competently too.

She'd also noticed the way Alexa couldn't seem to take her eyes off him, but hadn't spoken to him at all once Taylor had started flirting with him. Sierra just hoped that little triangle didn't get messy. Knowing Taylor, she'd have her fun and then move on. And knowing Alexa, she wouldn't say a word about it, always so eager to make everyone around her happy, often at the expense of her own happiness. Alexa was too sweet for her own good, and Taylor was too busy having fun to notice.

She set a plate laden with scrambled eggs, bacon, and pancakes in front of Sean, whose face lit up as if he'd just won the lottery. "Oh my God, this looks good." He looked up from his plate, and warmth suffused her at the expression on his face, all big smile and crinkling eyes. She passed him a knife and fork, and he cut into the pancakes and took a big bite, groaning softly as he chewed. Jesus. The man even made eating pancakes erotic. Or maybe she found a deep, raw sexual appeal in just about everything he did. She loved to watch him, no matter what he was doing. Pacing as he talked on the phone. Driving. Swimming laps in the pool. Leaning casually against a wall, little lines digging in between his brows as he read an e-mail on his phone. Pushing a hand through his hair when he was thinking.

The way he moved couldn't have been more appealing.

A couple of her metaphorical bricks started to crumble, and she scrambled to shove them back into place.

When he'd swallowed, he spoke again. "It doesn't just look good. This is delicious. Thank you." The words were so simple, and yet they tugged at something deep in her chest, his words like dynamite against her walls. Jack had never appreciated her cooking, always wanting to go out to eat so that they could be seen together. Her hurt feelings had only ever been a secondary consideration for him.

"You're welcome. I like to cook." She loaded up her own plate and sat down beside him, where they ate in companionable silence for a few minutes, her Motown playlist still humming softly through the speaker. Her phone chimed from its spot on the island a few feet away, and she reached for it.

She opened the text message, and her eggs turned to ash in her mouth. The message was from an unknown sender, and it contained a picture of her friends leaving her house last night. There was no text with the message. Just the picture, which spoke volumes on its own.

Someone had been watching her. Someone had taken a photograph of her friends. And that someone had been close by last night. Her hands started to shake as fear and anger boiled up inside her, her breakfast now sitting like a brick in her stomach.

"What is it?" Sean asked, his brow furrowed. Without a word she held out the phone to him, her fingers trembling.

"Son of a bitch," he growled, his voice low and dangerous as he took the phone from her. Despite her fear, that growl sent a thrill shooting through her. His expression darkened as he studied the picture for several long seconds. He pushed away from the island, her phone still in his hand. "OK, here's the plan. Tell your friends about this and have them be on the lookout for anything unusual or suspicious. Tell them to report anything out of the ordinary both to the police and to me. Change your number. I'll start going through the security cam footage from last night to see if we got whoever took this on camera. I'm also going to send a copy of this to Antonio Rodriguez. He's a detective with the LAPD."

"Can they trace the number?" If they could find out who'd sent the picture, they'd have an actual lead on who was harassing her.

Sean's mouth was a thin, firm line as he studied the message, tapping the screen a few times, calling up information about the date, time, and sender. Finally he let out a short sigh. "I'd bet my next paycheck that this came from a burner phone, but I'll get Antonio on it."

She balled up her paper napkin and threw it across the room, needing an outlet for the fear coursing through her. Hot tears stung her eyes, but she blinked them back, refusing to let them fall. "I'm sick of this! First they attack me, then they vandalize my home. And now they're making sure I know that they're watching not just me, but my friends, who have nothing to do with this."

Sean laid a hand on her shoulder, and she felt instantly calmer. Anchored somehow. "They're just trying to scare you."

"Yeah, well, it's working."

He tucked a loose strand of hair behind her ear. "As long as I'm here, I promise you that you have nothing to be scared of. I will do whatever it takes to keep you safe and to find out who's behind this. Nothing's going to happen to you or your friends."

She took a deep breath, and then another, barely fighting off the urge to press her face into his palm. "I know."

His eyes held hers for a few moments, her fear slowly melting until only a simmering rage was left.

"This makes me so angry, Sean. If they think this is the way to get me to back off from Choices, they've got the wrong idea." If Sacrosanct, or whoever the hell was behind these attacks, thought threatening her friends and scaring her was the way to go, it would soon learn the hard way that Sierra Blake didn't deal with bullies.

"I'm proud of you. Not everyone has your strength or bravery." He studied her intently, probably looking for signs she was cracking. But pride shone in his warm brown eyes, and she believed him.

She laughed softly. "I'm also incredibly stubborn."

He shrugged, and that lopsided smile she liked so much made an appearance. "Call it what you want, I'm impressed."

CHAPTER 10

It had been two days since Sierra had received the text message with the photo of her friends, and nothing had changed. Whoever had taken the photo had been well hidden in the shadows and wasn't visible on any of the security camera footage. As suspected, the number was untraceable. Sean was right—the call had been made from a burner cell, and according to the police, whoever bought it had paid cash for it. The cops were still working on the case, but no hard leads had turned up. They were no closer to finding out who was behind the harassment or confirming Sacrosanct's involvement than they'd been nearly a week ago.

Trying to push all that aside, Sierra walked down the bright, spacious hallway, her heels clicking against the marble floor. Sean's footsteps echoed a few feet behind her as they made their way toward the conference room at the end of the hallway. The Choices head office was housed on the tenth floor of an office tower on South Flower Street in downtown Los Angeles, and Sierra had been asked to attend a meeting with the board of directors. As she walked, she smoothed her slightly damp palms over the fabric of her black shift dress. She pushed open the glass door and glanced over her shoulder at Sean.

As it always did now when she looked at him, her heart fluttered helplessly in her chest as her stomach did a slow, enticing swirl. He tipped his head toward the door.

"I'll be right outside. Good luck." He winked, and the flutters and swirls kicked up a notch. She blew out a short breath, nodded at him, and stepped into the conference room. Despite her involvement with Choices, she'd never attended a board meeting before, and although she'd told herself over and over again that being invited was probably a good thing, there was a tiny part of her that was sure the board was going to get rid of her. The harassment had made the news, and maybe they'd figured it wasn't worth the negative attention to keep her around. Aside from an initial phone call after the harassment had started, no one from the organization had checked in with her, which had left her feeling slightly insecure.

The board was comprised of a dozen people, eight women and four men. Sierra had met many of them already—at fund raisers, functions, other meetings. She smiled politely as heads swiveled in her direction and she took a seat beside Vanessa Miller, a young ob-gyn who also acted as a spokesperson for Choices, tackling the more difficult medical questions Sierra wasn't equipped to answer.

Leslie Grant, the president and CEO of Choices, smiled and nodded at Sierra. With her elegantly cropped white-blond hair and slim-fitting navy blue suit, she looked every inch the corporate executive. Despite her friendly demeanor, Sierra found her intimidating. She always felt self-conscious and hyperaware of herself around Leslie, wanting desperately to earn her approval.

"Why don't we dive right in?" Leslie asked, and a young woman rose from a seat in the corner and passed out file folders to everyone. Sierra flipped hers open and began scanning down the page.

Whoa. This was big.

"As you can see from the information in front of you, we have the opportunity to apply for a large federal grant. Very large."

Sierra's stomach bottomed out when she saw the figure.

Fifty million dollars.

Leslie continued. "The purpose of the grant is to fund an initiative focused on improving the state of women's health across the country through awareness, education, and advocacy about things like contraception, STD testing and treatment, pre- and postnatal care, and cancer screening and prevention. Across our country, approximately seventeen million women are uninsured. The sex education offered in many states is, frankly, a joke."

She tapped the folder on the table in front of her. "This is the Jane Project, which is the umbrella name for the many subprograms we would be able to run with the grant money, all with the same singular focus and working within our already established framework: better health for women nationwide through improved education and access to services. Some of the subprograms include free STD testing, a teen pregnancy prevention program relying on evidence-based sexual education and ensuring access to a multitude of birth control options, free prenatal care for expectant mothers in targeted demographics, and free cancer screenings and health checks for women in correctional institutions, just to name a few. We've called it the Jane Project because every woman, regardless of age, race, or socioeconomic status, deserves access to the services we provide. Sierra, we'd like you to be the public face of this campaign."

"Really?" she asked, pride flowing through her.

"Absolutely. You're a wonderful speaker, and as we go forward in the grant application process, we'll need all of the public and political support we can get. You'll be speaking, lobbying, attending events. To start, there's the annual Choices fund-raising gala later this week, where you'll have the opportunity to speak to several influential politicians, and a symposium on women's health in Miami we'd like you to speak at next week. You've been tremendously influential up to this point in garnering support for Choices, and we think you're the perfect fit for this campaign. You're smart, well-spoken, and comfortable in the public eye. People like you. *We* like you," she added, smiling warmly.

Sierra bit her lip, not quite sure what to say. "Of course, I'll help in any way I can." She'd already been planning to attend the fund-raising gala with Rory, but now she was looking forward to it even more. There was so much they could do with fifty million dollars. So many women they could help, lives they could potentially save or change for the better with something as simple as a free Pap smear, or a free IUD.

"I'm glad you're on board. We need all hands on deck as we apply for this grant. We're not strangers to negative press." She paused, drumming her fingers on the table. "There's another organization also applying for the grant, and they have enough momentum behind them that they could potentially win it if they sway enough support their way. Have you heard of the Pregnancy Support Center?"

Sierra frowned, her mouth twisting slightly. "Don't they have those billboards? The 'Pregnant? Scared? We can help' ones?"

Leslie nodded, barely concealing a sneer. "That's them. They market themselves as a pro-choice women's health organization, but at the core, they're actually anti-abortion, anti–birth control, and anti–premarital sex. They believe women shouldn't have sex unless it's with their husband for the express purpose of making a baby. These are likely the same people who believe health insurers shouldn't have to cover birth control, and that employers shouldn't have to provide any kind of maternity leave." She shook her head. "I don't understand the logic of wanting all women to be mothers—whether they want that for themselves or not—and also refusing to support mothers with maternity leave or access to affordable health care. I shudder to think what an organization like that would do with fifty million dollars."

"I agree," said Sierra, shuddering right along with Leslie. She'd heard of organizations like the Pregnancy Support Center, masquerading as pro-choice but with ulterior motives. In some areas of the country, there were far more Pregnancy Support Centers than Choices branches. "Whatever you need, I'm your woman. I'm thrilled and honored to spearhead the public face of this campaign for you. I'll do my absolute best to make sure we get that grant. I promise," she added, so proud her ribs suddenly felt too big for her chest, poking at her and expanding outward as she filled up with pride, hope, and determination.

"Do the public appearances concern you at all?" asked Clark Nunes, the senior counsel for Choices.

A twinge of fear slipped between those puffed-up ribs like a tiny little needle, deflating her with the smallest prick. "It shouldn't be an issue. I've hired security, and I'll go over everything with them. I'm sure it'll be OK," she said, completely unsure it would be OK. Sean hadn't even let her go to the Chateau Marmont for a few drinks with friends. What was he going to think about a fund-raising gala? A speech at a symposium in Miami?

Shit.

"I hope it's not an issue. We need you," said Leslie, her long, slender fingers drumming the top of the table. "You've already been through enough because of your work for us. I'd hate to expose you to more harassment. Maybe this is asking too much."

"No. It'll be fine." It had to be. Choices needed this money; the organization could do so much good with it. "I want to do it." Despite the doubts she'd had since the harassment had started, she knew now that she couldn't back down. She couldn't let the bastards win, and she had the opportunity to help Choices and potentially make a real difference.

Hopefully, Sean would see it that way too.

After a few more agenda items, the meeting was adjourned, and Sierra rejoined Sean in the hallway. As always, her heart and stomach did their little roller coaster act when she laid eyes on him.

"How'd it go?" he asked, falling in a half step behind her, his hand at the small of her back. She wanted to ease back and melt into that simple, protective touch.

"They want me to head up a new campaign. They're applying for a grant, a huge one, and they've asked me to be the public face of it." Disbelief still tangled with pride. Sometimes she had a hard time believing that they really took her seriously. Knowing that they saw her as more than just an empty-headed actress meant a lot to her.

"Of course they did. They'd be crazy not to," said Sean, pressing the call button for the elevator with his thumb. As they stepped inside, she filled him in on the details, her excitement growing as she spoke. She paused before telling him about the necessary public appearances, hoping she wouldn't have to fight him on it, but prepared to if needed.

He sighed, his broad chest rising and falling as he pushed a hand through his hair. "It's not ideal, but I guess we have to make it work, don't we?"

"Yeah?" She looked up at him, and her breath stuck to her ribs. He smiled crookedly at her and she felt suddenly giddy with relief. And maybe something else too. Something she wasn't supposed to be feeling.

"Yeah. We'll figure it out. If this is what you want to do, I support you."

"Really?"

"One hundred percent. This is important."

The elevator doors slid open, and they walked out toward the lobby.

"Sierra?" She recognized Jack's voice instantly and turned around, spying him several feet away by a different bank of elevators. He looked much improved since she'd last seen him in person. His complexion was healthy, his black hair thick and shiny, and his piercing blue eyes clear, not bloodshot. Those eyes raked over her, and she was happy to find she felt nothing but a mild curiosity as to what he was doing here.

Those eyes had once seemed so appealing to her. But then she'd learned how they saw her, and everything had changed. He'd hurt her once, but the wound had healed, leaving scar tissue but no real pain. She'd loved him, and he'd never felt the same about her. He'd made her believe he had, though. And she'd fallen for it. She'd given him her heart, her trust, when all he'd wanted was her name and her body.

He approached, and Sean intercepted him, a hand extended. Jack flashed a megawatt smile and shook it.

"Sean Owens, Virtus Security," said Sean as Jack's eyes widened and he winced under Sean's grip. Now that he was standing with Sean, it seemed almost laughable how she'd once thought Jack so tall, so strong. He looked like a scrawny teenager compared to Sean.

"Jack Nikolaidis," said Jack, tugging his hand back, trying as subtly as possible to shake it out. He turned his attention back to Sierra and laid a hand on her shoulder, giving her a gentle squeeze.

"It's good to see you. You look great. Really great." He stood back and surveyed her again, smiling brightly. "What are you doing here?" he asked, slipping his hands into his pockets, his charm-o-meter cranked all the way up to eleven. He rocked back on his heels, watching her with genuine interest—an interest that was entirely one-sided. They'd broken up nearly six months ago now, and she hadn't forgotten his drinking and how bad it'd gotten. The nasty things he'd said. The way he'd tried to control her, bully her even. Yes, he was handsome, well educated, and ambitious, but he'd only ever been interested in her Hollywood connections and how good she'd looked on his arm at events.

And like hell she would ever settle for that. She'd rather be alone than with a man who wasn't all in.

"I had a meeting with the Choices board."

His eyebrows rose and he frowned slightly. "I heard about the attacks on the news." He shook his head, clicking his tongue in sympathy. "I had a feeling getting involved with them was a bad idea."

The urge to roll her eyes was so strong that she almost pulled a muscle restraining herself.

"You wouldn't know anything about those attacks, would you, Jack?" asked Sean, and she craned her neck to look up at him, wondering where he'd gotten that idea. His hand came to rest possessively on her lower back, and she relaxed into him, releasing tension she hadn't realized was there. Jack's gaze slid from Sierra to where Sean's hand rested and then up to Sean's face.

Jack's thick black brows drew together, his head tipping forward. "What?"

"You're well connected, and I was wondering if you'd heard anything. Rumors, maybe? Anything that could give us a more substantial lead." Sean studied him intently. What was he getting at? Sierra felt as though she'd missed something and was struggling to keep up with the conversation.

After a second, Jack shook his head. "No. I wish I could help you. You know, for a second there, I thought you were accusing *me* of being involved in the attacks."

Sean stared at him for several beats before speaking. "No, of course not. But if you could keep your ears open, use any connections you have to find out who's behind this, it'd be a huge help."

Jack nodded gravely, stepping a little bit closer and turning his attention back to Sierra. "Absolutely. If there's anything I can do to help, all you have to do is ask. Seriously. I care about your well-being."

"Yes, well. I *am* one of your constituents. And you know I vote."

He laughed, pointing a finger at her. "I always liked your sense of humor." He glanced at Sean again before smiling at her. "It really is good to see you, Sierra." He checked his watch. "I have to run. I've got a meeting, and then I've got to get back to Sacramento. Listen, I'm glad we ran into each other, and I'm glad you're OK. If I can help, call me. Please. And I promise to do the same if I hear anything."

"Thanks, Jack. I appreciate that." With a friendly nod and smile, he headed back toward the elevators. She appreciated his concern and his offer to help, but she knew she wouldn't be taking him up on it. Jack was firmly in her past, and she liked it that way.

"He seemed…" Sean frowned, his nostrils flaring slightly as a puzzled look crossed his face. "Nice, actually."

"You sound surprised."

"That's because I am."

They started toward the front doors of the lobby, and she debated how much to tell him. She'd never told anyone the whole truth about why her relationship with Jack had imploded. But with Sean…she knew she could trust him. She was surprised to find how much she wanted to tell him. "He *is* nice. Most of the time. When things are going his way and he hasn't been drinking."

Sean wrapped a hand around her upper arm and turned her to face him, bringing their steps to a halt. "He's a mean drunk?"

She nodded, fidgeting with the strap of her purse. "Oh yeah."

Sean's features tightened, and something burned in his deep-brown eyes. He dropped his voice to a near whisper. "Did he ever hurt you? Hit you?" His free hand curled into a fist, the skin tight over his knuckles.

"No. He never got physical. It was only ever verbal." She asked the question that had been pressing on her. "Why did you ask him about the attacks? That kinda came out of left field."

"I wanted to see how he'd react."

"Why? You don't think he's involved, do you?"

He shrugged. "I don't know. It's not impossible."

"Have you been talking to Taylor?"

"No, why?"

Sierra rolled her eyes. "She thinks Jack might have something to do with the attacks too."

"And you don't?"

"No. I think it's Sacrosanct." It was the most logical explanation, and putting an identity on her attackers gave her an ounce of comfort. At least that way she knew where to direct her anger. She knew who to blame. Without a target, she had nowhere to go with that anger, and it would sit inside her, burning a hole through her chest.

"Jack threatened you when you broke up with him."

She looked up at him and blinked slowly. "How did you know about that?"

He rubbed a hand over the back of his neck and glanced up at the ceiling. "I overheard your conversation the other night when your friends were over."

She couldn't help the flash of anger that rushed through her. "You were eavesdropping on me?" It was hard enough having him around 24/7, having to constantly wade through the quicksand of her attraction to him, being physically close to him and trying to keep some kind of emotional distance.

"Not on purpose." He reached out and wrapped his other hand around her arm, now holding her firmly in place with both hands. Funny how hard it was to feel annoyed with him when he was touching her with those hands. "Sierra, I want to find out who's doing this to you, and that means exploring every angle. If you want to be mad at me, go ahead, but I'm not sorry I listened in."

She blew out a breath and forced herself to relax, not wanting to pick a fight. "I'm not mad. Sorry I snapped at you. I think I'm just feeling a little…" She made her hands into claws, holding them up in front of her, trying to show him how she felt. "Caged. Which isn't your fault. I think all of this is getting to me a bit more than I realized."

"Completely understandable. Having 24/7 security can

feel oppressive. But it's the only way I can make sure you're safe."

"I know." She laid a hand on his chest, and his heart thumped against her palm, steady and sure.

* * *

Sean, Ian, and Sierra stared at the brown box sitting on Sierra's front porch. Sean studied the package, which had just been delivered by a private courier, looking for any signs it was dangerous. Sean and Ian had agreed that the package couldn't come inside, and Ian had already texted Clay, Virtus's investigator, to see if he could trace its origins. The box itself was about two feet tall and a foot wide and was unmarked except for Sierra's name and address. She reached out a hand toward it, and Sean grabbed her wrist.

"Don't touch it," he said, and the words came out gruffer than he'd intended. Not because he was annoyed with her but because each time his skin came in contact with hers he wanted to grab her and kiss her, and so, so much more.

"Clay says that the package was shipped anonymously, and whoever sent it paid cash," said Ian, his eyes on his phone, and Sierra's head whipped in his direction. "He's going to see if he can get security cam footage from the courier service so we can see who dropped it off."

"You're Scottish?" she asked.

"Aye."

"I don't think I've heard you speak before."

Ian shrugged in response.

Sierra crossed her arms in front of her, frowning as she studied the box. "How on earth did your investigator find that out so quickly?"

"Clay has a lot of connections, and he's very good at his

job," said Sean. "If this package was sent without sender information and the courier was paid cash, we have to treat this as a threat. The house is secure?"

Ian nodded. "Aye."

Sean tore his eyes from the box and swiveled his gaze back to Sierra. "I'm going to check it out. I need you to go in the house."

Her eyes widened, and she bit her lip. "If it's that dangerous, I don't want you touching it either."

He stroked a hand down her arm, trying to reassure her. "I'll be fine. I know what I'm doing." After completing the necessary training to be a licensed bodyguard, he'd continued taking courses. He knew how to deal with just about any kind of threat, whether it was from a person, from an object, or technological.

She rubbed a hand over her forehead. "Let's just call the police. Let them deal with it."

"We will. But if there's something really dangerous in here, I need to do something about it right now. And to do that, I need you to go in the house. Now."

She hesitated before finally nodding reluctantly, and he relaxed slightly, knowing she'd be safe from whatever the package contained. Surprising him, she reached up and laid her palm on his cheek. "Be careful." Something bright and intense shone in her green eyes, and his entire body tightened.

He nodded, and her fingers curled into him, her fingertips rasping against his beard. "Don't worry about me."

"I can't help it."

Despite everything, he came within inches of saying, "Fuck it" and grabbing her and kissing her. He struggled and failed to find something to say. He didn't have words for the conflicting jumble of emotions crashing over him, all blurring together. So instead he tipped his head toward the front door. "Go."

With big, worried eyes, she watched him as she unlocked the front door and let herself in the house, Ian following her. She appeared seconds later in the living room window to the right.

Sean quickly retreated to the SUV and retrieved a pair of black nitrile gloves from the box he kept in the trunk. After pulling them on, he crouched down in front of the package, studying it intently. There were no stains or leaks, no suspicious marks on the outside. The box itself was pristine, "Miss Blake" written in simple block lettering across the top in black marker. It was sealed with ordinary packing tape across the top, her address in plain type on a white label.

Leaning forward, he inhaled deeply, trying to catch the scent of anything unusual. Gunpowder, acid, the scent of almonds, which would indicate the presence of cyanide, or anything else out of the ordinary. But besides the papery scent of the cardboard, he couldn't detect anything. He cocked his head, listening for any sounds, like ticking, grinding, or beeping, but again, there was nothing. The leaves of the sycamore rustled softly, and a car horn blared several streets over, but nothing came from the box.

As carefully as possible, he lifted the box, testing its weight. It was light, almost insubstantial, but he could feel something shift inside as he picked it up. Given how light it was, it was unlikely to be an explosive, but he walked the box to the end of the driveway just to be sure. Reaching into his pocket, he fished out a Swiss Army knife and slit the tape down the center. With the tip of the knife, he eased back the flaps and peered inside.

Red. For a second that was all he could see. The box was filled with dismembered baby doll parts, all covered in red dye. His grip on the box tightened, the cardboard creaking under the pressure. "Son of a bitch," he bit out, trying to get a handle on the rage coursing through him. If he ever got his hands on whoever was doing this to Sierra...fuck. He'd probably end up in jail.

A note was taped to the inside of the box.

Seeing as you're all about choices, *here's one for you, Miss Blake: Back off now, and you won't get hurt. Refuse, and you just might end up like the millions you've helped send to the slaughter.*

The note was unsigned, but the message it contained made him think it had to be from Sacrosanct. Maybe he'd been barking up the wrong tree with Jack after all.

"Sean?" Sierra's voice from a few feet behind him almost made him jump. He spun to face her, trying to block her view of the box, wanting to shield her from the fear he knew the note and the box's contents would bring.

"You don't need to see this. It's from Sacrosanct. More of the same shit. We'll call the cops."

She narrowed her eyes at him and stepped around him, coming face-to-face with the disturbing contents of the box. He should've known better than to try to hide something from her. She froze as she read the note, her cheeks going pale.

Fuck. This was why he hadn't wanted her to see it.

"Oh, God," she breathed, fingers pressed to her mouth. "They're threatening to kill me." The words came out quiet and shaky, her eyes glued to the broken doll pieces, and his chest ached for her, over the shit Sacrosanct was putting her through. Her breaths came fast and shallow and then she was in his arms, her face pressed tight against his chest.

He wasn't sure who'd moved first, if he'd reached for her or she'd turned to him. It didn't matter. Instinct took over, and he turned his back on the box, sheltering her from it. He stroked a hand up and down her back, the other arm wrapped firmly around her. She shook in his arms, trembles racking her small body. She smelled warm and sweet, like vanilla and honey, and he pulled her tighter against him, wishing he could shoulder this for her. Wishing there were something he could do or say to make everything better. To take away the fear and the anger and the helplessness. And wanting, more than anything, to catch the assholes putting her through this.

The situation had shifted. They weren't dealing with a protest group intent on bullying her into silence. No, this was an actual threat, and he needed to do whatever it took to protect her from these assholes.

It didn't matter that he wanted her more than he'd ever wanted a woman in his life. It didn't matter that, although he'd known her for only a few days, he had feelings for her. It didn't matter that he couldn't remember ever connecting with someone so quickly and so easily. It didn't matter that she was the smartest, funniest, sexiest woman he'd ever met.

Keeping her safe and catching the bastards who were threatening his woman. That was the only thing that mattered. The only thing.

Somehow, once the trembling had subsided, he managed to release her, dropping his arms to his sides, but putting himself between her and the box, keeping it out of her view. She slid her hands up his chest, her breathing much calmer now.

"What do we do now?" she asked, tilting her head up.

"We call the cops and I keep you safe."

She closed her eyes and exhaled slowly, pressing her face

into his chest. "I'm so glad you're OK, Sean. I was freaking out watching you."

He felt his lips curl up in a smile, basking just a little in how sweet she was. "I told you I'd be OK."

She nodded. "I know I shouldn't say this, but I really want to kiss you," she whispered, and his world tilted a little. Heat flared low in his gut, and he had to stifle a low groan as his dick stiffened.

"You're a client, Sierra. It's not a good idea," he said, fighting for control, watching her mouth as he slipped his arms back around her. Shit. He hadn't meant to do that. But now that they were there, around her tiny waist, holding her against him, he wasn't sure he had it in him to let her go twice.

His heart slammed into his ribs like a sledgehammer as he struggled against how badly he wanted to give in and kiss her. He needed to stay professional, not just because she was a client, but because he needed—especially now, in the face of the escalating threats—to keep a clear head.

His cock pressed firmly against his zipper, making a pretty damn compelling argument for ignoring his brain.

She looked up at him, her green eyes bright. "I was scared you were going to get hurt. I was more scared of that than anything in the box."

Before he could talk himself out of it, he dipped his head until he could feel her breath fanning against his lips. He gripped her tighter, trying to hide the tremble coursing through him as he fought against what he wanted. Needed.

"I'm fine. Nothing's gonna happen to me, and nothing's gonna happen to you."

"Do you want to kiss me?" she asked, and her lips brushed against his bottom lip in a whisper of a kiss. Oh, hell, that felt good, just that tiniest touch of her lips to his, and it only made him hungrier for more.

"Yes," he growled.

And then he pulled back and put a few feet of distance between them. God, he was either a saint or the world's biggest goddamn idiot. He knew which one his dick was voting for.

CHAPTER 11

He sat back behind his desk, sinking into the black leather chair, his phone pressed to his ear.

"You sent her the picture?" he asked, scuffing one polished black shoe against the red carpet.

The voice on the other end responded immediately. "We did."

"Good. And the package was delivered?"

"Just a couple of hours ago, with the note, just like you asked."

"Perfect. That should make her rethink everything."

"You think it's enough to scare her off?"

"It should be. And without their star spokesperson, it'll be a lot more difficult for Choices to get the support they'll need to get that grant."

"And then the fifty million will be ours for the taking."

"Exactly. Keep your ears open, and let me know if you hear anything about her quitting or backing off. You got her new cell number?"

"Yep."

"Give her a few hours, and then send her a friendly little reminder that she can't hide from us. And find out what you can about that bodyguard she's got following her around. Sean Owens." The bodyguard was a potential wrench in the plan. A plan that needed to succeed if he was to have any hope of paying Fairfax back and keeping his kneecaps intact.

There was a pause on the other end of the phone. "You don't know who he is, do you?"

Irritation flared up, and he gripped the phone tighter, drumming the fingers of his opposite hand on the desk. "Why the hell would I know who he is?"

"You ever heard of Virtus Security?"

"Sure."

"That's him."

It was his turn to pause, and for the first time since they'd started trying to scare her off, the tiniest flicker of doubt rose up, like smoke from an extinguished candle. Insubstantial and almost invisible, but there all the same. "Shit. Really? How's she affording that?"

"No idea. Maybe she's fucking him."

He scoffed. "Unlikely." But he knew it wasn't impossible. Women were sluts, and he didn't doubt she'd whore herself out in exchange for security. "Wait, and then send the text. Call me when you've got more information."

"You got it."

The line went dead, and he tossed his phone on the desk, wondering how much she'd put up with before she threw in the towel. She couldn't last much longer. Women were weak, in both mind and body. She'd crumble soon under the onslaught of threats, and whether she was fucking him or not, there'd be nothing Owens could do about it.

* * *

"This is really nice of you. You didn't have to do this." Sean surveyed the spread of chicken wings, pizza, nachos, and beer spread out over the island in Sierra's kitchen, the food piping hot and the beer ice-cold. Off in one corner sat a few leftover cupcakes from Chloe's birthday a few days ago.

His stomach rumbled, and he smoothed a hand over his T-shirt, watching Sierra as she stashed the delivery bags and retrieved a stack of plates from a cabinet. She reached up, and her loose-fitting tank top rode up, leaving a swath of smooth, creamy skin exposed between the hem of her shirt and the waistband of her jean shorts. He knew exactly how well she fit in his arms, and it wasn't a stretch to imagine what that skin would feel like. How soft and warm it would be as he traced his fingers down the seam of her spine.

He glanced at the cupcakes again. Stupid fucking cupcakes.

"You guys have been awesome. I just wanted to say thank you." She'd invited the entire team over for a night of watching UFC fights and gorging on food and beer. Jamie was on duty tonight, though, so no beer for him. And Carter was on duty all day tomorrow. Sean had meetings he couldn't get out of, so he'd be spending the day at the Virtus offices. He trusted his team, and knew Carter could handle it, but he still hated to be away from the situation, especially given the new threat the package had brought that morning.

And he hated to be away from Sierra.

A round of cheers and groans erupted from the living room.

"Boss, get in here! You gotta see this knockout!" called Jamie.

Before he could duck back into the living room, Sierra was there, in front of him, her hand on his forearm.

"And I wanted to say that I'm sorry." Her voice was quiet,

pink spots rising on the apples of her cheeks. She cleared her throat before continuing. "For what happened this morning. I shouldn't have done that."

He didn't need her to clarify. He knew exactly what she was referring to. The memory of that tiny brush of her lips against his ghosted over him, and he could almost feel that touch again. That was the best part of the memory.

The worst? That was when he'd pulled away and seen something close off in her eyes, in her face, in her body language. One second she'd been open, vulnerable, and then he'd pushed her away. He'd had to, but it didn't matter. That look in her eyes, guarded and distant, had made him feel like an asshole.

And it was the second time he'd done it to her.

He felt like a caveman, brutal and clumsy. He'd had something beautiful in his hands, and he'd had the ability only to crush it. He could keep her safe, without a doubt. He could be her protector. He shouldn't want more from her, not when his focus should be on protecting her, but caveman that he was, he wanted it all. "No harm done."

"Good. Let's just pretend it didn't happen. OK?"

That was the last thing he wanted to do. It was also pretty much the only option, moving forward. "Sure. No problem."

She smiled, her nose scrunching up slightly, and she passed him a bottle of beer before hefting a tray laden with food and making her way into the living room. He watched her, and her laugh at something Jamie said hit him like a punch in the gut. He wrenched the cap off the beer, tossed it into the garbage below the sink, and drained half the bottle.

He followed her into the living room and dropped down onto the sofa between Carter and Zack. Ian and Jamie sat on the other sofa, Ian giving off his usual "nobody fucking talk to me" vibes. And as usual, the guys all gave him space and privacy without isolating him, respecting his grief. None of them knew the full story of what had happened to Ian, and no one was either brave enough or dumb enough to try to pry it out of him. Sean knew he was a former SAS paratrooper and medic, and that he'd had a fiancée back in Scotland at some point. He didn't know why he'd left the SAS or Scotland, or what had happened to the fiancée. Whatever the reason, he was willing to bet it was pretty damn bad.

Sierra passed out plates, and they all helped themselves to the food, mumbling their appreciation through full mouths. She curled up in an armchair, nursing a beer of her own, watching the fights.

She looked tired. A little paler than usual, dark circles visible under her eyes. She fiddled with the label on her beer bottle, peeling it away in little strips and letting the paper fall into her lap.

God, what he wouldn't give to be able to distract her from all the garbage of the past couple of days. To scoop her up, take her to his bed, and keep her there until she couldn't remember what she was worried about. Until she was completely relaxed and sleeping, naked in his arms.

His dick twitched in his jeans, and he grabbed a plate of food. He settled back and propped one ankle up on the opposite knee, forcing himself to focus on the fights and not Sierra, grateful for the distraction of two guys beating the shit out of each other.

"Whoa!" Sierra's mouth dropped open as one fighter landed a spinning kick to his opponent's head.

"Pretty impressive, huh?" said Zack, popping a cheese-covered nacho in his mouth.

"Yeah. I didn't realize how athletic it is."

"Zack and Jamie both do this, you know," said Carter, tipping his beer toward the TV.

"Really? You're both mixed martial arts fighters?" She glanced back and forth between the fight on TV, and Zack and Jamie.

Jamie nodded. "I do it as more of a hobby, but Zack's really good. How long you been fighting pro now?"

"A few months." He smiled cockily as he leaned forward, one eyebrow arched. "I'm undefeated."

"Wow. It looks...insane. But in a good way."

"You should come watch sometime," offered Jamie, smiling a little too warmly at Sierra for Sean's liking. Something hot and possessive unfurled low in his gut, and he took a sip of his beer, trying to extinguish it.

"Oh yeah?"

"Yeah. Winning's fun, but it's even better when you've got a beautiful woman cheering you on."

She laughed. "Laying it on pretty thick, there, Anderson."

Sean stifled a growl with a bite of pizza.

Jamie winked at her. "Can't blame a guy for trying."

She laughed again and rose from her chair, heading back into the kitchen. "Anyone want another beer?" she called over her shoulder. A few guys responded, and she disappeared around the corner.

"Hey," said Sean, leaning forward, his arms braced on his legs, his beer in one hand. Jamie turned to face him, guilt sliding across his face. "Knock it off."

"I was just kidding around."

"No flirting with clients." Christ, he was such a hypocrite. He was giving Jamie shit for some harmless flirting when he'd flirted with her, almost kissed her *twice*, and jerked himself off fantasizing about her. More than twice.

"You're right. Sorry, boss." The word *boss* rankled him.

He *was* the boss, and it was up to him to lead his team and set the right example.

Carter glanced toward the kitchen. "You hear anything from Clay or Antonio?"

"Nothing new. Still following up on the information they've got. Clay thinks he might be onto something, but he wasn't ready to share just yet."

"You still thinking it might be the senator?" asked Ian.

Sean grimaced, thinking, before finally shaking his head. "Pretty unlikely. We ran into him this morning, and I tossed a few questions his way about the attacks. Didn't seem fazed. Even offered to help if he can."

"Was she OK, seeing her ex?" asked Jamie quietly.

"Think so. It was all pretty civil."

"There's something about that guy I don't like," said Zack. "Every time I see him on TV, he seems so fake."

"He does," said Ian. "Something disingenuous about that bloke. No one's that perfect."

"That was Antonio's take too," said Sean, nodding in agreement.

Carter tipped his head toward the kitchen. "Does she think he could be involved?"

Sean took a sip of his beer and shook his head. "No."

"Oh, man," said Zack, his eyes glued to the TV. "Check out the ring girl. Damn."

They all watched in appreciative silence as a petite, stacked blonde walked around the caged octagon, holding a placard above her head.

Sierra came back into the living room, a couple of bottles of beer in her hands. And there was that tug in his chest again. That damn *need* he couldn't seem to shake. She avoided looking his way as she came in, handing a bottle each to Carter and Ian.

She pulled her phone out of her back pocket and froze. "What the hell?" She stood near the edge of the room, staring at her phone. Sean was on his feet immediately.

"What is it?"

She passed him her phone and paced away, her hands on her hips. One single text message, once again from an unknown, private number. Probably another damn burner.

We can always find you. You can change your number. You can hide behind security. But as long as you're working for Choices, you're not safe.

He followed Sierra into the kitchen and watched her slam things around as he forwarded the text message and its details to Antonio. Sean had spoken to him earlier that day, and he'd sent a patrol officer to come pick up the package. The police were now checking it for fingerprints and other evidence. So far Sacrosanct had been smart, covering its tracks thoroughly.

"How did they get my new number?"

"I don't know. We'll have it changed again."

"What's going on?" asked Carter from behind him, and he turned to find the entire team standing in the entryway to the kitchen.

"Another text message," said Sean, passing Sierra's phone over for the guys to look at.

"Bastards," said Ian, shaking his head.

"Yeah, well, those bastards are gonna have to get through all of us first," said Carter, crossing his tree-trunk arms over his chest.

"And like hell we're gonna let that happen," added Jamie, nodding emphatically.

Zack and Ian nodded too, and Sean stepped toward Sierra. "We've got you. I forwarded the text to Antonio so he can add it to the evidence. In the meantime we're going to keep doing what we're doing." He took another step closer, hating the guarded way she watched him. "You *are* safe. I promise. And I will do whatever it takes to keep you safe."

Something softened in her expression, some of the wariness in her green eyes receding, and then she pressed her hands to her face, her shoulders starting to shake.

Oh, shit. The guys all looked at each other with panicked expressions.

"I'm not crying because I'm scared," she said from underneath her hands after several seconds, hiccupping out a few sobs. "I'm just overwhelmed. With everything." She sniffled and rubbed her hands over her face, smearing her mascara. "Sorry."

"Don't apologize," said Ian, stepping forward and laying a hand on Sierra's shoulder. "Anyone would feel overwhelmed. It's only natural. You're handling it beautifully, lass. Truly."

She started to cry harder.

Jamie socked Ian on the arm. "Good job, Mac."

Sean couldn't take any more of Sierra's crying. Each tremble of her shoulders slammed into him, and he jerked his head toward the living room, silently asking his team to leave. They did, looking both worried and relieved.

"Shhh," he whispered, stroking a hand over her hair. She lowered her hands, her eyes raw and tired. Something passed between them, and even though she hadn't said anything, he knew what they both needed.

"Come here." He pulled her into his arms, and she didn't fight. He cradled her head against his chest, stroking a hand up and down her small back, not saying a word. Not trusting himself to.

He held her until her soft, shaking sobs subsided. Sacrosanct was going to fucking pay for this.

After a few minutes, she pulled back and laughed quietly. "I cried on you." She wiped at the small wet spot on his T-shirt in the center of his chest. She was so small that she didn't even reach his shoulder, and that made him want to shelter her even more.

"It's OK. I can handle a few tears."

She patted his chest and moved out of his arms. "Thanks." He saw the wall go back up, and she retreated to the bathroom, wiping her eyes as she went.

He knew he shouldn't, but he desperately wanted to knock that wall down.

CHAPTER 12

Sierra dipped her roller into the tray of light-sage paint, brushing a stray strand of hair out of her eyes with the back of one hand. She climbed up onto the small stepladder and rolled the paint onto the wall, wondering how many coats it would take before the bright-red "baby killer" didn't show through. Carter had kindly helped her put on a coat of primer that afternoon, and now that it was dry, she was starting in on the first coat of fresh paint. She'd finally gotten permission from the police this morning to paint over the vandalism, and although she'd originally been planning to hire painters, she'd decided to do it herself. If she was basically housebound, she might as well take on a project. She'd spent the day reading the script and pacing around her house like a crazy person. Sometime around four she'd convinced Carter to take her to the store to get paint and supplies.

And painting would give her time to think. To try to sort through everything. Sacrosanct. Choices. Her unnerving attraction to Sean, and the snarl of emotions that brought with it.

She'd never been so unquestionably drawn to someone before, and that had to mean something. But he kept pushing her away. And yes, she understood his need to stay professional. But she also got the distinct impression that there was more to it than that. Maybe he was using the whole "keep things professional" thing as an excuse. Maybe he'd found something lacking or undesirable in her.

And yet he'd *wanted* to kiss her. He'd comforted her. Been kind to her. Was obviously attracted to her, if the massive erection she'd felt the other day was any indication. So maybe it was just about professionalism.

She shouldn't have come on to him. It had been a mistake to open herself up like that, especially a second time, and it hadn't been fair to him after he'd told her he couldn't get involved with a client. Keeping her distance was the right thing to do. The respectful thing.

The safe thing.

So why was keeping her distance so hard? Why, if it *was* the right thing, did it feel wrong?

She rolled the paint as high on the wall as she could, stretching up onto her toes, grunting in frustration when she found she couldn't quite reach the seam where the wall met the taped-off crown molding that ran along the ceiling. She tried again, gripping the roller's handle a bit lower and stretching as much as she could. The stepladder wobbled, and she flailed her arms, trying to regain her balance, but it was no use. She let out a high-pitched "Eep!" as she braced herself for impact.

It didn't come.

Strong arms slid around her waist, and her back bumped against a wide, solid chest. A familiar scent washed over her, a crisp, woody aftershave, a hint of clean cotton, and something subtle and masculine, and she knew Sean had caught her.

"Easy there." Sean's voice rasped against her ear as he set her down safely on the ground.

She set her roller back in the tray and stepped away, needing a little distance. She glanced at him over her shoulder, raising one eyebrow. "Taking this protector thing to a whole nother level, aren't you?"

He saluted with two fingers. "Just doing my job, miss."

She ducked her head, trying to hide the smile tugging at her lips. He looked around, his hands on his hips. "Did you do this all by yourself?" he asked, surveying the large sideboard that had been pushed up against the dining room table in the center of the room. Drop cloths covered the furniture and the hardwood floor, protecting everything from paint splatter.

"Carter helped me move the furniture. He took me to get paint too."

"You didn't want to hire painters?"

"I needed something to do, and I really wanted this gone," she said, waving a hand at the shadowy remains of the "baby killer" message. She picked up her bottle of beer from where she'd set it on the floor and took a sip.

"You want a hand?"

"Are you asking because you're hoping I'll offer you beer?"

He laughed, and her stomach flipped over on itself. He was so gorgeous when he laughed like that, brown eyes crinkling, white teeth flashing. "I'm asking because I'd rather you not break your neck up on that ladder. And yes, I'm hoping you'll offer me beer."

"Well, I have lots of beer, and I'm not going to turn down an extra set of hands. Consider yourself hired."

"Let me go change. Be right back." He turned to leave, but she stopped him with a question.

"Were you standing there, watching me paint?"

He turned around and leaned against the doorway, his tie loose, a playful smile on his face. "I don't know. Do you watch me swim every morning?"

Her face flamed and she spun around, reaching for the roller again. She thought she'd been sneaky, but apparently not.

"It is *my* pool," she muttered, smearing her roller with fresh paint. Sean just laughed, the deep, rich sound washing over her like warm water. He left to go change, and she streaked paint across the wall in a wide W shape.

She had no idea if she was supposed to be happy, embarrassed, or turned on. She seemed to be in a constantly fluctuating state of all three around Sean.

She painted alone for several minutes with only the stereo for company, Jason Mraz floating through the speakers. When Sean reappeared, he'd changed into a worn gray Lakers T-shirt and navy blue sweatpants. He'd helped himself to a beer from the fridge, and he held something else in his other hand.

Her script. She'd been paging through it in the kitchen earlier, sitting at the island and reading it, trying not to let herself get excited about it.

"What are you doing with that?" she asked, loving the way the cotton of his T-shirt strained across his biceps as he moved.

Before Sean could answer, Ian poked his head into the dining room, a look of surprise flickering across his face at the sight of his boss in sweats, helping her paint. He surveyed them with a raised eyebrow before clearing his throat. He clearly felt as though he were intruding on something, and he shifted his weight from one foot to the other. "Oh, you're back. How'd your meetings go?"

"Fine. I'll send out an update tomorrow."

Ian nodded curtly and left, returning to whatever he'd been doing before. He was on duty tonight, which was why Sean was free to help her paint.

"I was flipping through it," he said, answering her question. "When's your audition?" He set the script down on the covered dining room table and picked up a fresh roller, running it through the paint tray.

She shook her head as she ran her own roller over the wall. "I don't think I'm going to audition, actually. Do you want the stepladder?" She glanced over at him, ready to scoot the ladder toward him. "Or not." He was easily able to reach the top of the wall. He wasn't even standing on his toes, just reaching one long, chiseled arm up and back down again, the muscles in his arm bunching and flexing as he moved. "Just how tall are you?"

"Six-five," he answered as he rolled paint smoothly onto the wall. "How come you're not going to do the audition?"

"You mean besides the fact that I already kind of have a lot going on?"

"Yeah. Besides that."

She shrugged, and the sleeve of her old, loose T-shirt slipped down over her shoulder. Sean's gaze slid to her exposed skin, and instead of hoisting it back into place, she left it. "I don't really act much anymore. My focus is on Choices. Especially right now, with the grant application."

"And?"

"And what?"

He took a sip of his beer and studied her, one eyebrow arched. Goddammit, he was hot. How was it possible for a man to be so bone-meltingly hot? "I get the feeling there's more to it."

She sighed and coated her roller in fresh paint. "Acting… I don't know. That whole industry, it…it didn't bring out the best in me. I didn't like who I was when I was deep into it. Sometimes I think I miss it, but then I remember how toxic it all was. How you can't trust anyone. If you want to survive, you have to assume everyone's out to screw you over, and then be eternally grateful when they don't." She'd learned from a young age that giving your trust to someone was a risky proposition at best, and it usually blew up in your face, leaving you alone, unemployed, and feeling like a complete fool.

He nodded, not saying anything, listening as he rolled paint onto the wall in long, even strokes.

"Right around the time my dad died, I wasn't making good decisions. I was hanging out with the wrong people, and I did a lot of stuff I'm not proud of."

She hesitated, and he urged her to continue. "I won't judge. We've all got stuff in the past we'd like to pretend isn't there." His features tightened, just for a second.

"When my dad got sick, and then died, I kind of came off the rails. I didn't know how to cope with losing him, and I just wanted to be numb all the time. I was seventeen, and I was going to bars, and smoking pot, doing coke, sleeping around…and everyone around me just kind of cheered me on, like I was doing something great. Like my self-destructive behavior somehow deserved to be celebrated, or glorified." She paused, scoffing out a quiet laugh. "The glorification of terrible behavior? That's Hollywood in a nutshell. I had money from *Family Tree*, and *Sunset Cove* was proving to be a hit. But that wasn't enough of a high for me, so I chased other highs."

"I know."

"You do?"

"You're a client. It's my job to know what information about you is out there."

"So why'd you ask?"

"You seemed like you needed to talk."

She chewed her bottom lip. "So you read up on me."

"I did. And for what it's worth, none of that changes what I think of you."

"Oh." She took a sip of her beer, not knowing what to say.

He didn't say anything for a few moments either as he dumped more paint into the tray and continued working his way around the room, painting the top third of the wall that she couldn't reach on her own.

"Besides. That role is…it's pretty incredible. I don't think I could do it justice," she added quietly.

"Why not?"

She chewed her lip, trying to figure out how to explain in a way that wouldn't sound self-pitying or as if she were fishing for compliments. "The character, Elle, she's so…strong. She sees something wrong, and she does everything in her power to stop it. She's brave, and she's tough, and smart, and—"

"She's you."

She froze as the compliment washed over her, somehow both soothing and exhilarating at the same time. She set her roller down and picked up her beer, taking a tentative step toward him. "That's really how you see me?" She pointed at the script, needing to know. "Like that?"

He set his own roller down in the tray and turned to face her. "You know what I see when I look at you?" He said it almost like a challenge, as though he was daring her to believe him.

"What?" she managed, her legs suddenly feeling wobbly.

He took a step toward her, closing the distance between them. His hand came up to cup her face, his thumb tracing over her cheekbone. "I see a beautiful woman, inside and out."

She laughed nervously, relishing the feel of his thumb brushing against her skin. "You barely know me."

"You barely know me. How do you see me?"

His eyes held hers, and for a second her brain stopped completely, as though it were devoid of blood and oxygen, despite the furious pounding of her heart and her quick, shallow breaths. "I see someone strong, and brave, and dedicated to his job. Someone who makes me feel safe and protected, despite everything that's happened over the past week." She swallowed, her mouth dry. She leaned forward slightly, needing to be closer to him, when he suddenly jumped back.

"Shit! I'm sorry," she said as she realized that she'd poured her beer all over him as she'd moved closer. She'd been so caught up in the moment that she'd forgotten she was even holding it, and she'd tipped it forward.

He held his wet T-shirt away from his skin, flapping it and revealing tantalizing glimpses of his abs. She darted into the kitchen and grabbed a towel, cringing at her clumsiness. When she stepped back into the dining room, Sean was naked from the waist up, his beer-soaked T-shirt balled in one large fist. His sweatpants hung low around his hips, revealing a deep-cut line on either side of his hips.

Sierra almost swallowed her tongue. "I…uh…towel," she stammered, shoving the kitchen towel at him awkwardly. He took it from her, their fingers brushing. It was as though an electric current passed between them, and every hair on her body stood on end. He swiped the towel over his abs, mopping up the beer that had soaked through the thin cotton of his now discarded T-shirt.

She hadn't realized she was going to touch him until her fingers made contact with his skin, her fingers brushing lightly over his ribs. She felt him suck in a surprised breath, but he didn't back away. She glanced up, and was nearly undone at the heat sparking in his brown eyes. She slid her hand up, resting her palm over his heart, and the heat only burned brighter.

She skated her hand lower, feathering over the ridges of his abs, and she felt him tremble slightly. "Do you want me to stop?"

In response he dropped the towel and grabbed her other hand, placing it on his bare chest. "No," he ground out, his voice strained, his eyes burning into her.

He held perfectly still as she walked around him in a slow circle, tracing the contour of every single muscle, every peak and valley, every inch of warm, smooth skin, drinking in the sight of all that masculine strength. The light from the setting sun filtered in through the windows, casting a warm orange glow over the room, and her mind flicked back to her candlelit dream. But this wasn't a dream. He was too solid, too warm, too perfect under her touch for this to be anything but reality.

Her hands slid up his back and to his hard shoulders, avoiding the gun tucked into the waistband of his sweatpants. The sight of the gun threatened to bring her back to reality, but she couldn't stop touching him. It was as though her skin were desperate to memorize his. She took her time exploring him, letting her hands wander over his chest, his abs, his back, his arms, his shoulders, marveling at the incredibly solid strength beneath her hands. She continued her slow circle, making her way back to where she'd started, dragging her fingertips over his skin as she did. Goose bumps followed her across the wide plain of his back, and he trembled slightly.

She was making this muscled beast of a man tremble. With her fingertips. A surge of power flowed through her as she came to a stop in front of him, her hands sliding up his bare chest, her palms scraping lightly over his flat brown nipples, his chest hair crisp against her skin. She wound her arms around him and tentatively brushed her lips against his chest, inhaling deeply, wanting to memorize his scent.

His nostrils flared, and he took a short, sharp breath. "Fuck, Sierra," he said quietly, his voice deep and raw. He threaded his fingers through her hair, and her breathing hitched as he gave her hair a gentle, electrifying tug, tilting her face up to his.

His eyes were dark, glittering with heat. He wanted her just as much as she wanted him, and none of the other shit mattered. The harassment. The past. The lingering doubts. Now that she'd tasted Sean's skin, how could anything else matter at all?

Crackling tension vibrated between them, the air thick and charged as before a storm. And it was about to pour.

"Fuck professional ethics." He dipped his head, a tiny up-and-down movement, brushing her lips with his, a tease of a kiss. But as desperate as she was, she didn't want to rush. No, she wanted to savor every single second of this.

Ian cleared his throat loudly from behind them, and Sean released her, turning away.

"I just picked something up on the security cam," said Ian, his hard blue eyes flicking between Sean and Sierra. With swift yet somehow casual movements, he checked the clip of the gun in his hands. "I think we've got a visitor."

Sean pulled his own gun free of his waistband, his eyes still dark, but with a different kind of heat now. "Stay here," he ground out, his voice rough. He looked like an action hero, shirtless and ripped, a gun clutched in his big hands, danger written in the hard lines of his face. "Where?"

"Coming round to the backyard." As if on cue, the alarm erupted with a continuous stream of blaring shrieks, and Sierra jumped, pressing a hand to her chest to keep her heart from leaping out of her body.

"Cover me." Sean made his way quickly across the dining room to the French doors in the kitchen, pressing his back against the wall and peering out. The sun had just about disappeared below the horizon, leaving the backyard in purple shadows. Ian mirrored Sean's actions, his back pressed against the wall on the other side of the doors. A crash sounded from the backyard, and with a nod at Ian, Sean pushed through the doors, his gun leveled at the intruder as he chased him down, his long legs eating up the distance in seconds.

Pulse pounding in her throat, Sierra raced to the window, practically pressing her face against the glass as she watched her own personal action hero grab the intruder around the waist, lift him, and slam him into the ground. Sean came down on top of the intruder, wrestling him onto his stomach and grabbing his arms, pinning them behind his back. Ian kept his gun trained on the man, approaching with quick, sure steps.

The intruder struggled against Sean, who held him down easily, muscles bunching and flexing in a show of strength that had her stomach doing a slow, scalding turn.

"Search him," Sean called over his shoulder to Ian, who dropped down beside Sean and began rifling through the man's pockets. Sierra's blood turned to ice as she saw Ian pull out a capped syringe and a small serrated knife. The threatening words of the note flashed through her mind, and she sank down onto the floor, too relieved that Sean had caught the intruder to do anything else.

CHAPTER 13

After showering and dressing the next morning, Sean strode into Sierra's kitchen, his phone pressed to his ear.

"He won't say a damn word to the cops," said Clay on the other end of the line. The intruder hadn't had any ID on him, and although he was currently sitting in a jail cell downtown, he wasn't giving the police any information. "But he doesn't need to talk for me to find out who he is," continued Clay, and Sean couldn't help but smile. Clay was expensive, but worth every fucking penny. "I used the security cam footage and was able to use the image to pull his driver's license."

"How the hell did you do that?"

"You really want to know?"

Sean paused. "Probably not. So who is this asshole?"

"Name's Judah Kirkham. He just moved here from San Francisco, and guess what? He was a confirmed member of Sacrosanct there. He's been arrested for obstructing access to Choices locations and criminal trespassing. He also just did a ninety-day stint in Pleasant

Valley State Prison for his role in bombing a Choices
clinic last year."

"So that confirms it. We're dealing with Sacrosanct."
Something hot and possessive washed over him as he remembered the syringe and the knife the fucker had clearly
planned to use on Sierra.

"Without a doubt."

He hung up, hating Sacrosanct even more than before.
Not only was it threatening his girl, but it had thoroughly
succeeded at cock-blocking him last night.

There was no doubt in his mind that if not for the interruption, he would've taken Sierra back to the guesthouse and
spent the night violating his professional ethics and exploring her, discovering exactly where she liked to be touched.
Kissed. Licked.

"Morning," called Sierra as she stepped into the kitchen,
still in her pajamas, her hair in a messy bun, no makeup on.
He liked her without any makeup because he could see much
more clearly the freckles that dotted the bridge of her nose
and the tops of her cheeks. He liked imagining kissing every
single one of those freckles, claiming every one of them for
himself. "Have you seen my phone?"

He tipped his head toward the dining room. "I think it's
still hooked up to the speaker in there."

She smiled her thanks and gave his arm a squeeze on her
way through the kitchen and into the dining room. She'd
barely disappeared around the corner when she came darting
back in, a bright, surprised smile on her face.

"You finished it?"

He'd been too keyed up to sleep after last night's intru-
sion, so he'd finished painting the dining room for her. He'd
needed something to do with himself, and he hated leaving
a job half finished.

He shrugged. "Yeah."

"You really didn't have to do that," she said, shaking her head but still smiling.

"I know how much you wanted the graffiti gone. It's no big deal."

"Thank you." Her eyes were soft and full of something he couldn't quite decipher. So he simply nodded.

"You're welcome."

She grabbed a cup of coffee and sat down at the island, her fingers curled around the mug.

Instantly Sean's mind went back to last night and the way she'd touched him, his skin coming alive under her fingers. The way she'd taken her time, exploring him, savoring him with a kind of sweet reverence that had left him incredibly hard and shaking with how much he wanted her.

She cradled her phone between her ear and shoulder, checking her messages as she sipped her coffee. Her movements slowed, and then stilled completely, and she froze. All the blood drained from her face, and Sean pushed up from his stool, his blood pressure skyrocketing.

"Sean?" Her voice came out like a croak, and she held the phone out in front of her. "You need to hear this." With trembling fingers she set the phone down on the island and played the message on speakerphone.

The voice was electronically scrambled, cold and robotic-sounding. "We told you that you couldn't hide from us. We will always be able to find you, you stupid, filthy, degenerate whore. Stop spreading your lies. Otherwise you'll leave us with no choice but to teach you what happens to women like you. Sluts who need to be taught their place in the world. The choice is yours. Choose wisely."

"*Fuck!*" Sierra yelled the curse and threw her spoon into the sink.

A surge of anger pushed through Sean, and he picked up the phone, digging into the call's details with a few taps on the screen. Once again the call had been placed from an unknown private number. It had come in the middle of the night, only a few hours after the thwarted attack.

"I'm going to make sure Antonio gets a copy of this, and we'll assign you a Virtus Security phone number this time. Sacrosanct obviously has connections and is working them to keep getting your number, but I can promise you that they won't be able to reach you at the VS number."

She nodded and sank down onto a stool. Sean's palms tingled, and he reached out and smoothed a hand down her back, rubbing the base of her spine in small circles. She relaxed into his touch, and he added an ounce of pressure. She closed her eyes and leaned into him, and he inhaled deeply, filling himself with her soft, warm scent. He wanted to kiss her. Touch her. Taste her. Fuck her until neither of them could walk.

And he would. As soon as he got his hands on the motherfuckers who'd made the mistake of targeting his woman.

CHAPTER 14

It was later than she'd realized when Sierra emerged from her office after spending the day working. She'd spent hours reading news articles, researching grant application procedures, making phone calls, preparing talking points, and reading up on the politicians who were going to be at the fund-raising gala tomorrow.

She wondered if those Sacrosanct assholes knew that the more they threatened her, the angrier she got. The more determined she became to help Choices. She might be scared, but that didn't make her weak. Fear itself wasn't weakness; only giving in to that fear was. And she refused to do that.

She could hear Sean talking on the phone as she neared the kitchen, and her body responded to the sound of his deep, warm voice, her spine tingling and heat prickling across her skin.

"No, I'm gonna have to miss it." He paused, listening, standing with a hip against the island, his phone pressed to his ear. "I know. But I'm working."

She stepped into the kitchen and waved silently. He smiled and tipped his chin at her, sending her stomach into a tailspin.

"Listen, I gotta go. Good luck. I'll try and make it next time." He listened for a second before hanging up, slipping his phone back into his pocket. Sierra poured herself a glass of water and took a sip, watching him for a second.

"I didn't mean to listen in, but what are you missing out on?" she asked.

"Just a baseball game. It's not a big deal."

"You have tickets?"

He shook his head. "No, I play."

"Oh." Guilt pulled at her, and she frowned. "I feel really bad that you can't go because of me." Her drama was taking over his life, and that wasn't fair. "You should go. Carter's here. I'll be fine."

He squinted and shook his head again. "That doesn't work for me. After the intruder, I'm not willing to take any chances."

"What if I came with you to your game? Then you'd know exactly where I was. Carter could sit with me."

"I could sit with you where?" asked Carter as he came into the kitchen, nodding at Sean.

"Sean's baseball game. Help me talk him out of skipping it."

Carter frowned, his eyebrows raised. "You're not gonna go? It's your night off."

"I wasn't planning on going, no."

"So I suggested that I could come too," said Sierra. "Then you won't have to worry about me."

"I'm still going to worry about you."

"But you'll be able to see me the whole time, and you won't have to miss your game."

Sean hesitated, pushing a hand through his hair, and she knew he was considering it. She sent Carter a "help me out here" look.

"It'll be fine, boss. I'll sit with her in the stands. I doubt Sacrosanct's hanging out in Griffith Park."

Sean rubbed a hand over his mouth, and finally he nodded, giving in. "OK. Fine." He turned to look at Sierra. "Thank you."

"Well, you did paint my dining room. And, you know. Kick that intruder's ass."

He smiled, his eyes crinkling. "My gear's in the car. I'll get changed, and then we can go."

Several minutes later the three of them stood in the driveway, gathered around Sean's SUV.

"I'm still not sure this is a good idea," he said, his hands on his hips. But Sierra wasn't really listening. She was too busy checking him out in his red baseball jersey and the white baseball pants that clung to his thick, muscular legs, framing his ass in a way that made her want to reach out and squeeze it, just to see if it was as firm as it looked.

God bless whoever had invented baseball pants.

"Are you really bad, or something? Is that why you don't want me to watch?" she teased, trying to lighten the mood.

Carter laughed and shook his head, but didn't say anything.

"No, I don't mind you watching." A hint of a smile tugged at his lips, and she liked that she'd put it there.

"Then it's settled. The alarm's set, Carter's coming with us, and you're ready to go. Besides, I could really use some fresh air. I want to go."

She heard him mutter something about a stubborn woman, and he held the rear passenger door for her. She slipped into the SUV, tucking the skirt of her white cotton dress around her and adjusting the sleeves of her denim jacket. Sean slid into the driver's seat and jammed a navy blue ball cap down over his eyes.

As they drove the short distance to Griffith Park, Carter showed her pictures on his phone of his eight-year-old son, Sebastian. He and his wife had split up a couple of years ago, and they shared custody. As he scrolled through the pictures—at Disneyland, at the beach, Sebastian sitting on Carter's shoulders, eating popcorn at a baseball game, the two of them making silly faces and taking a selfie—she felt as though a weight were pressing down on her chest, making her heart hurt a little.

She missed her dad.

And she hoped she got to do these things with her own child someday. She glanced at Sean in the driver's seat, and the pressure intensified. She was still getting to know him, but she had a feeling he'd be a good dad. He was kind, and smart, and he cared deeply about what was important to him. A vivid image of Sean cradling a tiny baby in his massive arms seared through her, and she found herself smiling.

Holy shit.

The image dissolved, and she was relieved.

"Here's the deal," said Sean, easing his SUV into a parking space in the lot lining the west side of a large baseball diamond in Griffith Park. "Stay with Carter, and I'll keep an eye on you the whole time. If anything happens, I've got you." Something in the way he said, "I've got you" sent little zings of electricity snapping through her. The three of them got out of the SUV, and she inhaled a deep breath, relishing the fresh air. It felt good to be out of the house.

"I seriously doubt anything's going to happen," she said, stretching.

Sean circled the SUV, coming to a stop right in front of her. "You're probably right, but I wouldn't be doing my job if I didn't keep you safe. And I *will* keep you safe." Her stomach bottomed out at the bright intensity shining in his eyes.

He turned and popped the SUV's hatch, slung his gear bag over his shoulder, and then slammed the hatch shut. "Carter, why don't you scout ahead, make sure everything's OK?" Carter nodded and took off at a brisk pace, surveying the parking lot and the baseball diamond as he went. After a moment Sean grabbed her hand and started leading her toward the diamond.

She laced her fingers through his and he squeezed, once. She loved the way his hand felt wrapped around hers—big and warm and strong. Natural. For a few blissful seconds, her world narrowed to where they were connected, happy tingles dancing up her arm.

"Didn't think you were gonna make it, dude!" An attractive Latino guy with short jet-black hair, a confident smile, and a uniform matching Sean's was headed toward them, a bat slung casually over his broad shoulders. He'd opened his mouth to say something else, but paused. A surprised look flickered across his face as his gaze dropped to their intertwined hands.

She expected Sean to let go, but he didn't. Instead he gave her another squeeze, his thumb rubbing across the back of her hand. Oh, God, that felt good. Such a small touch, and it did such big things to her.

"Changed my mind. I didn't want to risk our winning streak." A cocky smile that she found immensely appealing played across Sean's lips.

"You think we'd be doomed without you?"

"Nah. I *know* you would. This is Antonio, by the way." Sean gestured at his teammate, and Antonio extended his hand to Sierra. Unfortunately, taking it meant letting go of Sean's hand, so she did, and shook Antonio's hand.

"Antonio, as in Detective Rodriguez?"

"The one and only."

"It's nice to actually meet you in person." She laced her fingers with Sean's again, her hand slipping back into his as if that was exactly where it belonged. But then Carter came back toward them, and this time he did drop her hand. She tried to ignore how pathetically bereft she now felt without his touch, understanding how it might look if he were holding hands with a client in front of one of his guys. She wished him luck and headed off to the bleachers with Carter.

She almost laughed at how normal this all felt. As if she were nothing more than a woman watching her boyfriend's baseball game on a summer evening in Griffith Park. And it did feel like that, if she forgot about the facts that her bodyguard was sitting beside her, a crazy, violent protest group was trying to scare her into backing away from her job, and Sean wasn't her boyfriend. They'd never even kissed. Not really. Just those two tiny brushes that she kept playing over and over in her mind.

She watched Sean chatting and laughing with a few other players, tossing a ball back and forth. She didn't know a ton about baseball, but based on the athletic ease with which he threw the ball and the casual grace in his warm-up swings, he seemed to know what he was doing. Big-time.

"You know, he almost went pro." Carter's eyes scanned the bleachers and the field, on the lookout for any potential trouble.

"Really? Like, in baseball?"

"Mmm-hmm."

"What happened?"

He shrugged his broad shoulders. "Not really my story to tell. Ask him about it."

The sun was just starting to slide down the sky, casting the field in a soft, pinkish glow. The game started, and when Sean came up to the plate, a tingle of anticipatory excitement ran down her spine. He swung the bat gracefully up over his shoulder, tipping it in a small circular motion as he waited for the pitch. With an impressively powerful swing that caused the muscles in his forearms to bunch and jump, a sharp wooden crack rang out, and the ball was airborne, sailing toward the back of the field. He dropped the bat and began running the bases, slowing his pace when he saw the ball was gone. He rounded third base, glancing up at the bleachers and winking at her as he jogged by. The butterflies in her stomach cheered him on as he crossed home plate.

With each passing inning, Sean's team pulled ahead by a few more runs. He was far and away the best player on the team, and a tiny part of her wondered if he was showing off because she'd teased him, or if he was just always this good. His second at bat, he hit a triple, and his final time up he hit another home run. Defensively he was just as skilled. He made more than one diving catch in the outfield, marring his white pants with grass stains.

His team won, and she'd been completely riveted watching him, unable to tear her attention away from him. He was fist-bumping and high-fiving his teammates, and he pulled his cap off and ran his fingers through his hair, eyes crinkling as he laughed, his smile wide and bright. She liked seeing him like this. Relaxed and happy. Smiling and a little flushed.

Maybe that's what he looked like after sex.

God, she wanted to find out.

* * *

"Dude, somebody ate his Wheaties this morning," Antonio joked as he packed up his gear.

Sean laughed. "I'll buy you a box. Then maybe you'll actually hit the damn ball."

"Yeah, yeah, laugh it up. We both know why you played so well."

"We do?" Sean arched an eyebrow as he peeled off his batting gloves and dropped them into his bag.

"Yeah. Sierra, man." Antonio smirked knowingly at him.

"No idea what you're talking about," he lied.

"Deny it all you want, but you've got it for her. Don't think I didn't see you holding hands earlier. Dude, you should've seen your face, like holding hands with her was the best thing in the world. Like elementary school, playground-level bliss." It had been impulsive, and he'd half expected her to snatch her hand away. But she hadn't, and he'd wanted to keep holding it. He'd even risked Carter seeing them, which was stupid.

"You're so full of shit. She's just a client." A dull ache started at his temples.

Antonio scoffed, "So? I know you got your rules and shit, but man. You're lit up like a freakin' Christmas tree around this girl. You know what you should do?"

"What?" Finished packing up, Sean stood, swinging the bag over his shoulder.

"Now that you've held hands with her, you should like,

pass her a note. 'I like you. Do you like me? Check yes, no, or maybe.'" Antonio could barely get the words out through his laughter.

"Fuck you."

Mirthful glee lit up Antonio's face as he looked over Sean's shoulder. "Here she comes. You want a piece of paper?"

He flipped Antonio off and then turned around to face Sierra. Before he'd met her, he'd thought the whole "heart skipping a beat" thing was made up. But now he knew better, because it happened every damn time he looked at her.

When their eyes met, her face lit up and she quickened her pace, leaving Carter several paces behind her. "Sean! You were so awesome!" She held up her hand for a high five as she reached him, and he obliged her, fighting the urge to grasp her hand in his as he'd done earlier. "Let's go out for drinks."

He shook his head. "No, I don't think—"

"Oh, come on. We should all go celebrate. My treat."

"Not a good idea."

She held up a finger, a pleading look on her face. "One drink. And then we'll go straight home. I'm just…I'm having fun, not being cooped up."

She smiled up at him, happy and sweet and bright, and yet again, he knew he was going to cave, just as he had over her coming to the game. "Fine. One drink."

"You should come too," she said to Antonio, who nodded.

"Sure. It'll give us a chance to talk about the case. Why don't we go to the Clover? It's a little nicer than Frank's." Antonio smiled at Sierra, and the way his eyes raked subtly over her made Sean want to punch him. Hard.

"Watch it, or I'll tell Frank you said that."

Antonio laughed and headed toward the parking lot.

Plans made, they headed back toward his SUV, Sierra at

his side. He really wanted to take her hand again. The way
she'd slipped her small, delicate fingers between his had felt
so good. So simple. So right. He began to reach for her,
wanting to feel her skin on his again. Wanting to touch her
and have her close to him. But Carter was there, and he
couldn't.

By the time they arrived at the Clover, he'd convinced
himself that all of this was a colossally bad idea. He
shouldn't be bringing her to a bar. Hell, he shouldn't have
even brought her to his baseball game. But when she smiled
at him the way she had, he found he couldn't say no.

One of the many reasons it was stupid and dangerous to
fall for a client.

The four of them settled into a booth, Sean and Sierra
on one side, Carter and Antonio on the other. Sean made
sure Sierra was on the inside of the booth, practically hidden from view from the rest of the bar by his own body.
She nodded her head in time to the CCR tune playing while
she studied the list of beers on tap. The Clover was famous for its huge selection of craft beer from breweries
across Southern California. He leaned a little bit closer and
pointed at the Claremont Carlisle pale ale on the laminated
menu.

"This one's really good, and based on the beer you have
at home, I think you might like it."

She looked up at him, her nose scrunching slightly.
"Yeah? I'll give that one a try, then."

The waitress came over and took their order, and Sierra
slid the tiniest bit closer to him, her leg now flush against his
under the table.

He pressed his leg against hers, returning the pressure
when she rubbed her thigh along his, encouraging her. And
damn, it felt good.

"Hey, Sean, heads up," said Carter, his voice low. "Six o'clock."

Sean looked over his shoulder, angling his body in front of Sierra as panic shot through him. But it wasn't a threat headed their way. Just a major pain in his ass.

"Excuse me." He pushed up from the table and locked eyes with Colt Priestley, who looked just as surprised to see him. He stood several feet away, a beer in one hand, his other arm wrapped round a redhead with enough cleavage for three women.

"Will you give me a second...sweetheart?" Colt smiled down at the redhead, clearly unable to remember her name, and Sean couldn't help but roll his eyes. Some things never changed.

The redhead walked her fingers up his arm. "Don't be long." He watched her walk away before turning his attention to Sean.

"What are you doing here, Colt?"

He ran a hand over his short light-brown hair and cocked an eyebrow. "Uh, it's a bar," he said, as if that were explanation enough. Hell, knowing Colt and his proclivity for booze and women (and not always in that order), it pretty much was. "Listen, I'm glad I ran into you. I've been trying to get ahold of you."

"I know, and you're wasting your time. You can't have your job back."

He cursed quietly under his breath. "I'm sorry about the way everything went down. I fucked up, I know."

"You did." The memory of stepping into the fight that Priestley had caused flashed before his eyes. The chaos. The noise. The knife.

Colt sighed heavily and shifted his weight, dragging a hand over his mouth. "I know I don't deserve one, but I'm asking for a second chance here, man."

"That *was* your second chance. I refuse to take risks with client safety. The answer's no."

His nostrils flared, and Sean could see him struggling with his temper. He took a step closer to Sean. Although he was a few inches shorter, he was nearly as wide, and Sean was pretty sure Colt was too dumb to be scared of anything. "This have anything to do with the fact that your dad was on *my* side?"

Sean choked out a harsh laugh, refusing to take the bait. "You enjoy the rest of your night. We're done here."

Colt shook his head angrily. "Whatever." He stalked away with his slightly bowlegged gait, heading back to his date. Sean walked the few feet back to the booth and sat down. He grabbed his bottle of beer and took a healthy pull. His father had been the one to hire Priestley, but Sean had been against it from the start. Too many red flags. The temper, the reckless behavior, the drinking. But Patrick had fought him on it, overruling Sean. Not trusting his judgment.

And Sean had ended up nearly losing an eye.

"Who was that?" Sierra asked, her brow furrowed. She glanced back and forth between him and Carter. After another long pull on his beer, Sean answered.

"Colt Priestley. He used to work for Virtus."

"Used to?"

"I fired him."

"Oh. Um...for what?"

"Long story short, he made a reckless decision, and I ended up getting stabbed in the face."

Her eyes widened, and she laid her hand on his knee under the table. "*What?*" Her voice was quiet, her shoulders suddenly rigid.

He pointed to the faint scar that ran from the top of his

left cheekbone almost to his ear. She reached out tentatively and ran her fingertips over the remains of the scar, her bottom lip caught between her teeth.

"I'd noticed it, but…" She didn't finish her thought, just kept running her fingers over the scar. Funny how he was the one with the scar, and yet he wanted to comfort her.

"It's a lot better than it used to be. Pretty cool what they can do with lasers."

"I hate that you have such a dangerous job."

He'd been about to put his hand over hers when Antonio cleared his throat, smiling down into his beer. Carter studied a menu as though his life depended on memorizing it.

Shit.

A pink flush crept over her cheeks, and she took her hand back, wrapping it firmly around her beer. "So Carter tells me you almost played pro baseball? Is that true?"

"*Almost* is pretty generous, but yeah, sort of. I went to Cal State Fullerton on a ball scholarship, and I got drafted by the Giants. Mostly played in the minors, but I played a few games for them. It didn't work out, long term. Dad needed my help with the company, so I moved back." He took a sip of his beer and changed the subject, focusing on Antonio. "No updates?"

Antonio shook his head slowly. "I wish I had better news, but no. We're still trying to get anything concrete on Sacrosanct, but those bastards are slippery. Our buddy Judah isn't talking, and it doesn't matter what we threaten him with, or whatever deal we throw his way. He won't roll on anyone else, won't cop to anything. Everything else we've found is either a dead end or so circumstantial that we don't have a hope in hell of convincing a judge to grant us any kind of search warrant. Plus, we'd have to know where to search. Nothing's connecting. Yet. But it will." He smiled reassuringly at Sierra before tipping his beer at Sean. "Your guy Clay come up with anything else?"

"He's working a few leads, but no new information yet."

Sierra sighed heavily, trailing her finger through a streak of condensation on the table. "Well, that's disappointing."

"I know. Hang in there. We'll find them." Antonio nodded confidently. "It's only a matter of time."

CHAPTER 15

Sean turned onto Sierra's street, his gaze sweeping back and forth and landing on the black town car idling at her curb.

"You expecting someone?" he asked, catching Sierra's eyes in the rearview mirror.

She shook her head. "No."

Instantly on alert, he didn't say anything, just pulled the SUV into Sierra's driveway and threw it into park, wondering if he should grab one of the bats from his trunk. Carter pushed out of the SUV, his Glock already in hand and hanging by his side.

The rear passenger door of the town car swung open, and Jack stumbled out. The streetlamps cast eerie shadows over his face, but it was unmistakably him. Sean glanced in the rearview mirror again, needing eyes on Sierra.

"Stay in the—" But Sean didn't finish his sentence. There was no point, because Sierra had already hopped out of the SUV.

Jack slammed the car door shut, and his gaze swung from Sierra to Carter to Sean, and then back to Sierra.

Sierra took a step forward, her arms crossed. "What are you doing here, Jack?"

He laughed, the sound low and rough. "I came to see you and your new boyfriend," he said, his words running together. He leaned back against the town car, landing with a solid thunk against the car's body, his head bobbing.

He was fucking hammered. Great.

Sean stepped in front of Sierra, shielding her from Jack as his mind reeled back to what she'd told him about his drinking. "What do you want, Jack?"

He shook his head and laughed. "*You.* You're a piece of work, you know that? You think you can steal my girl, just fucking *swoop* in like some kind of fucking hero?" He laughed again. "You think you can have me investigated and that I wouldn't find out about it?"

Shit. Clay must not have covered his tracks as well as he'd thought. Or Jack had eyes in places they hadn't expected. Maybe a combination of the two.

"Let's get one thing straight here," said Sierra, her voice sharp and angry as she stepped out from behind Sean. "I am *not* your girl, Jack. I haven't been for months, so you don't get to come here and act all possessive. Nobody stole me away. I left you, and if you want to know why, I suggest you go home and take a good hard look in the mirror."

Jack laughed again, the sound hollow and bitter. Carter took a step forward, and a big guy in a suit stepped out of the front passenger side of the town car.

"Did you come here to make a point?" Sean stepped in front of Sierra again.

"You know, it's really charming, the way you're protecting her. But you can treat her like gold, and she'll still use you, and treat you like shit, and leave you when she's done with you."

It was Sierra's turn to laugh, but there was nothing happy about the sound. It was harsh and sarcastic. "Uh, excuse me, but if anyone was treated like shit, it was me, not you. Asshole."

"What did you call me?" Jack lurched forward, his eyes glued to Sierra. "Don't you dare talk to me that way, you stupid bitch."

Something in Sean snapped, and he closed the distance between himself and Jack in a few long, fast strides. "Leave her out of this. You wanna be mad at someone, be mad at me. Yeah, I had you investigated. And I'd do it again."

Jack's bodyguard approached, and so did Carter. Sean stared Jack down, and from what he could see in his peripheral vision, he knew Carter was doing the same with Jack's bodyguard.

Jack poked a finger into Sean's chest. "You fucked with the wrong guy. Do you have any idea the kind of power I have? The people I know? I could ruin your life with a phone call."

"Great. I'm real scared. Go home." He tipped his head toward the town car.

"No. I'm not done yet."

"Yes, you are."

Jack hesitated and then tried to step around Sean, who blocked him.

"Sierra, baby. I'm sorry I called you a bitch. I didn't mean it. You know I didn't mean it, right? I miss you, sweetheart. We were so good together."

Sierra didn't say anything, just stared at Jack, anger tightening her features. Jack took a step toward her, and Sean laid a hand on his chest, pushing him back against the car. No fucking way was he getting close to Sierra.

Sierra sighed heavily. "Just go, Jack."

Jack shook with anger, and once again tried to get around Sean. "You're nothing without me. You're pathetic. Weak. A used-up whore."

Sean's vision narrowed as heat flushed his body, feeding his already tense muscles.

"Screw you, Jack. I want you to leave. Now."

Jack's face contorted, and he let out an enraged snarl. "Listen, you stupid cu—"

Sean's fist connected with his jaw with a loud, wet crunch, cutting off the rest of his ugly words. Jack's hands flew up to his face, and his bodyguard lunged for Sean, but Carter intercepted him, holding him back. Grabbing fistfuls of Jack's shirt, Sean slammed him into the body of the town car.

"Here's what you're gonna do. You're gonna turn around, get in your car, and *fuck off. Now.*" He let Jack go with a hard shove against the town car.

"I'm going to have you charged with assault."

"Like I fucking care. You came here to be a bully and make threats. Don't show your face here again. You even so much as call Sierra, you'll have to answer to me."

"Poke your fucking nose into my business again, and you'll regret it." Rubbing a hand over his jaw, Jack wrenched the door open and dropped clumsily into the back of the car. Eyes flicking back and forth between Sean and Carter, Jack's bodyguard followed suit, slipping back into the front passenger seat of the car. It pulled smoothly away from the curb, and the three of them stood in silence, watching as the taillights shrank. As the adrenaline ebbed slightly, the reality of the situation washed over Sean.

He'd punched a senator. In the face. Shit.

Shit shit shit.

But then Sierra's small hand was on his arm, and just

for the way she was looking at him, with heat and gratitude and something else shining in her eyes, it had been
worth it.

"You weren't kidding about his drinking," he said, shaking out his right hand.

"That was pretty typical. He gets drunk, and suddenly the
whole world is against him. He's unpredictable and mean."
She rubbed a hand over his forearm. "I wouldn't worry about
him pressing charges. If he even remembers, he'll be so upset and remorseful that he won't follow through. He never
follows through with drunk threats."

Sean blew out a long, slow breath, trying to dispel the
adrenaline still charging through him. He shoved a hand
through his hair, closing his eyes briefly. "I probably
shouldn't have hit him."

She looked up at him, an incredulous smile on her face.
"He got exactly what he deserved."

He tucked a strand of hair behind her ear, letting the tips
of his fingers linger on her jaw. "You're OK?"

"*I'm* fine. But I think you might need some ice for your
hand."

He looked down and could see that his knuckles were red
and already starting to swell. "Carter, can you do a perimeter
check? I'm going to go in the house with Sierra."

"Sure thing, boss." He nodded, his Glock still in his
hands.

"And let's wait and see what shakes out, if Jack decides
to press charges or not. If he does, I'll deal with it, but in the
meantime, let's keep this between us."

"No problem. For what it's worth, that was a hell of a
right cross." Carter headed toward the side of the house,
making sure there were no other surprises waiting for them.

Sierra threaded her fingers through Sean's left hand and

led him into the house. Adrenaline still coursed through him, and he could feel each pump of his heart, a steady rhythm pounding inside him.

The adrenaline was from punching Jack in his arrogant, smug face. Not from Sierra's tiny hand nestled in his. Not from the almost overwhelming sense of protectiveness he felt toward her. He felt a warm tug low in his gut at the way she smiled at him as she unlocked the front door.

"I shouldn't have punched him," he murmured, following her into the house. She tapped her code into the alarm and flicked on the lights. Sean's eyes scanned the hallway and the living room, looking for anything out of place.

She glanced at him over her shoulder, and it was as if someone were tightening a vise around his ribs, his lungs. Around his heart. "I don't know what this says about me, but…it was kinda hot. No one's ever stood up for me like that before."

A plummeting feeling bottomed out in his stomach, as if he were standing on the edge of a cliff, trying desperately not to fall off the edge. He trailed behind her into the house, watching her small figure as she led him into the kitchen, her fingers still twined with his. The pulsing throb in his knuckles kept tempo with his thudding heart, and his blood hummed through his veins.

"I don't have an ice pack, but…" Her small, round ass stuck up in the air as she rummaged through the bottom freezer. Clutching a bag of frozen peas, she sprang back up. "Green Giant to the rescue." She hopped up on the island. "Come here."

He arched an eyebrow as he walked slowly toward her. "I can do it myself."

"Would you come here? I'm trying to say thank you."

The pressing need to wrap his arms around her vibrated through him. The vibrations turned into a warm tingle as she took his bruised hand in hers, holding the bag of peas over his tender knuckles. She turned her face up to his, her green eyes sparkling.

God, she smelled good. Like sunshine, warm and bright and life-giving.

He inched his body closer to the island, his hips bumping the edge. The insides of her bare legs grazed his legs as the skirt of her dress rode up.

"Thank you for sticking up for me. And for keeping me safe." She bit her lip and looked up at him through her lashes. His heart squeezed as he looked down at her, their faces only inches apart. Goddamn, she was beautiful.

"I meant it when I said that I've got you." With his free hand, he tucked a strand of hair behind her ear, tracing his thumb over her cheekbone. His eyes drifted down to her lips, and he couldn't fight it anymore. Clearly he was hell-bent on destruction tonight. He'd punched a state senator, and now, for the first time in his ten years as a bodyguard, he was going to kiss a client.

Cupping her cheek with his uninjured hand, he slowly dipped his head and gently, tenderly closed his mouth over hers. She responded immediately, returning the kiss with a soft sigh.

The peas slid to the floor with a crunchy plop and he slid his right arm around her, pulling her closer, growling quietly. She wrapped her arms around him as he deepened the kiss, parting her lips with his tongue. Finally he was touching her and tasting her just the way he'd wanted since the day they met. Finally she had her arms around him and was moaning softly into his mouth. Finally, and it was a thousand times better than he ever could've imagined. And he'd spent a lot of time imagining it.

He explored her mouth, savoring the sweetness of it as heat curled through his veins. His tongue caressed hers, and she gripped him tighter.

It was the best wrong thing he'd ever done.

Breaking the kiss, he buried his face in her neck, trailing his lips over her warm, soft skin, kissing and tasting, breathing her in. He sank his teeth gently into the curve where neck and shoulder met, nipping at her skin. She tipped her head back.

"Oh, God, Sean." Her words came out on a loud moan, breathless and hot.

Oh, hell yes.

She wrapped her legs around him, pressing herself against the erection straining against his uniform, and he rocked into her, the friction sending hot pulses through him. He kissed his way back up to her mouth, and as his lips pressed hungrily against hers, he felt as though liquid fire were slowly spreading through him. He rocked his hips against her again as the kiss became rougher, more urgent. His low moans tangled with hers, and their mouths melded together. She fisted her hands in the fabric of his jersey and yanked it free of his pants. Her hands slid up under his jersey, tracing the ridges of his abs as she softly bit his lower lip and then traced her tongue over it. He groaned as he caressed a hand up her thigh, pushing her skirt up as he went, wondering if she could feel his hands trembling with how much he wanted her. With how good she felt. How good she was making him feel.

He'd never had this kind of sexual chemistry with anyone. Ever. Kissing Sierra, he felt as though he were about to explode out of his skin with how badly he needed to be inside her. How badly he wanted to discover all the different ways he could make her come. With his hands, his mouth, his cock buried deep inside her.

She broke the kiss, her lips swollen, her eyes hooded and dark. "Your mouth feels so good." She brushed her lips across his jaw as she spoke, working her way up to his ear. "I want to feel it everywhere." She rocked her hips against him and shuddered slightly, her voice raw, coming out as a whispered half sob. "I want you so much."

He dipped his head, catching her mouth again, his nose brushing hers. "I've wanted you since the day I met you."

"I'm yours."

He had no words for the wave of possession crashing over him, so he kissed her again, slowly and hungrily, sliding a hand up her rib cage until he covered one small breast with his hand. He caressed in a slow, gentle circle, and she arched into him, her hips twitching as she whimpered against his mouth. Her nipple was a hard little bud against his palm, and he trailed his fingers across the top and down the side of her breast, memorizing the contours.

The front door opened, and they jerked apart.

Jesus Christ, he'd completely forgotten about Carter. She leaped down off the island, straightening her disheveled clothes as he quickly tucked his jersey back in, fighting to get himself together, adjusting the monster erection pressing against his tight baseball pants.

Damn baseball pants. They hid nothing. He circled around behind the island, knowing he'd have to stay hidden from the waist down until things were calmer south of the border.

She pressed a hand to her pink cheek, bending down and scooping up the bag of frozen peas from the floor. She straightened and quickly tossed it to him. Still breathing heavily, he caught it and pressed it to his groin, trying to get control of himself.

A surprised laugh burst from Sierra, her face bright. "For your *hand*," she whispered, gesturing frantically at his bruised knuckles.

Oh, right. He'd forgotten about that too. With a sheepish grin, he transferred the bag to his knuckles, trying to ignore the trickle of fear at just how easily and quickly he'd gotten distracted. She yanked open the fridge and stuck her head inside for several seconds.

At least he wasn't the only one who needed cooling off.

She emerged with a bottle of water just as Carter appeared. Sean hoped like hell he hadn't seen them kissing. Hell, they'd done more than kiss. They'd crossed second base and would've been well on their way to third if Carter hadn't come in. If he was going to violate his professional ethics, he'd rather his team didn't see him do it.

"Everything OK?" asked Sean, hoping he sounded a lot more relaxed than he felt.

Carter glanced from Sean to Sierra, who was guzzling her water as if she'd just hiked through the desert. "Everything's fine. How's the hand?"

"I'll live."

Carter's phone buzzed, and he pulled it out of his pocket. He answered and listened intently for a few moments. "I'll put you on speaker." He tapped the screen and laid the phone on the island. "It's Clay."

"Hey, Sean, I've been trying to call you. Everything good?"

"Yeah. My phone's in the car. What's up?"

"I think I found something. Can you come to the office?"

"Right now?"

"Yeah. I'm already here."

Sean pushed a hand through his hair, glancing at Sierra. He'd been so determined not to touch her until he knew she was safe, but with one kiss, that resolve had flown out the window. She was his to protect, and soon she'd be *his*. But not tonight.

CHAPTER 16

Sean pushed open the doors to Virtus's offices, slipping his key card into the back pocket of his jeans. Only one bank of overhead lights was on, leaving the corners in shadow. The row of offices was dark, giving the space an eerily empty feel. Clay sat at one of the computers at the table in the center, paging through what looked like surveillance photos and geotagging them as he went. As Sean approached, Clay stood, looking even scruffier than usual with his shaggy mane of dark-blond hair and at least a week's worth of stubble on his jaw.

"You find something?"

"You could say that. Not related to your case, though. I didn't want to say anything in front of Carter or your client." He tipped his head toward the back office, and tension radiated across Sean's shoulders.

"Shit."

"I'm heading out and didn't want to leave him on his own."

"Thanks." Sean clapped Clay on the shoulder as he

walked by him, making his way to his father's office. He pushed open the glass door, and the smell of scotch hit him like a punch in the gut. His father sat behind his desk, a tumbler clutched in one hand. A bottle of Glenfiddich sat on the desk beside him, glowing green in the light from the computer screen. He didn't look up as Sean entered and sank down into one of the leather chairs facing his desk.

"What the hell are you doing here?" his dad asked, the words slightly slurred. He dragged a hand through his hair and took a healthy swallow of scotch.

"Thought you might want a drinking buddy."

Patrick studied him for a second before nodding gruffly and pulling a second tumbler out from a drawer. He poured a small amount of the amber liquid into the glass and passed it to Sean, who took it and sat back in the chair, one ankle propped on the opposite knee.

For several moments they drank in silence. The scotch burned a path down the center of Sean's chest. He hated this. Hated seeing this man struggle so much with a pain that was entirely Sean's fault.

He took another sip, trying to burn away the guilt.

"Today would've been our fortieth anniversary." Patrick's voice was loud in the quiet office, the only other sound the whir of the computer.

Shit. Sean rubbed a hand over his mouth and set down his tumbler, leaning forward and bracing his forearms on his thighs. "I'm sorry."

His father nodded again and splashed more scotch into his own glass. He'd heard Sean say those two words so many times over the past ten years that they'd probably lost all meaning. But it didn't matter. Sean would keep saying them. It was his fault his mother was gone. His fault his father drank.

Patrick leaned back in his chair, a faraway look in his eyes. "She was so beautiful. So smart. So loving. I never quite felt that I deserved her. Maybe I didn't. I didn't get to keep her for nearly long enough."

Sean bowed his head, listening, knowing there was nothing he could say.

"She had the best laugh. And she never took any shit from anyone. I always loved that about her. She was so strong. But that strength didn't harden her. It just made her better."

"I miss her too."

Patrick leveled his gaze at Sean and let out a short, sharp breath. "You're sorry, and you miss her. What fucking good does that do me?"

Sean clenched his jaw, having known it was coming and refusing to get drawn into a pointless argument. "Let me drive you home." He stood and pulled his keys from his pocket.

"I'll take a cab."

"Dad." Sean crossed his arms. "Please."

His father just stared at him, his eyes burning holes right through him. "Leave me alone."

"I want to make sure you get home OK."

Patrick set his glass down with a loud clack, scotch sloshing over the side and onto his desk. "Just go." His nostrils flared when Sean didn't move. "Go! Get out!"

* * *

The next day Sierra sat in her master bathroom, mentally going over her talking points as her hair stylist and makeup artist fluttered around her. She would've loved a trip out to a salon or a spa to get ready for the gala, but with all the security precautions, it had just been easier to have them come to the house. She glanced up at her reflection in the mirror, her makeup almost done, her hair up in jumbo Velcro rollers. She wore a black satin robe and slippers, her gorgeous blush-pink gown of silk crepe and tulle hanging on the back of the door.

"Taylor, what time is it?" she called into her bedroom, looking up at the ceiling as the makeup artist lined her eyes.

"Almost six." Taylor lounged on Sierra's bed, flipping through a magazine. She'd come over earlier to help Sierra relax. They'd swum and eaten, and now Taylor was keeping her company as she got ready. "Hang on, your phone's ringing." Sierra heard her answer it, and then Taylor appeared in the bathroom, phone in hand. "It's Rory."

Sierra's heart sank, because she knew exactly why he was calling. She tapped the screen to put the call on speaker and laid the phone in her lap. "Hey, Rory. You're not going to make it, are you?" He'd texted her earlier saying that he'd gotten stuck on set and wasn't sure he'd be able to make it.

"I'm so sorry, babe, but I have to bail. We're still shooting."

"It's OK. It happens."

"I'm really sorry."

"It's not your fault." She tried very hard not to sound as if she was pouting.

"I really wanted to be there with you."

"I know you did. It's OK. I'll manage on my own."

"You're gonna knock 'em dead. You've got this. OK?"

"Thanks, Rory. How's the shoot going?" She chatted with him for a few more minutes as the hair stylist began taking out the Velcro rollers, leaving big, loose waves cascading down over her shoulders. She gave him a thumbs-up in the mirror.

Sometimes, in moments like this, she missed the fun,

glamorous parts of Hollywood. Just a little. She still needed to make a decision about the audition, but she was leaning more toward doing it and seeing what came of it than not. Maybe she did miss acting a bit. It was never something she'd chosen for herself, as she'd started so young, but now that she was away from it, she found she sometimes missed having that creative outlet.

She hung up with Rory and passed her phone back to Taylor, who stood in the bathroom's doorway, one shoulder propped against the doorjamb. "He's not coming?"

"He's stuck working. I'll be flying solo tonight."

Taylor paused, and Sierra could see the wheels turning. "Where's Sean?"

Sierra's heart did a little happy dance just at the mention of his name. "He had meetings and stuff all day, and he had something with another client tonight. He said he was going to try to get out of it, but he didn't think it was likely." They hadn't had a chance to talk about the kiss and what it meant. How things had changed between them with that kiss. At least things had changed for her. But he'd come back late last night, and she'd already been in bed. They hadn't found themselves alone at all this morning before he left, and he'd been gone all day.

"So he wasn't planning on going to the gala with you?"

"No. Zack and Ian. He wanted to be there, but it didn't work out. He was pissed about it." She'd overheard him on the phone, arguing with his father about it. She couldn't imagine how tough that had to be sometimes, having his dad as his boss. Especially given that Patrick had retired, and Sean was supposed to be in charge.

The hair stylist gave her hair a final spritz, and the makeup artist slicked on a coat of lip gloss before stepping back to admire her work.

"How come when I do the exact same stuff, I do *not* look like this?" Sierra smiled, checking herself out in the mirror, her hair falling in soft, loose waves around her face, her makeup flawlessly pretty. Polished and professional with a hint of sexy. The hairdresser and makeup artist started packing up their stuff, and Sierra stepped back into the bedroom, where Taylor helped her into the dress. The silk crepe bodice was delicately sequined and formfitting, with a slender cream-colored beaded silk belt separating it from the flowing tulle skirt.

She turned to check herself out in the mirror again, the skirt swirling around her ankles.

"Wow." Sean's voice came from the doorway, and she spun, her heart fluttering helplessly in her chest. He stood there in a white T-shirt and worn jeans, looking better than any man had the right to look. His eyes dipped up and down her body, a slow, appreciative smile curving his lips up.

"Thanks. I wasn't expecting to see you tonight. I thought you had another job."

"I did. I shuffled some stuff around, and I was going to see if Zack could trade off with me."

"Or you could go as her date," said Taylor matter-of-factly, as though it were the simplest, easiest thing in the world.

Sean raised one eyebrow. "Where's Rory?"

"Working. He can't come, so I'm minus one. It's not a big deal. Besides," Sierra said, giving Taylor her best "behave" glare over her shoulder, "it's black tie, so unless you've got a tuxedo with you, I—"

"I do, actually. In my car. I just picked up my dry cleaning on my way over."

"You have a tuxedo in your car."

"Must be fate." Taylor elbowed her.

"I don't mean to put you on the spot, but if you—"

"Yes. I'm in." He smiled, and when their eyes met, something passed between them, leaving Sierra feeling as though she were floating, just a little.

Sean left, and a knowing grin spread across Taylor's face. "You're welcome."

Sierra pressed a hand to her cheek, trying to control the giddy grin pulling at her mouth. She checked her appearance one last time, slipped on her gold pumps, and gathered her essentials, dropping mints, lipstick, and her phone into her clutch.

Taylor scooted around Sierra's bed and yanked open the nightstand drawer. She rummaged around, frowning.

"What are you looking for?"

"Condoms. You should put a couple in your bag."

Sierra laughed as her stomach disappeared somewhere around her feet. "We're going to a charity gala. It's a public place. We're not gonna need condoms." While swimming this afternoon with Taylor, she'd told her about kissing Sean.

Taylor shot her a challenging look, one eyebrow arched, a mischievous smirk on her face. "Really? Huh. You must not see the way he looks at you if you think you won't be needing any condoms tonight."

"How does he look at me?"

Taylor leaned forward, her eyes gleaming. "He looks at you like he can't wait to get inside you. Like he's imagining all the different ways he'll fuck you." She pointed at the doorway where Sean had just stood. "*That* is a hungry man, and you're his feast."

Sierra's brain disconnected from her tongue, and she pointed at the nightstand on the opposite side of the bed. Taylor opened the drawer and pulled out the box of Trojan Ultra Thins, dumping a couple into her hand. "I don't know,

Si, these are regular. Sean seems like he might be a Magnum kind of guy."

Sierra laughed and snatched the foil packets from Taylor, dropping them into her clutch as heat flushed across her chest. Given what she'd felt last night, Taylor might be right. "You're terrible."

Taylor winked, and they made their way down the stairs just as Sean stepped into the entryway through the kitchen, wearing a tuxedo that fit him perfectly, emphasizing his broad chest and shoulders. He'd parted his hair on the side and styled it with a bit of gel, and he looked like a cross between James Bond and Superman.

She stared at him and melted. "Not bad for ten minutes," she managed, her mouth dry.

"Do *everything* I would do," Taylor whispered in her ear before turning to Sean. "Zack still coming with you guys?"

"No, he's going to stay back and keep an eye on things here. Ian and I can handle the gala."

"Perfect. Have fun, kids." She waved over her shoulder as she disappeared into the house, probably seeking Zack out. Sierra was tempted to call out, "Don't have sex in my house," but decided that might embarrass them too much.

Sierra wasn't exactly in a position to judge, in any case.

The limo was already waiting outside, and Ian led the way, Sean offering her his arm as he escorted her down the driveway. He dipped his head. "You look incredible." His low voice rumbled over her skin, and she shivered.

She curled her fingers into his arm. "So do you." She wanted to say more, but they'd reached the limo, and the tiny, elusive moment of privacy was over as Ian hopped into the back with them. She struggled to keep her hands folded in her lap, but she couldn't give anything away in front of Ian.

"Don't be nervous." Sean laid a hand on her knee and sent her one of those lopsided smiles. "You're gonna do great."

She sent him a grateful smile in return, amazed at how a simple touch and two short sentences could make her feel so much better. "There are going to be so many influential people there. Politicians, journalists, people from other health-related organizations…it's a little intimidating. I just…" She trailed off and tried not to roll her eyes at herself. "I want them to take me seriously."

"They will. You're smart, dedicated, and you care about helping Choices. Just relax, and that'll all come through."

"If you embarrass yourself, I can create a distraction," said Ian, winking and easing a bit more of her tension. "Knock over a tray of drinks, step on some lady's dress, whatever."

She laughed, relaxing back into the seat. "I don't think that'll be necessary, but I appreciate the offer."

The twilit streets of Los Angeles slid by outside the window, the tall palms almost black against the lavender sky as the limo navigated its way downtown. The bright lights of the towering hotels and office buildings fought against the softer dusk, rising up into the falling darkness. As they crawled toward the Ritz-Carlton, the three of them slipped into easy conversation, Sean telling Ian about his meetings, Sierra asking them if they had any funny client stories they could share—with names changed to protect the innocent, of course.

By the time the limo rolled to a stop, she'd forgotten entirely about her nerves. Until the limo door opened, Ian and Sean stepped out, and she was faced with a blue carpet the same shade as the Choices logo.

"Ready or not," she muttered to herself, taking Sean's hand as he helped her out of the limo and into the cool night air.

CHAPTER 17

From a few feet away, Sean adjusted his earpiece and watched Sierra as she charmed the mayor, a few city councillors, a couple of journalists, and a handful of Choices board members. He couldn't hear what she was saying over the old-school R&B filling the Ritz-Carlton's massive ballroom, but it didn't matter. He was good at reading people, and he could tell the group was both interested in and impressed by what she had to say. Pride filled him, and he took a sip of his scotch, unable to tear his eyes away from her. She smiled and waved him over.

"This is Sean Owens. He's the director of operations and strategic planning at Virtus Security." She smiled up at him, her nose scrunching. "And my date this evening." Sean shook hands with everyone as Sierra continued. "He's the one responsible for getting me here in one piece tonight. I'm very lucky to have him."

He was pretty sure he was the lucky one to have found her. Lucky that she'd come to him for protection so that he could keep her safe.

One of the board members, a middle-aged Latino man, clasped his hand. "On behalf of Choices, we'd like to thank you. Someone from my office was supposed to reach out to you, but I don't think that's happened yet." He turned to Sierra. "Sierra, we've been discussing it, and we'd like to cover the bill for your security. You wouldn't be in this situation if it weren't for your position with us. The work you do for us is invaluable, and we'd like to do this for you."

"Oh, wow. Thank you so much. That would help a lot."

Sean smiled wryly. "I'll start charging overtime." The group laughed, and Sierra took a sip of her wine, laughing softly.

"So you think the harassment is coming from Sacrosanct?" asked one of the journalists.

Sean tipped his head, considering. "Most likely, yes. I know the LAPD are following up on several leads, and we have our own private investigator looking into any leads as well."

"You must be so scared." An elderly city councillor laid a hand on Sierra's shoulder, smiling with kindly concern.

"To tell you the truth, I am. But I also know that I'm in good hands. The best hands, actually." She smiled up at Sean again, heat flaring in her eyes this time.

"And you couldn't be handling this better," he said, letting his free hand come to rest on the small of her back. He felt her relax into him, and a possessive satisfaction shot through him, heating his blood and sending it all to his dick. One touch, one look, and he was ready to drag her away like a caveman.

He'd been on edge since he'd had to leave her last night, and he was counting down the seconds until he could get her alone and in his bed. He wanted her, and tonight he was going to take what he wanted.

"How do you feel about her continued involvement with Choices, given the situation?" asked the councillor. "I only ask because, if you were my daughter, or heck, granddaughter, I don't know that I'd want you to continue."

Sierra answered first. "I think that the work Choices does—promoting access to birth control, sexual education, and women's health—is not only important but critical, given the number of uninsured women in our country. In California alone, one in five women doesn't have health care, employer-sponsored or otherwise. So yes, the attention from Sacrosanct is awful, but it's worth it. And if I give in, we've let the bullies win, and what kind of message does that send?"

Sean tipped his head at Sierra. "What she said." The group laughed, and he waited for the laughter to die down before continuing. "I fully support Sierra's desire to stay involved. I agree that the work Choices does is important, and she's right about not letting the bullies win. I'm confident that Sacrosanct will be caught, and probably soon. They've already had branches shut down in San Francisco, New York, and Atlanta. It's only a matter of time, and until then, I'll make sure Sierra stays safe."

The talk turned to the upcoming mayoral election, and Ian's voice buzzed in Sean's ear. "Don't know if you saw him, but Jack Nikolaidis is here, and he's making a beeline for you."

Shit.

"Would you excuse me?" He smiled at the group, mouthing, "Be right back" to Sierra. As he walked away from the group, he locked eyes with Ian and tipped his head toward Sierra, indicating that Ian needed to keep an eye on her while Sean dealt with Jack.

He intercepted Jack about thirty feet later, feeling a swell of pride at the purplish-yellow bruise marring Jack's jaw, just below the corner of his mouth. "Do we need to go talk outside, Jack? Because I refuse to make a scene in here. I won't do that to her."

Jack shook his head, his hands raised in front of him in a placating gesture. "I didn't come looking for you to make a scene. I came to apologize."

Sean took a step back, rocked by surprise. "Apologize?"

Jack smiled ruefully and scrubbed a hand over his face. "I'd had a little too much to drink, and I...I shouldn't have shown up at Sierra's like that. And I shouldn't have taken out my anger on you. I'm still pissed that you had me investigated, but I get it. You want to keep her safe, and you can't leave any stone unturned. You care about her. I can see it."

"Of course I care about her. I care about the safety of all my clients."

"I'm not talking about safety."

Sean didn't respond, and instead drained the rest of his scotch and set the empty tumbler down on a passing waiter's tray. "Apology accepted. Sorry about the, uh..." Sean mimed a punch, and Jack snorted out a laugh.

"Believe me, I deserved it. I was being an asshole."

Sean pressed his lips together, wondering if agreeing would be a trap of some kind.

Jack rubbed a hand over the back of his neck, at least having the grace to look embarrassed. It seemed genuine, and if it wasn't, Jack could have a viable backup career as an actor if his political career didn't pan out. "It's OK. I was. I'm sure Sierra filled you in on the details of our breakup."

"I got the basic picture, yeah."

Jack sighed and glanced over in Sierra's direction. "I didn't realize how much I missed her until I saw her the other day."

Again Sean had no idea what to say. So he just nodded and shoved his hands in his pockets. "Let's just call it water under the bridge and move on."

"You know, I don't want to, but I like you, Owens." Jack wagged a finger at him. "I promise I'll stay out of your hair tonight, and…" He sighed again, once again glancing in Sierra's direction. "I know I blew it. I had something great, and I fucked it up."

"Sean?" Sierra's voice came from behind him, and he turned. Without hesitation she slipped her hand into the crook of his arm.

"What are you doing here?" Sierra frowned at Jack, one delicate eyebrow arching up.

"I'm here supporting a worthy cause."

Sierra stared at him, her mouth open. "I…I'm surprised."

"It wasn't that I didn't support Choices, Sierra. I think what they do is good. Important. Valid. I was just concerned about your involvement with them, and apparently rightfully so."

Sierra opened her mouth and then paused. She smiled and shook her head slowly. "Good-bye, Jack." She turned to Sean. "I love this song. Come dance with me." And without waiting for his response, she slipped her hand into his and led him onto the dance floor at the far end of the ballroom.

As "Midnight Train to Georgia" floated through the room, he slipped one arm around her waist, clasping her hand in his. She slid her other hand under his tuxedo jacket, stroking circles over the small of his back, electricity snapping up his spine at her touch. Even with heels on, she didn't quite reach his shoulder.

"You love this song?" he asked.

She laughed softly. "I wasn't even paying attention to

what was playing. I just didn't want to talk to Jack anymore."

"And here I thought it might've been an excuse to get closer to me."

She laughed again, louder this time. "Oh, it was that too." She looked up at him and slid her hand from around his waist and up his chest. "I can't stop thinking about that kiss, and, well, everything that followed it."

"Good."

She sighed, a soft little vibration, and laid her head on his chest. He dipped his head, inhaling her scent as they moved among the couples on the dance floor.

"You smell so damn good," he said, tightening his grip on her.

She made a soft sound, almost like a purr, and somehow managed to pull herself even closer. "So do you."

She skated her hands up and down his back, her body tight against his, and he knew he wasn't going to be able to wait until later tonight.

"Do you want to know what I'd planned for later tonight?"

She looked up at him, her eyes bright. "God, yes. Tell me."

He stroked a hand up and down her back, letting his hand dip a bit lower on each trip down. As his fingers grazed the top of her ass, her eyes fluttered closed for a second, her fingers digging into him.

He lowered his head, his lips brushing the shell of her ear. "I'd planned on giving Ian the rest of the night off so we could have the house to ourselves. So many possibilities with an empty house," he said, trailing his fingers over her exposed nape.

"Mmm," she sighed. "And then what?"

"I'd pull this zipper down," he said, tracing his fingers

over the zipper along the back of her dress, "and watch your dress fall to the floor. And then I would spend the next several hours exploring your beautiful body. I wonder how many times I could make you come? Three? Four?"

She trembled in his arms, and he smiled.

"I'd planned on making you mine tonight. On burying myself inside you as many times as you'll let me."

"Oh, sweet hell," she half whispered, half gasped. "But you're not still planning all of that? You keep saying *had*, as though it's not going to happen."

"Oh, it's going to happen. But I don't think I can wait until after the gala. Do you have any idea what you do to me?" He pressed his hips against her, his cock rubbing against her hip. "I am fucking desperate to get inside you, sweetheart."

She let out a soft moan. "Then let's go find somewhere to get desperate together. Please."

He smiled and stroked her back again. "That's my girl. I like the way you say please." He tipped her chin up to him. "Tell me what you want."

She licked her lips as her eyes met his. "You. Now. Please."

CHAPTER 18

With her hand nestled in his and heat pulsing wildly between her thighs, Sierra let Sean lead her through the dance floor, weaving her between dancing couples and finally out into the main hallway. Without pausing, he strode confidently down a smaller, narrower corridor.

She tried to speak, but her breath hitched as he stopped and pulled her into his arms. He caught her lips, his tongue caressing hers in a way that had her arching into him.

He kissed her with the hunger of a starving man, his mouth hot and urgent against hers. "God, Sierra. I'm losing my mind." He spoke the words against her mouth in a deep growl, his eyes dark pools, lust and need shining in their chestnut depths. He pressed his hips into her, the friction of his rock-hard erection dragging a moan from both of them.

"I know the feeling." An involuntary tremor vibrated down her arms, across her chest, and over her thighs, and he exhaled a shaky breath. Their eyes met, and it was as though someone had lit a fuse, the air between them hot and shimmering. Without a word he grabbed her hand, leading her farther down the hallway, around a corner, and into a service corridor. He tried several doors, and pulled her inside when he discovered an unlocked one.

They'd stumbled into a small, dark conference room. A mahogany table gleamed in the dim light filtering through the door's frosted window, and was surrounded by leather chairs. They stared at each other for one long, taut moment, and then he backed her against the wall and crushed his mouth to hers. Heat flooded her, her pulse thrumming at an insane tempo between her legs. His tongue slid hungrily against hers, and she whimpered, rolling her hips against him and sliding her arms around his deliciously hard torso, earning a low, gruff moan from deep in his chest. His mouth melded with hers and he kissed her until everything around her dissolved, and all she cared about was his lips, his tongue, his body pinning her to the wall. Hot, demanding lust thrummed through her veins as she moaned into his mouth, wanting the kiss and needing so much more from him.

He tore his lips from hers and nipped at her earlobe, sending shivers of pleasure over her skin. "I want you so much." Her stomach dropped as if she were on a roller coaster, excitement and desire spiraling through her. He trailed rough, urgent kisses over her neck, his beard prickling her skin as his fingers pinched her already tight nipple through the fabric of her dress. She arched into his hand, biting back a moan.

He lifted his face from the singed skin of her neck and closed his eyes. Exhaling a long breath, he opened them. "I need to be inside you," he groaned.

In response she slid her hand from around his waist and down, brushing her fingers against the hard bulge in his pants.

He dipped his head and kissed her again, hotly and urgently. She was melting into him, her body fusing to his under the skill of his mouth. God, she loved the way his arms felt around her, so big and strong. Coiling pressure burned low in her stomach and between her legs. She shifted and the silk of her thong slid against her, hot and damp. She couldn't remember the last time she'd been this wet this fast.

"Just so we're clear," he said between kisses, his voice rough, "I'm about to fuck you in this conference room. Is that what you want?"

"Yes." The word came out on a shaky sigh.

He rumbled out an approving noise. "Lift your skirt up. I need to touch you."

She'd unleashed something dark and primal in him, and a surge of power charged through her, making her feel more alive than she had in a long time. Alive, and like the sexiest woman on the planet. He nipped at her lips and then kissed her hard and deep, his hands skimming down her body. Raw need hummed through her, her nerve endings flaring and sparking under his touch.

She fisted her hands in the tulle of her skirt, and she eased it up until it was bunched around her waist.

He smiled, slow and sexy. "Good girl."

Two. Hottest. Words. Ever.

"Are you wet for me?" His fingers skated over her thong, a whisper of a touch that had her rolling her hips toward him. He cupped her, his palm hot against her.

She rocked her hips against his hand. "Mmm-hmm."

"Very good girl." Through half-closed eyes she saw him smile again, one side of his mouth tilting up in a cocky smirk as he drew his fingers in a slow circle over her aching pussy, the silk of her thong sliding against her. He kissed her again as he massaged gently, her legs trembling. Oh,

God, his hands were even better than she'd imagined. She stood pinned to the wall, her skirt clutched in her hands, trying to stay upright. He slipped a finger under her thong, groaning as he slicked it through her folds and around her clit.

"Oh, God, your hands, Sean. I need—" She gasped out the last word as, teasing and slow, he pushed her thong to the side and slid two fingers into her. She moaned as his thumb grazed her already swollen clit, writhing against his hand as he traced his thumb in a slow circle. He pumped his fingers, slow and deep, and she almost crumbled to the floor when he curled them inside her, igniting a fire in her core.

"These need to come off because I'm very close to ripping them." Slowly he pulled his fingers out, leaving her feeling empty and only intensifying the ache deep inside her. She nodded, unable to form words, and he hooked his thumbs into the waistband of her thong and pushed it over her hips, his eyes not leaving hers as he stripped her. Once her thong was around her ankles, she stepped out of it, her skirt still clutched in her hands. He pulled a condom from his pocket, unbuttoning his pants and pulling the fly down.

He held the foil square between two fingers as he released his gorgeously thick, long, hard cock. She dropped one side of her skirt and reached for him, wanting to touch him, to wrap her hand—hell, *hands*—around him, but he caught her wrist lightly, stopping her and guiding her hand back to her skirt.

"No. I can't take any teasing right now."

There was something beautifully debauched about the fact that they were in a public space, both still half dressed, in black-tie evening wear. She'd constructed dozens of fantasies about him, and this topped them all. Her fantasies had always failed to capture the searing need she felt, not just for sex, but for *him*. For Sean.

He ripped open the packet with his teeth and rolled the condom over his cock. Wrapping his arms around her, he kissed her, and she opened her lips eagerly for him. Cupping her ass, he lifted her up and pressed her back firmly into the wall. Her legs came up around him, her knee bumping into the gun holstered against his shoulder before settling around his waist. The idea that she was about to fuck a man with a gun strapped to him turned her on even more. She ran her hands up his chest to his shoulders, her hands skimming over the broad, hard planes of muscle, and pushed his tuxedo jacket down over his arms. He kept her pinned to the wall with his body and flung the jacket to the ground. The head of his hot, thick cock pressed against her, and he rocked his hips, sliding his hard length over her clit. She bucked and stifled a moan.

"I can't take any teasing either." To her own ears, her voice sounded far away, breathy and disembodied.

"Then let's stop teasing each other." His eyes held hers as he pushed into her, stretching and filling her, inch by delicious inch until they were fully connected. A sensation she couldn't quite name washed over her, a kind of exhilarating completeness. The tight fullness made every nerve ending sing and moan as he moved inside her with an impressively controlled thrust. Her body was on fire, dissolving and boiling and melting all at the same time, and she panted his name, over and over, like a chant. Like a prayer.

Nestled snugly—*very* snugly—inside her, he held still, his forehead pressed to hers. "Shit."

"What?" A snag of fear caught at her as she worried he'd pull away and leave her empty and sobbing for him.

He took a ragged breath. "I don't think I can last. You feel too good, and I've wanted you since the day I met you."

She squeezed her muscles around his cock, a throbbing wave of pleasure pulsing through her. "You feel so good inside me, Sean. So right."

"Christ." He ground the word out before pressing his mouth to hers. His fingers squeezing the flesh of her ass, he slowly slid almost all the way out before thrusting into her, his thick cock making her feel exquisitely taut and full. Over and over he stroked in and out of her, her skirt fluttering around them. She lost herself in the rhythm he set, wringing pleasure from her body with his. A deep, pulsing burn ripped through her core, and she rode the sensations, undone by the intensity in Sean's eyes as he filled her.

And in that moment, he possessed every part of her. Not because he'd taken it, but because she'd given it willingly. More than anything, she wanted to be his.

He kissed her hard and deep as her orgasm ripped through her, crashing with the force of a tidal wave.

"Yes. Come. Take it, sweetheart," Sean rasped against her mouth, and she moaned, shuddering against him, every muscle in her body rigid and straining as she climaxed. "Fuck. God, Sierra." He ground out her name as he came, buried deep inside her, holding her tight against him, his muscles tense.

His jagged breathing matched hers, their sharp exhalations the only sound in the dark conference room. Trailing light kisses across the hot, damp skin of his neck, she curled her fingers into his hair, brushing away the sweat dampening his hairline.

He didn't say anything, didn't pull out of her, didn't let her go. Just stared at her with full, dark eyes.

"Tell me you feel it too," he said, pressing his forehead

to hers again. Something bright and airy shimmered around them, sparkling and intangible, yet very, very real. It was beautiful and terrifying, perfect and messy all at once. Giving in hadn't sated her need for him. It had only made it stronger.

She nodded, swallowing thickly. "Yes."

She'd barely let the word out before he kissed her, softly and slowly. She returned the kiss, pouring everything she was feeling into it. The happiness and the hope, two words that felt too mundane for the emotions spilling over her.

* * *

Sean broke the kiss, savoring the feel of his body twined with Sierra's, of how tiny she felt in his arms. "We need to do this again, as soon as fucking possible." A hundred times. A thousand times. And yet he knew that wouldn't be enough.

She tipped her head to the side. "Mmm. I couldn't agree more."

He caught her earlobe in his teeth and tugged gently, unable to help himself. "In an actual bed. Or on that island in your kitchen. In the shower. On the floor. I don't care."

"Can I pick all of the above?" She ran her hands through his hair, tingles racing across his scalp.

"To start. But…" He trailed off, hesitating. "We need…" Oh, God. How to say this without sounding like a colossal asshole? "Maybe, until you're not a client anymore—"

She cut him off. "I get it. We need to be discreet." She smiled at him, her nose scrunching. "Sneaking around with my secret hot bodyguard boyfriend sounds pretty awful."

"Only until we get you out of this mess." He buried his face in her neck again, kissing a path across her skin. "Because I want everyone to know you're mine."

She sighed, and he felt her muscles tighten around his cock. "Yes." One syllable, full and heavy with meaning that went straight to all the important body parts: brain, heart, and dick.

"We should get back." Reluctantly he pulled out of her and eased her back down to the ground. He took care of the condom and retrieved his tuxedo jacket from the floor, laying it over the back of one of the leather chairs. His chest tightened as he watched her slip her underwear back on and smooth her dress into place, the fabric of her skirt a little wrinkled from being clutched in her hands. Her hair was messy, her lips were swollen, and her cheeks and chest were flushed and glowing.

She looked like a woman who'd been very thoroughly fucked.

By him.

Possessive satisfaction shot through him as he marveled at how beautiful she was. Even rumpled and disheveled like this.

Especially like this.

He needed to kiss her. He couldn't help himself, not anymore. He felt like a kid who'd never been allowed to eat candy must feel after his first chocolate bar. Happy and awake and buzzing with new awareness. Tucking his shirt in and zipping himself up, he stepped toward her and cupped her face in his hands. She sighed into him as his lips met hers, the kiss gentle and lingering.

"I don't know how I'm going to keep myself from touching you." She stroked a hand up his arm, her fingers tracing the contours of his bicep through his shirt. He slipped his hands around her waist and let out a long, slow breath.

"I know. Believe me, I know."

"Have you ever..." She bounced her eyebrows. "With a client before?"

"Never. You're the only one." He'd thought he'd feel guilty about crossing that line, but he didn't. With the euphoric happiness filling him, there was no room for guilt. Even though it had to stay a secret for now, it didn't feel *wrong*. Especially with the way she was looking up at him, her eyes soft, a half smile on her lips. He managed to tear himself away from her and slipped back into his jacket. Cautiously he opened the conference room door, poking his head out into the corridor. It was deserted, and he signaled for her to join him. They quickly made their way back toward the ballroom, and Sean slipped his earpiece back in. He'd taken it out while practically dragging Sierra off the dance floor. As soon as they stepped back into the ballroom, Ian was there, his arms crossed over his chest.

"Where the hell have you been?"

Sierra laid a hand on her sternum. "I wasn't feeling well. I think something I ate disagreed with me. I was in the bathroom." She grimaced and looked down, feigning embarrassment.

Ian frowned, looking from Sierra to Sean before relaxing slightly. "You *are* awfully flushed. You should have some water." He signaled to a waiter.

Sierra flashed him a grateful smile. "Thanks. I'm feeling a bit better now." She looked up at Sean, still feigning embarrassment. "Sorry."

He gave her shoulder a squeeze. "Just glad you're feeling better." He wanted to leave his hand where it was, but he couldn't, so he took it back and slipped his hands into his pockets. Thankfully, Ian appeared to buy Sierra's excuse. Sean hated lying to his team, but it was for the best if he and Sierra kept what was going on between them secret. At least until she wasn't a client anymore. Maybe it was selfish, but it was simpler this way.

A sound like a loud bass drum rumbled through the room, shaking the floor, followed by a loud, sharp bang. Instinctively Sean grabbed Sierra, sending her glass crashing to the floor. Light flared and he dove to the floor, sheltering her with his body as an explosion tore through the ballroom.

CHAPTER 19

Sierra tried to catch her breath, her brain scrambling to make sense of what had happened. Sean covered her body with his, his arms tucking her head against his chest. Every couple of seconds, another blast tore through the room, shaking the walls and the floor. The music had stopped, and screams erupted from every corner of the ballroom. Eerie shadows flickered across the swath of floor Sierra could see, the massive chandelier swinging back and forth precariously, crystals tinkling like wind chimes.

Debris fell around them, chunks of the wall smashing into the floor. Sean grunted as a piece hit him in the back, but he held his position, not moving away from her. Another bomb went off, this one closer, and the force of the shock wave slammed into her like a freight train. She felt it everywhere, in her jaw, in her ribs, in her joints. Her ears hurt, as though someone had jammed ice picks through them and into her skull. The ballroom shook again, and the chandelier came crashing down, shattering on the floor, shards of broken crystal flying across the room. Her bones felt brittle, as though they were made of hollow metal, and she felt every tremor, every crash, every movement as if it had the force of a sledgehammer.

Dust trembled in the air as silence descended over the room.

"Shallow breaths," whispered Sean. He lifted his head, his eyes frantic with worry. "Are you hurt?"

She shook her head, dizziness rocking her. "I...don't think so." She could barely get the words out around her racing heart. If it didn't slow down soon, it would explode, shattering just like the chandelier. Her stomach felt as though it were filled with cement. She reached up to touch Sean, her hands shaking uncontrollably.

"Are you OK? Something hit you."

"I think it was a small piece of the wall. I'm OK. Let's sit up." He pulled the white pocket square from his tuxedo jacket and handed it to her. "There's a lot of dust. Breathe through this."

She pressed it to her mouth, still taking shallow breaths. Across the room people slowly stirred, rising from the floor and from underneath tables. She saw Jack sitting on the floor about a hundred feet away, looking dazed, with blood trickling from one ear. Her own ears still felt as though they were packed with cotton.

Sirens erupted in the distance and she jumped, the sound jarring in the stunned silence of the ballroom. She knew it was stating the obvious, but she needed to say it out loud to try to make it sink in.

"Those were bombs."

Sean nodded. "I counted seven, all from different points around the room. Probably little pipe bombs."

"They didn't feel little."

"No."

The sirens wailed closer and Sean helped Sierra to her feet, his eyes raking over her. And then he pulled her into his arms, cradling her against him. "We need to get you checked out by a doctor."

"I'm OK, Sean."

"Most injuries from bombs aren't from shrapnel or debris, but from the concussive wave of pressure the bomb creates. It can cause internal bleeding."

"Fine. But only if you get checked out too."

Several more pieces of the wall and ceiling fell around them, kicking up more dust. Around them, huddled women were crying, and a man lay on the floor moaning, clutching his head. Ian approached, covered in dust but otherwise OK.

"I'm going to stay and help," he said. "You should get her out of here." Sean nodded and tucked Sierra against him, joining the crush of people flowing out of the ballroom.

"He's staying to help? Isn't that dangerous?" she asked, slipping her hand into Sean's as they descended the stairs with everyone else.

"He's a former Special Air Service medic. He knows what he's doing."

She merely nodded and squeezed his hand. He squeezed back.

"I just want to go home," she said, her mind still reeling. Less than fifteen minutes ago, she'd been in that conference room with Sean. It felt as if it had happened hours ago, days ago even. It was as though the bombing had destroyed any concept of time.

"As soon as we get you checked out by a doctor, I promise I'll take you home."

After what felt like an eternity, they pushed out into the cool night air, red and blue lights bouncing off every surface, the road clogged with police cruisers, ambulances, and fire trucks. A huge black truck marked "LAPD Bomb Squad" was parked front and center, lights flashing. Paramedics were triaging people, sending the obviously injured directly to the hospital, and checking out others on the scene. A young Asian guy in dark-blue paramedic scrubs approached them.

"You guys OK?" he asked.

"I think so, but we were close to a couple of the blasts."

Nodding, the paramedic tipped his head toward an ambulance with its doors open. He quickly checked them over, taking their blood pressure while he checked their eyes and ears. He held out his hand to Sierra.

"Squeeze my hand," he said, and she did. He did the same with Sean.

"Any pain in your chest or abdomen?"

They both shook their heads no, and he had them take several deep breaths while he listened to their chests with his stethoscope.

"You guys seem OK. You experience any symptoms, like light-headedness, shortness of breath, vomiting blood, swelling of joints, or unusual pain or bruising, go to the emergency room. Are your ears ringing?"

They both nodded.

"It should pass. If it doesn't, see your doctor. You're free to go, but the police will likely contact you for a statement. They'll probably be in touch with everyone on the guest list."

Taking her hand, Sean led her away from the chaotic scene. The streets in the immediate vicinity of the hotel were closed, and traffic was jammed on the open streets around them.

"You OK to walk a little?" he asked, tracing his thumb

over her knuckles. She nodded numbly. Walking a mile or two until they could get a cab or get someone to pick them up would be far from the worst thing that'd happened to her today. Sean led them northeast up South Figueroa Street, the crowds thinning and the traffic opening up more with each passing block.

"We were just in a bombing. Someone bombed the gala. Someone tried to kill everyone." Her voice sounded distant and robotic, especially when mixed with the metallic ringing still buzzing through her ears.

"I don't know if the intent was to kill, or to scare and make a point. I didn't see anyone with any shrapnel injuries. Normally when you make a pipe bomb, you fill it with all kinds of dangerous shit, like BB pellets, scrap metal, nails, screws, broken glass."

She nodded, taking that in, concentrating on just putting one foot in front of the other and on the solid comfort of Sean's hand around hers. She sucked in a shaky breath, and she knew the adrenaline was wearing off. Something clenched in her chest, and she started to sob.

Without a word Sean stopped and pulled her into his arms, holding her against him. "You're OK," he murmured, stroking her hair. "You're OK, sweetheart. I've got you." She felt his lips graze the top of her head, which only made her cry harder.

"You could've been hurt," she managed to choke out, but saying the words out loud only made her cry harder. It made them that much more real. "Or worse."

"Hey." His voice was gentle, and he tipped her chin up. "I'm OK."

She sniffled, trying to catch her breath, knowing how irrational it was to cry over something that hadn't even happened. He'd protected her, and they were both OK. Both safe.

"I really, really want to go home. I just want to have a shower and crawl into bed. I don't want to be out here, in the open."

"We should be far enough away now. I'll call Zack to come get us. I don't like our chances of getting a cab right now." She nodded and sank down onto a bench in front of an office tower. They'd made it about six or seven blocks from the hotel, and it was as though they'd entered an entirely different world. A world where an explosion hadn't just happened. Traffic slid by around them, the street brightly lit. A few pedestrians walked down the sidewalk, talking or listening to headphones. A bus rumbled by, its brakes squealing as it pulled to a stop across the street. The sky glowed an eerie blackish orange, lights shining from the office tower behind them. Everything felt so absurdly normal.

She hated that normal was now absurd.

"Zack's on his way." Sean sat down on the bench beside her and pulled her into him. She went willingly, craving the solid comfort of his body.

"Do you think this was Sacrosanct?" she asked, tucking her head against his chest.

"They'd be the most likely suspects, yeah."

Sierra's phone buzzed from inside her clutch, which had only survived because she'd had it in her hand when Sean had pulled her to the ground. She pulled out her phone to answer it, not caring about the cracked screen, but her hands were still shaky, and she managed to spill the clutch's contents at her feet.

Including the condoms.

She let out a small laugh as Sean scooped them up and handed them back to her with a raised eyebrow. "You were more optimistic than me. I only brought the one." He smiled that lopsided smile she loved so much and she let out another laugh, louder and stronger this time. He pulled her in and kissed her temple, holding her as she answered her phone and assured her mom she was OK.

Despite everything that'd happened, with Sean's arms around her, she felt better than OK.

She felt safe, and whole.

* * *

Sean and Sierra piled into Zack's Jeep, Sierra slipping into the back while Sean folded himself into the front passenger seat. Before he even had his seat belt on, all three of their phones began buzzing at the same time. A bolt of adrenaline coursed through Sean, snapping his spine straight, and he pulled his phone out of his pocket. Sure enough, it was a notification from the house's alarm system, indicating it had just been triggered. He'd known he was taking a risk having Zack come and get them, but he'd been so desperate to get Sierra home that he'd gone ahead with it.

"Drive." Sean nodded grimly at Zack, who floored it, and then turned in his seat to look at Sierra.

"The alarm?" she asked, her face pale. His gut twisted as hot, prickling anger flooded him. He hoped whoever had broken in was still there when they arrived so he could beat the shit out of them. Sierra was his, and he was damn well going to make whoever was behind this pay.

He nodded and reached a hand back, giving her leg a squeeze.

Almost twenty long minutes later, Zack pulled into the driveway, and the front door stood wide open, the alarm shrieking.

"Sierra, stay in the car with Zack." Before she could protest, he pulled his Glock out of its holster and made his way toward the house, eyes darting into every corner, looking for movement in every shadow. Sean stepped cautiously into the house, his gun raised in front of him. Nearly every single light was on, and immediately Sean saw what had happened.

Sierra's house had been trashed. He sucked in a breath as he surveyed the carnage of the living room. The leather couches had been gutted like fish, stuffing spilling out of them. A pile of feathers lay on the floor beside a slashed throw pillow, now sadly deflated. Several lamps had been smashed, and the floor was strewn with broken shards of glass and ceramic. Moving into the kitchen, he saw that all the windows facing the backyard had been smashed, glass and splinters of wood littering the counters and floor. Each white cabinet bore a different epithet in bright-red paint.

BITCH.
SLUT.
WHORE.
MURDERER.

And across the surface of the island: SHUT YOUR MOUTH.

Quickly he went through the house and cleared the rest of the rooms, ending with Sierra's bedroom. The door was ajar, and he pushed it the rest of the way open, his gun trained directly ahead of him.

A distinct coppery scent hung in the air, and, stomach churning, Sean flipped on the light. He inhaled sharply at the sight before him.

Sierra's bed was covered in guts. Entrails. Organs. Intestines. Many of the parts looked far too large to be human, making him suspect someone had hit up a butcher shop for castoffs. Breathing through his mouth, he checked out the closet and the master bathroom.

Anger ripped through him, and he paused, closing his eyes and trying to get a handle on his temper. He wanted to hit something, or someone. He wanted to smash things, to punch a hole through the wall. He hated that she'd need to come in here and see this. What fucking good was his protection if he couldn't protect her from the horror of seeing her house trashed and vandalized?

With a heavy heart, he headed back downstairs, knowing that whoever had done this was long gone. They'd be on the security camera footage, but Sean wouldn't be surprised if they had been wearing masks. They weren't dealing with inexperienced amateurs who were likely to expose themselves or do something stupid like leave fingerprints. He signaled for Sierra and Zack to come in the house.

She stepped inside, Zack right behind her, and she erupted as she laid eyes on the damage, a string of curses that would've made a trucker blush flowing from her mouth. She blew out an angry breath and balled her fists, her mouth a thin, tight line. "I'm so sick of this garbage. I'm sick of it! Goddammit!" She kicked at a slashed ottoman.

"The cops should be here any minute," said Zack, his face tight with disgust and anger as he looked around the trashed living room. "Fuck. This is my fault."

"No. I called and asked you to come pick us up. This isn't on you." If anything, this was on Sean.

"Clearly they were watching the house and waiting for the opportunity." Zack shook his head, his hands on his hips.

"Do you think they've been watching the whole time?" Sierra's face was pale as she stared at the slurs written on her kitchen cabinets.

"It's possible." Sean came up behind her and laid his

hands on her shoulders. "Sierra, I'm sorry, but there's damage in your bedroom too."

She glanced at him over her shoulder, her eyes wide. He felt the tremble course through her, and he tightened his grip on her.

"I want to go see." Without another word she pulled away from him and made her way up the stairs, her skirt clutched in her hands.

"Stay down here and wait for the cops," he called over his shoulder to Zack as he followed her up the stairs.

She stood in the center of the room, hugging herself as she stared at the vile destruction, and his chest ached at the look on her face. As if someone had kicked her puppy and told her there was no Santa Claus. Sad and hurt and vulnerable. Immediately he crossed the room and folded her into his arms, kissing the top of her head as she slid her arms around his waist and pressed her face to his chest. He stroked her back with one hand, cradling her head with the other.

"I'm not going to let anything happen to you. I've got you and I'm not going anywhere."

She took a shuddering breath and he tightened his arms around her, wishing he could take the hurt, the fear, the sadness for her. Because he would gladly shoulder it all for her if it would mean she was OK.

"I hate this. I feel like I'm stuck. If I quit, they win. If I don't, this keeps happening."

"I know." He pressed another kiss to the top of her head. He wished he had something more to say, but she was right.

"Sean, I…" She pulled back slightly to look up at him. "I'm really glad you're here."

"Me too." He pulled her back into his chest, not wanting to let her go, not even for a second. Because right there, in that moment, she was safe. She was his, and she was safe.

"Where am I supposed to go? I don't want to stay here, and I'm kind of off hotels right now." She looked up at him again and he tucked a strand of hair behind her ear.

"And hotels are still too public. We don't know what kind of connections Sacrosanct has. It could potentially be easy for them to find out your location."

"So where should we go?" She chewed her bottom lip, her eyes huge with worry.

"For tonight we can stay at my place. It's very secure, and I know I can keep you safe there."

"And we'd be alone." She pressed her face into his chest, the move both sweet and sexy.

"Mmm. We would."

"I really, really don't want to sleep alone tonight. Not after all of this. I want to feel you beside me all night."

The idea of spending the night holding Sierra made him feel as though he were standing in the sun after months of cold, it was so warm and welcome.

"Cops are here," Zack called up the stairs, and Sean led Sierra back down to the kitchen.

"Are you guys OK?" Antonio stood at the island, surveying the damage and taking notes. A forensic photographer took pictures of everything, while a woman dusted for fingerprints. Two uniformed cops were talking to Zack, who was leading them toward the garage so they could access the security camera footage.

"Yeah, we're OK," said Sean.

"I heard about the bomb. Scary shit."

"It was." Sierra's voice was quiet, and her eyes had a hollow look to them. Sean knew she was remembering, and he wanted to pull her into his arms. He settled for laying a hand on her arm. Her eyebrows shot up, as though something had just occurred to her. "You know, I think this means that we can definitively rule Jack out as a suspect. He was at the gala, and he was injured in the bombing."

"He was?" asked Sean.

She nodded. "I saw him on the other side of the room with blood coming from one ear. He looked pretty dazed."

"Hey, did you see this note?" The forensic photographer came over, a piece of paper pinched delicately between his gloved thumb and forefinger. Sierra shook her head.

"Where did you find it?" asked Antonio.

"It was stabbed into the cutting board over there with a knife. I took pictures before I removed it."

Sierra peered at the note, her brow furrowing as she read.

If Choices wins that grant, you'll end up like the animals on your bed. You, and everyone you care about. Your friends. Your family. Everyone. So back off now or face the consequences of your choices.

"The grant," she whispered, and then looked up at everyone. "Choices is applying for a major government grant, and so is another organization called the Pregnancy Support Center. What if this isn't Sacrosanct at all, but the PSC?"

Antonio nodded, studying the note. "It's worth looking into, for sure. How much is the grant worth?"

"Fifty million dollars."

Antonio let out a low whistle. "People have done worse for a lot less money."

"Right, but what are the chances that this other organization would bomb the gala?" asked Sean, pushing a hand through his hair.

"That does seem in line with Sacrosanct's MO." Antonio nodded, drumming his fingers on his notepad. "But that information about the PSC is good. We'll look into it, see what we can find out."

"And I'll get Clay on it too. See what he can dig up." Sean turned his attention to Sierra. "Go pack a bag, and let's get the hell out of here."

CHAPTER 20

The elevator doors opened onto the fourth floor of Sean's condo building, and he smiled that lopsided smile—Sierra's favorite smile—as he squeezed her hand and led her down the hall. Once they'd finished giving their statements to the police, she'd quickly gathered up a few things in an overnight bag and they'd left. Zack had stayed behind at the house, watching for any suspicious activity. On the short drive over, she'd answered dozens of text messages from worried friends and family who'd heard about the bombing on the news, assuring everyone that she was unhurt.

Sean unlocked the door to number 410 and pushed it open, ushering her in ahead of him. With easy familiarity he shut the door behind him, flipped the dead bolt, punched his code into the alarm, turned on the lights, and dropped his keys onto a table beside the front door, all in a series of fast, fluid motions.

"Oh. Sean, this is so nice." She toed off her heels, her feet practically crying in relief, and padded into the condo across the gleaming black walnut floor. The kitchen was immediately to her right, dark-gray cabinets lining the walls and framing the stainless steel appliances. Light-gray granite countertops complemented the black subway-tile backsplash.

Moving past the kitchen, she walked into the large, open living room. Floor-to-ceiling windows lined the far wall, with sliding doors giving access to a balcony. A flat-screen TV dominated the wall to her left, surrounded by built-in shelves stuffed with books. She stepped closer to study them, tracing her fingers over the spines. One shelf was overflowing with what looked like mysteries and thrillers, another with science fiction paperbacks. Cookbooks, sports biographies, and a variety of military, political, and law enforcement memoirs lined other shelves. More fiction filled the remaining ones, a mix of hardcovers and paperbacks of various genres. Facing the TV sat a dark-blue sectional, and she noticed a neat stack of magazines piled on the coffee table in front of it, issues of *Sports Illustrated* and *Men's Health*.

Just when she'd thought she couldn't be more attracted to him, Sierra found out he was a reader. The sudden image of sitting cuddled up with him on that big sectional, wearing sweats and reading, curled through her, warming her like a shot of whiskey.

It was wholly and completely different from Jack's place, which was huge and showy, almost ostentatious in its over-the-top decor and expensive…well, expensive everything. Not to mention almost completely devoid of books. But this…it was airy, yet cozy. Sleek, yet comfortable. She'd never really felt fully at home at Jack's, always feeling as though she were in a museum, lots of pretty things to look at, but not to touch. But Sean's place was immediately appealing and welcoming.

Maybe she felt that way because it was *Sean's*, and everything about him was appealing and welcoming. She spun to face him and saw that he'd taken off his shoes and tuxedo jacket and was loosening his bow tie.

"Do you mind if I have a shower? I want to wash this night off of me."

"No problem." He pointed to the hallway that led away from the living room. "Bathroom's on the right, towels are in the cabinet under the sink. Are you hungry? I can make us something to eat."

She thought about it for a second and was surprised to find she was, so she nodded. "Actually, I am. Thank you."

"Take your time."

She grabbed her bag and headed down the hall, feeling as though she were in some kind of wonderful, safe, cozy cocoon. She stepped into the bathroom and closed the door behind her. It featured a large walk-in shower with a gleaming glass door, tiles the color of linen covering the floor and the interior walls of the shower. She reached in and turned it on, cranking the faucet as hot as it would go, wanting to scald everything away and scrub at her skin until she was shiny and new, and not someone running on the fumes of fear and adrenaline.

She pulled a couple of white towels from the vanity and slung them over the towel rack before stepping under the spray. She tipped her head up, closing her eyes as the water pelted her skin. It felt so good that she wasn't sure how long she stood like that.

In typical guy fashion, the only two toiletries Sean had in his shower were a bottle of two-in-one shampoo and conditioner and a bar of Zest. She washed her hair and did her best with the soap, missing her loofah and body wash. Men had no idea what they were missing.

She stepped out of the shower and toweled off, pulling on a T-shirt and yoga pants. She twisted her wet hair up into a messy bun as she walked.

While she'd been in the shower using up the entire building's hot water supply, Sean had changed into worn jeans and a blue T-shirt and had made them each a grilled cheese sandwich with bacon. Two plates sat beside the stove.

"That smells so good. Have you got any ketchup?" she asked, opening his fridge, which was pretty bare.

"You want ketchup for your sandwich?"

"Yup." She saw a bottle of Heinz at the back and snagged it. When she turned to face him, he was staring at her with one eyebrow cocked. She pointed at him with the bottle. "Hey, don't knock it till you've tried it." She squirted a little mound of ketchup on her plate and put the bottle back in the fridge. "Like this," she said, picking up half her sandwich and dunking the point of it in the ketchup. She took a bite and closed her eyes. "So good," she mumbled around the big mouthful she'd taken.

Still eyeing her skeptically, he picked up his own sandwich and tentatively dunked a tiny part of it in her ketchup. He took a bite and chewed, his eyebrows shooting up. "That actually is pretty good," he mumbled, dunking his sandwich again and taking another bite. He set his sandwich down and picked up both plates, heading into the living room. They settled next to each other on the sectional, plates in their laps.

"Stick with me, I'll show you all kinds of things," she teased, dunking and biting again. That earned her a hot, intrigued look.

"I don't doubt it." He winked and dunked his own sandwich in her ketchup again, taking another bite. He grabbed the remote from the coffee table. "You mind if I put the news on?"

"No, go ahead. I want to see too."

He turned the TV on and flipped to CNN, which was covering the bombing with a blaring "breaking news" headline. A reporter was on the scene summarizing what had happened.

"The bombing of the Choices gala here at the Ritz-Carlton happened about three hours ago. A total of seven bombs were detonated inside the ballroom and in its vicinity. There have been no reports of any deaths so far, but dozens of people are injured, some critically. The hotel has been evacuated while the LAPD bomb squad investigates. There is a heavy police presence downtown tonight, but there have not been any reports of additional threats.

"The attacks are being attributed to radical right-wing protest group Sacrosanct, who posted a video online just moments ago taking credit for the bombing. Police are investigating and are asking anyone with information to please come forward. Police are also asking the public to stay away from the downtown district as a precaution."

Sean turned the volume down as the reporter continued to talk, giving background information about Sacrosanct and Choices and speculating about the bombings. Sierra stared at the screen, feeling numb.

"We were so lucky." She swallowed the last of her sandwich, forcing it down.

Sean took her plate and set it on the coffee table with his. "I'm not going to let anything happen to you."

"*You* could've been hurt." The idea that he could've been seriously injured—or worse—was almost too much. Her chest knotted tightly and she reached for him. She kissed him, softly at first, but it quickly turned into something deep and hungry. He pulled her into his lap, and she straddled his hips.

"I'm OK," he whispered, stroking a hand up and down her back.

"I hate how much danger this puts you in." Fear threatened to swallow her whole. Not fear of Sacrosanct, but the fear of losing Sean. Yes, he was strong and smart and capable, but awful things happened every single day. And she knew she couldn't handle losing him. Not when she'd just found him. When they'd just found each other. And although what was happening between them was new, she knew it was different. Special. Rare.

She was falling in love with him.

"I want to see your back. Take your shirt off." She climbed off his lap to make it easier for him, sitting on her knees beside him. After hesitating a second, he complied, sitting forward and reaching behind him with one hand, yanking his T-shirt off. He turned, and she sucked in a breath. Already a nasty bruise was coming through on the upper left-hand side of his back. Mottled angry red and blue, it was bigger than her hand. "Oh, Sean. I'm sorry."

He tossed his shirt on the floor and pulled her back into his lap. "I got it protecting you. Worth it." He cradled her face and kissed her again, his lips soft but firm against hers. Sierra didn't have any words for the emotions tumbling around inside her, so she kissed him back with everything she had. Sean's hands left her face and skated down over her arms, the sides of her breasts, her ribs. He pulled her T-shirt up over her head, tossing it on the floor beside his. "I will do whatever it takes, Sierra. I will protect you, no matter what." He unhooked her bra and added it to the growing pile of clothing.

She kissed him again, harder and deeper, their tongues sliding together, and his hands cupped her breasts, his thumbs playing across her already peaked nipples. She melted into his touch and deepened the kiss even further, thrilling at the sensation of his hands on her bare breasts for the first time. He groaned, the sound washing over her like warm water, and she traced her hands down over his torso, touching and exploring, reveling in each muscled ridge, in each crisp hair beneath her fingertips.

He broke the kiss and trailed his lips down her neck and across her collarbone. "I need to be inside you again."

"I need that too." He trailed one large, warm hand over her breast and down into her yoga pants. With one hand spanning her back, he held her and closed his mouth over her nipple. He stroked her through the cotton of her panties and she writhed against him, the touch maddeningly gentle. "More," she breathed, and he slipped his hand under the cotton. He kissed his way from one breast to the other, circling her nipple with his tongue before scraping over it with a delicate bite. With deft movements he slid a finger between her folds, circling around her clit. She bit her lip and whimpered, her eyes fluttering closed as she ground against his hand.

He made a low sound, an approving growl. "You're so wet already." He began to torment her, circling and stroking, his mouth hot and wet over her nipple.

"For you," she managed to rasp out. He must've liked her answer because he gave her more of what she needed, sliding two fingers into her and stroking his thumb against her throbbing clit. He caught her mouth with his, kissing her with a raw intensity that turned her on even more. His fingers caressed her, creating an exquisite pressure that already was pushing her to the point of eruption. Her hands gripped his arms, fingers flexing and digging in as she tried to anchor herself somehow. He stretched and pressed from the inside while stroking her on the outside, making her feel as if she were melting into his hand.

"Fuck, Sierra. I want to bury myself inside you, you're so hot and sweet." His voice was low and rough. Her hips bucked as she came on Sean's hand, hot, throbbing pleasure radiating outward from her core. He held her as her muscles shook, tightening his free arm around her waist. She sat like that for several seconds, letting her orgasm wash over her while she caught her breath, his fingers still inside her. A gorgeously sexy smile played across his lips, and then he dipped his head and sucked her earlobe into his mouth. He slipped his fingers free and wrapped his arms around her.

And then he stood effortlessly, despite the fact that he was holding her against him. She slipped her legs around his waist and he headed down the hallway toward his bedroom.

* * *

Sean focused on making it to his bedroom and the king-size bed waiting for him and Sierra. If he didn't, he might just drag her to the floor and sink his painfully swollen cock into her. Squeezing her ass, he held her tight against him as he walked. He marveled at how perfectly she fit around him, despite how small she was.

"I fantasized about you, you know." She pressed her lips to his neck as he made his way down the hall.

"Really?" A jolt of pure happiness rang through him.

"Mmm-hmm." She nuzzled the answer into him, her lips and tongue setting fire to the skin under his ear.

He bumped open the bedroom door with his shoulder. "Did you touch yourself when you fantasized about me?" He reached the edge of the bed, but didn't set her down.

"Yes. I made myself come, thinking about you." She kissed his ear, teasing his earlobe with her tongue.

He eased her down onto the bed on her back, but didn't

go down with her. "Show me how you touch yourself when you think about me."

"Only if you take your pants off. I want to see you." She rose up on her elbows, a playful smile on her gorgeous, flushed face as she shoved her yoga pants and panties down over her hips, kicking them off.

He returned her smile and opened the button on his jeans. She lay back on the bed and bent her knees. He eased the zipper of his fly down, and his jeans sagged around his hips. Slowly she spread her legs, revealing the soft, pink flesh there, swollen and wet. She dipped a hand between her legs and began to tease herself, her other hand palming her breast. She pushed a finger inside herself and moaned.

"Tell me what you fantasized about." He hoped she didn't hear the slight tremor in his voice as he barely held himself together. He pushed his jeans down and stepped out of them. He hadn't bothered with any underwear when he'd changed. She moaned again, and he watched, enraptured, as she massaged her swollen pussy. She looked up and met his gaze, her eyes hot and dark.

"How good you'd look with your face between my legs."

He let out a low, gruff groan, fire licking up his spine. She stroked herself faster, in a circular motion. Her muscles began to tremble and her breathing became rough and shallow.

"Doesn't have to be a fantasy anymore," he ground out, and then fell to his knees in front of the bed and hooked his arms under her splayed legs, tugging her toward him. She arched her back off the bed and cried out as his mouth closed over the tender flesh between her legs.

"Christ, you taste good." He moved his lips against her as he spoke, her hips writhing as a shuddering moan escaped her throat. He licked her slowly, pressing his tongue against her, circling around her clit before licking back down. He took his time, savoring her as he discovered what she liked, paying attention to her little trembles, to her breathing, to the way her hips jerked when he swirled his tongue over her clit in a lazy circle. Fuck, he could do this all night.

She thrust her hands into his hair. "Oh, God, Sean. Your mouth feels so good, I can't—" He sucked her clit into his mouth and swirled his tongue over and around it, and her hips jerked off the bed as she moaned loudly. She came again, pulsing and throbbing against his tongue, every muscle in her body taut.

Feeling like a goddamn king, he trailed light kisses along the insides of her thighs as she slowly came down, her fingers still clenched in his hair.

"That was incredible." She propped herself up on one elbow to look at him with heavy-lidded eyes, raking her fingers through his hair and sending tingles racing across his scalp. He climbed up on the bed beside her, kissing his way up her body, lingering over her breasts, wanting to taste every inch of this woman. His woman. He hissed out a breath as her small hand closed around his throbbing cock. She traced her index finger over his swollen head, massaging the bead of pre-come into the tip before pumping her fist up and down.

He basked in her touch, closing his eyes as she stroked him. It felt so good that he didn't want to tell her to stop, but he knew he had to. Gently he pushed her hand away and kissed her, hotly and deeply, pulling her against him. His chest swelled almost painfully at the sensation of her naked body against his. Everything was colliding. His need to protect her. How much he liked everything about her. Lust.

Love.

They were all swirling together until they were connected, each one feeding into the other. Indistinguishable.

All that mattered was Sierra. Her name hummed through his veins as he lost himself in her.

In that moment he needed to connect with her. To be inside her, to feel her body around his. Joined. Whole.

Reaching over, he yanked open the nightstand drawer, grabbed a condom, tore open the package, and rolled it on. He guided her up to the head of the bed and eased his weight down carefully on top of her. Hungrily he closed his mouth over hers, the throbbing pressure in his balls becoming almost unbearable.

She wrapped her legs around his hips and kissed him, pressing herself into him. "Now, Sean. I need you." Her entire body shook, her voice trembling, and he knew she needed the connection just as badly as he did.

Unable to wait a second longer, he eased into her, her flesh hot and wet and deliciously tight around him. Skin to skin and fully connected with her, he kissed her, sweetly, tenderly, slowly. He didn't want to move, didn't want to stop kissing her. He didn't want to let this moment go.

He brushed a lock of her hair out of her eyes, and what he saw nearly undid him. They were full of lust, and passion, and something deep and true that both thrilled and awed him.

Something a hell of a lot like what he was feeling. "My beautiful Sierra," he murmured, stroking in and out of her once.

"Call me that again."

"You're beautiful." He kissed her again, unable to get enough of her delicious mouth.

"No. The other part. Yours." She shuddered out a sigh as he thrust again.

"My Sierra." He withdrew almost all the way before sliding back into her, his breathing heavy.

"Your Sierra. I like that."

He teased in and out of her, wanting release but not wanting this to be over. "That's what you are. You're mine." He kissed her again.

Her eyes shone in the dim light of his room, bright with emotion, and she held him tighter. His release began to burn through him, narrowing his vision. Pressing his face into her neck, he pumped into her, hard and deep, her hips rising to meet him.

"Oh, God, you feel so good. Fuck me, Sean." Her voice was high, almost a whimper, as she moaned into his ear.

He felt the first pulse of his orgasm and thrust into her deeper, harder, grinding into her. Her muscles tightened around him with her own orgasm, and she nipped at his shoulder as his cock pulsed deep inside her. He held himself above her, and she bit at his bicep.

"Oh my God, Sean." She whispered the words as she looked up at him, her cheeks rosy, and he pressed his forehead to hers.

"I know. Do you have any idea how happy I am that you came to my office that day?"

"Hopefully, as happy as I am."

A euphoric weakness overtook him, and he pulled out of her and rolled onto his back, pulling her into his side. She laid her head on his chest and wrapped herself around him, flinging her free arm and top leg over him. He stroked a hand up and down her back while she trailed her fingers back and forth across his chest. The moment was both heavy and light, their connection filling up the room and negating the need to say anything. They belonged to each other now.

She nestled into him, and he felt a tremor vibrate through her.

"Are you cold?"

She laughed softly. "Hardly. You're like a furnace."

"You're trembling."

She lifted her head, her eyes locking with his. "I know."

A happy thrill shot through him, as if he were sitting in the front car of the world's tallest, fastest roller coaster, about to rocket down that first drop. He rolled so that she was once again beneath him, and he pinned her arms above her head, tracing his tongue around her nipple. She squirmed happily, and he exhaled, blowing across her skin and teasing her pebbled nibble to an even harder peak. She moaned, arching her back up, pressing her small breasts into his face. He closed his mouth over the opposite breast, sucking her nipple into his mouth and swirling his tongue over her. She cried out as he closed his teeth around her nipple and tugged gently. They'd just finished, and he wanted her again. Needed her. Couldn't stop touching her, kissing her, tasting her. It was need, yes, but something more. It was comfort. It was joy.

It was everything.

She tensed at the sharp staccato of someone knocking on his front door. Immediately he was on his feet. "Stay here. I'll be right back." As fast as he could, he disposed of the condom, yanked on jeans and a T-shirt, retrieved his Glock from its holster and shoved it into his waistband.

CHAPTER 21

Sean peered through the peephole and stood back, flipping the dead bolt and opening the door for his dad. "How'd you get in here?" Sean had brought Sierra to his condo because it was secure. Only residents could access the underground parking, and a doorman was stationed in the lobby twenty-four hours a day.

Patrick held up a white key card. "You gave me this."

Right. He had. So long ago that he'd completely forgotten.

Surprising him completely, his dad threw his arms around him and pulled him in for a hug. Sean couldn't remember the last time his father had hugged him. Years ago, for sure. Before…everything.

"Thank God you're all right," he said, letting him go. "I saw the news about the bomb on TV, and then I couldn't get ahold of you on your phone."

"Oh, shit. Sorry. I didn't mean to scare you." His phone had likely been buzzing with his dad's missed calls while he'd been in bed with Sierra.

"Zack filled me in. I knew you were alive, but I wanted

to see for myself. He told me about what happened at Ms. Blake's too." He shook his head. "Sick sons of bitches."

Sean nodded in agreement. "You said it."

"And she's here?"

"Yeah. Sleeping." He tipped his head toward his bedroom. God, he felt like shit lying to his dad this way, but they'd be dealing with a second explosion tonight if Patrick found out Sean was sleeping with a client.

A tense silence hung between them, filling the space. Sean turned and headed for the fridge, and Patrick followed him into the kitchen.

"You want a beer?"

"Sure."

Sean popped the caps off two bottles and extended one to Patrick, who accepted it and took a long pull.

"How's she doing?"

"Better than you'd expect." Sean took a sip of his beer. "She's…" He paused, wanting to find exactly the right words to describe her. "She's tough. Strong. She'll be OK. And I'm not letting her out of my sight." A swell of hot, possessive pride crashed through him.

Patrick nodded, leaning against the counter, his back to the sink. They sipped their beers in a silence that stretched on for a few long minutes before Sean decided he needed to ask the question weighing on him. "So you seriously drove all the way over here because I didn't answer my phone? You were that worried about me?" He hadn't meant to sound so cynical, but he was genuinely surprised.

"All the way over here? I live in Encino. It's twenty-five minutes away." Patrick waved his hand, batting away Sean's question instead of answering it, which was answer enough itself.

"I know where you live."

Patrick scowled, picking at the green label on his bottle, now softened with condensation. A jab of guilt poked Sean in the ribs.

Jesus. They couldn't go five minutes without sniping at each other.

Patrick sighed heavily. "Yes, I wanted to make sure you were OK."

"Sierra and I are both fine."

Patrick nodded, worrying a strip of green between his thumb and forefinger. "Good." He took a breath and looked up at the ceiling, visibly hesitating for several seconds before he spoke again. "You know that I don't blame you, right?"

Sean froze, his beer bottle halfway to his mouth. He had no idea what he was supposed to say to that. He *didn't* believe that his father didn't blame him for the accident. How could he not? Sean sure as hell blamed himself. So he didn't say anything, just sipped his beer.

"Sean. Say something." Patrick set his beer bottle down on the counter and pushed his hands through his short hair.

"Why are you telling me this right now?"

"Because you need to hear it. I thought I might've lost you tonight, just like…"

Sean completed his father's unspoken thought. "Just like you lost Mom. Which *was* my fault, and you *should* blame me."

The scene came rushing back at him. The rainy night. The driver who'd run a red light, whom Sean hadn't seen in time. The horrible, gut-wrenching sound of squealing tires, crunching metal, and shattering glass. His frantic efforts to stanch the blood flowing from his mom's wounds. The way she'd told him she loved him just before the light went out of her eyes.

How his dad had refused to look at him in the days following her death. They'd each grieved alone, and a wall had gone up between them, Patrick blaming, and Sean accepting the blame.

In the weeks following his mother's death, Sean had watched his father fall apart. Drinking. Gambling. Neglecting the company. So he'd quit playing semipro baseball and come home to help with the business. Giving up baseball had been his penance for what had happened.

So now a simple "You know that I don't blame you" was hard to swallow. Maybe it was true right now, tonight, but Patrick had blamed him, and Sean had blamed himself all the more because of it.

"You resent me, and I don't blame you for that either." Patrick studied him, his arms crossed.

"You think I resent you?" Sean frowned, not entirely comfortable with this conversation. Deep down he probably did resent his father, but it was more complicated than that, because the resentment was tangled up with guilt, remorse, and grief.

"I resent the hell out of myself for the position I put you in after Mom died."

"You didn't force me to do anything." Sean took a long, deep pull on his beer.

"Didn't I? You'd just lost your mother, and I couldn't keep it together. I didn't leave you much choice. I let you down. I should've been there for you, and instead I fell apart and it was up to you to keep everything together. I should've done better by you."

Patrick's words settled over him, the truth in them seeping into the cracks Sean hid, buried deep inside.

"I'm the one who let her die, Dad. I'm the one who was driving, and I'm the one who couldn't save her."

"So, what? You came home because you felt guilty?"

Sean shrugged, sipping his beer. "Partly, yes."

For some reason that seemed to make Patrick angry, and he stalked into the living room, his hands on his hips as the newly closed emotional distance gaped once again between them. He froze, his eyes glued to something on the floor.

He bent down and picked up Sierra's bra from where it lay on top of their discarded shirts. "Interesting spot for this."

Shit.

He tossed the bra onto the couch, shaking his head in anger. "Are you sleeping with a client?"

There was no point lying about it, so he nodded, and Patrick exploded. Just as Sean had known he would.

"I can't fucking believe you! Do you have any idea how unprofessional this is? How dangerous?"

Sean exploded right back, the anger, the anxiety, the fear that maybe his father was right ripping through him. "Yes, I know! OK? I know! What do you want me to say?"

"For starters, that she's not going to be your client anymore. And second, that you won't continue sleeping with her. Jesus, Sean."

He licked his lips, fighting back his anger. "I can't do that. I won't remove myself from this assignment."

"How are you supposed to protect her if you're only focused on getting her into bed? You're putting her, yourself, and the other guards in danger."

"I can handle it." And although he knew he could, he also knew Patrick would never believe him.

"I thought you knew better. Apparently I was wrong. You're off the case!" Patrick sliced his hand through the air, his shout echoing off the walls.

Something snapped in Sean, and he was suddenly inches away from his father. "You don't get to make that decision. You're supposed to be retired, for fuck's sake! This isn't even any of your goddamn business."

"She's a client, and it's *my company*, so it is *absolutely* my fucking business!"

"I'm *not* stepping aside."

Patrick's lip curled, his face red with anger. "You're jeopardizing the company's reputation, your reputation, and her safety just so you can get your dick wet. I didn't raise you to be so selfish."

"Oh, so now I'm selfish? When a second ago I was too much of a martyr for your liking? How is it that nothing I do is ever fucking good enough? I can't ever win with you, and you know what? I'm sick of it."

"And how are you going to martyr yourself when this all goes sideways, huh? What kind of fucked-up punishment are you going to saddle yourself with then? When she ends up hurt, or worse, what are you going to do? You want to fuck her, or protect her? Because you can't do both, Sean." His father jabbed a finger into Sean's chest, challenging him.

"Get the fuck out. *Now*."

Patrick stood still, barely breathing. Abruptly he spun and exited, slamming the door behind him. Sean stood with his hands on his hips, breathing and staring at the ceiling, trying to sort through and compartmentalize everything, trying to push a little bit more of the anger and the hurt away with each breath out.

He knew it was wrong to sleep with a client. He also knew he was falling in love with Sierra. He knew he needed to stop blaming himself for what had happened to his mom, but he also knew that as much as he pretended not to, his dad did blame him for what had happened, regardless of what he said. It colored every single interaction between them, on both sides.

He knew that he resented having had to give up his dream of playing professional baseball, but he also knew it had been the right thing to do. Given the option, he'd make the same choice again. Yes, he'd come home partly out of guilt, but also because he wanted to help his dad. Now they'd both spent so long living with all of it—the guilt, the blame, the resentment, the loss—that they didn't know how to communicate without it. Anytime they made baby steps forward, something happened to send them spiraling back.

It had become clear that Patrick felt just as guilty about how everything had gone down as Sean did, and nothing would ever change until they forgave both themselves, and each other. And Sean wasn't sure he could ever forgive himself for letting his mother die, leaving them at an impasse.

"Oh my God, Sean. I'm so, so sorry. I didn't mean to cause a problem between you and your dad. Are you OK?" Sierra stood a few feet behind him in the hallway, wearing his favorite Dodgers T-shirt, her fingers pressed to her mouth.

Need vibrated through him, and he closed the distance between them. Cupping her face, he crushed his mouth to hers. After several long seconds, he broke the kiss. "I am now."

"What do you want to do?" she asked as he traced his thumbs over her cheekbones.

"About us?"

She nodded, biting her lip. "Do you want to stop—"

He kissed her again, soothing the bite with his tongue. "I want to go back to bed."

* * *

Guilt ripped at Sierra even as Sean led her back to his bedroom. She'd heard every single word of that fight, and each word had sliced into her like a knife.

I'm the one who let her die, Dad. I'm the one who was driving, and I'm the one who couldn't save her.

Her heart ached for Sean over what he'd gone through losing his mother. She couldn't imagine the pain he'd been through. Couldn't fathom the pain he still carried every single day.

"Wait." She tugged on his hand and stopped just before they entered his bedroom. She bit her lip and shifted her weight from foot to foot. "Maybe we shouldn't."

Sean's face fell, and he dropped her hand. "If you don't want to, then we won't."

"It's not that I don't want to, Sean. Trust me. I want to. But I don't want to do anything to put you or the guys in danger, or to threaten your job. I don't want to do that to you. It's selfish."

He sighed and led her gently into the bedroom and pulled her onto the bed with him. Sitting up against the headboard, he tucked her against him. Several moments passed before he spoke.

"I'm going to be completely honest with you. Yes, we're taking a risk by getting involved right now. Part of the reason bodyguards shouldn't get involved with clients is because of the distraction. If I'm thinking about how I can't wait to get my face between your thighs, I might not be paying attention to important details. It's a legitimate risk."

His voice was a low rumble in his chest, vibrating gently against her cheek. She closed her eyes, instantly soothed by the warmth of his body, the rhythm of his breathing, the steady beat of his heart, the security of his arms around her.

"But then there's the other side of it, the potentially good side. I'm personally invested in your safety in a unique way, and I'm damn well not going to let anything happen to you. I have additional motivation now beyond doing a good job and getting a paycheck.

"And in terms of jeopardizing my job, it's a moot point. Whether he likes it or not, Dad officially handed control of the company to me over a year ago. Virtus is *my* company. No one can fire me. I get why he's upset, but we fight. It's just what we do. If it wasn't about this, it'd be about something else.

"I'm confident that I can keep you safe and we can keep seeing each other, because I'm aware of the risks. Now that you're mine, there's no way in hell I can let you go."

He was the one who'd just had a huge argument with his father, and he was comforting and reassuring her. She wasn't sure what she'd done to deserve this man, but it must've been something pretty amazing.

She lifted her head from his chest and kissed him, slowly and tenderly, wanting to give him some of the comfort and reassurance that he'd just given her.

"I don't want to make you choose between me and your father."

"You're not. He's angry now. He'll get over it and find something else to be angry about. Trust me."

"I do." She kissed him again. "And I don't want to stop being yours."

Her words must have unleashed something in him, and with a low growl, he kissed her again, the kiss raw and urgent. He broke it and rose, and she watched his gloriously sexy body come into view as he shed his T-shirt and jeans. He grabbed another condom from the nightstand and came around to the foot of the bed.

"Come here, sweetheart." He tossed the condom onto the bed, and she pulled the shirt off over her head. She crawled across the bed toward him, smiling at the look of pure hunger on his face. "Holy fuck, that's a gorgeous sight." He ran a hand down her back, and she rose onto her knees.

His cock rubbed the insides of her thighs, her breasts pressed against his chest. He took his cock in one hand and rubbed it through her folds, slicking her wetness over himself.

She nipped at his neck, savoring the perfection of his skin under her mouth. "I want you deep inside me." She pulled back to look at him. "I want you to take what's yours."

He caught her mouth in a searing kiss and guided her down onto her back on the bed, her legs dangling off the edge. Still standing at the edge, he took her ankles and spread her wide open, a sexy, possessive smile on his face.

"Mmm. So fucking pretty." He laid her ankles on his shoulders and rolled on the condom, pressing the head of his cock against her entrance. He teased her, almost pushing in and then slipping away to rub himself through her folds. He licked his thumb and circled her clit, causing her hips to writhe against him. It was as though he already knew exactly how to touch her. As though their bodies had been made for each other.

He slipped first one and then a second finger into her, teasing her and testing her readiness. She clenched around his fingers and he smiled that lopsided sexy smile. She knew he could feel exactly how turned on she was, and spread beneath him, she felt both vulnerable and powerful. He slowly pulled his fingers out and pushed his cock into her, stealing her breath. With her ankles on his shoulders and his thick, long cock driving deep, the burn bordered on painful at first. He held still, giving her a second to adjust around him as he continued to circle his thumb around her clit. He pulled slowly out of her, almost all the way, and then slid back in, filling her and hitting every pleasurable spot she owned. She moaned out his name, and he grabbed her hips, guiding her onto his cock, deepening the angle even more, and with each thrust, a shattering sparkle of pleasure burst over her skin.

Each stroke was slow and impossibly deep, and she

arched up off the mattress. Something she'd never quite felt before was building deep inside her, an intense yet wholly pleasurable sensation fanning out across her skin and through her entire body.

She'd had a feeling sex with Sean would be hot, and fun, and probably pretty damn good. She'd had no idea that it would be off-the-charts intense like this. It was addictive—not just the pleasure, but the high of belonging to someone who belonged to her.

Waves of pleasure crashed through her as he thrust into her, and his eyes held hers. He shifted his grip on her hips, and with a deep thrust, an orgasm crested over her, pleasure exploding through her. Every muscle went taut as she rode out the orgasm, her skin tingling from head to toe. Her body felt like ten thousand tiny miracles, all shimmering at once.

"You are so goddamn beautiful," he breathed, sweat dotting his hairline. He thrust into her again and she kept coming, each thrust hitting something deep inside, and she felt as if her heart were on fire. He continued his slow, steady, deep thrusts, and she rode the peaks and valleys, holding nothing back. Her body, her mind, her heart—they were all wide open and his for the taking.

And he was taking. Taking and claiming and cherishing. And she was giving, wanting him to have every piece of her. Wanting every piece of him in return.

Her entire body shook, pleasure sparkling over her until everything was a blur, and the only thing anchoring her was Sean's body inside hers. He pumped harder, faster, deeper, and ground out her name as he came. She trembled still, aftershocks of what had been the most intense orgasm of her life coursing through her.

Minutes later, tucked against the solid warmth of his bare chest, she fell into a deep sleep.

CHAPTER 22

Sean pulled his SUV into Sierra's driveway, Sierra in the passenger seat beside him. In less than twenty-four hours, she'd gone from being Sierra, the client, to being *his* Sierra. He hadn't wanted to bring her back to her vandalized house, but she was leaving for Miami tomorrow and needed to get her stuff together for the trip. He'd reviewed the travel details and decided that he and Jamie would accompany her. Given that Sacrosanct didn't have a known presence in Miami, the risks associated with the trip were fairly minimal, but he wasn't willing to take any chances.

His father's words from the night before echoed through his mind, but he pushed them away, doing his best to ignore the tiny shard of doubt lodged somewhere deep in his brain. His father was wrong, and after last night, the idea of leaving her safety up to someone else was unbearable. Excruciating. Unthinkable. She was his to protect, and he'd do whatever it took to keep her safe.

She sat with her eyes glued to the screen of her phone, reading what looked like an e-mail. She must've felt his gaze on her because she looked up, her brow furrowed.

"There's a protest rally in support of Choices all day today at City Hall. I want to go."

"I don't think that's a good idea."

"I know, but I really want to show my support. And I think, as one of their key spokespeople, it's important for me to be there."

"I get that, but there are too many variables. It's an open, public space, Sacrosanct is still out there, and you'd be vulnerable. I'm sorry, but no." The police had reviewed the footage from the security cameras, and just as he'd predicted, the creeps had been wearing ski masks. The police and Virtus were both doing everything they could to get a lead on Sacrosanct, but so far they'd come up empty-handed. Given everything that had happened, protecting her was challenging enough. The fact that he was protecting her from shadows and ghosts made it that much more difficult.

"Even if you and one of the other guys come with me?"

"Even then. I don't want to scare you, but what if there's another bomb? What if Sacrosanct is there and tries to hurt you?"

She hesitated, chewing on her lip. "Going to stuff like this is part of my job, Sean. And right now, after last night, it's important for us to show strength, and solidarity. To show that we won't be bullied. It's at City Hall, and I'm sure there will be tons of security."

He paused, turning the idea over in his mind. Everything was getting muddy. Was he hesitant because it truly was a bad idea, or because he didn't want the woman he was falling in love with to be in danger? Was he making the same decisions he'd make if Sierra were just a client?

Of course he wasn't.

Once again his father's words echoed through his mind, casting doubt over his decisions.

"How did you find out about the rally?" he asked, turning the SUV off.

"Choices e-mail blast."

He blew out a breath. "Let me see who else is available. If I can get someone else, then…" He trailed off. "I'm still not sure, Sierra. Let me think about it."

She nodded and hopped out of the car. He followed Sierra into the house, and he was proud of the way she didn't hesitate, just walked straight in and right up the stairs. But he didn't miss the tension in her slender shoulders or the slight jerkiness to her movements as she opened her closet and yanked a small suitcase out. Barely looking at what she was touching, she tossed clothing into the suitcase at lightning speed. The worst of the mess had been cleaned up already by the crime scene cleaning team Antonio had called in, but the metallic smell of blood still hung in the air.

"Do you not want me to go to the protest rally because you think it's dangerous, or because you're worried about me because of…because of us?" she asked, giving voice to the exact thoughts spinning through his head. She stepped into her bathroom to gather more toiletries.

"Both. It's risky. Very risky. I understand why you want to go, I just don't think it's a good idea." He leaned his shoulder against the doorjamb, watching as she threw more stuff into her suitcase. "I'd never forgive myself if something happened to you."

She paused with a curling iron in one hand and a can of hair spray in the other. "You do that to yourself, don't you?" she asked softly, and something in his chest clenched. Apparently she'd heard more last night than he'd realized.

"We're not talking about that right now." His voice came out a bit gruffer than he'd intended. "We're talking about your safety."

"I know. But we're also talking about my job. It looks bad if I don't show up today. With this grant on the line, they need all the support they can get."

He sighed and nodded, pulling his phone out of his pocket and stepping out into the hallway to make the calls. As he spoke with Carter, and then Jamie, his heart sank, just a little. They were both in and didn't think it would be an issue to keep her safe at the rally, proving to Sean just how clouded his own judgment was becoming when it came to Sierra.

He was going to have to let her go to the damn rally.

She was just zipping up her suitcase when he came back into her bedroom. "Both Carter and Jamie are going to come with us to the rally."

Her head snapped up. "So I can go?"

His mouth was dry, and he licked his lips before he spoke. "Yes."

She flashed him a grateful smile. "Thank you."

Unable to help himself, he returned the smile and tipped his head toward the stairs. "Come on. Let's get out of here."

* * *

He leaned back in his leather desk chair, his gaze riveted to the television screen mounted on the wall and tuned to CNN. The bombing at last night's gala was still one of the top stories, and although no one had been killed, several people had been seriously injured. Too bad that fucker Owens hadn't been one of them.

Bombing the gala had been a risk, but it had gone off without a hitch, and it had made a hell of a statement. Choices had no idea who they were messing with, and last night had been a wake-up call.

What he hadn't anticipated was the showing of support from the public, including that damn protest rally at City Hall. And if their little star Sierra showed up, it would galvanize support even further. He could feel the grant—and his life, if he didn't get the money—slipping through his fingers.

So the solution was simple, really. She couldn't make it to the rally.

The phone on his desk buzzed, and he lowered the volume on the TV. "Yeah?"

"We got eyes on her. She's at her house right now with the bodyguard."

"Is she going to the rally?"

"Unconfirmed. She must know about it. Maybe she'll be too scared to show up."

He laughed. "Unlikely."

"What do you want us to do?"

"I don't want her to show up at that rally. It would be bad for us." He drummed his fingers on his desk, thinking. "Follow her and the bodyguard when they leave. If they head toward City Hall, take them out. And make it look like an accident."

He sighed heavily. He didn't want to kill her. He really didn't. But it was becoming clearer and clearer that getting rid of her might be his only option.

"The bodyguard too?"

"Especially him." His lip curled, and tension radiated down his neck. "I want Sean Owens dead."

* * *

Sean and Sierra headed back down the driveway, her suitcase in Sean's hand. He opened the hatch and tossed it into the back before climbing into the driver's seat. He was about to press the ignition button when he froze.

As a rule he kept his car neat. No garbage, no extra stuff, nothing. Not even an air freshener. So the sight of a screw and a tiny bit of wire on the floor under the steering column set off alarm bells in his mind immediately. His blood rushed through his ears, his heart pumping frantically as he realized someone had tampered with his vehicle.

"Get out of the car." He glanced at Sierra, silently imploring her not to argue.

"What? Why? What's wrong?"

"Get out of the car."

Some of the color drained from her face and she nodded, opening the passenger side door and sliding out. Sean did the same, and without a word, he took her hand, led her back into the house, and locked the door behind him. He drew his gun and flattened his back against the living room wall, peering cautiously out the window.

Sierra laid a hand on his arm. "What's going on?"

"Someone tampered with the SUV. We're being watched, and whoever did it is probably still nearby. We were only in here for fifteen, maybe twenty minutes." She went to go look out one of the living room windows, but he held her back. "Stay away from the windows. I'm going to call the cops and the team to let them know what's going on."

She nodded and sank down onto the stairs, watching him as he made two quick phone calls to Antonio and Carter.

"If someone's watching us, I don't want to stay here. My car's locked up in the garage. We can take it to the rally and get out of here."

"I agree that we shouldn't stay here. You sure you still want to go to this rally?" He sent up a silent prayer that she'd changed her mind.

She nodded. "I'm not backing down."

He stifled the curse he wanted to bite out. "We'll take your car. Where are your keys?" She slipped a hand into her purse and tossed them to him, leading him into the garage, where her little blue Lexus sat. He did a quick perimeter check of the vehicle, but there were no signs it had been tampered with, and the garage was secure. He dropped down behind the driver's seat, and he had to duck his head and wedge his knees up against his chest to fit. With a mirthless chuckle, he adjusted the seat for his much longer legs and torso, his eyes scanning the interior of the car.

"Do you see anything out of place?" he asked her. "Things that weren't here before, stuff that's been moved?"

She studied the interior of her car, her eyes narrowed. Finally she shook her head. "No, it all looks normal to me."

Sending up yet another silent prayer, he slipped the key into the ignition and the engine came to life. Sierra clicked open the garage door, and Sean pulled quickly out of the garage and down the driveway and took off down the street, his eyes darting back and forth between the road and the rearview mirror to make sure no one was following them. But there were no cars pulling onto the road, and after several minutes he relaxed slightly. He headed for the 101 South, the most direct route downtown. He glanced into the rearview mirror again, and his grip tightened on the steering wheel.

A black SUV bore down on them, accelerating way too fast. He took his eyes off the road for a second to make sure Sierra had her seat belt on.

"We might have company. Stay low in your seat."

He floored it, weaving smoothly between two other cars, waiting to see if the SUV would follow.

It did.

"Fuck. He's following us. Hang on."

He punched the gas even harder, swerving away from the on-ramp at the last second and veering onto Franklin Avenue. With horns blaring, the SUV managed to do the same, tires squealing behind them.

"There's a police station about a mile away. We'll go there." He'd barely finished speaking when the car was rammed from behind, jolting them both against their seat belts. Sierra shrieked and gripped the handle above the window. With his heartbeat thrashing in his ears, Sean pushed the gas as far down as it would go, the car's engine grinding as he wove through traffic. But the SUV had more power, and it swerved out from behind them, ramming into the rear passenger side of the car and sending them into a spin.

It was as though everything had dropped into slow motion as the nose of the car spun into the path of oncoming traffic. A truck blared its horn, and Sean eased off the gas and steered into the spin, regaining control of the car and barely managing to get out of the truck's path. The smell of burning rubber filled the air when he hit the gas, and they came out of the spin. Sean jerked the car back into his lane. Sweat ran down his back and pain shot across his knuckles from his grip on the steering wheel.

With the other vehicle still speeding behind him, he knew he needed to take a chance. He had to get them out of here. He had to get *her* out of here.

He turned the wheel sharply to the right a split second before he yanked on the hand brake, executing a 180-degree turn as the SUV sped by. Releasing the hand brake, he floored it, driving as fast as possible, weaving through traffic and earning several horn blasts and middle fingers as he took turn after turn, taking a circuitous route to the police station on Wilcox, eyes flicking back and forth between the road and the rearview mirror, but there was no sign of the SUV. Tires squealing, he pulled into the parking lot and drove around to the back of the building, out of sight of the main road. With shaking hands he put the car in park and cut the ignition.

Slowly he flexed his hands and forced air into his lungs, blinking away the dots flaring and fading in front of his eyes. He couldn't hear anything except his blood surging through his ears.

Sierra touched his arm and he jumped, lost in the memories of the night he'd lost his mom, and how close they'd just come to…fuck, he couldn't even think the words. He checked the rearview mirror again, even though they were now parked out of sight of the road.

"Are you OK?" she asked, her voice loud in the silent car. She pressed a hand to his cheek and forced him to look at her. "*I'm* OK, Sean. This isn't the same thing. I'm OK. We're safe now, thanks to you."

As the adrenaline eased, a wave of dizziness rocked him, and he needed to anchor himself. He grabbed her and kissed her, hard and a little roughly. He needed to touch her, taste her, feel her. He couldn't seem to catch his breath, his lungs screaming for air, and he broke away.

He flung open the car door and came around to Sierra's side, cringing at the damage to her car. He opened her door and gathered her into his arms. "Are you sure you're OK?"

"I'm fine, I promise. Because of you."

His voice shook, and there wasn't a damn thing he could do to stop it. "That was very, very close to ending very, very badly."

"But it didn't." She laid her head against his chest. "I trust you to keep me safe."

As her words seeped into him, they warred with the lingering guilt over his mother's death, and for the first time in years, he wanted to let some of that guilt go. As though keeping Sierra safe were some kind of atonement. Which was fucked up, but there it was.

He kissed the top of her head, his hands still shaking, and led her into the police station.

"You can forget about that rally, sweetheart."

CHAPTER 23

The next day Sierra settled into her business class window seat on the flight to Miami. She was a nervous flier at the best of times, and with everything she'd been through in the past few days, she was even more on edge than usual. The trip to the airport had been tense, as though Sean had expected the black SUV to reappear or someone to grab her as she walked through the airport, but after yesterday's chase, there'd been no further threats.

Sean stowed their bags in the overhead compartment and then sat down beside her. Just his presence beside her unknotted some of the tension from her shoulders. Jamie sat in the aisle seat across from them.

After they'd filed the police report about the car chase yesterday, they'd learned that Sean's SUV had, in fact, been tampered with. The brake and fuel lines had both been cut, and several electrical wires had been frayed. Those frayed wires would've produced sparks that might have ignited the leaking fuel. Sean's attention to detail had saved them. She shuddered to think what might've happened had he not noticed the screw and the bit of wire that had been left behind in haste.

According to the security footage, his SUV had been tampered with by yet another man in a ski mask. The police had checked for fingerprints, but hadn't found any that didn't belong to Sean, Sierra, or other members of Virtus. She'd arranged to have her smashed-up car towed, but she wasn't optimistic it could be repaired. The damage, at least to the body, was fairly extensive. But it was a small price to pay to be alive.

Yesterday had been yet another reminder of how dangerous this entire situation was, not just for her, but for him. She hated the idea that he was in danger because of her. Hell, she hated the idea that he was in danger at all. It hurt just thinking about what she'd do if something happened to him. The only solution was to catch Sacrosanct. Neither of them would be safe until it was over. And while he was focused on protecting her, who would protect him?

She'd e-mailed Jack, making sure he was all right after the bomb blast, and asking if he'd heard anything that could help them catch Sacrosanct. After being injured in the bombing, he'd likely be out for Sacrosanct's blood too. She felt a little weird e-mailing her ex-boyfriend behind Sean's back, but she knew he wouldn't approve, and she wanted answers. Jack, with all his connections, could maybe provide some. As a politician, he could apply pressure to law enforcement and grease the right wheels. He was a good ally to have, even if he was her ex.

She'd spent the night at Sean's again, and that had suited both of them just fine. Waking up in his bed, in his arms, was something she could get used to. Something she *wanted* to get used to.

"What are you thinking about? You're a million miles

away." Sean's hand landed on her knee, his thumb tracing gentle circles on her skin. He'd told Jamie about their relationship, but as far as she knew, he was the only one on the team who knew about them. It would've been hard to hide it in front of him on this trip, and she knew Sean hated lying to his team.

She sighed. "Everything. The bombing. My house. The car chase. Us." She laid her hand on top of his. "I want this over so we can have our lives back."

"I know. Do you have any idea how much I'd love to just take you on a date?"

It was such a simple thing to say, but her heart melted a little. "I'd really like that. Dinner, a movie, or a walk on the beach." She slipped her hand into his, marveling at how much bigger his hands were than hers. "We could go away someplace for the weekend, just the two of us. Santa Barbara, maybe?"

He brought their joined hands to his mouth and kissed her knuckles, just once. "Mmm. Or what about a week in Mexico? I haven't had a vacation in a while."

Her stomach flipped over on itself. "Oh, God, that sounds amazing. Just us and the beach, and fruity drinks, and—"

He cut her off with a low whisper, his breath tickling her ear. "A nice big bed."

She bit her lip, stifling a laugh. "That goes without saying."

His brown eyes glittered warmly. "It's settled. As soon as this is over, we're going to Mexico."

"You better buy me dinner first. We're doing everything out of order."

He cocked an eyebrow, a teasing smile on his lips. "You didn't seem worried about that last night when I—"

"Shhh!" She smacked him lightly on the arm, her cheeks heating.

"You are adorable." He kissed her on the forehead before settling back in his seat. As they prepared for takeoff, she laid her head on his shoulder and dozed off.

* * *

Humid air poured into the cabin of the jet as soon as the door opened. Heat shimmered on the tarmac, visible and thick. Sean ushered Sierra out of her seat, and with Jamie in front of her, Sean behind, they made their way off the plane and into the overly air-conditioned airport.

They hadn't checked bags, and they made their way directly to the waiting limousine the symposium had arranged for Sierra. He knew she was frightened of Sacrosanct and nervous about her speech, but she walked through the airport with her head held high. She was so strong. So brave. And he was so proud.

And at least a little bit in love.

He took a deep breath as they stepped outside, and it felt as if the air were sticking to the insides of his lungs. He knew that the likelihood of any Sacrosanct attention here in Miami was low, but he wasn't willing to take any risks with her safety. Between the harassment, the bombing, and yesterday's car chase, she'd been through enough. More than enough.

"So I have a press meet and greet by the pool, and then the speech at the symposium dinner tonight. And then back home tomorrow." It was a quick in-and-out trip, and Sean found himself wishing they could just stay in Miami until everything with Sacrosanct was resolved. But he knew she needed to get back. She'd be needed for more public appearances as the grant application process ramped up.

"Jamie and I are going to be there for both events. At the

press event, we'll try to blend in as best as possible so that you can keep the focus on Choices, and not Sacrosanct. If we're front and center, it'll distract from what you want to talk about."

They settled back into the limo, watching the Miami skyline in the distance. A few dark clouds hung low in the sky, floating by and casting the occasional shadow on the otherwise sun-drenched landscape. A humid haze hung over the skyline, obscuring the tops of the tallest buildings. Lush palms lined the roads, fronds swaying lazily as traffic rushed by.

As they made their way toward the hotel, they went over the security plan, including the contingencies should anything go wrong. They'd gone over it earlier this morning too, but it was worth repeating. Annoyed and bored was far superior to injured, or worse.

When they arrived at the hotel, Sierra and Sean checked into a suite, and Jamie checked into the room across the hall. The suite had two bedrooms, but Sean had a feeling that second bedroom would go unused. After checking in, Sierra quickly got herself organized for her press event, changing into a pretty green sundress. She tied her hair up and plopped a straw fedora onto her head.

She turned to face him and froze, her mouth half open. "Is that…is that what you're wearing?"

He looked down at his navy blue swim trunks. "What's wrong with this? We're going to the pool."

She approached him, a coy smile on her face that he'd already learned meant the best kind of trouble. It was the same smile she'd worn while crawling naked toward him the other night. Tracing her fingers over the ridges of his abs, she placed a kiss in the center of his chest. "How am I supposed to concentrate on doing press for Choices if you're walking around like this? Mmm." She trailed her mouth across his chest, scraping her teeth lightly over a nipple.

And now he was hard. Shit. "If you don't stop, I'm about three seconds away from throwing you down on the bed and making you sorry for teasing me."

She looked up at him, her fingers toying with the waist-band of his swim trunks, a naughty smile on her face. "Promise?"

They were interrupted by a loud knock on the door, and Sean reached down and adjusted himself, planning all the ways he was going to make her pay for that little tease later.

With Jamie in tow, they all headed down to the pool, Sierra flashing her symposium badge at the security guards Sean was happy to see vetting everyone attending. As Sierra went off to do her thing, he and Jamie settled themselves near the pool, trying to blend in while keeping an eye on both Sierra and the entire situation. Tropical pop music floated through the air, echoing over the water and reverber-ating against the glass windows of the hotel rising above the pool. The scents of chlorine and sunscreen mingled with the humid air, and he allowed himself the luxury of daydream-ing about lying by the pool with Sierra at some secluded resort in the Riviera Maya.

Across the pool she sat with a group of reporters, talk-ing animatedly as she sipped at a drink with a wedge of pineapple and a little umbrella sticking out of it. She looked over at him, and he had to remember to breathe. Damn. It wasn't only her touch he was becoming addicted to. It was the sound of her laugh, her warm, feminine scent, how happy and whole he felt when he was with her. He craved her, every aspect of her, and the more he got, the more he needed.

Eventually she and a few of the younger female reporters moved closer to the pool, snagging a few lounge chairs. No wonder they were all so taken with her. She didn't talk to them as if she had to be there, but as if she were having fun, catching up with girlfriends. Her passion for the organization and the work it did shone through, and he could see the appeal for the reporters.

He looked over to find Jamie grinning at him. He sat on the edge of the pool, his feet dangling in the water.

"What?"

Jamie shook his head, still smiling. "Nothing. I just think it's funny how you tried to hide that there was something going on between you two, seeing as you're the one who trained us all to be observant."

"What do you mean?"

"Dude, *everyone* saw it. Ian. Carter. I think Zack might've been the only one who didn't see it, and that's because he's been too busy with the rocker chick."

"Zack's hooking up with Taylor?" asked Sean, his eyebrows shooting up.

"Yeah. I don't know how serious it is, but it's been going on for at least a week. Guy's been showing up wrecked for training sessions."

Sean laughed. "So everyone knows, huh?"

"Yeah. And before you get all defensive, we're happy for you, man. I know you broke your own rules to be with her, and if I know you, you're beating yourself up about the example you're setting for the rest of us, but I'd bet my next paycheck that this isn't just a casual hookup."

"No," Sean confirmed. "It's not."

"Good. Because Sierra's awesome."

He laughed again. "Yeah, she is."

Jamie looked at him expectantly, clearly wanting more. It

was funny how women thought they were the only ones who liked to gossip.

Sean gave in, shrugging. "I've…I've never met anyone like her. She's smart, and funny, and just so strong and tough. But she's sweet too. Really sweet, actually."

"Not to mention gorgeous."

Sean smiled. "That too." But while the attraction had started out as purely physical, it had quickly grown into something much, much deeper. Something much more powerful. He had the feeling that even if he were blind and had no idea what she looked like, he'd still love her.

He glanced over at her again and saw her smiling at the reporters.

Yeah. He loved this woman. His woman.

"So what about you? You're not seeing anyone?" he asked Jamie.

Jamie shrugged. "No." He hesitated before continuing. "Before I moved down here from Napa, I was actually engaged to someone."

"Really? It didn't work out?"

"You could say that. Breaking it off was for the best, but it sure as hell pissed my family off. She was a Forsythe, as in Forsythe Wines." Jamie's family owned one of the biggest, most renowned wineries in Napa Valley. According to *Forbes*, Jamie's family was worth almost ten billion dollars, but Jamie seemed to want no part of it. Sean knew he'd had a falling out of some kind with them years ago, but he'd never pried more info than that out of him.

"I'm sorry. That's rough."

"Yeah. Well, I was already on pretty rough footing with my family. Things aren't always what they seem."

"Oh, I know."

"Does your dad know about you and Sierra?"

Sean huffed out a breath. "Yeah. He knows."

Jamie snorted, swirling his feet in circles in the water. "That conversation went well, I see."

"Oh yeah. Just great. Just like all our conversations."

"Sucks, man. Don't let him get to you."

Sean nodded and returned his attention to Sierra, who was shaking hands with the reporters and moving on to the next group.

His father, Sacrosanct, jealous ex-boyfriends, his own fucked-up past—nothing could tear him away from Sierra.

* * *

Sierra flipped through her index cards again, her eyes scanning over the bullet points she'd jotted down. She was slated to speak for twenty minutes, and she was ready. Well, as ready as she'd ever be. She'd spent hours and hours working on her speech, running it by one of the PR advisors at Choices before finalizing what she planned to say. She wanted to make sure she was on message and hitting all the right notes.

She stood backstage in the hotel's ballroom, and although she tried to stop it, her mind flashed back to the bombing and how suddenly it had happened. She knew it was extremely unlikely that another attack would happen here, but she was nervous all the same.

She heard her name called, and she smoothed her hands over her light-blue blouse and dove-gray skirt and stepped out onto the stage. She glanced back over her shoulder once, and Sean winked at her from his spot in the wings. She knew Jamie was in the audience somewhere, but thanks to the bright lights illuminating the stage, she couldn't see past the first row of round tables. As the audience clapped, she made her way toward the glass podium and shook hands with the woman who'd introduced her. She set her cards down on the podium, took a deep breath, and began, her pulse pounding in her throat. Her limbs felt a little shaky, but she brushed it off, falling back on her years of acting experience and focusing on the moment and the message.

"Good evening, ladies and gentlemen, and thank you for inviting me to speak here tonight." She began talking about her past and how she'd come to be involved with Choices. She talked about what the organization meant to her on a personal level and how it had helped her through an incredibly difficult time in her life.

She then broadened her focus, talking not just about herself, but about all women, and the impact an organization like Choices could have on their lives. She also tied in the topics being covered at the symposium, and how the medical community and organizations like Choices could work together. Then she got to the meat of her speech.

"I want everyone in this room to sit back for a few minutes and imagine with me. Imagine you're a college student struggling with student loans, who can barely afford to eat. That student can visit Choices for low-cost birth control and annual checkups that may save her life. Imagine you're a single, uninsured mother of a newborn baby. That mother can visit Choices for postnatal care for both herself and her baby. Imagine you're the victim of a horrible, violent crime. That woman can visit Choices for counseling and support while she decides if she wants to have her rapist's baby.

"Imagine being told that you don't get a say in what happens to your body. This is a reality women across our country face on a daily basis, and at Choices, we believe this is wrong."

She outlined their services and continued. "Currently our organization is under attack, both literally and in the media. As I'm sure you saw on the news, our annual gala was bombed. But the concept that women should have autonomy over their bodies is one that we will continue to support, threats or no threats. Women's health is not a feminist issue, and it's not an issue relegated to the medical community. It's a human rights issue, and one that I'm proud to support. I hope you'll join me. Thank you."

Within seconds the entire audience was on its feet, loud applause crashing over her. She glanced to the side of the stage and saw that Sean was clapping too, beaming at her.

She practically floated offstage.

CHAPTER 24

Jack clicked replay on the YouTube video, starting it over from the beginning. Sierra's face filled the screen, and he couldn't suppress the snarling growl rumbling deep in his chest. He sipped his scotch and watched, desperate anger clawing at his insides. Although it had been uploaded only a couple of hours ago, it already had tens of thousands of views. Sierra's little speech at that fucking symposium had gone viral, rallying even more support for Choices being awarded the grant.

He couldn't let it happen. He couldn't let Choices get the money. He didn't really give a shit what women did or didn't do with their bodies. If you were a slut, you deserved what you got, in his opinion, but this wasn't about that. This was about fifty million dollars. He'd aligned himself with the right people, and with cleverly disguised moves, the fifty million dollars could be his. It would be more than enough to pay off the gambling debts he owed, more than enough to pay Fairfax back for rigging the election, and more than enough to prevent the bank from foreclosing on his house.

In one fell swoop, he'd get the Golden Brotherhood and the bank off his back. He almost laughed, wondering what people would think if they knew who Jonathan Fairfax really was. But very few people knew the truth, including his daughter, whom Fairfax protected fiercely. Everyone who dealt with the Golden Brotherhood knew that Alexa was off-limits.

Disgusted, Jack slammed the lid of the laptop shut and rose from the desk in his elegantly furnished office. With long strides he crossed the room to the sideboard and poured himself another drink.

There had to be a way to use that e-mail. But how? He couldn't give her any additional information without tipping his hand. But she'd reached out to him. Despite their history, she trusted him, and there had to be a way to exploit that.

He wondered if Owens knew about the e-mail. Staring down into his glass, he swirled the scotch, watching the amber liquid as it sloshed up the sides.

No, maybe the e-mail wasn't the way to go. Maybe one last scare tactic would finally put her off. But the video had already gone viral, and she'd done a lot to boost support for Choices, so maybe scaring her wasn't enough at this point. Maybe she'd need to be silenced.

He smiled into his drink, thinking about it. He'd been reluctant to go down this path, but now that he'd allowed himself, he didn't know why he'd hesitated so much before. He could use the e-mail to lure her to him, and then he'd have both his revenge and his victory. Not to mention an outlet for the stress he'd been carrying around for weeks now. It had been a long time since he'd allowed himself to indulge his twisted, sadistic side.

But it wouldn't hurt to scare her a little more in the meantime. Then she'd be even more likely to come running when he told her he could help her.

Scotch in hand, he sat back down at the computer and started typing.

* * *

"So how about dinner?" Sean leaned against the wall, his arms and ankles crossed, and Sierra felt her blood hum just looking at him. After her speech, she'd been so busy talking to everyone at the party that she hadn't had time to eat her own meal. Now it was nearly nine, and her stomach was about to eat itself.

"Yeah?" she said, emerging from the bathroom. She'd taken off her serious clothes and high heels and changed into a short peach-colored sundress and flat silver sandals. Sean had also changed, out of his suit and into khakis and a light-blue button-down shirt that hugged his shoulders and emphasized his muscular physique. It was the kind of shirt that made her want to take it off, especially with the way he had it rolled up around his elbows.

"Yeah. Have dinner with me. I was serious when I said that I wanted to take you on a proper date."

She finished putting her earrings on and smiled at him in the mirror hanging on the wall. "Does Jamie have to come with us?"

"No. It'd just be us."

"Then yes. I'm in. Not that I don't like Jamie, but I want you all to myself."

He stepped up behind her and slid his hands around her waist, bending to drop a kiss on her bare shoulder. "I'm all yours, Sierra."

Her stomach dipped and swirled, and she turned and kissed him. The kiss started out soft and sweet and quickly grew into something hot and hungry, urgency building between them like wildfire. He picked her up, his hands palming her ass, and pressed her back against the wall. Her legs slipped around his waist as she fit her body to his. He was so *big*, so strong, and she didn't have words for how safe and sheltered she felt with his body surrounding her.

Her stomach growled loudly, ruining the moment. She felt him smile against her mouth, and he gently set her down.

"We better get you fed."

She was too hungry to argue, and they hopped into a cab in front of the hotel. Sean gave the driver the name of the restaurant and laced his fingers with hers. His hand was so wide that it stretched her own hand to fit her fingers through his, but she liked it. More than liked it. A sudden giddiness sneaked up on her, her skin hot and tingling as the cab wove its way toward the water. The sun was long gone, but the humid air lingered, filtering through the open windows of the cab. Heavy clouds obscured any stars, and a soft flicker of lightning lit up the sky several miles away, so far that the rumble of thunder never reached them. The entire city glowed in the night, buildings striped with blue and green neon lights, palm trees lit up from below.

They arrived at the restaurant, which looked out over Dinner Key Marina. Yachts bobbed in the dark, lights from the shore shimmering against the water's surface. Their table was outdoors on the edge of the patio, but sheltered by gauzy fabric that hung from the patio's steel rafters. The fabric fluttered dreamily around them, matching the tempo of her heart as Sean held out her chair for her, his hand lingering on the nape of her neck for just a second before he sat down across from her.

The waiter came, and they each ordered a glass of red wine, falling into easy conversation. Before long the waiter returned with their wine and took their orders. Sean picked up his wineglass and clinked it softly against hers.

"I want to know everything about you." He leaned back in his chair, and he looked so sexy that Sierra almost couldn't breathe. The breeze ruffled his thick hair slightly, and his brown eyes were soft and warm in the candlelight from the table. The top buttons of his shirt were undone, leaving it open at the collar. He smiled at her, that lopsided smile she loved so much, and she took a mental picture of this moment.

She took a sip of her wine, hoping she'd be able to swallow it. Her heart was so big right now that it was pressing up into her throat. "I want to know everything about you too."

"We haven't had much time to just…talk…with everything going on." It went unspoken that, when they were alone, they were usually too busy going at it like teenagers to talk, but she felt the flicker of heat pass between them. She knew he was thinking the same thing.

"Why don't we play firsts?" Sierra took another sip of her wine, looking at him over the rim of her glass.

"Firsts?"

"Yeah. First job, first kiss. That kind of stuff. Rock-paper-scissors to see who starts?" She held out her fist. He smiled in response, holding out his own much larger fist.

"One, two, three!" Her fist sprung open, making the symbol for paper, covering his rock. She closed her hand over his, letting her fingertips linger against his knuckles. Faint bruises were still visible from when he'd punched Jack, and she felt a tug deep in her stomach.

"Hmmm. So what do I want to know about Sean?" She leaned back in her chair and tapped her mouth with her fingers. "First job."

He took a sip of his own wine before answering. "Washing dishes at a restaurant when I was sixteen. I really wanted a car, and I knew I'd have to save up for it myself." He smiled, remembering. "God, what a shitty job that was. It was hot as hell, and a lot of the dishes were really gross. I had to wear these rubber gloves that smelled like old tires, and my hands got so sweaty they looked like overgrown prunes by the end of my shift."

"Did you save up enough to buy a car?"

He nodded. "Yep. I became the proud owner of a 1987 mud-brown Chevette. It was a total piece of shit, but I loved that car. What was your first car?"

"Uh...well, I had a Mercedes CLK convertible." She looked down into her wine for a second.

He let out a low whistle. "Nice."

She shrugged. "I bought a car because all of my actor friends had cars." She waved her hand dismissively. "First crush? Like, real crush. Not playground crush."

He sat back in his chair and rubbed a hand over his mouth, remembering. "Laura Zimmerman. Freshman year of high school. She was cute. Blond. Sweet. It took me weeks to work up the courage to ask her to the movies. She ended up being my girlfriend for three whole weeks, which is pretty serious when you're fourteen." He winked at her, and she smiled, melting a little. "Same question to you. First real crush."

"Steven Simmons." She bit her lip, waiting for the reaction.

He choked on a laugh. "The guy who played your older brother Brian on *Family Tree*? Isn't he gay?"

She blew out a breath and shook her head, laughing. "So, so gay. But twelve-year-old me wasn't picking up on that. He was fifteen at the time, and I had this really intense crush on him. He was older, and he was so cute, and smart and cool. I think I was probably a pretty huge dork about it. First kiss?"

"Laura Zimmerman, again. We went to the movies, and I did the classic stretch and put my arm around her. It was pretty smooth, if I do say so myself."

"Well, you did date for three whole weeks, so it must've been a pretty good move."

He laughed. "OK, you. First kiss."

She sighed and toyed with the stem of her wineglass. "It was actually while I was filming a scene for a TV movie. I was fifteen, and…to be honest, it's always bothered me that this big moment happened while I was pretending to be someone else, with someone who didn't even want to kiss me, for all I know. So technically that's my first kiss, but I'm not sure if it counts. I guess it must."

He laid a hand over hers. "Nah. I don't think it counts."

"Really?"

"It was acting, not real life," he said gently. "What was your first real kiss?"

She could feel the heat rising in her cheeks. She hesitated for a second, but she knew she could open herself up to Sean. She wanted to. She wanted to show him all the different parts of her, and it was only fair, because she wanted to see all the different parts of him. "I won't tell you his name, but I was sixteen and he was twenty-two. I was going through a rebellious phase, and we met at a club. We ended up dating secretly for a while. He was my first real, offscreen kiss, and my first…well, my first everything."

"You won't tell me his name?"

"He's, like, crazy famous now. I probably shouldn't."

He scoffed. "Now you *have* to tell me. And then you have to tell me more about this rebellious phase."

They fell into silence as the waiter set down their meals in front of them.

"He wasn't really famous at the time. He's Canadian, and

he was on a sitcom that filmed in LA. He…" She looked around, making sure no one was listening. "He may or may not have been in a huge superhero movie that flopped several years ago. He's married now, and has a daughter."

"I think I know who it is, but I won't say anything." Sean paused, chewing and swallowing a bite of steak. "Is that something that you want?"

"You mean getting married and having kids?"

He nodded, his eyes holding hers, and she swallowed, hoping they were on the same page. She knew she'd come crashing down if they weren't. So she took a deep breath and nodded. "Yes. Very much. Is that—"

"Me too." He set down his fork and scooped her hand up, holding it across the table. He brought her hand to his lips and kissed her wrist. "For a long time, I thought I knew what I wanted out of life, but I know now that I was wrong."

Her breath caught in her throat. "What changed?"

He caught her eyes, his gaze full of meaning. "You." He kissed her wrist again before setting her hand back on the table, her entire body tingling with an awareness that was deeper than sexual.

She'd never experienced falling in love with someone like this before, each moment feeding into the next, making everything bigger and brighter and shinier until she thought it couldn't possibly get better. And then it did. She wondered how many more untold levels she'd find with him.

"So this rebellious phase…" He leaned forward, his elbows on the table.

"I was working sixty-hour weeks, my dad was dying, and I had no freedom. So I went out and found some." She told him a bit more about how she'd come to be involved in Choices and how she'd gotten sick of the toxic Hollywood environment.

"Have you decided if you're going to do the audition?" he asked, slicing into his baked potato.

"I want to, if we can get the timing to work out. There's so much going on with Choices right now that it's a little tricky." She took a bite of her chicken and swallowed before steering the conversation back on track. "My turn. First time you had sex."

He took a sip of wine before he spoke. "I was seventeen, and my girlfriend and I snuck into the Hollywood Reservoir." He shook his head, smiling ruefully. "It lasted about forty-five seconds, and while I thought it was awesome, it was probably pretty disappointing for her."

"Well, I think it's safe to say your skills have improved greatly over the years."

"I should hope so." He winked and signaled to the waiter for more wine. Thunder rumbled softly in the distance, and they started comparing favorite books, movies, TV shows, and music, finding things in common and teasing each other about the differences.

Even though they were doing things backward, it was the best first date Sierra had ever had.

* * *

Water lapped against the docks as Sean and Sierra walked around the marina, the air cooling significantly around them as the storm rolled in across the water. Palm fronds rustled quietly, and although he could practically smell the rain in the air, the last thing Sean wanted to do was bring the date to an end. With Sierra's small hand tucked into his, he'd be perfectly content to walk like this with her for hours. He'd have been hard-pressed to believe it could feel so damn good just to be with someone, but now he knew better. He felt as though all the pieces of his life were falling into place, and it was all because of her.

She tugged him to a stop, and they sat on the edge of one of the slips, their feet dangling above the water below. The soft floral scent of her perfume mingled with the night air, and he inched a little bit closer, wanting more.

"Will you tell me about your mom? About what happened?" Her voice was quiet, and she looked straight ahead, giving him the tiniest bit of space.

It wasn't something he wanted to talk about, especially not tonight, but he also knew he owed her the truth. She had the dots of the story, and she wanted to connect them. In her shoes he'd probably feel the same way. So he ripped the bandage off, willing to show her his scars.

"It happened ten years ago. I was living in Fresno, playing for the Giants' farm team. My mom came up to visit me, and that's when the accident happened. We'd gone out to dinner, and I was driving us home. It was raining, and another driver ran a red light. I didn't see him in time, and he smashed into us." He swallowed. "Into the passenger side of the car. We were pinned against a lamppost, and I couldn't get out of the car. My left leg was stuck, and I couldn't reach her."

Sierra's hand had tightened on his, but she stayed silent, listening.

"I…she was three feet away from me, and I couldn't save her. I couldn't get to her to stop the bleeding. I let her die."

"Oh, Sean." Sierra's voice was barely a whisper as she slipped an arm around his waist, and he leaned into her, taking the comfort she was offering. "It's not your fault. I'm so sorry. You shouldn't have to carry that." She held him tighter. "I'm so sorry for putting you through all of this."

He closed his eyes, waiting for the usual crush of pain,

of guilt, of regret that came with thinking about that night, but it didn't come. There was a distant kind of sadness, but nothing more, and he knew it was because of her. Because of Sierra.

"You have nothing to be sorry for, sweetheart." He turned, his heart beating fast and hard in his chest, and kissed her. A loud thunderclap startled her, and she pressed closer to him. Even though his eyes were closed, he saw another flash of lightning burn through the sky. Raindrops, soft and warm, started to fall on them, and he broke the kiss.

"I think I'm in love with you," she whispered, and he didn't care that the rain was falling harder around them now. He crushed his mouth to hers and pulled her against him, amazed at how light he felt. How free.

"I think I've been in love with you since the day I met you," he said, speaking the words against her mouth, not wanting to break the connection. She made a soft whimpering sound and kissed him back. She must've been able to feel his heart beating, it was going so crazy trying to leap free of his body and into her hands.

They sat on the edge of the dock, kissing as rain fell around them, and Sean felt both lost and found at the same time. Lost in her, but found with her, and he knew he never wanted to let her go.

Another clap of thunder echoed through the sky, and Sierra jumped again. He pulled her to her feet and, laughing, they ran down the dock and out to the street, where he flagged down a cab. They tumbled in, soaking wet, and his mouth didn't leave hers the entire ride back to the hotel.

CHAPTER 25

The door to their hotel room had barely latched behind them before they began quickly shedding their soaking-wet clothing. Naked, Sean ducked into the bathroom and grabbed two of the fluffy white towels from the rack. He handed one to Sierra and then dried himself off, racing to finish before her.

Dry enough, he dropped his towel on the floor and then pulled her toward him with her own towel. He kissed her, rubbing his hands over her shoulders, over her arms, down her back. He worked the towel over her breasts and stomach, kneading her hips and pulling her against him so that his hard cock slid against the soft skin of her belly. She slid her hands up his chest and over his shoulders, and she made that quiet, humming purr that drove him crazy. He deepened the kiss, his mouth hungry against hers, and the now familiar urgency began to spread between them, so he gentled the kiss. He wanted it slow and sweet, wanted her begging for him as he made love to her as many times as she'd let him.

"Tell me again." She trailed her lips over his prickly jaw,

nipping at him in between words, and he knew exactly what she wanted to hear. He was happy to oblige.

He let her towel fall to the floor, and he pressed his lips to her neck, kissing and sucking. She shivered when he teased the spot below her ear with his tongue. "I'm in love with you, Sierra." He kissed her again, a slow, sweet, lingering kiss.

She broke the kiss and threaded her fingers through his, guiding him to a sitting position on the edge of the couch in the suite's living room. Holding his gaze, she sank to her knees in front of him. He looked down at her and ran a hand through her hair, his breath hitching in his chest. She kissed a path across his abdomen, starting at one hip and ending at the other. His erection twitched against her cheek, and she smiled, trailing her mouth over the muscles along his hip. She slipped her hand around his cock, her touch light and teasing, and she looked up at him, her beautiful green eyes glittering. "I'm in love with you too."

Sierra feathered kisses over the tip of his cock, dragging her lips against him. He watched her, transfixed. She swirled her tongue around the head of his cock, and pleasure flared up his spine, heat pooling low in his gut. Cupping his balls with one hand, she stroked down his length and pressed the tip against her lips. In one smooth movement, she took him into her mouth as deep as she could, and a ragged moan tore from his throat.

She looked up at him again, and his heart unraveled at the sight of her on her knees in front of him, his cock filling her mouth. She pulled slowly back, a naughty grin on her face.

"Oh, fuck. Do that again." His voice was rough, maybe even shaking a little, and his hands cradled her face.

She stroked him once before taking his length into her mouth a second time. He gathered her damp hair away from her face, holding it in a loose fist against the back of her head, encouraging her with the slightest pressure. She swirled her tongue over him, teasing and tasting. Gently massaging, she fondled his balls, and he was amazed he was still sitting upright. His vision narrowed and his muscles tensed under the intense pleasure. The wet heat of her mouth, coupled with the sight of her lips stretched around his cock, was almost too much, and heat fanned out across his skin.

Once more she took him as deep as she could, and a groan rumbled from his chest as she found a steady rhythm, through with teasing. The urge to pump his hips told him he was close, and he let go of her hair and squeezed her shoulders, pulling her up from her knees. Immediately his mouth was on hers.

She broke the kiss, her breathing heavy. "I wasn't finished."

"Not tonight. I want to come inside you."

She smiled at him, biting her lip, and a fresh wave of arousal rolled through him. He scooped her up and cradled her against his chest, carrying her to the nearest bedroom in the suite. She looped her arms around his neck, and she kissed his chest, her mouth lingering over his heart, which felt as if it were about to burst.

He eased down onto the bed, still holding her, with his back against the headrest. She turned to straddle him, and they both let out a low moan when his cock slid against the slick flesh of her pussy. She settled against him, threading her fingers in his hair as they kissed. He'd never get enough of her mouth. She rocked against him, and he was about to push up into her when he remembered that the condoms were in his bag, which was still by the door.

She rocked against him again, her voice a breathy moan

when she spoke. "Don't make me wait, Sean. I'm about to lose my mind."

Need pulsed through his veins, and he ground his hips up into her. "Condoms are in the other room. I'll be right back." He kissed her neck and then started to move her off him, but she shook her head.

"No."

He pulled back, his eyebrows raised. "What?"

"I don't want to use one. I'm on the pill." She pulled back to look at him. "What do you think?"

His head spun for a second, his hands trembling slightly at the idea of being bare inside her. "Are you sure?"

"I want to feel you, Sean. I don't want anything between us."

"Fuck," he groaned, his cock already in his hand. She lifted her hips, and he lined up the bare head of his cock at her impossibly hot, slick entrance.

She pressed her forehead to his, her eyes holding his as she slowly sank down onto him. They each let out a shuddering moan.

"Yes," she hissed out, rocking up and then sinking down even farther. His hips rose up off the bed, and he closed his eyes, trying to center himself against the onslaught of intense pleasure rippling through him. She clenched around him, and he groaned, able to feel every pulse, the slick heat of her with nothing between them better than he could've imagined.

"You feel incredible inside me." Her voice was soft and breathy, and throbbing pleasure radiated through him as she stretched to accommodate him. He kissed her, nearly overwhelmed by the intimacy of the moment.

He managed a low chuckle. "I don't even have words for how good this feels."

She kissed his neck. "And how right." She rocked her

hips, and he flexed his hips up, pushing deeper into her and drawing a long, loud moan from her. Their mouths met, and his tongue slid against hers in a rhythm that echoed the slide of his body into hers. His hands caressed her back as she moved against him, and he let go of everything he'd been holding on to. He didn't have room to love her and carry the rest of the shit he'd been dragging around for so long.

And he chose to love her. Given the opportunity, he'd spend the rest of his life choosing to love her.

He ground deliberately against her clit every time he thrust into her, bringing her closer and closer, her muscles fluttering around him. Gradually their tempo increased, becoming faster and more frenzied until their skin glistened with sweat. Sierra shuddered and bucked her hips against him as she came, a refrain of "Oh, God, Sean," falling repeatedly from her kiss-swollen lips. He thrust one final time, and his cock pulsed inside her as he came.

They stayed still for a moment, chests rising and falling. She pressed her face into his neck, trailing featherlight kisses across his skin and then resting her head on his shoulder. He dipped his head and inhaled her addictive scent, wanting to memorize this moment. He caressed his hands up and down her back and kissed the top of her head, and she sighed, snuggling into him a little more. They basked silently in the afterglow, and an intense rush of euphoria washed over him.

* * *

Several hours later Sierra lay with her head on Sean's chest, her fingers trailing through his chest hair. Her muscles were weak, her body limp from the pleasure Sean had spent hours wringing from her. A white-hot bolt of lightning burned its way across the sky, a booming echo of thunder following closely behind. Rain pelted the window, soft and rhythmic.

They were inching closer to dawn, but she was too alive and awake to even think about sleeping. Every single time she closed her eyes, she saw Sean, rain dripping down his face, telling her he'd loved her since the day he'd met her, and her entire body bloomed all over again. And she knew, after the way he'd made love to her, after the raw intensity in his eyes as they'd connected with nothing between them, that he was telling the truth. She saw the way he looked at her, and it only made her love him more. Love him harder. Love him bigger than she'd thought possible.

After each time they'd had sex, they'd lain in each other's arms, talking about everything and anything. She'd told him more about her dad, about growing up in Hollywood, about the shows she'd worked on. He'd told her more about playing baseball, getting drafted by the Giants, and even playing a few big league games. They'd swapped college stories—he'd gone to Cal State Fullerton, while she'd gone to UCLA—and talked about their families. She'd told him about dating Jack, and he'd told her that he didn't really date much. The conversation had drifted to work, and he ran a hand down her back as he told her about running Virtus.

"It must be challenging, working with your dad," she said, tracing a circle around his nipple.

He sighed. "It can be. He's not good at letting go, and neither am I, so that's not a good combination. I think he does respect the work I do. There's just so much other shit between us that gets in the way."

She nodded against him, breathing him in, wanting to wrap herself in his scent. Her heart still hurt for him over everything he'd been through losing his mother, and the havoc it had wreaked on his career plans and family life. She wanted to take that hurt for him so that he wouldn't have to shoulder it alone. She could help him carry it, just as he'd helped her carry so much already.

"Once this job is finished, I'll talk to him. I'm OK with it if he still wants to be involved with the company—I mean, it's his baby, I get it—but I know that we need to find a way to communicate that doesn't involve yelling and slamming doors."

Sierra pushed up onto an elbow. "What happens once this job is finished?" A completely irrational surge of jealousy charged through her. "Will you be protecting someone else?"

He pulled her back down to him, settling her against his chest. "Yes. Once this job is finished, I'll be working with another client, or several other clients, depending on what business we've got coming in. Sometimes I'm not out in the field, but in the office, doing the more administrative stuff. It depends." He tipped her chin up, forcing her to look at him. "But once this job is finished, that doesn't mean you and I will be. We're just getting started."

"I know, but…" She trailed off and tried to look away, but he held her gently in place.

"What's wrong, sweetheart? Tell me."

She bit her lip. "This sounds so silly."

He smiled crookedly. "Tell me anyway."

"I guess I…I'm having a hard time with the idea that you'll be protecting someone else. Putting yourself in danger for someone else."

"It's my job. And yes, it's dangerous, but you don't need to worry about me. I know what I'm doing."

"I know, but…you're *mine*, and I don't like the idea of you getting hurt for someone else. I don't like the idea of you getting hurt at all, but—"

He silenced her with a soft, sweet kiss, and she felt instantly calmer. Not completely calm, but calmer. The kiss deepened, and her sense of possessiveness only grew, tangling with the guilt she felt at how much danger she'd already put him in.

"Are you jealous?" he asked, rising up over her and then beginning to kiss his way down her body, his mouth blazing heat over her breasts and down her stomach.

"A…a little, yes. And a little worried. When you're out risking your life, who'll protect you to make sure you'll come home to me?" He nipped at her hip bone, and she found it harder to think.

He flipped her over and started kissing a new trail down her back. "I'll protect myself, sweetheart." His teeth sank into one of her ass cheeks, and she moaned, arching her hips up off the bed. He licked and sucked at the spot to soothe the bite before moving to her other cheek to repeat the delicious torment. Sliding his hands under her hips, he pulled them up off the bed so that she was lying ass-up and facedown and feeling wickedly, amazingly exposed and open to him. She knew he was about to claim her, and her arms shook against the mattress.

He slicked his thumb through her folds and she moaned into the mattress. He laughed softly. "It's cute that you're a little jealous, Sierra, and very, very hot that you called me yours." He circled his thumb around her clit, and she arched into his touch. "But you've got it all mixed up, sweetheart. It's because you're *mine* that I'll always come home to you."

She moaned again, and she felt the mattress dip behind her. And then his tongue was on her, licking a slow, deliberate path over her folds. He slipped a finger into her, and then another, working them in and out in time with his mouth as he swirled his tongue over her in a steady rhythm. A tremble crested through her, and her legs shook, pleasure vibrating through her. He groaned against her, adding to the vibrations, and tension began to coil low in her belly. He gave her ass a playful slap, warm tingles emanating outward from the contact, and she swore she could feel her bones melting.

"I need…to…more…" She panted out, her eyes closed as she focused entirely on Sean's mouth and what it was doing to her.

"Tell me what you need," he said, swirling his tongue over her again.

"I need…need to come," she managed, and he sucked her clit into his mouth, scraping his teeth over it and sending her over the edge. Her entire body bucked as she came, and she screamed his name into the mattress. She felt the head of his cock slide against her swollen lips, and she pushed up onto all fours. His teeth nipped her earlobe, and he growled as he pushed into her.

"I love you, Sierra. That's my motivation for staying safe."

Her heart came undone, unspooling like ribbon as he slid home, his hands tight around her hips. She looked at him over her shoulder.

"I love you, Sean." She couldn't get the rest of her thought out around the lump pressing against her throat at the tenderness and passion in his eyes.

She heard his breathing hitch, but he continued to move, stroking in and out in a deep, deliberate rhythm. Suddenly he pulled out of her, flipped her over again, and sank back into her, his mouth urgent against hers. She wrapped her legs around his hips as they lost themselves in each other, the sounds of soft moans, the creaking mattress, and the gentle slap of skin against skin filling the room.

"Say it again," he said, sliding his hands up to twine them with hers above her head.

"I love you." She blinked and felt a tear slide down her cheek. He dipped his head and kissed it away, slowing his rhythm.

"Don't cry, sweetheart." He kissed her neck. "Nothing to cry about. I'm here, and I've got you. I'm not going anywhere."

Every single cell in her body buzzed, and she couldn't think straight. Everything was a jumble inside her, and all she knew was that she needed this man the way her lungs needed air, the way her heart needed blood, the way her body needed food. *He* was her air, her blood, her food. He was everything, and she knew that, if they didn't deal with Sacrosanct, all of this could be snatched away from her, and she couldn't bear the thought of losing Sean. She was so in love with him that the idea of anything happening to him caused her actual physical pain.

She would do whatever it took to protect not just him, but what they'd found together.

* * *

Sierra stretched her sore muscles, not wanting to open her eyes. The soft glow behind her eyelids told her the room was bright, and she could hear a housekeeping cart rumbling down the hallway. She turned and reached for Sean, her arm thumping against the mattress. Cocking one eye open, she listened, relaxing when she heard the quiet patter of the shower in the adjacent bathroom.

She'd drifted to sleep a few hours ago in his arms, unable to stop touching him. Wanting the comfort and reassurance of his skin against hers. She wished that they didn't have to go back to Los Angeles this morning, that they could just stay curled up in this hotel suite together for the foreseeable future.

Her phone began to ring from her purse by the door, and she ran to answer it. Taylor's name scrolled across the screen.

"Hey. I'm surprised you're up. Isn't it like, five in the morning there?" Sierra hopped back into bed, pulling the duvet around her.

"Yeah. I couldn't sleep, so I thought I'd try and write for a while, but I got nothing. Distract me?"

"Still blocked?" She snuggled deeper into the soft mattress.

"Ugh. Yes. I haven't written a song in months now, and I feel like I've forgotten how."

"Patience. It'll come. I think if you try to force it, you'll make it worse."

"Maybe. I don't know. Anyway, I didn't call to whine about being blocked. How's Miami? I saw your speech online, and you killed it."

"Really? You saw it online?"

"Yeah, have you been living under a rock for the past twelve hours? It went viral, dude."

"It did? Wow." A thrill shot through her at the idea that thousands of people were watching her speech. If that didn't help galvanize support for Choices' getting the grant, she didn't know what would.

"Yeah. Where's Sean?"

"In the shower." She cringed as she spoke the last word, knowing that she'd just given them away.

Taylor laughed, the sound deep and husky. "So you weren't under a rock, but under a hot bodyguard."

Sierra laughed too, relieved Taylor didn't seem hurt that she'd kept it from her.

"As a penalty for holding out on me, you owe me details."

"Oh, really? Such as?" Sierra challenged, not really wanting to share parts of Sean with anyone else.

"Is he proportional? I mean, he's such a big dude, that I can't help but wonder...if...*you know*."

Sierra laughed, and even though she was alone, her cheeks warmed. "Get real. I'm not telling you how big he is."

"Oh, come on. Ballpark. I don't need specifics."

"Are you that deprived?"

"Deprived? No. Depraved? Yes."

She laughed again, smushing a hand against her face. "Like, on the Sierra Blake scale of penises?"

"Yes. Although the data on your scale probably isn't as comprehensive as the Taylor Ross log...log. Ha. Log log."

Sierra laughed even harder. "You should copyright that."

"Uh-huh. Enough stalling. Spill."

"Fine. On the Sierra Blake scale, he falls somewhere between holy shit and *unnnggnnnf*." She made a Homer Simpson–like groaning, drooling noise.

Taylor laughed, one sharp burst. "Very scientific, this scale of yours."

Sierra began to make an even raunchier joke when a muffled male voice on the other end of the phone stopped her. "Everything OK, babe?"

"Yeah, couldn't sleep. Sorry." Taylor came back on. "Still there?"

"Um, excuse me, but *who* was that?" She had a feeling she knew, but she wanted confirmation.

"Uh...it's Zack."

Sierra was about to ask for more info when Sean emerged from the bathroom wearing nothing but a white towel knotted low around his hips. Water droplets still clung to his chest, chasing each other down his glorious muscles. Every single thought flew out of her brain.

"I have...to...go..." she said, watching with anticipation

as Sean strode slowly toward her, a wicked smile on his gorgeous face.

Taylor laughed again. "I assume Sean is naked, because it sounds like your brain is sliding out through your ears."

"I think it is. We'll catch up when I get back."

"Have fun with Mr. Unnnggnnnf."

Sierra slid her thumb across the screen to end the call, watching as Sean dropped the towel to the floor.

Her phone began to buzz again from where she'd dropped it on the bed, and she glanced over at it, wanting to put it in silent mode, but froze when she saw the name on the screen: Detective Rodriguez.

She glanced up at Sean and knew that he'd seen it too, the wicked smile having been replaced with a frown. He nodded for her to answer it.

"Sierra." Antonio's voice was hoarse, and the hair on the back of her neck stood on end.

"Antonio? Is everything OK?"

She could hear the sound of sirens and crackling radios in the background, and he cleared his throat before speaking.

"I'm sorry to tell you this, Sierra, but there was a fire last night. Your house is gone."

CHAPTER 26

Sierra stood at the edge of her driveway, trying to make sense of the smoldering wreckage in front of her. A few of the exterior walls still stood, crumbling and charred along the tops. The roof was gone, having collapsed into the house and taking out most of the second floor with it. White smoke still rose into the sky from the ashes, although the fire had long been extinguished. They'd flown back to Los Angeles on an earlier flight than planned, but even still, it had taken nearly eight hours for them to get back from Miami. Worry and guilt had gnawed at her the entire trip.

Carter had been in the house when the fire had started. Someone had thrown several Molotov cocktails in through a window, and the fire had spread far too quickly for Carter to do anything but get out.

He could've died. She thought of the pictures of his son, and she wanted to throw up. She took a small step forward and noticed the graffiti scrawled across her driveway.

BURN IN HELL BITCH

She stared at the ruins of her home, trying to wrap her head around the fact that everything was gone. All her furniture. Her clothing. Her personal items. Things that couldn't be replaced, like photographs, her grandmother's engagement ring. Gone. She was trying to feel something, anything, but looking at the smoke still rising into the air, she felt numb. Distantly she knew that she was probably in shock, but she didn't know how to shake herself out of it, or if she even wanted to.

Antonio approached with Carter and a man wearing an LAFD uniform, all with smudges on their faces.

She looked over at Sean, who was talking to one of the other men from the LAFD. He must've seen her looking because he broke away and came toward her. Clearly any concern for confidentiality was gone because he slipped an arm around her waist and tucked her against him. With his solid, strong body sheltering hers, some of the numbness started to recede.

"Clearly this was a targeted attack," said the LAFD officer. "I don't know if anything from the security cameras is salvageable, but we'll do everything we can to speed up the investigation."

"That's Virtus's security system," said Sean, "and everything backs up remotely to one of our servers. I'll get someone working on getting you that footage ASAP. What time was the fire started?"

"Around three in the morning," answered Carter. His voice was hoarse from smoke inhalation, dark circles bruising the skin under his eyes.

Sierra nodded, starting to shake. Sean excused them, clapping Carter on the shoulder, and led her away from the scene. He pulled her into his arms and kissed her temple.

"I'm so sorry, sweetheart. I'm so sorry."

Now that the numbness was wearing off, she missed it. Numbness was better than the terror churning through her and making it difficult to do anything except shake and try not to cry.

"Everything's gone," she choked out, pressing her face into his chest. His arms tightened around her, and he stroked her hair. She pulled back slightly and looked up at him. "What if we'd been home? What if it wasn't just *stuff* that was gone? What if Carter…" She trailed off, unable to keep speaking around the sobs now racking her. She glanced over at what was left of her house and cried harder, letting the loss, the fear, the sense of powerlessness pull her under.

"Shhh." He kissed her forehead. "It's OK, sweetheart. You're OK."

She pulled out of his arms, suddenly needing space. She paced away from him, hugging herself again. "I know, but I'm sick of this shit, Sean!" She pointed at the house. "If we'd been in there, we could've died. Carter could've died. And even though that didn't happen, I've lost everything. I'm homeless because of this fucking garbage, and I can't do it anymore. I'm at my wits' end with all of this, and something has to give." Tears made tracks down her face as she voiced the thoughts that had been churning through her the entire way home. Now, seeing the wreckage, she couldn't keep it in anymore. She sank down onto the curb and sobbed, both for what she'd lost and for how much worse it could've been.

He sat down beside her, but didn't pull her back into his arms. "I know. I'm sorry if it sounded like I was brushing everything off." Something darkened in his eyes as he looked back at the house. "I'm so angry about this that I'm just trying to keep it together and not lose my shit on everyone here. That won't help anything."

She managed a tiny smile. "No, but it might entertain me."

He returned her smile, and she brushed at a tear with the back of her hand. "I just feel like this isn't ever going to end, and that I can't win. If I back down, that's not a guarantee they'll leave me alone. Not after the video of my speech went viral. But if I don't, this kind of shit will keep happening. They've tried to kill us more than once now." She slipped her arms back around Sean's waist and leaned her head against his broad shoulder. "This can't keep happening."

"The police are doing everything they can, but they don't have a lot of concrete evidence to go on."

"Sierra? Are you OK?" She turned at the familiar voice as Sean's arms tightened around her, not letting her go. Jack strode toward them, his face pale, his eyes worried. His pace slowed as he took in the charred remains of the house. "Oh my God. I'd hoped it wasn't true." He rubbed a hand over his mouth and then studied her. "You're OK?"

She and Sean stood. "I wasn't home. I'm OK." She looked at Sean. "We're OK."

Jack glanced upward for a second before rubbing his hand over his mouth again. "Thank God." He blew out a heavy breath, his hands on his hips as he surveyed the damage. "Listen, I got your e-mail, and I might be able to help."

Her stomach dropped, and an itchy prickle of heat raced over her skin. She hadn't told Sean about the e-mail, and now it looked as if she'd gone and deliberately e-mailed her ex-boyfriend behind his back. Which, OK, was kind of what she'd done, but only because she was trying to get both of them out of this situation. She chanced a glance over at Sean, whose brow was furrowed.

"What e-mail?" he asked, and she knew he was angry at being left out of the loop.

"Sierra e-mailed me asking if I could help with the investigation into Sacrosanct, that's all. And," he said, turning his attention back to Sierra, "I have a lead on someone who used to work for them. Someone who can give us names, descriptions, even addresses. If I can arrange a meeting, are you interested?"

"Yes, if—" said Sierra at the same time that Sean gave an emphatic "No." Both she and Jack looked at him. He pushed a hand through his hair, shaking his head as if in disbelief. "It's way too fucking dangerous. No way am I letting you anywhere near anyone from Sacrosanct, former member or not. Not gonna happen."

Sierra opened her mouth to speak, but Jack beat her to the punch. "I understand. I'll keep working my connections, see what I can dig up." He pulled Sierra in for a quick hug. "I'm glad you're OK." He got back into the waiting town car and sped away. When she turned back around, Sean's mouth was pressed into a thin, tight line.

"You e-mailed Jack?"

She bit her lip, guilt churning her stomach. "Are you mad?"

His expression softened, but she could still see a flicker of anger in his eyes. "No. I just wish you'd told me." He walked back toward Antonio, and she pressed a hand to her chest, wishing she could rewind a few minutes. Hell, wishing she could rewind back to yesterday, when she'd still had a home.

After a moment Sean came back, his hands shoved in his pockets. "We can go. They'll call you with any updates or if they need any information." He raised a hand and cupped her cheek. "You can stay with me as long as you need."

She leaned into his touch. "I only e-mailed Jack because I

want this to be over. I didn't tell you because there was nothing to tell. I just want to get us out of this." She wasn't done making her case for reaching out to Jack's potential contact, but she knew that now wasn't the time. She also knew that she didn't have the mental or emotional energy for it right now. Losing her home had left both her brain and her heart feeling heavy and sluggish as she tried to process the reality of it.

"I get it. But in the future…"

"I won't keep stuff from you."

He kissed her, and she felt as though they were back on an even keel. Relief trickled through her. "That's all I ask. Come on. Let's go home."

* * *

Sean had lied to Sierra, and he felt like shit about it, but he didn't know what else he was supposed to say. Her house had burned down, for fuck's sake, and he wasn't going to pile on by admitting that, yeah, he *was* pissed she'd e-mailed Jack behind his back. Not because he had issues with her talking to Jack, but because she hadn't told him about it. She hadn't trusted him enough to tell him, and that hurt. Especially after everything they'd shared the night before. After all the times she'd told him she trusted him.

But right now wasn't the time to poke into any of that. He needed to focus on keeping her safe, and they could sort through everything later.

He dropped his keys on the table by his front door and locked it behind him, setting the alarm. She'd been quiet on the drive over, her expression unreadable, and he hated how powerless he felt. There was nothing he could say, nothing he could do to make what had happened any less horrible.

She'd lost her home and was in shock. Soon enough the devastation of what had happened would creep in, and he'd need to be there for her. That was more important right now than any anger he might be feeling.

He headed into the kitchen to rustle up some food, and she settled on the sectional in the living room, still quiet. When he returned a few minutes later with sandwiches, she was lying on the couch, staring at the ceiling with a thoughtful look on her face, her phone in one hand, the other toying with the shooting star pendant she'd told him her father had given her shortly before he'd died.

"I can't do this anymore," she said, still staring at the ceiling. He set the plates down on the coffee table and sat down, pulling her feet into his lap. "I can't keep living my life like this, and neither can you."

"We'll get through it, Sierra."

"I need to put an end to this." She sat up and curled her feet under her. Away from him. She held up her phone. "I had a text message from Jack. His contact is willing to meet to give information. But he'll only talk to me. He doesn't trust anyone else."

"If he has information to give, he should go to the cops. Or, hell, why can't he just give the information to Jack? I don't understand why he needs to meet with you. I don't like it."

She reached out and laid a hand on his cheek. "I want to do this. For me, and for us."

He laid a hand over hers. "No."

"But what if this could put an end to everything? It would just be a meeting, and we'd do it as safely as possible. If this guy has information that could stop Sacrosanct, I need to see this through so that I can have my life back. So that dangerous shit doesn't keep happening to us."

"No, Sierra. There are too many variables, too many un-knowns. It's a terrible idea. It's my job to keep you safe, and I wouldn't be doing my job if I let you meet with some stranger, even if I was with you. God only knows what we'd be walking into."

"Well…you wouldn't be there. Like I said, Jack's contact will only talk to me, so I'd have to go by myself."

Sean let out a mirthless laugh and pushed up off the couch, pacing to the window with his hands on his hips. "You've gotta be fucking kidding me with this, Sierra." He shook his head, watching the traffic below and trying not to lose his temper. "I'm not letting you out of my sight. This entire idea sounds incredibly dangerous and stupid, not to mention suspicious as hell."

"I thought you didn't suspect Jack anymore." She stood a few feet away, her arms crossed.

"My answer's no. How do you not see what a fucking ter-rible idea this is? You're smarter than that. I know you're scared, I know you're frustrated, but no way is this happen-ing. No fucking way." He sliced his hand through the air, hoping that would be the end of it.

But, to be fair, she had warned him that she was stubborn.

"You're damn right I'm scared! You're damn right I'm frustrated! You're not hearing me, Sean. *I. Want. My. Life. Back!* And yes, I know this plan isn't ideal, but it's a shot, and I want to take it. I need to put an end to all this!" She threw her phone down on the couch and it bounced against the cushions before landing on the floor with a quiet thud. She took a breath, and then another. "I want to do this."

He clenched and unclenched his hands, trying not to let his anger and frustration get the better of him. "I've kept you safe up to this point, and I'll keep protecting you until this is behind us. You said you trusted me. Is that still true?"

Her expression softened, and she bit her lip. "Of course I trust you. This isn't about that."

"Really? Is it because you trust me that you e-mailed Jack behind my back?" Well, shit. He hadn't meant to throw that in there, but it was too late to take it back now.

She stepped closer, only a few inches away. "I e-mailed Jack behind your back because I can't take watching you put yourself in danger for me."

"I can protect myself, Sierra. I can protect both of us."

"But what if we can put an end to this?" she asked, cycling back to the beginning of the argument.

He crossed his arms over his chest. "*No.*" He took a breath, trying to get a handle on his rising temper, heat beating through his veins.

"Because you're mad I e-mailed Jack?"

Something in him snapped, and he pulled her roughly against him. "Because you're *mine*."

Immediately his mouth was on hers, rough and demanding, and she opened her mouth hungrily. She'd never kissed him quite like this before, and he kissed her like a drowning man trying to breathe. His erection pressed firmly against his zipper and he backed her against the wall, wanting to cage her in, to keep her and protect her from everything. The desperation brought on by the argument hadn't eased, had only become brighter and hotter, fueling the fire between them.

"I fucking love you, Sierra." He spoke the words against her mouth, his teeth scraping against her lips.

"Sean." She moaned out his name on a half sob, and his hands circled her ribs before sliding up, his palms rubbing against her peaked nipples. She choked out a moan and deepened the kiss.

She pushed at his T-shirt, her fingers scraping over his

stomach, and he yanked it over his head, dropping it to the floor. As he kissed her with greedy hunger, she raked her nails down his back, the sting of her touch only ratcheting up the intensity sparking between them. She broke the kiss and pressed her mouth to his chest. He sucked in a breath as her teeth nipped at his skin, and he laid his hands against the wall on either side of her head, trying to hold himself upright under the weight of need crashing down on him. Need to protect her. Need to make her understand. Need to be inside her.

"Take your clothes off. Now."

Eyes holding his, she pulled off her T-shirt, bra, and denim shorts, leaving only a pair of light-blue cotton panties. Without waiting for further instruction, she pried open his belt buckle and shoved her hand into his pants, underneath his boxer briefs, firmly gripping his hard cock.

She met his eyes as she stroked him. "It's because I love you that I want this over."

With her hand still in his pants, he shoved them down and stepped out of them, amazed at the level of coordination he had, considering her fingers were curled around his cock. Her words fueled his hunger for her, and he squeezed her breasts and buried his face in them, sucking and nipping across her skin, savoring each shaky breath, each throaty moan, each shiver. His teeth raked over her nipple, and she cried out, arching into him.

Words were failing, but maybe he could make her understand—that she was his to protect, that he would do whatever it took to keep her safe—with his body. Maybe then she'd let this dangerous idea go.

He shoved his boxer briefs down, and his cock snapped against his stomach, thick and heavy.

He pulled her into his arms and led her over to the couch,

kissing her as they walked. When they reached the back of
the sectional, he spun her around, his cock pressed against
the smooth flesh of her ass. With one hand he bent her forward over the couch while he teased his cock over the fabric
of her panties with the other. Pushing the cotton aside, he
slipped a finger into her. He took a shuddering breath as he
slowly eased in and out of her, adding a second finger and
drawing a long, loud moan from Sierra.

She glanced up at him over her shoulder. "Fuck me,
Sean." His breathing hitched, and dark lust seared through
him.

Roughly he pulled at her panties, but he tugged too
sharply, and the fabric tore. Unable to stop himself, he let out
a low growl and tore them all the way off before plunging
into her, hard and deep. She cried out, moaning his name and
a string of curse words. She was so hot around him, so tight
and wet, that the pleasure of being inside her was almost too
much to take, and he moaned loudly. He thrust into her, es-
tablishing a brutal, thrilling rhythm that had every muscle in
her body quivering. Caressing a hand up her back and into
her hair, he pulled gently, and she arched her back, giving
him even deeper access. He pulled again, a little harder, and
she screamed out his name.

His breathing harsh, he pounded into her, driving her
higher and higher. He smacked her ass with his free hand,
and she pushed her hips back into him, riding him.

"Tell me you're mine." His voice was hoarse, full of emotion and lust that was echoed back to him when she spoke.

"I'm yours. God, Sean, I'm yours."

"Mine." He ground the word out as he drove into her, sav-
age and possessive. She started to come on his cock, pulsing
around him and setting all his nerve endings on fire, burning
as he took her, hard and deep. Her muscles clenched around

him, and he buried himself deep inside her, her name tearing from his mouth on a loud, harsh groan as his orgasm rocked through him.

Mine. The single syllable beat through him like a drum, over and over again, hypnotic and rhythmic.

Mine.

CHAPTER 27

Sierra lay in Sean's arms on the couch, a blanket thrown over them, neither of them speaking. She stroked her fingers through his chest hair as he ran a hand up and down her back. She pressed her cheek against his chest, reassured by the steady thump there, breathing in his scent as she held him tighter.

She'd never loved anyone more in her life than she loved this man. She closed her eyes and tried to figure out what to do. She knew that he'd never agree to her plan—that much had been clear. She also knew that meeting with Jack's contact was potentially a chance to get them out of this situation.

He kissed her forehead and pulled her tighter against him, and she knew they were clinging to each other because the way they were living now wasn't sustainable.

An idea zapped through her, and her heart sank.

She could go over his head. She could call Antonio… Patrick. If she could get them on board with meeting Jack's contact, maybe Sean would see that she was right. And then they could put all this behind them.

If he ever forgave her for going behind his back. She

knew she'd hurt him with that e-mail. This would be ten times worse. A hundred times. If Antonio and Patrick agreed to her plan and it worked, it might get them out of this situation, but what would their future look like if she went around him? He'd be furious with her.

But if it kept them both out of harm's way, maybe that was justification enough. She loved him, and she couldn't let him keep putting himself in danger for her.

He kissed the top of her head, and her heart lurched. Given his relationship with his father, involving him without Sean's consent was basically taking a stick of dynamite to the relationship they'd just started and blowing it to smithereens. But she also knew that Patrick was the only one at Virtus who held any kind of authority over Sean.

Maybe Sean would see that she'd had no other choice, and they could rebuild.

So many maybes and ifs. Too many. So she focused on the certainties.

She loved Sean. She wanted, more than anything, to get them both out of this situation. To keep him safe.

Sean loved her, and as long as Sacrosanct was still out there, he'd put himself in danger time and time again to protect her.

Maybe he would understand that she was doing this not just for her but for him. That she was doing this to protect him so that they could have a future together. That she was doing this because she loved him.

Another big maybe.

She was desperate, and with a sinking feeling in her stomach, she knew she had to take this chance. Take it and deal with the fallout once everyone was safe.

She sniffled, fighting back the tears stinging her eyes. Sean tipped her head up with a finger under her chin.

"Hey. Shhh. It's OK. I've got you."

She let the tears fall, savoring the feel of his arms around her while her heart tore itself to shreds. She wasn't sure how long they lay like that, holding on to each other. Not long enough before he moved to sit up.

"I should hit the grocery store. The fridge is pretty bare. Anything you want me to pick up?"

She sat up and wrapped the blanket around herself, smiling weakly. "Some new underwear?"

He nodded and chuckled. "I won't be gone long, and the building's secure. Set the alarm behind me and call me or one of the guys if you need something." He kissed her once, a brief, sweet kiss on the lips, and then started pulling his discarded jeans on. A few minutes later he left, and she watched the door click shut behind him. She picked up her phone, tears streaming down her face.

She called first Antonio and then Patrick, telling them about the informant Jack had managed to track down who wanted to meet with her to give her information on Sacrosanct. As she'd expected, both of them immediately jumped all over the plan, and she invited them to come over, hoping they could sway Sean to their side. But even if they couldn't, she was still going through with it. They finally had a solid lead on Sacrosanct, and she intended to do her part in bringing it down. How could she not, after all the shit it had put her through?

Antonio and Patrick arrived together before Sean got home from the store, using Patrick's key card to get into the building. She let them in and they all sat down around the small dining table adjacent to the kitchen.

"Where's Sean?" asked Antonio, leaning forward on his elbows.

"He went to get groceries."

"And what does he think of this?" Patrick eyed her skeptically.

She forced herself to meet their eyes. "We talked about it earlier, and he's against it."

"Wait, so you're going over his head?" Antonio frowned at her.

"Yes. Sean and I don't agree about this."

"That's because he's not thinking clearly." Patrick stabbed his finger against the table's surface, shaking his head. "*This* is why you don't get involved with clients. No offense."

"None taken."

At the sound of Sean's key in the lock, they all turned, watching as he walked in with several bags from Ralph's. He paused, his eyes jumping from her to Antonio to Patrick, and back to her. He dumped the bags on the kitchen counter and strode toward them, his hands on his hips.

"What's going on? Did something happen?"

With her heart hammering in her chest, Sierra stood, knowing she was about to set fire to the best thing in her life. She just hoped the foundation they'd started would be enough to rebuild on.

"No, nothing happened. I called them to tell them about Jack's contact, and they're on board with the plan to meet with him."

* * *

Sean's stomach hardened into a rock, his throat constricting painfully as he tried to think through the anger beating through him and making it hard to breathe, hard to see. Hard to think.

"I…" He took a deep breath, his teeth clenched painfully

together. "Can you give us a minute?" he asked his father and Antonio, tipping his head toward the balcony. Without a word they rose from their seats and went outside. For several impossibly long seconds, he and Sierra stared at each other, anger swirling through him because she'd gone over his head. Anger that after everything they'd shared, she didn't trust him. That he was a goddamn fool who'd fallen for a woman who didn't love him. How could she if she didn't even trust him? He exhaled a long breath through his nose and pushed a hand through his hair. He didn't know what to say, how to put into words the heavy disappointment pressing like a weight on his chest.

"What the fuck, Sierra?" His voice was quiet, shaking a little with barely leashed anger.

"I'm sorry. You didn't leave me any other choice." She looked down at her hands, her fingers twisted together.

He closed the distance between them in a few long strides and pulled out a chair, sitting down hard, his pulse pounding in his ears. "So this fucked-up mess is somehow my fault? No one forced you to e-mail Jack, and no one forced you to do this." He crossed his arms and leaned back in his chair, staring at the woman who, although he'd known her only a short time, he'd started imagining a future with. A future that was now quickly fading and slipping out of his grasp.

"No, I didn't mean it like that."

He frowned, struggling to stay on an even keel. "How did you mean it? I thought you trusted me. I thought we were a team."

"I do. We are."

He leaned forward, shaking his head, anger and frustration tensing every muscle in his body. "No. If we were a team, you wouldn't have gone behind my back like this. If you trusted me, you would've listened when I told you that this plan is a really bad fucking idea."

She laid a hand on his arm, and he shrugged off her touch. He couldn't think with her hands on him, and he was already having a difficult enough time wading through the angry fog clouding his brain.

She looked down and bit her lip, a tear sliding down her cheek. And fucking idiot that he was, he had to steel himself against reaching out and wiping it away. He'd fallen in love with a woman who didn't trust him, who didn't believe that he could keep her safe. Had all those times she'd told him she trusted him been lies?

Had Miami been one big lie? Had what had just passed between them less than an hour ago been a lie? She'd told him that she was his, but she wasn't if she didn't trust him to protect her. She wasn't his, but he was still hers, and that disconnect…damn. It fucking *hurt*.

"I did it because I love you," she whispered, tears still falling, and something broke open in his chest, and all the anger, all the hurt he'd been trying to hold back flooded out.

He leaned forward, his voice barely above a whisper. "Bullshit. You did it because you're determined to get your way."

"It's not bullshit! It's the truth! Do you have any idea how hard it is for me to watch you put yourself in danger, time and time again, and then to be told to sit back and do *nothing* when I have a chance to put an end to this?"

He scoffed out a mirthless laugh. "Do *you* have any idea how hard it is for *me* to find out that the woman I love doesn't trust me? Doesn't trust my judgment, or my ability to keep her safe?"

Her face crumpled. "I do trust you! Sean, I do."

He shook his head. "I don't believe you."

More tears fell, and even though his anger was completely justified, he felt like an asshole.

"I know you're angry, but let's just get through this and then we can…"

"And then we can what? I don't know where we go from here."

She sucked in a sharp breath and pressed her fingers to her mouth. "What are you saying? That you want to end this?"

He rubbed a hand over his face. "No. I don't know. I need to think." His heart kicked weakly against his chest, and he leveled his gaze at her. "I'm so fucking pissed at you right now."

She nodded, swallowing thickly. "I know. I deserve that. But I only did this because I love you and I want this over with. I hope you understand that, and I'm so sorry for hurting you. I don't want this to be the end, Sean."

His hands shook, and he could feel his world unraveling. Nothing made sense anymore. Without saying anything, he rose from the table and let his father and Antonio back in, both of them glancing warily between Sean and Sierra.

Patrick pointed at Sierra. "She's right, you know. We need to pursue this lead."

Sean stalked to his fridge, and even though it was only midafternoon, he grabbed a beer and wrenched the top off, crushing the metal cap in his fist. The teeth dug into his palm, sharp little points of pain that centered him, preventing him from getting lost in the anger and the pain pounding through him. He took a long pull and then sat down at the table again, not looking at Sierra.

"What I want to know is why this contact will *only* talk to Sierra. That doesn't make sense to me," said Sean, watching a drop of condensation trail down the outside of his beer bottle. "I don't like it."

Antonio nodded. "If Jack's got an informant, I can talk to him instead. That would be safer. I'm with Sean. I don't like the idea of you meeting with this guy alone."

Sierra shook her head. "He won't talk to the police. Jack thinks he's wanted, and he doesn't trust cops. He wants the information about Sacrosanct to get out, but he's scared. He knows I'm not a threat."

"Why is he willing to talk at all?" Sean paused, trying to articulate the bad gut feeling he had about the situation.

"He used to be part of Sacrosanct, and he doesn't agree with what they're doing."

"Again, why doesn't he just talk to the cops?" Sean looked up at the ceiling, his jaw clenched.

"You've seen what Sacrosanct can do. In his shoes I'd be scared too." Patrick drummed his fingers on the table and looked at Sierra. "What do you want to do?"

She bit her lip, twining her fingers together. "I'll call Jack and tell him to arrange the meeting. We'll find out when and where, and then I'll go, get the information, and report everything to the police."

"For the record," said Sean, taking another long pull of his beer, "I *fucking hate* this plan."

"I think what Sean's trying to say is that you can't go by yourself." Antonio tented his fingers.

Sierra met Sean's gaze, and he looked away, some of his anger fading just the tiniest bit as he thought of everything she'd been through. While he didn't condone the way she'd gone behind his back, he could kind of see why she'd done it. There was something sweet about the way she was so worried about him, so concerned for his safety when she was the one under fire.

But he was still angry. This plan was still stupid and dangerous, and the fact that she'd gone over his head still hurt, mainly because it showed him things about their relationship he didn't want to see. The lack of trust. The now uncertain future.

"We can outfit her with an earpiece, and we'll be nearby, ready to jump in if anything happens," said Patrick, as though it were the simplest thing in the world.

"And just send her in alone, unarmed?" Sean snorted. "Abso-fucking-lutely not. Not happening."

"You don't...I mean...I know you're not on board." Sierra cleared her throat, her eyes still a little red. "You don't have to participate."

Sean's eyebrows shot up, fresh anger coursing through him. "Are you fucking serious? I'm not letting you do this without me." Pissed or not, she was still his to protect, something she didn't seem to grasp. And now she was telling him he could bow out? *Fuck.*

"Even though you're angry at me right now?"

"Yeah, I'm angry, but that doesn't mean I'm going to leave you unprotected. I hate this plan, but like hell you're doing it without me."

She sent him a tentative, sad smile, and he felt a little bit more of his anger dissolve. Given the chance, he knew she'd chip away at that anger, and he turned away from her, not ready to let it go.

"If this guy really is an informant, we don't want to spook him," said Antonio. "Outfitting her with an earpiece and stationing ourselves close by is the best option."

"And if he's not?" Sean crossed his arms again, feeling restless.

Antonio and Patrick exchanged glances, but it was Sierra who spoke. "It's a risk we have to take."

CHAPTER 28

Sierra fiddled with the earpiece nestled snugly in her ear and was greeted by Antonio's voice.

"Don't touch the earpiece. You'll give it away. Try and forget that it's there."

She nodded as she stepped into the lobby of the Omni Hotel and then realized that was stupid, because no one could see her. It felt strange to be out in public on her own, without Sean by her side.

Her heart clenched just at the thought of his name. He was barely speaking to her, barely looking at her, but still taking care of her. When she'd called Patrick and Antonio behind his back yesterday, she hadn't been fully prepared for how hurt and angry he'd be. She'd thought she knew what she was getting into, but she'd been wrong.

He'd slept on the couch last night, avoiding her as much as possible in the one-bedroom condo. He'd made dinner for both of them and then taken his out onto the balcony to eat, leaving her alone in the kitchen. She'd cut into her baked salmon, tears streaming down her face, not tasting her food

as she ate. She didn't know where they stood, and she was
terrified to bring it up. He'd probably tell her that they were
through if she pressed him, so for now, she was willing to let
it be.

He'd only spoken to her while going over today's plan,
again and again, to make sure she had it straight. She'd
called Jack to tell him to arrange the meeting with his contact, and he'd set everything in motion. She was to come to
the Omni Hotel, alone, at seven the following evening. Jack
would meet her there, and he'd take her to meet with his contact in one of the hotel rooms.

As far as anyone—including Jack—was concerned, she
was there alone. Except she wasn't. With the earpiece she
was connected to Antonio, stationed in the hotel's parking
garage in an unmarked van with Sean and Patrick.

Originally she'd wanted to loop Jack in on the plan, but
Sean had vetoed that immediately. He'd fought tooth and
nail against giving Jack any additional information, and she,
along with Patrick and Antonio, had given in. It didn't hurt
to play things close to the vest.

She saw Jack across the lobby, and anxiety raced through
her like flames licking across gasoline, leaving her skin hot
and itchy, but she couldn't chicken out now. She'd ruined
the best thing that had ever happened to her to see this
through, and if she backed out now, it would all have been
for nothing.

Jack met her in the center of the lobby, and she wiped her
sweaty palms on her jeans, wondering if Antonio could hear
how furiously her heart was pounding.

"I wasn't sure you'd show." Jack studied her.

"I want answers. You say that this guy can give me
some." She shrugged, focusing on her breathing, on keeping
her voice steady. Jack glanced around the lobby.

"And you're alone?"

"Yes. I'm alone," she lied, despite the fact that she felt alone.

"Good. This guy's jumpy as hell." He gave her shoulder a reassuring squeeze before tipping his head toward the elevator. "Let's go."

As they crossed the lobby toward the elevators, Sierra felt as though all her senses had gone into hyperdrive. The lights were too bright, the sound of Jack's shoes clicking against the marble floor too loud, the scent of the gardenias in a massive vase on a nearby table too strong. Her stomach roiled, and she took a deep breath as subtly as possible, calling on every single ounce of acting ability she possessed.

She almost jumped at Antonio's voice, but caught herself in time, covering it up with a cough. "You're doing good, Sierra. Don't forget, you need us, you say *lucky* and we're there in a heartbeat."

The safe word had been Sean's idea too. Her chest hitched again, and she wondered if there was any way to fix what she'd broken. Maybe the fact that he was still looking out for her was proof that he still cared.

Or maybe it was just proof of how good he was at his job. She wasn't sure anymore.

She stepped into the elevator, and as Jack hit the button for number fifteen, she was keenly aware of how vulnerable she was. For the second time in the space of five minutes, she desperately missed Sean's presence by her side, and a fresh wave of pain and sadness rocked into her.

The elevator doors slid open with a soft ping, and Jack led her down a hallway. The back of her neck prickled, but she kept going, wanting to talk to the informant. It was all she had, and she clung to the idea that talking to him would put an end to the hell her life had become thanks to Sacrosanct.

Jack took out a key card, swiping his way into a room not far from the elevator. He ushered her inside, and her skin buzzed with awareness.

Why did Jack have a key card? Why hadn't he just knocked?

The door closed behind him, and he turned, slowly.

There was no one else in the room. There was no informant. She licked her lips, her mouth dry.

"You know, fifteen's my lucky number." She barely managed to get the last word out before he grabbed her by the hair and slammed her head against the wall, pain exploding through her skull. As the room tilted momentarily around her, she felt him rip the earpiece out. Distantly she heard a crunch as he crushed her only connection to safety beneath his shoe.

And then he laughed, a cold, joyless sound she'd never heard from him before. Fear flooded her, and she shoved Jack away, as hard as she could. He stumbled back, but not nearly far enough.

He laughed again, a smirk on his face, his eyes cold. "You stupid bitch."

Every joint in her body stiffened with panic. She felt as if she were watching from underwater as Jack stalked toward her. For one long, terrifying moment, she was paralyzed. Everything was happening in slow motion as he pinned her against the wall.

"I didn't want it to come to this, but now that it has, I'm gonna enjoy it." He slapped her across the face so hard that tears sprang to her eyes, her ears ringing.

It hurt, but the slap jolted her out of her shocked stupor, and everything shifted from slow motion to fast-forward. Adrenaline surged through her, momentarily chasing away the paralyzing fear. She kneed him in the groin, ducking away as he yelped in pain, scrambling for the door. Jack grabbed her arm and flung her away from the door as she screamed. The closet to her left was open, and she grabbed the iron mounted above the ironing board and spun to face him, swinging it as hard as she could. It connected with Jack's cheek, and he lurched backward a few feet, stunned. She bolted for the door.

Her fingers closed around the handle as a pair of strong arms circled around her from behind, squeezing all the air out of her lungs. Wildly she swung her right hand back and caught him in the eye with her fingers.

"Fuck!" He stumbled back, gripping his face. She scrambled for the door again, but he grabbed her hair and slammed her head into the door. Her vision slid sideways, and dark spots danced in front of her eyes as she fell to the floor, her legs giving out. A metallic taste flooded her mouth, and she struggled to get to her feet. Pain exploded down her side as Jack's foot connected with her ribs. He kicked her again, and she almost passed out from the pain. He moved to kick her a third time, and she managed to roll out of the way just in time, her ribs screaming in agony.

Desperately she shot a hand up and grabbed his balls, squeezing and twisting as hard as she could. He screamed and fell to the floor, clutching his groin. She staggered to her feet, and her vision blurred red around the edges, hot with pain. Seeing her on her feet, he grabbed her by the ankle and pulled her down again, maneuvering himself on top of her. His hands closed around her neck, and she clawed at his face, struggling to get free as pressure built in her temples and behind her eyes. He leaned forward slightly, and she sank her hands into his hair, ripping a handful out. He fell beside her, clutching his scalp and cursing.

Sierra stumbled to her feet, gasping for air, careening

forward into the hotel room. She picked up the iron she'd
dropped, and as Jack came at her again, she swung it a second
time. With a sickening crunch, it connected with his jaw. He
shook his head and kicked her in the stomach, sending her tumbling to the floor as she gasped for air, pain shooting through
her body. He grabbed the iron from her, and she was too over-
come by the pain screaming through her to fight anymore.

The last thing she saw was the iron swinging down toward her.

* * *

Sean sat in the van, his hands clasped tightly in front of him,
his shoulders rigid.

Maybe he was being overprotective. Maybe he was letting his uncertainty over his future with Sierra color everything. Maybe he was assuming the worst-case scenario,
being overly suspicious of what could potentially be a solid
lead.

His phone buzzed from his pocket and he fished it out,
swiping a thumb across the screen to answer it.

"Clay, what's up?"

"You need to get her the fuck out of there. Jack *is* Sacrosanct. He's part of it. It's been him this whole time." A
buzzing filled Sean's ears, and he missed the rest of what
Clay said.

And then Sierra's voice, shaky and high, came through
the van's speaker, and his heart plummeted into his stomach.

"You know, fifteen's my lucky number."

A muffled thud filled the speakers, followed by static.
The earpiece was gone.

"Fuck!" Sean pushed out of his chair and grabbed his gun
from its holster, checking the clip. "I'm going in."

Antonio stood too, worry etched into his features. "You can't just go in there guns blazing. I'll call for backup and we'll get her out of there."

Sean snorted and shook his head. "You're fucking crazy if you think I'm going to sit here and wait around while she's in trouble. I'm doing this my way."

"It's not a good idea."

Sean slid his Glock back into the holster and pushed open the van's door, meeting Antonio's eyes. "Try and stop me."

"I'm coming with you." Patrick hopped out of the van behind him, his Beretta in hand. They ran for the stairs, feet pounding on the concrete of the hotel's parking garage, Sean's heart beating so hard he thought it might explode. They tore up the stairs and burst into the lobby, earning a few curious stares, but no one moved to follow them. He put a hand on his father's arm.

"We can't attract attention. We don't know who Jack has watching the lobby."

Patrick nodded. "Elevators?"

"You think she meant the fifteenth floor?"

Patrick hit the call button for the elevators. "That'd be my guess."

"We'll take the elevator to fourteen, take the stairs the last flight up."

The doors slid open, and Sean punched the button for floor fourteen. He paced in the small car, unable to keep his legs still as anxiety shot through him. He shoved a hand through his hair, trying to breathe. But he knew he wouldn't be able to breathe until he got eyes on Sierra. Until he knew she was OK.

He'd never felt so fucking frantic in his life.

His father's hand landed on his arm, and Sean stilled. "We'll get her out. She'll be OK."

Sean nodded curtly, not trusting himself to speak. Wanting to believe his father, but unable to escape the nightmare playing over and over in his mind. Blood everywhere, Sierra's body limp and lifeless, and the knowledge that he'd once again failed to protect someone he loved.

He couldn't let it happen. It didn't matter that she'd hurt him. He'd do whatever it took to save her.

The elevator doors opened on fourteen, and they stepped out, running for the stairwell at the end of the hall, slamming into the door and pushing it open. They ran up the flight of stairs, and when they reached the door with a large 15 emblazoned on it, they stopped. Cautiously Sean nudged his shoulder against the door, easing it open a few inches, his Glock in his hands. Two men in black suits stood in front of a door at the other end of the hall, closer to the elevator. Not only did Jack have Sierra in the hotel room, he had the room guarded as well.

"Here's the plan," said Patrick. "You go back down to fourteen and take the elevator up. They probably know what you look like, but not me. I'll come out of the stairwell and make my way toward them like I'm a guest going to my room. When I hear the elevator doors open, I'll take one, you take the other. We'll have the element of surprise."

* * *

Sierra's head throbbed woozily as it bobbed against her chest, and she struggled to open her eyes. Pain threatened to split her skull in two, and a wave of nausea rolled through her. She tried to push her hair back from her face, but she couldn't move her arms. The red-tinged fog began to lift, and she forced her eyes open.

Her head bobbed down again, and she discovered why

she couldn't move. She was tied to the desk chair, her arms pinned painfully behind her, her ankles fastened to the chair legs with coarse rope. Everything hurt. Her head, her face, her ribs. Hot, terrified tears stung her eyes as she struggled uselessly against the rope holding her in place. She'd been gagged with a piece of fabric, and she forced herself to breathe through her nose, trying not to choke on the cotton wad stuffed into her mouth.

Jack emerged from the bathroom, a cloth pressed to his face.

"You know," he said, wiping at his face, welts visible on his cheek and jaw from where she'd nailed him with the iron, "my original plan was just to kill you quickly and get it over with, but after that little demonstration back there, I think I'll take my time. I've always wanted to teach you a lesson." He smirked, and her blood ran cold. He stuck his head out the door. "Have you got my kit?"

Someone passed him what looked like a leather briefcase. With calm, sure movements, he set it on the bed and opened it. Her entire body shook, and she tried to scream around the gag, her eyes bulging as Jack pulled out a cordless drill with a long, sharp spiral bit attached. She choked on her scream and pulled frantically against her ropes, feeling the tiniest bit of give.

Pain throbbed through her head as the same horrifying thoughts chased each other around in circles.

He's going to torture you and kill you. You're never going to see Sean again. You're going to die, horribly and painfully, and you'll never get the chance to make things right with him.

With an almost painful flash of clarity, she knew that Sean was the love of her life, and she'd do anything to fix what she'd broken.

A silent sob racked her, and Jack laughed.

"Poor little self-righteous princess." He shook his head in mock pity.

He pulled the chair closer to the bed, and then he sat on the corner, the drill clutched in one hand. A gun lay on the bed beside him. He stroked his fingers over her cheek, and she recoiled from his touch, her mind reeling, trying to make sense of everything, trying to figure out a way out of this. Without a word, he set the drill down on the bed, raised his arm, and backhanded her, hard. Lights flashed in front of her eyes as her head snapped back.

"You were always such a stubborn bitch." He stroked her face again, her skin stinging under his touch. "If I take this gag out, do you promise not to scream?" He ran the tips of his fingers over the gun. "You're not stupid enough to scream, are you?"

She shook her head, the room blurring around her, and he pulled the fabric out of her mouth. She sucked in several breaths, her blood rushing through her ears and throbbing against her temples.

"Why, Jack?" she croaked out. "I just want to know why." If she could keep Jack talking, maybe there was a chance Sean could find her before it was too late. She wouldn't have thought she had room to feel anything beyond the terror clogging her senses, but a shard of guilt pierced right through it. He'd been against the plan from the start, and she'd gone around him and hurt him in the process. And now look at what she was putting him through.

But she knew he'd come. Despite the shit between them, he'd come for her. She knew it the way she knew her name, the way she knew the sky was blue.

Jack picked up the drill, examined the bit, and then set it down beside him. He braced his forearms on his knees and leaned forward, a cold, sadistic smile on his face. "Is this the part where I tell you my evil plan?" He shook his head, laughing at her.

"If you're gonna kill me, I at least want to know why. Is this because of us?"

He rolled his eyes as if he were placating a child. "Don't flatter yourself. It's about money."

"Money?"

"Well, we couldn't let Choices get that grant."

"We? Jack, I don't understand."

"The Pregnancy Support Center. Or I guess I should say Sacrosanct. They are the same thing, after all, although that's a secret, so you have to promise not to tell anyone." He pressed a finger to his lips, laughing at his own morbid joke.

"And you're part of it?"

"Sacrosanct recruited me years ago. I'd like to think I've been a good asset for them, with my political connections. Probably why they put me in charge."

Her mind spun, and she felt as though she were wading through mud, trying to understand. Jack was in charge of Sacrosanct, and Sacrosanct was behind the Pregnancy Support Center. All of this had been about the fifty million dollars.

"But why target me?" She had a feeling she knew the answer, but she wanted to keep him talking. Her pulse throbbed in her throat.

"Because you were our biggest obstacle. You were the one gaining support for Choices. Initially the plan was to scare you into shutting up, you know, because I did like you once, but as I said, you're a stubborn bitch. Stubborn to the point of stupid." He shook his head and sighed happily. "Now that you'll be out of the way, the grant will be ours."

"You think turning me into a martyr will hurt Choices? You're delusional."

"I think killing you will devastate the organization and completely derail them, leaving the fifty million dollars for us. No hard feelings, though. I just really need this money."

"Sean is going to beat the shit out of you when he gets here."

He raised his hand to hit her again, but froze when the unmistakable sound of gunfire erupted in the hallway outside.

She smiled.

Sean.

* * *

The elevator doors slid open, and Sean emerged just as his father took a flying leap and tackled the guard closest to him. They hit the ground with a crash, grunting as fists swung. As they struggled on the ground, Sean charged at the second guard, who leveled his gun at Sean. He ducked into a doorway, his back plastered to the door, as two bullets disappeared into the wall a few inches from his head. He stepped out and fired two shots, narrowly missing the second guard, who was raising his gun to return fire. Sean stepped into the doorway again, adrenaline surging through his system. The second the gunfire stopped, he charged out from the doorway and fired again, managing to hit the second guard. The man stumbled backward, his hand clutched to his shoulder. His father, who'd beaten the other guard unconscious, kicked his gun away and trained his Beretta on him.

The hotel room door opened, and Jack stuck his head out. Anger beat hotly through Sean's veins, and Jack's eyes widened. Leaving his father with the two guards, Sean barreled into the room, his only thought getting to Sierra and getting her the hell out of here. Jack tried to shove the door closed, but Sean kicked it open, sending it slamming into the wall. Jack scrambled backward, grabbing for a gun lying on the bed, and Sean chased him into the room, desperate to get to Sierra.

She sat tied to a chair beside the bed, her hands bound behind her back, wriggling furiously against her bindings. Sean raised his gun and trained it on Jack just as Sierra managed to tip her chair over, crashing to the floor. With a glance at Sean, Jack leveled his gun at Sierra. The sight of the gun pointed at her caused Sean's heart to stop, fear pulsing through him.

Sean dove, launching himself between Jack and Sierra, and Jack fired.

CHAPTER 29

Sierra stared in horror as Sean dove in front of the gun, her heart clenching as he grunted in pain and landed with a heavy thud on the floor, blood flowing from his left arm.

"No, Sean!" she screamed, shaking as she watched her worst nightmare come to life. Her vision blurred as tears filled her eyes, guilt, regret, fear, and misery all swamping her and obliterating everything except his name, beating through her brain in time with her frantic pulse.

Sean pushed quickly to his feet, seemingly indifferent to the fact that he'd been shot in the arm. He'd dropped his gun when he fell, but he lunged for Jack, tackling him to the floor and slamming his face into it, wrenching the gun free from his hands, and landing a few bone-crunching punches in the scuffle. The gun skittered away, and with one more hammer-fisted punch, he knocked Jack unconscious, leaving him limp on the floor.

Sean rushed over to her, his face tight with worry, and undid the knots still holding her to the chair. Carefully he helped her up from the floor, his hands skimming everywhere, over her bruised face, her arms, and her torso, and up and down her back.

She couldn't hold back the sobs, and he pulled her into his arms, not saying anything. She gulped in breath after breath, trying to calm down enough to talk. "I'm so sorry for dragging you into this, Sean. I know you're furious with me, and you should be, but I need you to know how grateful I am. For everything. For you."

"I know."

She glanced up at him, trying and failing to read his expression. Blood still flowed from his arm, and she pulled away, grabbing a pillow and pulling off the pillowcase. Wadding the fabric, she pressed it over his arm, trying to stanch the blood.

"I'm so sorry, Sean. I never meant for any of this to happen. I'm so sorry."

"I know. Shhh. I know." The tiniest hint of a smile quirked up the corner of his mouth, and a seed of hope took root deep in her chest.

"I should've listened to you. I should've trusted your judgment. And now you're hurt because I didn't. I was trying to protect you." She swallowed thickly, adjusting her grip on the fabric. "For what it's worth, I knew you would come. I at least trusted that much." A sense of just how close they'd come to catastrophe rocked her, and the room spun for a second as the adrenaline started to wear off.

"Of course I came. I love you."

The seed of hope bloomed. "Even though you got shot because of me."

He looked down at his arm and then placed his hand over hers, a familiar gleam in his brown eyes. "Worth it." He brought his mouth down to hers and kissed her so gently that her heart broke open, leaving her completely vulnerable and exposed.

"I love you so much, Sean. I'm so sorry that I...I ruined things between us."

"You didn't. I'm not going anywhere. I've got you."

* * *

Sean sat on the edge of the ambulance, grimacing as the paramedic cleaned the bullet wound.

"You're lucky. It didn't hit the bone, and the damage seems to only be to the muscle. You'll need surgery, but you'll live. You need a tetanus booster and antibiotics too." He finished dressing the wound with gauze and helped Sean fit a sling around his neck, easing his injured arm into it. "I can take you to the hospital now, if you want."

"Do you mind waiting just a minute? I need to check on my girlfriend." His entire body vibrated with the need to get eyes on Sierra, even though he knew she was only a few feet away in another ambulance. Before he could stand, Patrick approached, fresh stitches above his eye, his bottom lip split and swollen.

"You did good today," his dad said, laying a hand on Sean's uninjured arm.

"Thanks. And thanks for your help. You kicked some ass back there. I couldn't have done it without you."

Patrick smiled and shook his head. "That was more fun than I've had in years."

Sean laughed. "You have a fucked-up sense of fun."

"Oh, probably."

A silence hung between them for a moment before Patrick spoke again. "None of this is your fault, you know."

Sean sighed heavily, nodding slowly. "I know." Objectively

he knew that, but he still felt responsible for the fact that Sierra had gotten hurt. Still blamed himself for what had happened.

"Just like the accident wasn't your fault." Patrick sat down in the ambulance beside him, looking straight ahead. "I was lost when she died, but I never blamed you. I'm truly sorry if you felt that I did. I didn't, and I don't now. You take things, and you carry them, Sean. It hurts to watch. You need to forgive yourself, and you need to let go. And so do I."

Sean took a deep breath, turning his father's words over in his mind, examining them. He decided he wanted to keep them instead of rejecting them. They felt good. True, even.

"I'm proud of you." Patrick clapped him lightly on the back and tipped his head toward Sierra, who was making her way over from the other ambulance. "I think someone wants to talk to you."

Before he could slip out of the ambulance, Sean caught his father's arm and met his eyes, the same shade of brown as his own. "Thanks, Dad."

Patrick nodded, a wistful smile on his face. He stepped away from the ambulance and headed back toward the cluster of police officers several feet away.

"Hey." Sierra's voice was quiet as she sat down beside him, clutching a blanket around her shoulders. She had a bruise on her cheek, and another at the corner of her mouth. Her wrists had been rubbed raw by the rope and were now wrapped in gauze.

Then she smiled, and relief filled him, mirrored back to him in Sierra's eyes. For a moment they just stared at each other, drinking each other in. They'd gone through hell together, but in the end, it'd been worth it, because they'd found each other.

"I'm so sorry for putting you through all of this, Sean. Really, I am."

"I know. And I get why you did it. But for future reference, I like it a hell of a lot better when we're a team."

Her face lit up. "Future reference, huh?"

With his good arm, he pulled her closer. "Damn right."

She stared at him, wonder in her eyes. "I can't believe you took a bullet for me."

He kissed her, being careful of her bruised mouth. "I'd do it every goddamn day for you. This barely hurts compared to how I felt when I thought I might lose you."

"You're never going to lose me. I'm yours, remember?"

He kissed her again, a little harder this time, unable to help himself. "I want you to move in with me. As long as you don't mind playing nurse." He shifted his injured arm, indicating the sling. It hurt like a motherfucker, and he didn't care.

She kissed his jaw and snuggled into him. "For you, I'll even wear a naughty nurse outfit."

He laughed, and everything in the world settled back into place.

CHAPTER 30

Waves lapped at the sandy shore, a light breeze stirring the dried palm leaves covering the *palapa* above them. Sierra sat back in her beach chair and adjusted her sunglasses, taking a deep breath and inhaling the scents of salt, coconut sunscreen, cigar smoke, and tropical flowers, all mingling together to create her new favorite smell: On the Beach in Mexico with the Sexiest Man Ever. Patent pending.

The month following the shooting had gone by in a blur, but life was good. Really good. Jack had confessed to his involvement with Sacrosanct, and his confession had had a domino effect on the entire organization, effectively shutting it down across the country, including the deceptive Pregnancy Support Centers. Choices had been awarded the grant, and the money would be put to good use.

Shortly after the shooting, she'd made the decision to go forward with the audition for *Bodies*, and to her complete shock, she'd won the role. The dog-eared script sat in her lap, pages fluttering in the ocean breeze, and rehearsals were due to start in a few weeks. Thankfully, the movie was scheduled to film in and around LA, which meant she wouldn't have to leave Sean. After everything that had happened, she was taking a little break from Choices and was looking forward to acting again.

She'd moved in with Sean, who was still on medical leave for the next several weeks, and as soon as the arson investigation was finished, she planned on building a new house on her land. One for her and Sean.

He was recovering well from his surgery, and his doctor was pleased with how the wound was healing. He'd be in the sling for another month or two, and then he'd start his physical therapy. She knew the wound caused him pain, but in time he'd make a full recovery, and she didn't have words for how grateful she was. They'd fallen into an easy, happy rhythm, cooking meals together, running errands, going on dates—to dinner, to a movie, on a drive up the coast—spending the evening together on the couch, reading or watching TV.

Oh, and the sex. Oh, good Lord, the sex. They couldn't keep their hands off each other. Frankly, she was amazed she could walk.

Over the past few weeks, they'd had dinner with the guys from Virtus a couple of times, and even once with his father, who seemed to be making a genuine effort with Sean. She was proud that he was returning that effort, and he and his father seemed to be on much better footing than just a few weeks ago.

They'd had dinner with her friends a couple of times too, and Taylor had managed to tear herself away from Zack long enough to join them one night. Despite her assertions that they were only casual, Sierra had a feeling Taylor was falling for him. Hopefully, it would work out.

Since Sean was on leave and she was a few weeks away from rehearsals, they'd figured it was the perfect opportunity to take that trip to Mexico they'd talked about. Just as at home, they'd fallen into an easy, happy rhythm, walking on the beach, swimming, eating and drinking anything and everything they wanted.

Oh, and the sex. Oh, good Lord, the sex. It was pretty incredible what that man could do with only one arm.

She glanced over at him, his large frame casually sprawled out on the beach chair beside her. With a cigar between his lips, wearing nothing but aviator sunglasses and the same black swim trunks he'd worn the first day she'd seen him swimming in her pool, he looked like pure sex. He sat with his good arm propped behind his head, one leg bent with a tablet leaning against it. A faint sheen of sweat clung to his gorgeous bare chest, and she contemplated dragging him back to their suite. Again.

Yeah, life was very good.

The waiter came by and set down two margaritas on the table between their beach chairs, and they both sat up, Sean setting his cigar in the ashtray on the table. Condensation dripped down the sides of the plastic cups, and cool water dripped onto her bare stomach as she raised the cup to her lips. Sean pushed his sunglasses up on top of his head, and his eyes tracked the drop as it traced a cool path toward her bikini bottoms.

It still felt unreal sometimes that this man—this smart, brave, strong, loyal, incredibly sexy man—was hers.

She leaned forward and kissed him, knocking her cup lightly against his.

"To taking risks," she said, biting her lip. His eyes darkened slightly, and he kissed her again, setting his cup down.

"And enjoying the payoff." He tucked a strand of hair that

320 TARA WYATT

had escaped from her braid behind her ear and kissed her
again.

A surge of happiness charged through her, and her eyes
stung for a second. "I love you," she whispered against his
mouth, and with surprising speed, he took her cup out of
her hands, set it down, and curled his arm around her waist,
hoisting them both up. He started toward the water, and she
wrapped her legs around his waist, amazed at his strength,
amazed at how perfectly she fit around him. He kissed a trail
down her neck, and she felt the first cool drops of ocean
water hit her feet, the sun blazing above them. The water sparkled around them, the faint strains of tropical music
floating out to reach them, and she felt as though she were in
a sun-drenched fairy tale.

"I love you too," he said, just before he closed his mouth
over hers in a searing kiss.

Life wasn't just good; it was perfect.

Rock star Taylor Ross doesn't need a babysitter, let alone some muscle-bound hunk, to stay focused on her music. But her new bodyguard Colt is a tall, gorgeous, mouth-watering distraction—and there's no telling how hot things will get…

Please see the next page for a preview of

Primal Instinct

Taylor Ross drummed her fingers against the table, the red tablecloth absorbing the restless rhythm she tapped out. She blew out a breath and reached for her Jack and Coke, averting her eyes from the blinking light on her phone, which lay on the table in front of her. She took a sip of her drink and then ran her finger across the screen, frowning at the numerous text messages, e-mails, and Google Alerts all begging for her attention. She took another sip and, with a fingertip, flipped several pages of the notebook that lay open on the table in front of her, scowling at the scribbled and hastily scratched-out chord progressions and lyrics.

It was going to happen tonight. She could feel it. Almost taste it. The dry spell would end, and things would go back to normal. Tonight. What she needed shimmered around her, in front of her, and if she reached out her fingers, if she touched the gauzy inspiration floating in the air, she'd finally be able to write music again.

She didn't want to think about any of it—breaking up with Zack, the stupid video that had gone viral, or her inability to write. If her life was a sentence, the past few months had been a semicolon. An interruption, a pause, joining what happened before with what was to come. The past and the future linked by a tiny little wink in time. She was still waiting for the wink to end, so for tonight, all she wanted was to catch a buzz so that she could numb the pain, the doubt, and the loneliness that were always simmering just below the surface.

She rested her chin in her hand as she scanned the dim interior of the Rainbow, a favorite LA hangout for rockers, groupies, some locals, and the occasional tourist. Red vinyl booths lined the walls, which were covered with rock paraphernalia. Autographed pictures, gold records, vinyl albums, all encased in glass and staring down at her. She knew that if she wandered over the garishly carpeted floor to a corner near a window, she'd find a picture of herself and two assholes, all glaring moodily at the camera. She remembered autographing that picture. Hell, she remembered posing for that picture, full of the kind of cocky swagger only a twenty-two-year-old with a hit record can pull off.

How had ten years gone by so damn fast?

She glared up at the plants lining the ceiling, a row of lights shining from underneath them. Frustration rolled through her as her eyes landed once again on her phone. She was gripped by a sudden urge to hurl it across the room, but she forced herself to pick up her drink and drain it instead. She certainly wouldn't be the first rock star to throw a tantrum at the Rainbow, but it wouldn't accomplish anything. She'd only be embarrassed, and then get drunk, and then do something even more stupid. As usual.

She shook her head and forced herself to focus on the blank page in front of her. Her brain scrambled for an idea, a melody, a lyric, a hook, *anything*, but the harder she tried to pull a song out of her brain, the more she felt as if she were spinning her wheels in mud. Sweating and working and stressing and getting nowhere fast. Factor in the added pressure of the album being six months overdue, and real panic began to set in. If she couldn't deliver this album, there was no question that the label would dump her, and she'd be out on her ass. And then what?

She sifted through the scraps of ideas littered throughout the notebook. She'd hoped maybe coming to the Rainbow and sitting where so many greats had sat would inspire her. As if sitting in a sticky vinyl booth would somehow miraculously move her to finally write a new song. Lips pursed, she shook her head again. She had nothing. Her brain spun emptily, filled with nothing but frustration and disappointment and fear.

Shoving the notebook aside, she scrolled through a series of texts from Jeremy Nichols, her manager, and then opened the Google Alerts, which were set to notify her if anything new was posted online about her. Given that just a few days ago she'd managed to get herself booted off a plane, there was lots to sort through.

Like pressing on a bruise, she pressed play on the video of her in-air meltdown. She'd already watched it several times; she couldn't seem to stop watching it. It had all started because she'd been trying to get numb to everything she didn't want to feel. Because when she felt good, whether it was a high from sex or from booze, she didn't *hurt* so much. And God, she hurt. Several months ago she'd started casually dating bodyguard Zack De Luca, and much to her surprise, she'd fallen fast and hard for him. For the first time in years, she'd wanted something more than casual. But Zack hadn't, and even though he hadn't meant to, he'd broken her heart.

So, to numb the pain of walking away from Zack, she'd hooked up with the super-hot copilot. She'd been in the process of retreating to her first-class seat when a flight attendant—and the copilot's ex-girlfriend, it turned out—had confronted her, calling her a dirty slut. Never one to back down from a fight, especially when drunk, Taylor had said some pretty filthy things to the flight attendant about her ex-boyfriend's stellar performance, and just as the air marshal had come over to see what the commotion was about, the flight attendant had called her a white trash whore. So she'd slapped the flight attendant across the face, and the confrontation had devolved into flailing limbs and hair pulling.

The air marshal had had to separate them, and she'd accidentally caught him in the throat with her elbow.

Not her finest moment.

She'd been escorted off the plane, and to her complete and utter humiliation, the video had gone viral almost immediately. She'd had to figure out a way home from Lincoln, Nebraska, which was where she'd been booted off her NYC-bound plane. Jeremy had been *pissed* when she'd told him she wouldn't be able to meet with the label executives that night.

To console herself, she'd gone to a bar in Lincoln and gotten spectacularly wasted. Because what the hell else was there to do in Nebraska?

She shook her head and closed the video. Her pulse throbbed ominously in her temples, warning her of an oncoming headache. Everything was falling apart: her career, her love life, her reputation. And hell if she knew how to fix it.

A tall guy with a slim build approached her table, his phone in one hand, and the headache bloomed across her skull. His dark-brown hair was long on top and shaved close on the sides, his plain white T-shirt and jeans boring but clean. A surge of irritation pushed up through her chest, and she forced herself to take a breath. He was probably just a fan looking for a picture. She should be grateful she still had fans.

"Hi, um, Taylor? Taylor Ross?" His voice was higher than she would've expected.

"Yeah, hi," she said, wanting to get this interaction over with.

"Can I, um, get a picture?" His eyes darted around the bar, oddly bright, and the hairs on the back of her neck prickled. He pushed his big horn-rimmed glasses back up his nose and made an awkward, fluttering gesture with his hand before shoving it in his pocket. She glanced around, trying to figure out what he was looking at.

She plastered a smile on her face that she hoped didn't look as fake as it felt. "Sure." Pressing her palms against the table, she stood from her booth.

He slipped his arm around her, and a slight chill shivered down her spine, making her shrink away from him a little. Raising his phone in front of them, he took the picture. Relieved, she started to move away from him, but his arm tightened around her. He smiled shyly.

"One more." She held still for the picture and didn't smile this time, hoping that if she appeased him he'd leave her alone. As soon as he'd clicked the button, she pulled away. He let her this time, his fingers trailing over her waist and leaving her feeling as though she'd been slimed. "Can I buy you a drink?"

"No thanks." She'd turned away and moved to slip back into the booth when he tapped her on her shoulder. She spun, ready to tell him to fuck off, but froze at the look on his face, his eyes blazing, his lips curled into a thin sneer.

When he spoke, his voice was quiet and determined. "But I want to. You have to let me."

Anger melted her fear, and she scoffed out an impatient laugh. "I don't have to let you do sh—" But the rest of her words died as he grabbed her, curling a surprisingly strong hand around her arm, and her heart leaped into her throat. There had been a time when she hadn't gone anywhere without security, but those days—that fame—were long behind her.

"Get off me," she growled through clenched teeth, jerking away from him. His fingers dug in harder, and she raised her knee, ready to hit him in his tiny balls.

"What's going on here?" At the sound of the deep voice, the creep released her.

"Nothing." The creep stuffed his phone back into his pocket and stalked away through the bar, disappearing quickly into the crowd. Taylor let out the breath she'd been holding, her shoulders slumping slightly. Her skin itched, a physical remnant of the anxiety.

"Are you OK?" The man's voice was deliciously warm and rumbly, washing over her and chasing away the chill the creep had left behind.

"Yeah, I...thanks." Taking another deep breath, she ran her hands through her hair and turned to face her rescuer. For the second time in as many minutes, her heart was in her throat, but for an entirely different reason.

Taken individually, the man's features were all so pretty. The intensely green eyes with the long lashes. The perfectly formed nose. The high, sculpted cheekbones. The lush, tempting mouth. The thick, short, light-brown hair. And yet together, all prettiness disappeared, coalescing into the most handsome male face she'd ever seen. Her eyes scraped down his body, and she took in the way his black Led Zeppelin T-shirt was stretched tight over strong, broad shoulders and hugged his biceps. His muscular right arm was covered in a sleeve tattoo consisting entirely of intricate, detailed feathers overlapping each other. The T-shirt fell straight down over his flat stomach and narrow waist, leading to strong legs clad in denim.

He looked...sturdy. As if he'd been made to lean on.

She couldn't remember ever having that initial impression of a guy before. Hot, yes. Sexy, sure. But sturdy? That was a new one.

"I...need another drink." Taking a deep breath and trying to get her heart to slow down, she grabbed her purse and jacket out of the booth and made her way toward the bar at the back of the room. Her rescuer followed a few feet behind.

"Jack and Coke, please." She tipped her head at the bartender and could feel the gorgeous guy's eyes on her, leaving her skin tingling with excitement.

"You sure you're all right?" He turned sideways to face her, leaning one arm on the bar, and she finally had the chance to drink him in up close. Never had a man looked so good in an old T-shirt and jeans. Never. And never had a man been so immediately appealing. It was the model-worthy face paired with that deep, rumbly voice; the strong, muscular body with the relaxed, confident posture; the alertness in his gaze and his slow, easy smile.

"I'm fine. Really, he should be thanking you. It's because of you that his balls are still intact."

He chuckled, the sound low and warm. "Trust me, there isn't a doubt in my mind that you can take care of yourself."

She arched an eyebrow, twirling a finger around the rim of her fresh Jack and Coke. "So why'd you come over?"

"I was worried about the guy's balls." He winked, and she found herself smiling as her heart flickered in her chest.

The man scrubbed a hand over his hair and smiled, flashing a row of straight white teeth, and the skin around his light-emerald eyes crinkled in a way that had her stomach doing a slow turn.

She sat down on the barstool, crossed her legs, and ran her hands through her hair again. "I'm Taylor."

He nodded and picked up the bottle of beer the bartender had set down in front of him. "I know." He took a swig of the beer, and she watched his Adam's apple bob as he swallowed. A faint layer of stubble covered his jaw, and she found herself wondering what that stubble would feel like beneath her fingertips or against her neck, rasping over her skin. "I'm Colt. So, uh…you come here often?" He smiled again as he leaned in a bit closer.

Her heart gave a little kick against her ribs, and she laughed. "I used to, but tonight's kind of put me off. Thanks again for stepping in." She signaled to the bartender and pointed at Colt's beer. "You can go ahead and put that on my tab."

He smiled at her again, a cocky half grin that was doing funny things to her stomach. "You trying to get me drunk?"

She shook her head, returning the smile. "Just trying to say thank you."

"Well, in that case, you're welcome." He leaned in even closer. Jesus, he smelled good. Like warm leather and something else both mouth-watering and masculine. Whatever cologne he was wearing could've been marketed as a panty-dropping aphrodisiac for the effect it was having on her. She bit her lip and looked down into her drink.

"Hey, I was just teasing with the 'you come here often' thing. If you want me to screw off, I get it."

It was her turn to lean in, and she smiled sweetly, looking up at him through her lashes. He was hot, kind, and funny. The last thing she wanted him to do was screw off. No, her mind was quickly veering to another kind of screwing. "Nah. You vanquished a creepy nerd for me. Have a seat."

He touched his thumb to his lips as his eyes traveled up and down her body, and a slow smile turned up the corners of his mouth, his eyes crinkling once again. "Sure."

He sat down on the barstool next to her, pulling in close, his broad body angled toward her, but instead of crowded, she felt sheltered. Her eyes slammed into his, and heat flared through her.

Oh, holy hell, but this man was trouble.

"So you didn't know that guy?" The way his low voice rumbled over the words sent a warm shiver down her spine and curled her toes.

She shook her head. "No. Just a fan, I guess."

"Lucky you."

She chuckled down into her drink and then met his eyes again.

Lucky her, indeed.

* * *

Sweet son of a bitch, but this couldn't be real. No way. This had to be a dream. Because there was no way that Taylor fucking Ross would be flirting with him in a bar in real life. Nope. He'd probably fallen asleep on the couch and was going to wake up alone and hard as concrete, and this would all turn out to have been a dream.

But no. The reality was, he'd just spent the past hour flirting like crazy with Taylor Ross, rock goddess. Making her laugh. Making her blush. Making her forget about the asswipe who'd grabbed her.

Fighting the urge to pinch himself, Colt took a long pull on his beer, his eyes once more roving over Taylor's long, lean body. She was so tall, almost as tall as him, and as he was six-two, that didn't happen very often. His eyes kept sliding down to her long, slim legs, wrapped in black denim. For now. Soon they'd be wrapped around him, if he got his way. And when it came to women, Colt almost always got his way.

Damn, but he needed this. Needed the release. Needed the temporary oblivion of hot sex with a gorgeous woman. He didn't want to think. Not tonight. Hell, not most nights.

Huey Lewis began thumping through the bar's speakers,

and Taylor made a face, scrunching her cute little nose. "I thought this was a rock bar."

"Hey, don't rag on Huey Lewis. He had some great hits." Colt smiled and bopped his head with cheesy, put-on enthusiasm in time to the music. She touched her fingers to her mouth and stifled a laugh before her eyes found his, and suddenly her hand was on his chest. Hopefully she couldn't feel his heart pounding harder than a damn kick drum.

"I would've thought with this"—her fingers traced over the Led Zeppelin logo on his T-shirt—"and this"—the fingers of her opposite hand trailed up his right forearm, over his tattoo—"you'd have better taste than Huey Lewis."

He tried to think of something sexy, something flirty to say back, but his eyes were glued to her mouth, and goose bumps were trailing up his arm where she touched him. He cleared his throat and flashed her a smile.

She bit her lip and looked up at him, amusement flashing in her huge blue eyes. "Did you know that Huey Lewis and the News were originally called Huey Lewis and the American Express? They had to change it when the credit card company threatened to sue them."

"Now who's hip to be square?" He shot her a teasing smile.

She flung her head back and laughed, a throaty, husky sound that sent blood flowing straight to his already heavy cock.

"Touché," she said, taking another sip of her drink.

God, he couldn't take his eyes off her. The bar could've been on fire and he wouldn't have noticed. He wanted to fist his hands in all that blond hair and pull her close, taste her mouth, feel her skin against his and lose himself in her. But just for tonight.

It was all he could offer. All he had any right to want.

He watched her as she took another sip of her drink, trying to memorize the exact way her hair was falling over her shoulders, the precise shade of blue in her wide, bright eyes. The sound of her laugh. A heavy sadness tempered his excitement, resting like a weight across his shoulders. For the first time in a long time, he wished he could offer more.

"So why feathers?" Her fingers still trailed over his arm, sending little sparks of lust shooting through him.

Fuck. Nope. Not talking about that. Not with her, not tonight. He'd come here not to think about all that shit. He'd come here to find a woman, or get drunk, or start a fight. All three worked in varying ways to keep him on an even keel. Colt knew that as long as he kept the demons fed, he wouldn't have to feel anything he didn't want to feel.

And there was a lot he didn't want to feel.

"You like it?" he asked, dodging the question. If she noticed, she didn't seem to mind.

"Mmm. I do." Her voice was beautiful, rich and sultry with a slight rasp to it, and he couldn't wait to find out what she'd sound like moaning out his name. He wanted it so badly that he was already imagining the feel of her fingers digging into his shoulders, her heels pressed into his ass as he sank himself deep inside her.

He forced himself to take a breath and a swallow of beer.

"You have any?" he asked, relieved she hadn't pressed him about the meaning behind his own ink.

She slipped out of her leather jacket, rolled up the sleeve of her denim shirt, and flipped her arm over. A swirled line of black stars decorated the inside of her right wrist. "And," she said, and swept her hair up, showing him the Egyptian ankh on the back of her neck, just below her hairline. "I have a couple of others." She let her hair drop back around her shoulders, the blond waves fanning out around her.

His eyebrows rose. "Oh yeah? Where?"

She leaned toward him and took one of his hands in hers. He watched, transfixed, as she laid his hand on her rib cage. Instinctively his fingers flexed into her, and her eyes fluttered closed for a second. "Here." She was warm and soft through the fabric of her shirt as he caressed his hand up her side, still not quite able to believe that this wasn't a fantasy.

"Where else?" His eyes held hers. She slipped off the stool, erasing all distance between them, and slid his hand from her ribs up and around to her shoulder blade.

"Here." Her warm breath tickled his ear, and he clenched his jaw against the need to bury his face in her neck, right here at the bar. "What about you? Any others?"

He leaned back slightly and took one of her hands in his, placing it over his heart. "Here."

Her long fingers curled into the cotton of his shirt, and heat crackled in the air around them. His stomach bottomed out, and if he was reading her right—and he would've bet a bottle of fifty-year-old scotch he was—she wanted him as much as he wanted her.

Time to test the waters.

He slid a hand up to her face and grazed his lips against hers, a tease of a kiss. She held stone-still, her eyes fixed on his mouth, her lips slightly parted. All the noise around him seemed to drop away, and in that moment, Taylor was all that existed for him. Well, her and the erection doing its damndest to bust free of his jeans.

He closed his mouth over hers and felt the vibration of her sigh against his lips. He fought back a groan when she slid her tongue against his and heat exploded over his skin as he tasted her, drinking in the soft warmth of her mouth.

He couldn't remember the last time he'd been so aroused from just a kiss. His chest tightened, and as he deepened the kiss, he pressed down the cold, hard knot of fear eating at him. Already he knew sticking to his one-night rule would suck, big-time. She felt so good, so perfect, so fucking *right* kissing him, her fingernails scraping lightly down his back.

He shouldn't want this. He shouldn't *do* this. Taylor was going to be too much for him, and he knew she'd probably leave a new scar instead of helping him forget the existing ones. He knew, and he wanted it anyway. As if he had a choice.

She opened her mouth to him a little more, which he immediately took full advantage of, greedily claiming everything she offered him. He caressed her mouth with his tongue, and she moaned softly, her body swaying into his when he parted his legs, letting her hips nestle snugly against his. He wove his fingers into her hair and crushed his mouth against hers as arousal and lust and need all sang through him. Lips and tongues melded together with increasing urgency, and the kiss seared through him. She rocked against him and bit gently at his lower lip.

Fuck, this was going to be good.

"Get a room, why don't ya?" the bartender chirped at them, and Taylor broke the kiss, pressing her forehead against his. For a second they just stood there, trying to breathe.

She was pretty much a total stranger, and yet the intensity of that kiss had been off the charts. Hot and bruising and so, so promising.

He swallowed, trying to find his voice. "Come home with me."

She nodded against his forehead, and his dick rejoiced.

* * *

From his little table in the corner, Ronnie watched Taylor walk out of the bar, her fingers laced with those of the brute from earlier. He finished the rest of his Coke and slammed the empty glass down. Possessive anger coupled with an almost blinding jealousy churned through him. It'd been hard to watch that interaction, and now she was leaving with him? He'd been much happier watching her while she'd been alone, even if she'd looked sad.

He knew he shouldn't have gone over and talked to her, but he couldn't help himself. He'd been warned, but no one knew what they were talking about. They didn't see. They couldn't see. He loved her, and she loved him. Soon everyone would know, and everyone who'd called him crazy and obsessed and delusional would fucking see.

Ever since he'd first heard her sing, he'd known he was listening to the future mother of his children.

He dropped a five on the table and pushed his way out of the bar, getting in his car just in time to follow Taylor. He had to. He couldn't let her go off alone with that brute, unprotected. And if she was going to betray him, he needed to know. He needed to see.

Because Taylor was his. Every part of her. Her gorgeous blond hair, those huge blue eyes, the long, lean body. The incredible voice. The skilled hands. Her mind. Her soul. Her body.

She belonged to him.

Fall in Love with Forever Romance

PLAY TO WIN
by Tiffany Snow

In the third book of bestselling author Tiffany Snow's Risky Business series, it's finally time for Sage to decide between two brothers-in-arms: Parker, the clean-cut, filthy-rich business magnate…or Ryker, the tough-as-nails undercover detective.

Fall in Love with Forever Romance

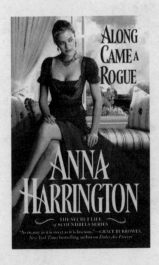

ALONG CAME A ROGUE
by Anna Harrington

Major Nathaniel Grey is free to bed any woman he wants…except his best
friend's beautiful sister, Emily. But what if she's the only woman he wants?
Fans of Elizabeth Hoyt, Grace Burrowes, and Madeline Hunter will love
this Regency romance.

Fall in Love with Forever Romance

NECESSARY RISK
by Tara Wyatt

The first book in a hot new action-packed series from debut author Tara Wyatt, which will appeal to fans of Suzanne Brockmann, Pamela Clare, and Julie Ann Walker.

SEE YOU AT SUNSET
by V.K. Sykes

The newest novel from *USA Today* bestselling author V.K. Sykes! Deputy Sheriff Micah Lancaster has wanted Holly Tyler for as long as he can remember. Now she's back in Seashell Bay, and the attraction still flickers between them, a promise of something *more*. Their desire is stronger than any undertow...and once it pulls them under, it won't let go.